Dear Reader:

FBI agent Nicholas Drummond and his partner, Mike Caine, are deep into an investigation of COE—Celebrants of the Earth—a violent group known for widespread bombings of power grids and oil refineries across the country. While Drummond and Caine investigate a civilian tip about a possible bombing plot, the Bayway Refinery in New Jersey explodes. Nicholas and Mike race to the scene and barely escape being killed by a secondary device.

Returning to the tipster's home to continue their interrogation, they discover the man—and the FBI team left to guard him—dead. While Nicholas calls in the assassinations, COE strikes again, this time launching a cyber-attack on several major oil companies and draining their financial and intellectual assets.

CIA agent Vanessa Grace is undercover in COE; her assignment is to steal the tiny undetectable bombs invented by the COE's leader, a brilliant young scientist. Someone else has infiltrated COE: the infamous assassin Zahir Damari, whose mission is not only to steal the bombs for his Iranian and Hezbollah clients, but also to assassinate the president and the vice president.

Nicholas and Mike, working with Dillon Savich, Lacey Sherlock, the CIA, the Secret Service, and Mossad, must counter each move until they reach the end game, where either side could win.

So enjoy yourself with this intense, wild, and woolly chase for two crazy-smart bad guys. Be sure to play The Game of the Century *(each chess move at the top of each chapter). Do let me know what you think at facebook.com/CatherineCoulterBooks, or e-mail me at readmoi@gmail.com.*

Catherine Coulter

continued . . .

"*The End Game* was mind-blowing! I wait with eager anticipation for your next book. Please keep writing. *The End Game* is a winner!"   —L. Benjamin

"*The End Game* was great! Wonderful! I couldn't put it down and I can't wait to see what happens next."
   —P. Earl

"I raced through *The End Game*. Awesome story—I loved it! I absolutely loved the ending. You and Ellison are the best."
   —P. Sweeney

PRAISE FOR THE BRIT IN THE FBI NOVELS

"The authors juggle marvelous action with stellar character development and intriguing history to spin another great tale. Both are excellent writers, but together they are in another league."   —The Associated Press

"Readers will be terrified and on the edge of their seats throughout the book."   —*Crimespree Magazine*

"Coulter and Ellison have created a new son of Bond licensed to shine in future thrillers. Genre fans will find the action nonstop."   —*Kirkus Reviews*

"Impossible nail-biting situations that are resolved by ingenious means."   —*Library Journal* (starred review)

THE END GAME

CATHERINE COULTER
AND J. T. ELLISON

JOVE   NEW YORK

A JOVE BOOK
Published by Berkley
An imprint of Penguin Random House LLC
375 Hudson Street, New York, New York 10014

Copyright © 2015 by Catherine Coulter
Penguin Random House supports copyright. Copyright fuels creativity, encourages
diverse voices, promotes free speech, and creates a vibrant culture. Thank you for buying
an authorized edition of this book and for complying with copyright laws by not
reproducing, scanning, or distributing any part of it in any form without permission.
You are supporting writers and allowing Penguin Random House to continue to
publish books for every reader.

A JOVE BOOK and BERKLEY are registered trademarks and the B colophon
is a trademark of Penguin Random House LLC.

ISBN: 9780515156300

G. P. Putnam's Sons hardcover edition / September 2015
Jove premium edition / September 2016

Printed in the United States of America
3   5   7   9   10   8   6   4   2

Cover design by Andrea Ho

J. T.—

May our upcoming adventures in Italy prove as spectacular as the wild roller coaster in *The End Game*. It's wonderful to know that our two writer brains will always find a way.

—*Catherine*

For Laura Benedict and Ariel Lawhon. You know why. And for my Randy. You know why, too.

—*J. T.*

ACKNOWLEDGMENTS

As always, to Karen Evans, my partner in synergy, always there at my side, at my back, always supportive, helpful, always positive. Thank you.

To my sweetheart of a husband, always ready to brainstorm, to throw around ideas, to be the rock.

And to my wonderful household: Lesley DeLone, Catherine Lyons Labate, and Yngrid Bejarano. Thank you for all you do—your energy, your positiveness, your laughter, your steady hands on the rudder.

Thank you all,
Catherine Coulter

What a fun, glorious ride this collaboration has turned out to be. I have to thank Catherine first and foremost, for bringing me on board, for constant laughter and fun, and for always challenging me to be the very best writer I can be. We make one helluva team, lady, and I can't wait to see what we cook up next!

And to the usual suspects: I couldn't do it without you. This means you, Scott Miller, Chris Pepe, Laura Benedict, Ariel Lawhon, Sherrie Saint, Karen Evans, Amy Kerr, Jeff Abbott, and darling husband. And for my parents, for listening, and listening, and listening.

—*J. T. Ellison*

THE END GAME

PROLOGUE

United States–Mexico Border
Three Months Ago

Zahir Damari watched the coyote turn to face the ragged band of Hondurans on the sloping Texas side of the Rio Grande. As the last Honduran climbed up the bank, pulled up by his father, Zahir saw hope now dawning on the dirty faces, saw the relief in their tired eyes at surviving the nightmare trip. They'd made it; they were in America.

The coyote, Miguel Gonzales, eyed them with contempt—nothing new in that, he'd treated this group with unveiled scorn since the beginning of their trek eight days before. Gonzales stuck out his hand to the leader of the group, an older man, a father of two younger sons. He waggled his fingers.

"Pagenme porque ustedes son unos miserables."

He wanted the other half of the money owed. No, the thieving scum wanted more. Gonzales had upped the payoff. Zahir saw the Hondurans' shock, their fear, saw them talking among themselves, voices rising.

Gonzales pulled a pistol, aimed it at the group, and held out his hand again.

Zahir smiled at Miguel Gonzales, a brutal man with stained teeth and black eyes that reflected Hell. He walked up to him, his hand outstretched with bills, and as the coyote grabbed them, Zahir stepped in quickly and gently slipped his stiletto into Gonzales's filthy shirt. Gonzales didn't make a sound because Zahir's knife was always true. It slid under the breastbone, directly into the coyote's heart. Gonzales simply looked up into Zahir's face, dropped the pistol, fell on his side, and died in a mess of dry shrubs.

The Hondurans were frozen in place, too terrified and shocked to move. Zahir leaned down, pulled out his stiletto, cleaned it on Miguel's filthy jeans. He calmly went through Miguel's pockets, pulled out a big wad of bills, handed them to the young woman closest to him, and smiled.

"Buena suerte"—good luck—and he gave them a salute and walked away, toward El Paso, only three miles to the north.

The day was brutally hot, but he didn't mind since he'd been raised in the worst desert heat imaginable.

In his shirt pocket was a small notebook filled with information and strategy from Hezbollah's top enforcer,

Hasan Hadawi, the Hammer, about a brilliant young scientist named Matthew Spenser, and how Zahir could use him to help him cut off two heads of the hydra. It made Zahir's heart speed up to think about the actual doing of it, the awesome pleasure that would course through him when he'd succeeded.

Zahir knew most of the intel and strategy was from Hadawi's Iranian master, Colonel Vahid Rahbar, openly committed to the obliteration of anyone who wasn't a Shia, which would leave a small world population indeed.

Zahir knew Spenser and his small group were hiding near Lake Tahoe. Spenser, according to the Hammer, had gone off the rails years before when his family had been killed in London's terrorist subway bombing in 2005. Now he led a small group called Celebrants of Earth, or COE, their goal to eliminate oil imports from the Middle East, but no murder, no casualties. *The idiot ideologues.* Until recently, Zahir knew the group had operated in Britain and Europe, blowing up only mid-sized oil refineries, small crap. But now they were here, in America, their message to the media after each bombing always the same:

**No more oil from terrorist countries
or you will pay the price.**

Both the Colonel and the Hammer believed Spenser was an unsophisticated anti-Muslim zealot, and ripe for manipulation. Over the Hammer's favorite gin and countless

French Gauloises, he'd told Zahir to become Matthew Spenser's best friend, his mentor, a man he would come to trust implicitly, a man he would follow. "You will gently mold and manipulate this fool's penny-ante goals until they become your glorious ones"—that is, until Spenser became a murderer. Zahir knew it would be a challenge, but one he would win. He knew he wasn't as smart as Spenser in science, but he was years beyond Spenser in strategy, planning, execution, and sheer balls. But unlike the bare-fisted Hammer, Zahir was never guilty of underestimating an opponent, or reducing him to faults and weaknesses and strengths. He knew when to use a hammer, when to use a simple lie.

It was over the Hammer's fourth gin that he'd told Zahir with a snicker that Spenser might have a possible weakness—a woman named Vanessa, a beauty, late twenties, red hair, milk-white skin, and blue eyes, and the Hammer showed him a photo of her. She hardly fit the image of a wacko bomber, but the Hammer assured him she'd been building bombs with an Irish IRA git named Ian McGuire and his faction. Both groups hated what they saw as radical Islam's encroachment into their world, and according to the Hammer, this common cause united them.

With another snicker, he told Zahir the woman and Spenser were probably lovers and his grin split his mouth wide enough to see the gold filling in his back molar. He suggested Zahir seduce Vanessa away from Spenser, but Zahir couldn't figure out what that would gain him, certainly not Spenser's trust and friendship. He would see.

But it was Iranian colonel Vahid Rahbar who'd told

him his most important goal: to steal Spenser's amazing invention, a bomb that looked like a gold fifty-cent piece, no larger, and, according to their sources, would be undetectable. Nearly perfected, they'd heard, and the minute it was perfected, he wanted it. The colonel had rubbed his hands together. "You, my friend, will light the fuse that will begin the war, then we will explode their cities, kill millions, and none of them will even know how it was done. Our casualties—it is nothing compared to what we will gain. When it is all over, we will rule the world." Unspoken was *Shia will arise from the ashes and control the earth's destiny.*

Zahir didn't really care if Shia ran the world or if Buddha took over. His specialty would always be in demand.

Zahir whistled as he got into another stolen car, lifted from a side street in Reno. He would steal another car in a place named Incline Village, drive into the Sierras, and find Spenser.

He wondered which head of the hydra he'd manipulate Spenser into killing—the president or the vice president.

The game was about to begin.

1

KNIGHT TO F3

Grangemouth Refinery, Scotland
Four Months Ago

Vanessa was crouched down, staring into the night, her muscles tense and cramping in the night chill. It was her first job with Matthew, her first bomb built especially for him. It would work, she knew it would, but deep down she had doubts, and hated it. She shook her head, knowing she'd produce a lovely explosion for him as she watched for Ian and his boys. The Firth of Forth was to her left, salt and brine mingling with the sharp scent of unrefined oil.

The darkness was broken only by the lights of the refinery, always running, even after the sun went down. The lighted metal poles mingled with security lamps and boom lights to halo the bobbing headlamps on the workers' helmets. The whole scene looked fantastical, a stage setting in an artificial gloom.

Vanessa looked at her watch. Five minutes to go. Ian was placing the bomb, and at his signal she should be the one to detonate it, but not this time. Matthew told her he was going to be the one to blow up the night sky.

Well, let him, if it gave him a kick. Or was it this particular refinery? Even though it was her job, she smiled at him as she handed over the trigger. It didn't matter, she knew her baby would work just fine.

Vanessa didn't yet understand him, but it was early days. She recognized his genius, his facility with ideas and each step they had to consider before moving ahead with his selected target. She also knew his amazing bomb wasn't yet perfected. If it was, surely he'd want to test it.

She looked at her watch again, said aloud to Matthew, "Where is Ian? He should be out by now. The security guard will circle back around in thirty seconds. He's cutting it too close."

Matthew Spenser, the Bishop, a moniker he'd been given by Ian a long time before, because, as Ian had explained to her, he'd learned that Matthew existed in a master's chess realm that was always ten moves ahead of everyone else, and so didn't he deserve the name? *Why not King?* she wondered, but didn't say anything. Matthew was tall, lean, and hyper, sharp as a poised knife, he liked to think. She felt the excitement coming off him in waves. He was about to score another win.

He said to Vanessa, "Ian's never failed me. He'll be along. He knows what he's doing."

Three minutes now. They couldn't use comms; radio frequencies could set off the bomb.

She saw movement by the perimeter, and her adrenaline spiked. No, it wasn't Ian. Where was he? She felt gut-wrenching fear that something had gone wrong, that he'd been caught. Or, almost as bad, that she'd messed up and the bomb was somehow defective. Or, at the very worst, she'd been found out. No, she had to calm herself. Her beautiful, powerful Semtex bomb would work and Ian was a master at this; he'd get it set in place and get himself and their guys out of the plant. All would go well.

She let out her breath. Since her prints were all over the bomb and Ian always wore gloves, the message would be clear and received. Her bosses would know it was her group who'd blown up Grangemouth.

Two minutes.

Matthew squeezed her arm, gave her a quick smile. "Your first bomb for me." She could only nod. He felt to her like he was ready to jump out of his skin, or his brain, maybe both, but she felt it, too, this manic brew of emotions that roared through both of them. She wondered if in the aftermath of the explosion he would try to get her into bed, to celebrate scoring this victory by scoring her. She'd hold him off, waiting, waiting, trying to judge if she would have to go the sex route to find out what she needed to know.

She took one last look at her watch. "We're out of time."

"Vanessa, look there."

Ian was running across the field toward them, his now-empty backpack flying like wings behind him, a crazy smile stretched across his face, three of their men behind him.

She put in her earplugs.

Matthew was watching her as he stuffed in his own earplugs. Then, without a word, he grinned down at her and handed her back the trigger with a flourish. "Have at it, Vanessa, have at it."

Why had he changed his mind? What did it prove? Had he planned to see if she'd lose her nerve, not be able to detonate the bomb? Well, it hardly mattered.

Vanessa looked up at him as she depressed the trigger, a button on her cell phone.

A fraction of a second later, she felt the explosion. It started in the soles of her feet, pounded up her legs as the ground began to shake and an earsplitting roar tore through the silence. The night sky became day.

The concussion knocked both of them backward. They landed hard, their breath knocked out of them. When Vanessa managed to pull air into her lungs, she scrambled to her hands and knees, facing the heat of the blaze raging in the refinery. It looked like a bonfire on steroids, much stronger than she'd expected. She saw Ian and his men crouched down behind distant refinery trucks, did a quick head count. Everyone was accounted for.

So fast, all of it, so fast. The bomb had done its job, and she'd been its builder. She'd proven herself, established herself once and for all. Now she would be in with Matthew Spenser; now he had to accept her into his inner circle. After all, she was the one who'd engineered this marvel for him, and he would know there were more marvels to come. He had to trust her now.

He was screaming something at her, his voice wild, filled with alarm.

She couldn't hear him, pulled out her earplugs, but it didn't help much. The bomb's concussion had deafened her.

Then he leaped on her, rolling on top of her, slapping at her head.

"Your hair is on fire!"

Her hair was on fire? She knew she should be panicked, she should freak out, but she didn't move, and let him worry about it. Matthew jerked off his shirt and smothered her head in it.

When he pulled his shirt off her head, he stared down at her. "It's only the ends of your hair. Are you all right?"

She stared up at him, smelling her burned hair, listening to the roaring flames, and she started to laugh. She rolled away from him and dropped her singed head to the scrubby, ancient land and laughed and laughed.

Matthew lay beside her, panting, watching her. He rolled up on one arm, raised his hand and fingered the ends of her burned hair. "Vanessa, are you all right?"

"Oh, yes, I'm perfect," and she laughed again.

Ian, his dark hair coated in ash, his men behind him, appeared to their left. "What a blast that was, Van! Wasn't expecting it to roar like a dragon. What are you two waiting for? It's time to go. Coppers will be here in a flash. Van, what'd you do to your hair? I told you never to stand so close, and look what you've done."

Vanessa stood, ran a hand over the crispy ends of her hair, brushed the dirt from her jeans. She looked at the two men—one dark, one light, both crazy like foxes, both grinning at her.

"Satisfied, Mr. Spenser?"

Matthew rose slowly, wiped off his hands on his jeans as she had, and smiled down at her. "Oh, yes," he said, his voice filled with pleasure. "I'm more than satisfied." And he stared down at her, at her mouth, his eyes hot and manic.

Monday

11 p.m.–4 a.m.

2

KNIGHT TO F6

FBI Special Agent Michaela Caine drove the black Crown Vic with one hand, tucked a hank of loose hair back into her ponytail with the other, then shoved up her glasses.

It was late and she was tired, ready to go home and crash. But no chance, since they'd gotten a credible tip off the hotline. She looked over at her partner, Special Agent Nicholas Drummond, tapping on a laptop balanced on his knees, doing a background check on their tipster.

She said, "I'm praying with all my might we're not on a wild-goose chase and this guy isn't a thrill chaser."

Nicholas looked up. "I'm inclined to think he isn't.

Ben said the man was convinced he had information on COE, and a possible bombing. At this point, I'm willing to listen to anyone, even if it means missing one of Nigel's dinners. He called me earlier, said it was prime rib."

Mike laughed. "Oh, my, that sounds even better than the scrumptious three-day-old chicken salad sandwich I was planning to have at home." She paused, then sighed. "We've been working this case for two weeks now, Nicholas, and gotten nowhere. I hate that. Several oil refineries out west and no leads. I only wish we could keep the frequent-flier miles earned from flying all over the country. And what do we have? This group's mission statement, over and over, the same thing: No more oil from terrorist countries or you will pay the price.

"And now, out of nowhere, this guy pops up in our own backyard with information on COE? On a possible bombing? Do you really think this Hodges character is for real?"

He looked over at her. "My gut is starting to agree with my brain and say yes. You know what else? I think it's also about time that we have our turn at bat."

Baseball metaphor from a Brit? No, he probably meant cricket. Were you at bat in cricket? She didn't know. She grinned. Either way, he was right, it was their turn, and if Hodges was for real, it was possible they'd have a chance for a home run.

Nicholas looked back at his laptop. "Mr. Hodges appears solid, an accountant for a local Bayonne engineering firm. His wife died three years ago, breast cancer."

She took a left into an older residential neighborhood,

thick with trees and small, well-manicured lawns. Mr. Richard Hodges's house was on a quiet dead-end cul-de-sac that backed up to the Hudson River. To Nicholas, the block looked like any other older development in a small eastern American town—thirty-year-old single-story houses, comfortably settled in with their neighbors. Amazing how quiet it was, considering its proximity to Manhattan. He supposed the lapping water dampened the sound.

They saw the curtains twitch.

Nicholas closed his laptop. "I see we're expected."

Mike turned off the engine. "Okay, I'm thinking positively. I'm up at bat and Mr. Hodges is going to give me a perfect pitch."

The door opened before they had a chance to ring the bell. A man dressed in jeans and a white polo shirt waved them in and closed the door quietly behind them, as if he didn't want to wake someone. A habit from when his wife was ill?

The interior of Mr. Hodges's house was neat, looked clean, but it smelled musty, somehow sterile, and Mike doubted there'd been another woman living here since his wife's death. She didn't see any photos or knickknacks on any surface, only piles of newspapers and newsmagazines. The house, she realized, was now only a place where a lonely man lived off his memories.

"Mr. Hodges? I'm Agent Caine, and this is Agent Drummond. We were told you have some information about the terrorist group known as Celebrants of Earth, or COE, and a possible bombing."

Hodges was a smallish man with a bald spot and a heavy

five-o'clock shadow. He looked solid, calm, no indication that he was an alarmist or a wild-hair. Maybe they had finally caught their break. She smelled bacon and toast, a single man's dinner. She felt a punch of pain for him.

"It's nice to meet you," he said. "Thank you for coming. Shall we sit? Can I get you coffee? I have some already brewed."

"We wouldn't say no to a cup, sir. Thank you."

He gestured toward the kitchen.

Mike and Nicholas took a seat at an ancient table with one leg shorter than the others, held steady with a pile of magazines. Moments later, they both had mugs of coffee and a plate of chocolate-mint Girl Scout Cookies. Nicholas took one to be polite; they'd been floating around the office for the past few weeks and tasted like wax to him.

Nicholas sipped his coffee, then set the cup on the table. "So, Mr. Hodges, tell us what you know."

Hodges blinked at him. "You're British? I didn't know people from England could be in the FBI. Are you some sort of special case?"

Mike nodded, grinning. "Yes, sir, he is indeed a special case."

Nicholas sat forward. "My mother was American. The story, sir, please."

Mr. Hodges nodded. "I was at the Dominion Bar tonight, having a drink after work. There was a man there—I don't know his name, but I've seen him around before. He's works at the Bayway Refinery—doing what, exactly, I don't know. He'd obviously been drinking a while, looked pretty drunk to me, and I wondered why the bartender, that's the owner, May Anne, hadn't cut him off. He was shooting his mouth off, you know the kind of person, they get loud when they've had too much to drink and, well, lose all sense. I heard him tell his friend he was celebrating. He'd gotten a big payoff, a lot of money, and more to come, and he was going to retire and move to an island somewhere and have women in bikinis wait on him, and not take his wife and whiny kids with him.

"I thought that was a pretty crappy thing to say—I lost my Miriam three years ago and I miss her every day—and I didn't want to listen to him, so I tried to tune him out. But he was sitting in the booth directly behind my stool, and I couldn't help but hear. His friend asked where the money came from, and he shushed him and lowered his voice like drunks do, whispered real loud that he couldn't tell, it was top secret. But something really big was going to go down, like what had happened to that oil refinery in Scotland a few months ago—Grangemouth, he said.

"His friend asked if he was breaking the law, and he started to laugh, sounded like a hyena, so drunk he couldn't keep it together. I paid for my drinks and left, but all the way home I couldn't help thinking about what he said. I knew this group COE claimed responsibility for the Scotland refinery bombing, they'd sent their statement to the news media, and it's the same as the one they always use here in the U.S. And like I said, I knew this drunk guy worked at Bayway Refinery. That's why I called your FBI tip line. Thank you for taking me seriously. Do you think this is a real threat?"

Mike felt the surge of adrenaline to her toes. This was it, the break they'd been waiting for. Nicholas was right, this could be their home run.

She knew Nicholas felt the same, but his voice was cool and calm. "If you would, Mr. Hodges, please run through it again for us. Every word you remember the man saying."

Hodges repeated everything again, then remembered more at their questions, then gave them descriptions of the drunk man and his friend. When they knew the well was dry, Nicholas stood, clapped Hodges on the shoulder, and shook his hand.

"Thank you, sir, for calling us. We'll let you know."

Hodges walked them back to the front door. "You think this is serious, don't you? He wasn't bragging, he knows something is going to happen?"

Nicholas said, "We're certainly going to check it out. We'll know soon enough if it's serious when we find the guy. So keep thinking about everything you heard and saw, and if you would, please, write it all down. Agent Caine and I will have a visit with the Dominion bartender, see if she knows the customer's name as well as his friend's." He handed Mr. Hodges a card. "And please keep this to yourself."

"I sure hope nothing happens. It would be a real problem if they blew up Bayway like they did Grangemouth. What would it do? Raise our oil prices some more? Burn down houses? Make the air we breathe toxic for a year?"

"We'll do our best to see it doesn't happen, Mr. Hodges," Mike said. "Good night, and thank you again."

Mike had her cell to her ear before they got in the Crown

Vic. "Ben, we've got a real live lead on COE. You need to get a team of agents to Mr. Richard Hodges's house in Bayonne." She gave him the address. "I'm also thinking it would be smart to get a sketch artist out here, too, in case we can't get an ID on the drunk guy from the Dominion's bartender. But the protection for him is the most important. Just a precaution, but it'd make me feel better."

Ben was now as hyped as they were. "Come on, Mike, what did the guy tell you?"

"Not good, Ben. There may be a bombing at Bayway."

3

PAWN TO C4

Mike pulled in across from the Dominion Bar on Broadway in Bayonne, not five minutes from Mr. Hodges's house.

Nicholas checked out the cozy-looking neighborhood bar, heard no wild yells, no blaring music. "Maybe they have food. A pizza would be good. I'm ready to chew off my arm at the elbow."

"If they don't, there's a pizza place next door that's still got its lights on. We can get a slice."

"A slice? You're talking like a girl. I want a whole pie all to myself. I'll bet you could eat a whole pie, too."

He was right about that. "Bartender first, then stomachs."

Inside, the Dominion Bar was all dark wood, dim lights, and a long varnished copper bar with wine bottles lined up on shelves along the mirrored wall. There were twenty stools and six booths. It was a place for local couples on dates, or people stopping in after work before heading home, or for widowed men to feel comfortable to have human contact, and Nicholas wondered: Did the drunk live in the neighborhood?

Mike read his mind. "Mr. Hodges said he'd seen the guy before, which means he's a regular. Since this place isn't a dive, I can't imagine he's a low-on-the-food-chain roughneck. Probably he's at least a supervisor at Bayway, otherwise he wouldn't fit in here."

They walked through the large room, checking out the few remaining Monday-night customers. Mike checked everyone out. "I don't see any guy here who remotely fits Mr. Hodges's description. Or the guy's friend."

Mike showed her creds to the Dominion bartender, the owner, Mr. Hodges had told them, a tiny woman who looked like a middle-aged Peter Pan. She was wiping down the bar, humming an old Elton John tune under her breath. Over a healthy right breast was a nametag: May Anne.

Mike introduced both herself and Nicholas.

They saw instant alarm. "What's the matter? I didn't do anything, I promise. I own this place and I've never had any health violations, ever, and—"

"No," Mike said over her. "We simply need information. Do you know a Mr. Richard Hodges?"

"Dicker? Well, yes, of course I do. He comes in most every night. He always has the house merlot, tells me how his day went, asks me how I'm doing, and then goes home to bacon sandwiches. It's a shame about his wife; she was such a nice lady. Listen, I know Dicker wouldn't have done anything, really—"

Nicholas lightly laid his hand on her arm. "No, Mr. Hodges is fine, he's in no trouble. He was here earlier tonight?"

"Yes, he was. Is he okay? Has something happened to him?"

"No, no, he's fine, May Anne. We need your help. Now, we need to know if you remember a man who was sitting right behind Mr. Hodges, in a booth, a very drunk man. Tall, on the thin side, grayish hair, middle-aged—"

"Oh, yeah, that's our local idiot, Larry Reeves." May Anne rolled her eyes. "God sent him to punish me, I know it. He doesn't even live in the neighborhood, but he comes here maybe twice, three times a week. He's always pushing the limits on the weekends, drives me nuts. I was about to cut him off tonight when his friend took him out to drive him to Bayway; that's where he works. It was odd, though, because I've never known Larry to get that drunk before his shift, and here he is a night supervisor. Why? What's the fool done?"

Nicholas's heart revved. "You said he was going on shift?"

"Yes, he's third shift, a supervisor, like I told you. But you know, I think his friend had to take him home first, to shower and sober up. No way he could show up in that condition."

Mike leaned over the bar. "Do you know his friend's name?"

"Can't say I do, he's fairly new to the bar. Does he live in the neighborhood? I can ask Clem, he's back cleaning up in the kitchen. He knows everything about everybody." May Anne turned and called out, "Clem, please come out a minute. I need you!"

The floor started to shake, rippling in waves, like an earthquake, and a muffled roar filled the bar. Nicholas's mind registered *explosion* before he hit the floor, pulling Mike beneath him. He yelled, "Everyone get down!"

Bottles shimmied and dropped, glasses and bottles skidded off tables and crashed to the floor to shatter, spewing glass everywhere. The windows flexed and burst, sending shards of glass hurtling through the air. May Anne was grabbing bottles as they toppled, but it was a lost cause. The few customers were yelling, diving for cover, hands over their heads. Nicholas felt a shard of glass slice into the back of his hand. He realized Mike was struggling to get out from under him.

The shuddering stopped.

"Get off me, Nicholas, get off. What blew up?" But she knew it had to be the Bayway Refinery, as Nicholas did.

He rolled off her, yelled, "Is everyone okay?"

People started to stand, all of them clearly shaken. May Anne came out from behind the bar to help brush off her customers, soothing them as best she could. As Mike and Nicholas ran out of the bar, she heard May Anne yell, "Everyone, calm down. You're all okay. I've got insurance! Drinks are on the house!"

Mike and Nicholas rushed outside to hear car alarms, loud and piercing, and people shouting, pouring out of their homes, out of the pizza parlor. Glass littered the sidewalks. Nicholas jerked open the driver's-side door and shouted, "We can help, Mike, hurry. You drive."

Mike was turning the key in the ignition when their cells began to ring. She floored the Vic down the street as Nicholas answered his. It was their boss, Milo Zachery.

"Sir, is it the Bayway Refinery?"

"Yes, a huge explosion. No reports in yet, so I don't have any idea how bad it is. Where are you and Agent Caine?"

"We're nearby, sir. We'll be on-site in five minutes. Listen, we met with a man who tipped the hotline." Nicholas told him about Larry Reeves, gave Zachery the description Hodges had given them, found Reeves's home address on his laptop, and read it off to Zachery. "Sir, we need agents to be on the lookout for him. There's little doubt he's involved in the bombing."

"Got it," Zachery said. "Report back as soon as you can. And don't do anything stupid—that means heroic—either of you. Catch these guys."

"Will do, sir."

Mike drove fast over the Bayonne Bridge, past Newark Airport and into Elizabeth. They saw flames and black smoke visible from the tip of the island, lighting up the night sky like a huge torch. As they neared the refinery, they saw broken glass all over the sidewalks and streets, dozens of people crowded outside, staring toward the refinery. The flames made it bright as day.

It had taken Mike less than ten minutes to get to the refinery, and they spoke once the whole way. Mike said, "You know it's COE, has to be."

"Of course it was. Up until now, it's been small stuff, refineries away from where people live, and the grids haven't impacted too many people, either. But now they've upped the ante. This is a big leap, Mike. They're now saying they can cause us grave hurt."

Nicholas and Mike had taken over from a small task force that had gotten nowhere, until now. And they hadn't been in time. Even with Hodges's tip, their home-run break, they hadn't been in time.

COE had to know there were people working in the refinery, and that meant injuries and deaths. Why had they suddenly become bona fide terrorists?

Nicholas stared at the swelling orange flames that were turning the air acrid and bitter, the thick billowing black smoke scorching the very air they sucked into their lungs.

This was going to be bad.

4

PAWN TO G6

Bayway Refinery
Elizabeth, New Jersey

They arrived on scene along with most of the first responders. Mike speeded through the gates of the refinery, onto the long road leading to the huge converters, closer and closer to the fire. When the road ran out, blocked by a large chunk of metal, she pulled to a stop and flew out of the car, running toward the flames, Nicholas beside her, both dodging the debris still raining down. Nicholas grabbed her arm, jerked her back to him. He pulled off his leather jacket, ripped off his shirtsleeve, and wrapped it around her face. "Tie it tight."

He ripped off the other sleeve and covered his own nose and mouth. Still, the choking black smoke seeped in, making them wheeze and cough. And then they were off.

It was like running through a battlefield toward a wall of flames, he thought, as he shrugged his jacket back on. It wasn't much protection, but some. Mike was wearing her motorcycle jacket, heavier than his, and that was good.

They sucked in their breaths and kept running. He heard Mike scream, "Over here, Nicholas!"

He changed course, dodging flying rubble, banging his hip against a concrete pylon, there to ensure the security of this place, only it hadn't done any good. The bombers had gotten in despite all the safety precautions.

Nicholas saw a man pinned under a piece of the wreckage. His skin was deathly white and blood seeped from his legs, black in the night.

Nicholas moved behind the man, nodded to Mike. "One, two, three," she yelled, and Nicholas pulled up the stinging hot metal, burning his hands, heaving with all his strength while Mike tugged the man clear. He dropped the metal back to the ground with a crash barely heard in the hellish chaos around them.

"Bloody hell." He shook his hands, rubbed them together, wincing at the blisters that had popped up. He hadn't thought to get gloves from the car's boot, brain that he was.

"There's another man over there!"

Nicholas saw a large chunk of metal sticking out of the man's neck and the odd angle of his head. "He's dead. Keep moving."

Mike swallowed, nodded. They wound their way closer to the center of the blast site. The heat was incredible, the flames shooting madly into the night, singeing their arms and hair, but they kept moving, picking through the rubble, looking for survivors.

"Here's one," Nicholas shouted, and they dragged the man free, picked him up by arms and legs, and ran him back to where firemen had set up a protected space for the arriving EMTs to tend to the wounded.

They lost count of the men they'd carried back to the staging area. Finally a firefighter stepped in their way, hands up.

"Hey. Stop, both of you. I don't know who you are, but you don't have the right equipment. Get back away from here, now. I don't want the two of you hurt as well."

Mike shouldered her way past him. "These men are going to die if we don't get back in there. Help us or get out of the way."

The firefighter opened his mouth to yell at her when Nicholas grabbed his arm, saw his name on his jacket. J. JONES. "Don't bother, mate. She's unstoppable. Come on, we could use your help. We'll tell your supervisor you were escorting us. Move it, now."

Without waiting to see what the man did, Nicholas ran after Mike into the flame-lit night.

Twenty minutes after the bomb went off, the scene looked like a Hieronymus Bosch nightmare scape. The air was still ripe with the scent of carnage, men stumbling from the converters, others slumped silent on the ground, bloody, groaning, so many others more seriously hurt and bleeding in the staging area. In that instant, this hell shot Nicholas back to a place more than three years before, in another part of the world, and the terrible mistakes made, and he felt a ferocious hit of pain and guilt.

The firefighter who'd tried to stop them, Jones, was at his elbow, pointing and shouting. Nicholas whirled round. He thought they'd cleared everyone in this quadrant. He couldn't see any more bodies in the hellish light.

"What is it? I don't see anyone."

Jones yanked on his shoulder, pulled him backward, shouting, "No, look, over there. Bomb, bomb!" and Nicholas saw a black backpack on the ground, with wires sticking out of the top. His heart froze.

Mike was a good twenty feet in front of him. He sprinted to her, caught her, grabbed her hand, and dragged her as fast as he could away from the backpack into the darkness, yelling, "Secondary device, run, Mike, run!"

They ran toward Jones, who was still screaming at everyone to fall back, fall back.

The backpack exploded, and the world around them shattered.

5

KNIGHT TO C3

Nicholas barely had time to fling his arms up to protect his face before he was hurled backward to the ground, unconscious. A year, a day, moments, he didn't know, but when he came to, he was lying facedown on the oily tarmac. He shook his head, pulled himself together. He saw Mike lying ten yards away, sprawled on her back, legs and arms flung out, Jones lying beside her. Neither of them was moving. He saw something dark and wet on the ground near Jones's head—blood, yes, *blood* was the word he was looking for—and Mike still wasn't moving. He tried to stand up but couldn't, he had no balance.

He crawled to Mike, pressed his filthy fingers to the pulse in her neck. She was breathing, thank the good Lord.

He pulled her onto his lap and held her close, rocking her. "Come on, Mike, wake up, come on, sweetheart, you can do it."

She began to moan low in her throat and he said over and over, "Come on, Mike, come back to me, you can do it. I've promised a dozen years of good works if you'll be okay. Come on, Mike, wake up, do it now before I stroke out." Finally, she twitched and opened her eyes. He looked into her beautiful blue eyes, now vague with confusion, and knew such relief he wanted to shout with it. He wondered if this was how she'd felt in Geneva, with him out cold on the ground, the building exploding behind him? Her glasses lay on the ground beside her, incredibly unbroken. He handed them to her, watched her shove them back on.

They'd both lost their shirtsleeve masks. Mike's hair was sticking out in all directions. Her face was grimed with soot, but he could clearly see the big bruise on her cheek and the beginnings of a black eye.

Amazingly, she smiled up at him. He pressed his forehead to hers, knowing his heart was still pounding too fast, the fear still eating deep. "Tell me you're okay. Promise me you're okay."

"Yes, don't worry, Nicholas, I'm only battered a bit. You look pretty scary. Can you believe it? My glasses aren't broken. You okay?"

He nodded. "But our savior, Jones, he doesn't look good."

Together they crawled to where Jones lay motionless. He was still, too still. Mike leaned close, said over her shoulder, "He's breathing. He lost his hardhat, but he's wearing his fireman's jacket, it cushioned his fall." Mike patted his face, ran her hands over his head, down over his shoulders, while Nicholas felt his arms and legs. She patted his face again. "Mr. Jones? Come on, wake up, tell me you're okay."

A few moments later his eyelids began to flutter, and he was back with them. "Wh-what's happening?"

"Don't worry about it," Nicholas said as he pulled a handkerchief out of his pocket, amazingly still snowy white. "Here, your nose is bleeding."

Mike sat back on her knees, watched Jones take a swipe at the blood. She said, "Hey, way to get out of the way, dude."

He gave a ghost of a laugh. "Do I look as bad as you guys?"

"Probably worse," Mike said. "You have blood smeared all over your face."

"Feels like I busted my nose again. Weird, but it doesn't hurt like the first time. You guys all right?" He sounded like he had a bad cold.

"Bumps and bruises," Nicholas said. "Can you stand?"

They hauled him to his feet, all three clinging to one another for balance. Mike said, "You know the drill, keep pressure on your nose. What's your name?"

That took him a minute, then he grinned. "Jimbo, everyone calls me Jimbo."

"Okay, Jimbo," Nicholas said. "I'm Nicholas and this is Mike. Let's get you back to the EMTs."

The scene behind them hadn't worsened after the second blast. Since they'd been closest, and they were alive and nearly walking, it hadn't been a very strong bomb. Nicholas thought back to the placement—the backpack had been lying on the ground out in the open, almost as if it had fallen off the wearer's back. Perhaps it was the bomber's and he'd been running away from the first blast.

Nicholas said, "This is curious. I mean, a second bomb—that's the MO normally used by terrorist organizations to achieve maximum death tolls by taking out the first responders. What's going on? COE has never pulled this trick before."

"No, they haven't." Mike looked around at the devastation. "This makes no sense. If it's COE and not a new wild-hair come to the party, they've changed their ways. Up until now, that second smaller bomb should have been the one and only one detonated, not that big honker first bomb. This is scary, Nicholas, really scary."

A gaggle of firefighters was headed their way, shouting. Nicholas waved them off. They were fine, no reason to waste resources. Jimbo still had Nicholas's wadded-up handkerchief pressed to his nose, was using his other hand to brush the dirt off his uniform.

Nicholas said, "Thanks for spotting the bag, Jimbo. You saved our lives."

Jimbo Jones grinned, showing a mouth and teeth rimmed in blood. "Buy me a beer sometime, guys. Now, you two need to get out of here, to safety. Really, I'm okay now. You can leave the rest to us." He started to hand Nicholas back the handkerchief, shook his head at himself, and jogged off in a drunken zigzag pattern to rejoin his company.

More fire trucks were arriving, a parade of red and white lights, sirens shrieking.

"How many fire companies do you think have been called, Mike?"

"I don't know. Of course Bayway has their own resources for this type of emergency, but they need all the help they can get tonight. This explosion was certainly much bigger than anything Bayway's people could handle alone."

"Has an explosion on this massive a scale ever happened before here at Bayway?"

"There was a major explosion in 1970. For a while, everyone believed it was the work of revolutionaries, since the FBI received a call from a man who claimed to be a member of the United Socialist Revolutionary Front. His demand: release of political prisoners. The FBI dug deep, but it turned out to be an accident, not a bomb. Then a smaller explosion ripped through the refinery in '79. Again, a suspected bomb, but it turned out to be another accident." Mike looked around her. "But this wasn't an accident. This was a huge purposeful hit."

Nicholas tried to wipe off her face, but it didn't do much good since his hands were black with soot. "COE designed this hit for maximum damage and disruption, and they didn't give a crap about innocent lives."

Her hand tightened on his arm. "We've done all we can, Nicholas. Let's regroup and find these bastards."

6

BISHOP TO G7

They made their way toward the car, feeling like salmon swimming upstream with all the rescue personnel and cops and firefighters rushing toward the scene.

Nicholas said, "I wonder how COE managed to pull this off—a bombing in our own backyard, at one of the most secure refineries in the country, under close scrutiny and additional security."

Mike was feeling pain in every inch of her body, screaming at her for aspirin or something much stronger, but she ignored it, no choice. "That first bomb was so powerful, why bother with the small secondary bomb? And no deaths before, but now I'm afraid to know how many people died tonight. Why have they done this? Nicholas, we need to track down Larry Reeves right away, open him up like a can, find out who paid him the big bucks."

The farther they were from the blast site, the better the air became. She stopped, sucked in deeply. "I hadn't realized—Nicholas, if Mr. Hodges hadn't called us—"

"Then more people would have died, so we did some good, Mike. You know, it strikes me as odd—sneaking someone into this facility is certainly doable, if one were properly motivated, but still very risky for Reeves. How could a man so drunk he staggered out of the bar manage to pull it off?"

"Well, it doesn't sound like he was faking being drunk—I mean, flapping his mouth like that—sounds like he gave his COE contact access before his little celebration party with his buddy." She shook her head. "Still, what a moron, shooting off his mouth for anyone to hear. Good for us, though."

Nicholas looked up at the video cameras on the light poles. Several had been blown off their mountings and were hanging by their wires. "Ah, there are a couple of good ones, thank the good Lord." He pointed them out to Mike. "Here's hoping they still function after the blast and we'll have enough footage to recover."

"Good eyes, Nicholas. I'll get Gray Wharton on it. Digits crossed the blast didn't knock out the connections."

She put her phone to her ear as she walked. Nicholas paused for a moment, looking back, and he sent up a prayer of thanks that he and Mike were both unharmed, a prayer for the health and happiness of Mr. Hodges, and a prayer to mourn the men who hadn't made it.

At the car, Mike reached in for her bag, drew out a wad of hand wipes, started scrubbing at her face, making comical streaks in the black. Nicholas took one from her, swiped it over his own face, felt the grit and dirt and whatever else pebble beneath the wipe. He breathed in the scent of antiseptic mingled with blood and death and acrid smoke. A nightmare, and they'd been in the middle of it, playing with death. Too late—they'd been too late to stop it.

He leaned against the car and watched the orange flames funnel into the night sky, still ferocious and lethal, and he wondered when the firemen would manage to finally kill it. He hoped by morning. Then all the experts could get closer, find the ignition point, find the elements that could lead them to the bomb maker.

"Too bad we can't summon a bloody hard rain to come down and help."

Mike said, "With all the oil on fire now, it wouldn't help much."

"Have I ever told you about the fire in Farrow-on-Grey?"

"You haven't. When was it? Was anyone hurt? I can't imagine your lovely home damaged. Breaks my heart."

"It was the town itself, not Old Farrow Hall. It happened in 1765, nearly one hundred years after the great fire destroyed London. Our fire damaged many of the buildings, but the town was spared because of several quick-thinking young lads who'd been playing whist in The Drunken Goose. There used to be a large lake on the grounds of Old Farrow Hall, where the gardens are today. Family lore says they emptied the lake to save the town."

"I assume one of the quick thinkers was the Baron de Vesci at the time?"

He smiled. "The third Baron, yes. Colin Drummond.

He quickly organized the whole town—women and children, too—into a fire brigade. They saved the church and the pub, and the lower two-thirds of the town."

"So you're telling me firefighting's in your blood?"

He coughed out a laugh. "Apparently I am."

She cleared her throat. It hurt, hurt deep. She was quiet for a moment. "Nicholas, our information was that COE had threatened to take out Rodeo San Francisco next, not Bayway."

"For whatever reason they changed their minds. You know what? I think they've made a big mistake coming to New York. Now they're here on our turf and shoving their god-awful destruction right in our faces. They're going to regret ever screwing with the FBI."

"I agree, Agent Drummond." SAC Milo Zachery walked out of the night. They hadn't heard him drive up over all the noise—helicopter rotors and car alarms and the shrieks and calls of the first responders and the roar of the fire. Mike realized he was nearly shouting to be heard, supposed she and Nicholas had been shouting at each other as well. The flames outlined Zachery in an orange mantle.

"Sir." Nicholas pushed off the car, stuck out his hand, realized it was burned and black with soot, and shrugged.

Zachery's voice was flat and angry. "We went to talk to Larry Reeves. Seems someone beat us to him."

7

PAWN TO D4

Near the Bayway Refinery

From atop a nearby hill, Vanessa stood rigid, numb and disbelieving, as she watched the Bayway Refinery burn. When the tenth ambulance left the facility without its lights and sirens, signaling it was carrying another dead body, she fell to her knees, dropping her ATN NVG7 night-vision monocular to her chest, hugging herself. She had to get it together, had to.

Her Semtex hadn't done this. The small second explosion, that had been her bomb. She didn't want to believe what she was seeing, but the horrific flames, the shouts, the screams were all too real.

No deaths. That was her rule, Matthew's rule. No deaths.

Well, it had been Matthew's rule until tonight. Now they had blood on their hands, real blood. She wanted to scream with grief, with fury. She heard her uncle's voice telling her, *"Nessa, don't blame yourself, sometimes things will simply be out of your control, awful things that you'll simply have to learn to live with. Follow your training, Nessa, you won't go wrong, not in the end."*

But these were innocent people's lives, no way around it. However could she learn to live with that?

And she knew what it meant: Matthew had perfected his small gold-coin bombs and used a tiny part of one as a test. Thank heaven he hadn't used an entire gold coin, it would have wiped out countless thousands and reduced the landscape to rubble.

She knew to her gut it was Darius who'd kept after Matthew to finish perfecting his bomb, Darius who'd decided to test it tonight. It hadn't taken her long to recognize Darius for what he was—a born soulless killer who didn't care how many people died. But this time she knew he'd had a reason. To see for himself how powerful Matthew's new bombs were because he wanted them for himself.

She breathed deeply, again and again, until she calmed. She wondered what Matthew was thinking as he looked out over the killing field and knew it was his creation that had brought it about. Was he as horrified as she was, or was he with Darius, and very likely smiling and nodding at the success of his bomb? *All the deaths.* And it was up to her to stop both of them.

She rolled over onto her stomach and raised the monocular again. She'd been watching the two civilians. Now they'd been joined by another man, and she realized who they were. Not civilians, no, they were FBI.

Over the past two weeks, she'd memorized files on all the FBI players. The older man was Milo Zachery, head of the Criminal Investigative Division for the New York Field Office. The younger, taller one was that Brit, Nicholas Drummond. Of course she recognized the woman who could double as a biker chick in her black boots and black-framed glasses—Michaela Caine. She'd watched them on the news after they'd helped stop a nuclear attack in Europe. Of course, even without the media flood, Vanessa would recognize Mike Caine. Even back in the day, Vanessa remembered her as a burning light, smart, funny, unforgettable.

Of all the people she didn't want to see, these two were at the top of the list, but here they were—not more than a hundred meters away, witnesses to the horror that her group had brought about. And here she lay, one of the anonymous deathmongers. And how would she ever learn to live with that?

She remembered the Matthew Spenser she'd met only a little more than four months before. That Matthew hadn't believed in collateral damage, had abhorred the thought of killing anyone, accidently or on purpose. He'd been gaining more and more attention from the small-scale bombings, as he wanted. And then Darius had come, dumped a million dollars in his lap, and begun manipulating him, changing him. And now this. She knew Darius—or whatever his name was—had a plan, and now he'd sucked Matthew, sucked all of them, into it, made them all murderers, made them all—terrorists. Didn't Matthew realize he was now no better than the terrorists who'd killed his family?

Matthew had told her so little, and she hadn't figured out how to get him to open up to her. Sex wasn't in the cards now, even if he put the moves on her. She simply couldn't bear to think about his hands on her now, not with the horrible stench of blood and death filling her nostrils. The Matthew she knew was quick to anger, just as quick to laugh, a man who could spend hours concentrating his genius brain on something he was creating. She'd believed he liked her, maybe even coming to trust her, at least until Darius came along. But now she realized he was headed toward something unimaginable, something horrific, and that something involved Darius. She had to find out what it was before it happened, and somehow get her hands on Matthew's bombs and his formula, or her assignment would be a failure. Now, that was a small order to fill, wasn't it?

Matthew had almost told her his plans yesterday at their apartment in Brooklyn. They were talking about the logistics of the Bayway bombing, and Matthew, as was his habit, was skillfully weaving a gold coin through his fingers over and over again, like a magician. Wily, no-nonsense Ian had rolled out the blueprints a night supervisor had provided them—Larry Reeves had cost them the rest of their ready cash, though Andy always got his hands on more; it never seemed to be a problem. Matthew and Vanessa ran through the last of the logistics, drinking Bud Light because that's all Luther from Belfast, one of the boys, had bought at the corner market.

She'd taken a sip from the bottle, eyed him, and thought, *Careful, careful.*

"Matthew, what's next? You already have the attention of the world. Every law enforcement organization is looking for us. People are afraid of what you might do next. We'll have much more destruction at Bayway, a much bigger statement. The FBI will be in an absolute frenzy. What are we going to do to top Bayway?"

He'd reached over and tucked a strand of loose hair behind her ear. "Tomorrow the plan will be in place, and no one will be able to stop it—"

And then Ian had come back into the room and Matthew backed away from her and once again was weaving a coin through his fingers. She remembered the first time she saw those gold coins, no larger than a fifty-cent piece, remembered how Ian McGuire, her compatriot from Belfast, was so excited to tell her how he'd met a fellow terrorist-hater all those years ago, and he'd recognized his genius, and he'd happily offered her up to make bombs for him.

She could deal with Ian, but what to do about Andy Tate, that wild ungoverned boy who'd set fires since he was seven years old and, even more, was a computer genius, a hacker of incredible talent, probably more valuable than she or Ian was to Matthew, since he procured the money.

Vanessa saw another ambulance silently leave. Another dead. Had Matthew known what Darius was going to do? Or had Darius simply taken one of Matthew's bombs and used it? Would Matthew be as livid as she was? Or had he changed that much? She'd never forget what he'd said when Ian had brought her into the group, "No innocents can die, Muslims included, Vanessa. I'm not like those terrorists who kill wantonly. I'll make my point without death."

She looked out over the burning refinery. Everything had changed now. It didn't matter which of them was responsible, or if both Darius and Matthew were complicit. It had to stop.

8

CASTLES

Where was Darius? He was supposed to meet her, and she hadn't seen him come out of the refinery. She would wait another ten minutes, then she had to clear out because she knew law enforcement would be searching the area soon. Could he possibly be dead, burned up in his own fire? Wouldn't that be fine irony? And one less terrorist she had to deal with.

Darius had caught her once, walking back to their cabin in the mountains near Tahoe, and she knew his intent immediately. She'd said only, "You force me and I'll cut your balls off." And she'd waited, looking at him, emotionless, to see what he would do.

"So you prefer your brainy little boy to a man, do you?"

"I'd prefer Satan himself to you." Not smart, given what she knew to her gut he was, but she also realized, the moment the words were out of her mouth, she'd say them again.

He'd laughed and walked off, giving her a little finger wave over his shoulder. "Later, love," he'd said, but after that, he'd ignored her.

She'd managed to take a full-frontal photo of him, stepping out of a field shower, the only clear shot she'd ever gotten of his face. He was always careful, and why was that? He was dark, muscular, very strong, his eyes black and cold. Middle Eastern heritage, but he'd been educated in England, given his Brit accent. She'd sent his photo in two weeks ago, hoping for word about who he really was.

Now, as she waited, Vanessa remembered how he and Matthew had been talking together, voices low, before they'd left for the refinery. When she'd come into the room, they'd shut up. In hindsight, she realized of course they'd been finalizing their plans to test the gold-coin bombs, which meant Matthew had been turned and was now a willing murderer.

Vanessa looked at her watch: nearly twelve-thirty. Time was up. She had to get back to the rally point. She couldn't wait any longer to see if Darius emerged like Lazarus from the flames. *Be dead*, she prayed. *Please be dead.*

She bagged up her things, slipped her backpack onto her shoulders, started off down the hill at a steady jog, thinking hard.

Caine and Drummond were going to be a problem. Caine especially, since Vanessa knew the woman was a pit bull—a brainy, relentless pit bull. Now that COE had killed, the FBI would redouble their efforts. Time was running out. She had to get Matthew to tell her his plans, what he was going to do with his magic gold-coin bombs, and she had to do it now.

Matthew was waiting in the mud-caked Toyota Corolla. He'd disabled the dome light, so when she opened the door, there was nothing but the squeak of the hinges and his harsh breathing. He'd turned off the scanner, was staring straight ahead, unseeing, into the night.

He nodded to her. "Ian and his boys checked in, all of them safe. We need to send our statement to the media now—"

Her voice was wonderfully calm. "Matthew, you just did a test run for your bombs. Do you have any idea what kind of carnage you've created? People are dead, Matthew, by your hand, not mine."

He didn't say anything, didn't look at her. "Send the media statement, Vanessa. Now."

She kept hold of her temper. "Darius didn't come out of the bombing. You even killed your mentor, Matthew."

9

BISHOP TO F4

Bayway Refinery

Both Mike and Nicholas leaned in so Zachery could hear. "What did you say, sir? Reeves is dead? He was killed?"

Zachery said, "No, but he's missing. His wife said he didn't come home from the Dominion Bar to change before his shift. His friend's name is Chuck Metter; we're looking for him now. No luck yet. Jersey police are canvassing the neighborhoods, the few who could be spared from this mess.

"We're running Reeves's financials now, trying to see if there's a money trail. Either he decided to bolt or he's been kidnapped or killed."

Nicholas said, "Ten pounds says he came back to the refinery to do whatever he was supposed to do to let in the bombers. He obviously needed some liquid courage to pull it off. He may be among the dead or injured. He may be in hospital. I'll leave word with the EMTs, see if anyone fitting his description was taken away." Nicholas paused. "Or COE is eliminating witnesses and took him out. They didn't count on him shooting his mouth off in a bar."

Mike kicked the tire of her car. "He was our only lead. I hope security has been increased on Mr. Hodges as well. Given what these people have done tonight, their sheer disregard for human life, we don't want to take any chances with his safety."

Zachery said, "Nor do I. With any luck, COE doesn't even know about Mr. Hodges, but just in case, I now have three agents with him. He'll be fine."

"You're thinking revenge?"

Zachery shrugged. "I don't know, Nicholas, that or an overall cleanup. I plan to have him moved to a safe house later tonight. Now, have they found the initial blast site yet?"

Nicholas said, "They have to get the fire put out first, then it will still be too hot for a few hours. We'll go in the moment they clear us."

"New Jersey bomb squads are here; New York is close. They'll find the ignition point." Zachery touched both his agents on the shoulder. "I've been told what you two did tonight, how you didn't stop. I met a firefighter named Jimbo who said you were both maniacs and saved his life. I realize you're both frustrated, exhausted, and angry, but know this—you saved lives otherwise lost if

you hadn't been here, if you hadn't been who you are."
He paused. "Thank you both. I'm thinking there might
be commendations coming to you for this night." He
paused again. "That is, if you catch these scum."

Nicholas looked down at his hands, covered in soot,
the flesh pink and raw, blistered in places, and at Mike,
who was staring back into the flames again, also covered
in black ash, her blond ponytail gone brunette with small
silver streaks. "We're going to catch them, sir."

Mike asked, "Has COE claimed responsibility yet?"

"Not yet. But I'm sure they'll follow the path of the
last few bombings—give the media maybe an hour to
speculate before their signature letter is splashed all over
the Internet and blaring out from newsrooms." He paused
for a moment. "What really concerns me is, unlike the
other bombings, people died tonight. At least fifteen, last
count, and COE has never killed before. And the bomb
itself was more powerful, much more powerful, plus there
was a second bomb, lying in the open, almost as if it had
been dropped."

Mike nodded. "Tonight they changed, and I keep
wondering why. Why murder people when they never had
before? It's not like they weren't getting lots of attention.
People were getting alarmed, there were politicians beginning to talk about reducing oil imports from the Middle
East, the refinery bombings on everyone's mind."

Nicholas said, "Maybe there's something else going
on, maybe they now have another, grander plan—"

Zachery nodded. "Yes, or another person is now on board.

Another player, perhaps, one with no qualms about killing. Or maybe a separate group entirely, using COE's MO?"

Nicholas said, "The last bit of chatter in the darknet warned specifically of a California hit, near San Francisco. But now this happens here at Bayway. No, I still think it's COE. Another player now involved, someone far more violent who's now calling the shots? That sounds possible."

Mike shook her head, sprinkling ash down onto her shoulders. "We're going to have to—"

Zachery interrupted her, his hand on her arm. "Stop. Listen, Agent Caine, both you and Agent Drummond go home, take a shower, get some rest. Nothing will happen until the fire is out, which could take hours. Since you two are our leads on these bombings, JTTF will want to be briefed in the morning. You know they'll be expecting a full report, so you need to power down and get some sleep."

Mike had worked for Zachery long enough to know he meant what he said, so she nodded slowly. But she still wasn't ready to fold her tent.

"Yes, sir." Mike ran her hands across her face. They came back still streaked black with soot. "I've got to hose myself down before I hit the sheets. Maybe get a power wash."

"We'll find a place where they can turn a hose on both of us," Nicholas said, and gave her a wink.

"May I also suggest you put some ice on that shiner?" Zachery said. He patted her shoulder once again, shook Nicholas's hand, then set off to talk to the firemen at the triage center.

"Get the chemical ice pack out of the first-aid kit in the boot, Mike. It's quicker than stopping off for a bag of peas."

She quickly found the ice pack since all the pool cars had the same equipment. She broke the pack as she climbed into the front seat, pressed it against her face and leaned her head back against the headrest, and felt the blessed freezing begin.

She said, "You don't have any sleeves. Dare I ask what Nigel will have to say to you?"

He laughed, and it felt good after this nightmare of a night—well, at least for a moment.

He fired up the Crown Vic and headed back for the bridge.

Mike lifted off the ice pack and pulled down the passenger mirror. She really didn't want to look, but she had to. *Oh my, not good.* At that moment, she saw her mother staring at her, horror clear on her face. She lightly touched her fingers to her cheek. Bruises galore, and a lovely plus—her skin was lobster-red from the few minutes with the ice pack. She groaned and slapped the visor closed. She looked over at Nicholas. Sure enough, he was smiling, a brow arched. "I shouldn't have looked. The truth doesn't always set you free. Sometimes it terrifies."

He laughed. "You do look like you went rounds with Lord Queensberry himself."

"Isn't Queensberry one of your grandfather's swanky friends?"

"Possibly, though a few generations removed. He's a famous British boxing enthusiast. You've heard of Queensberry Rules?"

"Yeah, yeah, it figures it would be a Brit who decided the proper, most civilized way to go about killing each other."

He reached over and lightly touched his fingers to her cheek. "Even though you look a bit rough, Agent Caine, all those men you rescued tonight would agree an angel saved them. The ice pack should help."

She said, "When I'm done with it, you can use it. You're a bit on the edge yourself." She paused, then, "And they'd say you're an angel, too."

He shot her a grin with a raised eyebrow, his teeth shiny white against his soot-black skin. "Have I ever told you you're fierce?"

She gave a small laugh. "You want to tell me what you mean by that?"

"Let's say if you were my mom, I'd know to my core you'd keep me safe."

She felt a warm glow all the way to her belly. "Thank you."

Once over the bridge, he said, "What's the fastest way to your place?"

"You're kidding, right?"

"Well, yes, of course. Despite the three agents, we're going to make certain Mr. Hodges is safe and sound and hasn't thought of anything else useful. But if Zachery finds out, I'm telling him it was all your idea."

10

PAWN TO D5

Richard Hodges's house
Bayonne, New Jersey

Nicholas retraced their steps to Bayonne. Mike, her face set, stared back at the burning refinery.

"We weren't in time, Mike, but we did good. Are you all right? No broken bones you're keeping from me?"

"No, nothing," she said, still staring back.

"I ask because you're practically vibrating."

Mike gingerly pressed the ice pack back to her cheek. "Yeah, I guess I am. I'd like to hit something. I hate what we saw tonight. So much death, so much destruction."

He gave a humorless laugh. "I feel precisely the same way."

She turned to face him, drawing her legs up on the

seat. "I'm sorry, of course this would remind you of your past as well."

Some things were better left unsaid, so he simply shook his head. "You've seen this kind of destruction before?"

So he didn't want to talk about the huge betrayal in Kabul. She knew enough. She said, "My dad was in Oklahoma for work when McVeigh bombed the Alfred P. Murrah Federal Building. I was ten. I spent hours watching it on television, and when he came home, he showed me some of the pictures his team had taken, not of dead children, of course, even though I knew of their deaths, just as I knew he'd taken out many of the really bad photos, but it was still too much. All of it brought about by a misguided madman.

"I was sixteen when Nine-Eleven happened." Her voice rose, and she smacked the dashboard with her closed fist. "These sons-of-bitches and their bombs and attacks, it still makes me so mad I knew if I had them in front of me, I'd blow off their worthless heads." She sucked in her breath, knew her blood pressure had spiked to the stratosphere. "Sorry, but it really pisses me off. Unlike you, I haven't ever been in the middle of it, but I've seen enough."

"Is this why you became a copper?"

"Not really. You know my dad's a cop, so I knew the life, knew I wanted it. Dad was all for it. But my mom, do you know she's still known in Omaha as the Gorgeous Rebecca? Yes, Nicholas, unhoist your eyebrow. Mom was a beauty queen, Miss Nebraska, as a matter of fact. My mom the beauty queen had great plans for me, her only daughter. She wanted me to be some sort of model or maybe a movie star, although I could never act my way out of a paper bag, or maybe marry a rich guy and have beautiful kids. But even as a bratty teenager, I never gave her vision of my future serious thought." She paused. "When I was accepted to Yale, she decided maybe a high-falutin education would be just the ticket. She saw me marrying some eastern politico, I think.

"But she's come around, likes to talk about her daughter, the FBI special agent who lives in New York City. She and Dad come to town at least once a year and see an endless round of Broadway shows and eat at fancy restaurants where all the waiters gawk at my mom, and my dad just sits there, shaking his head, and grinning."

"You look like your mom?"

"Ha. In my dreams, but I guess I look like her more than Dad. And she still looks like my older sister."

"And then there's your younger brother, Timmy, who also lives here in New York. You said he's a wannabe actor, right?"

Where were all these coming from? To distract her, Mike realized. He was good, she had to admit it. "Timmy—well, he's another matter entirely." And she shut it down, as he had before.

Nicholas saw that she was relaxing, that she was rebooting, getting back her balance. "And then you went to the FBI Academy and blew everyone away. Yes, I read your dossier. You made the New York CID office at twenty-six, one of the youngest agents to fill such a position. From personal experience I can add that you're pretty hot stuff, Agent Caine."

Hot stuff? She'd rather be fierce. "How in the world did you get ahold of my personnel file?" She smacked his arm, his bare arm, which was as black as his face. "You and your hacker talent. Don't whine, you deserved the punch."

"Well, that, plus your instructors in Quantico loved to talk about you. I think you might have broken a couple of hearts. Believe me, I grilled them, since no way I wanted to be partnered with a slacker. They said you were pretty good, Agent Caine. Actually, Mr. Filbert, the shooting range supervisor, said I'd have to bust my butt to keep up with you."

"Those instructors, Mr. Filbert especially, they're jokers, experts at spotting gullible marks, plus you're the freaking Brit who rescued the Koh-i-Noor diamond. They figured you had to be full of yourself and wanted to cut you down to size. Trust me, they were putting you on. Now, talk about making his bones at the Academy, you walked away with an award or two yourself."

"Only one." That got him a smile. At last.

But the laughter died a quick death when Mike looked out the window yet again to see the orange plume of flame still reaching into the sky.

He said quietly, "We're going to stop them, Mike. They don't stand a chance against the two of us."

He reached over and took her hand, gave it a squeeze.

He rocked with surprise when she said, in the most

vicious voice he'd ever heard, "If Reeves isn't dead when we find him, I'm going to slam his ass up against the wall, maybe knee him a couple of times to show him how serious I am, and he's going to split right open and tell us everything in that pea brain of his."

That's my girl. "Remind me not to get on your bad side. See, like I told you—fierce."

Five minutes later, Nicholas pulled in front of Richard Hodges's house. It was quiet. No lights were on. No draperies twitched, no shadows moved into defensive positions because of an unscheduled visitor. Even the air had stilled. The silence was eerie.

Both of them went on red alert. Mike already had her Glock in her hand, and fear in her belly.

She whispered, "Do you think maybe they already moved him to a safe house?"

He didn't answer, he was calling it in, speaking low. He hung up, shook his head. They stepped quietly to the red front door. Nicholas tried the knob. The door opened easily. Not good. He mouthed, *One, two, three,* and they went in.

11

QUEEN TO B3

On the road to Brooklyn

Matthew drove like a Sunday grandmother, always on the alert for cops.

Vanessa turned in the seat to face him. "Matthew, talk to me. Do you think Darius died in the fire?"

He shook his head. "Don't worry about Darius."

Everything inside her sharpened to pinpoint focus. The way he'd said those words. "Why?"

He shrugged. "You might as well know. Darius is alive and well and moving into position for our next step. He's done everything I asked tonight."

Or you did everything Darius asked? She felt pounding rage; she wanted to tear his throat out. No, she had to be calm, she had to keep it together, she had to find out what was going on. *Next step of what?*

Time to try the spurs. "I see. First, you didn't bother to tell me that you were going to test out your bombs tonight and kill people, and then second, you didn't bother to tell me Darius was just fine, thank you? This small detail somehow slipped that genius brain of yours? I laid on that hill for an hour waiting for him to come out, watching the dead and the injured being ambulanced out, and it was all for nothing because you couldn't be bothered to tell me?" He looked taken aback. She poured on more, slammed her fist on the seat. "Didn't it occur to you that I could have been taken? The FBI was there, and wouldn't they have done a happy dance if they'd nabbed me? Why didn't you tell me, Matthew? About the bomb? That you'd finally perfected it? That you were going to test it out? About Darius? Why?"

He had the gall to laugh at her. "Oh, I perfected it a while back. What, are you jealous, Vanessa?"

"No, you moron. What I am is sick and tired of being kept out of the loop, always trying to prove myself, which I have, over and over, always trying to make you trust me. I've done everything you wanted and done it well, yet you treat me like some sort of outsider.

"Then Darius shows up with a bag of money and you fall all over him. Who is he? Do you even know? I know, I know, I've heard his rhetoric—he hates the terrorists as much as you do, wants them to choke on their oil. I've heard the both of you having a cursefest against them, but so what? I'm your bomb maker. I've been with you since Belfast when Ian brought us together. You always said you needed me because this bomb you were building—you weren't going to use it because you didn't want to take any chances you might hurt someone, you wanted it for leverage, to force our government into stopping oil imports.

"So what happened, Matthew? Darius changed your mind, obviously. Where is Darius and what is he doing? What are you two planning?"

His hand shot out and gripped her knee, hard. She felt equal parts surprise and pain. Should she break his hand? She wanted to, but she didn't move, said only, her voice perfectly calm, "You're hurting me."

"I need to make my point clear, apparently. You are a soldier, Vanessa, my soldier, to be told where to go and what to do. Don't you understand? We are at war with radical Islam, with all the jihadist fanatics who would destroy our world and us with it. I had to make a big point tonight that if our country continues to import their freaking oil, they're as bad as the terrorists. And I made it, and about time, too.

"And like you said, sweetheart, I didn't search you out, Ian brought you to me, promised me you wanted in, promised me you were good."

"And you trust Ian. You worked with him for years. Why don't you trust me? Ian does. Even crazy Andy does. You didn't search out Darius, either. He came to you, like I did."

"Come on, Vanessa, you told me yourself you wanted a chance to right the wrongs, to mete out well-deserved punishment to the terrorists and those fools who import their oil. I'm the leader of our group and what I do with

Darius is none of your business. I make the decisions, select the targets, whip up the media and hopefully the public. Not you. You do what I tell you to do. Do you understand me?"

Had Darius pumped him up into this little Hitler? "I'm not your enemy, Matthew. Why are you treating me like one? After three months together, we were getting close, but then Darius showed up and everything started to change. You were closeted together for hours at a time. Some of the guys wondered if you were cozying up, screwing your brains out."

He laughed. "No one thinks that; you're making it up because you're pissed at me. Darius didn't want to screw me, he wanted to screw you, but you didn't screw around with any of us, including me, even though you know as well as I do we'd be good together."

Where had he gotten this scenario?

"You want to know what I told him? *'Good luck, man, but know she'd yank out your eyeballs if you tried to force things.'* So, tell me, Vanessa, did Darius have the nerve to try anything with you?"

"Yes, once. I left his eyeballs intact. That's not important, it was nothing." *Try again, try again.* "Matthew, listen to me. I've worked hard for you and the cause, done everything you've ever asked, and more. Stop treating me like this. Other than Ian and Andy, I'm your only friend. Not Darius, and if you believe he gives a crap about you, you're as crazy as Andy. He's using you; he's manipulating you. He has his own agenda, you're simply too blind to see it. Or he's blinded you too much to see it. Or he's got you to buy into what he wants to do. And tonight? It was really your idea, Matthew? Or his?"

"Enough of your whining. COE is not about friendship or lovers. It is not about trust. We're on a mission, and we each have our jobs to do. Get in line, Vanessa, or you'll regret it." *More Hitler.*

Now he was threating to kill her? Then, fast as lightning, he grinned, his hand once again on her knee, now caressing rather than hurting.

"Come on, babe, you're getting all upset for no reason. You're special, Vanessa. I've never said otherwise. You know I care about you. You're a great talent, easy on the eyes, too, and you're fun to be with, until now anyway. Be patient, okay? You'll come around because you'll see the payoff is worth it. Then who knows? Maybe you and I can have some time together. Maybe I'll tell you everything you could ever want to know."

He'd turned on a dime. He'd done it before, but never this fast, this radically. *What has that monster made you? Who are you now, Matthew?*

But she couldn't let him see she was both afraid and killer angry. She said nothing more.

In another twenty minutes, in the dead of night, Matthew parked the car in the derelict lot next to the building—a car repair shop with an apartment on the second floor. It was a dump, but perfect for his uses. He looked over at Vanessa, still and silent, and got out of the car. He looked up at their darkened apartment, above the auto repair shop with its smelly bays. The whole place stank of gasoline and oil and old sandwiches and dirty men, but it was out of the way, and the owner of the shop had been more than happy to take the wad of cash Matthew had pressed into his greasy palm and shut down the business for an extended European vacation.

Matthew hoped the owner was enjoying himself, since if it came down to it, if necessary, he'd have Andy torch the building, and whoosh, no more business.

He hoped all his other men were cozied in their three different assigned motels in Brooklyn, none more than a mile away from here.

He didn't like Vanessa's silence. He knew she was pissed, sulking, but he also felt it was something more. This silence of hers—after a bombing, she was usually on top of the world, but not tonight. Well, things had changed. She'd get used to it. She'd come around. Then he realized that Ian, Andy, all of the men were quiet after Bayway and all the deaths. No, he realized they'd all been on edge before tonight, and he understood now it was because of Darius. He knew all Ian's men were afraid of Darius, and they were right to be. Matthew knew there was a killing lust in Darius that ran deep, and was as automatic as a snake striking out.

No, it would be all right. They would stick to the plan, the grand plan he and Darius had devised.

But still, Matthew worried about Ian, his best friend, the one man he'd trusted for so long. He thought of those long-ago days when the two of them had traveled through Europe, guns and bombs in their backpacks, targeting those electrical grids and oil refineries that relied heavily on Middle Eastern oil. But now he'd come to see that destroying them in his perfectly executed little bombings had been petty, nearly meaningless in the grand scheme of things, and they hadn't accomplished very much at all.

But Darius had showed him the way, the new way, and he wanted it so bad he could taste it, the final revenge for his family. Close, so close now. No looking back, only forward, ever forward. He and Darius would stop the madness once and for all, and because of them the world would change. It made him tremble to think about what he was going to do. And he felt, deep down, where it counted most, fear and pride and a sense of infallibility. What he would do was righteous.

He called Vanessa to help him. Silently, they unloaded the car, pulled a dirty tarp over it, and placed a large rock on the hood so it blended in with the other cars on the dingy repair lot, and then went up the oily, stinking stairs to the apartment. It was the middle of the night, no one to see them.

There were blackout curtains on the windows, a good thing, because inside, the apartment pulsed with gleaming monitors and equipment that took up every available flat surface, their screens glowing blue in the night. Andy Tate, firebug and computer expert, too young to be as crazy as he was, always wired, no coffee necessary, was leaning back in a broken leather chair, his legs crossed on top of the kitchen table, alternately playing with a Zippo lighter and eating an apple.

He saw them, raised a fist, and shouted, "I am the master of the universe!"

Matthew felt his heart pound as he hurried over to him. "Does that mean you're in?"

"Tango down, bitches. Oh, yeah, dude, I pulled down their drawers and slipped it right in. My baby has already infected all the terminals and servers, corrupted all their precious files. I have control of the master boot records. Everything's offline and I should have all the data downloaded in another hour, two tops. They won't know what hit them. They'll be scrambling for days trying to track us, and we'll be long gone, with everything we need in place."

"Good. Good. Well done, Andy." He turned to Vanessa. "Go shower and start packing. We leave as soon as Andy has the information downloaded."

She gave him an emotionless look and went down the narrow hallway, fear scoring deep at Andy's announcement. This, at least, she'd known about, but now it was reality. Andy had gotten into all the major oil companies' computer systems. Truth be told, she hadn't imagined he'd be able to do it. Well, she'd been dead wrong. She had to send in an alert right away that it was no longer a plan, it was done. It would happen.

She nearly ran into Ian as he came out of the bedroom, his hair still wet from his shower. He gave her a loud smacking kiss on each cheek, hugged her tight.

"We did it, Van, we did it." His Irish accent was thick tonight, but then he frowned. "But all those men, dead. I didn't like that at all. I mean, they weren't those wanking Muslim gits taking over Belfast."

"No, they weren't," she said. "They burned to death;

innocent people shouldn't have died. Too much death, Ian, too much, and we all swore we never wanted that."

"It wasn't your doing, Van, or mine, so don't feel guilty. It was that maniac Darius, he's the one who pushed Matthew into using one of his new coin bombs at Bayway. At least we now know what a tiny part of one of Matthew's coins can do. Still, it was too close. I nearly didn't make it out in time since that arse Darius put the bomb too near the room I was in. Nearly burned to death—now, what a thought that is. And I heard the screams." He shook himself. "Hey, come help Andy and Matthew load the cases in the van."

Say something, say something. "I'm very glad you made it, Ian. I'll be out in a minute to help."

"Listen, Van, we'll make it to Tahoe, and maybe things will go back to the way they were before, since Darius is gone now. We'll lay low and plan our next attack, the right kind of attack."

Matthew came into the hallway, heard Ian, and nodded. "Yes, we need to leave, but we're not going back to Tahoe, we're heading south. It's time to take this to the next level."

Ian eyed him. "You mean you still want to do Yorktown?"

"Oh, yes."

Ian shook his head. "I don't know, Matthew, I don't know. Tonight was—bad."

"I promise you and Vanessa, no major bombing like tonight at Bayway." Matthew pumped his fist in the air. "Life's an adventure, Ian, our adventure. Don't turn coward on me now."

The power plant at Yorktown? Vanessa hadn't known. Neither Ian nor Matthew had told her. Did Andy know?

Matthew was still pumped, thrilled with himself. "Andy is breaking down his computers, then you can help him get everything into the van. You know what he did, right, Ian?"

"I know all I need to know—he crippled the buggers. Hey, even if you explained it all to me, I wouldn't understand it." He grinned, clapped Mathew on the back and left him and Vanessa alone in the dim hallway.

12

PAWN TAKES C4

Vanessa turned away from him, said over her shoulder, "I'm going to shower and pack. Five minutes."

"We need to talk."

"Later, Matthew. We have plenty of time to talk on the road south. To Yorktown."

She left him, already writing her text message in her head as she went into the bedroom to get clothes and her special phone she'd stashed in a tampon box, the safest place in the universe when surrounded by men. She was scared, excited, knew at last things were coming together. Yorktown? Was that where Darius had gone? But why split apart from the group?

She took the tiny phone out of the box, grabbed a towel and clothes, and went into the small bathroom. She turned on the shower, leaned into the noise, turned on the phone. She saw there was a response to her last text, the one she'd sent with Darius's photo.

> Need more information. Nothing in
> databases. Ghost.

She couldn't believe it—no records at all? She knew Darius was a criminal. Surely he'd been arrested at some point, fingerprinted and photographed. He'd even once told her about a prison in Turkey—had they contacted Interpol? Of course they had.

She texted back.

> 911, coin bombs already perfected,
> Bayway test run. Darius did not return
> with us. Don't know where he is.
> Heading south.

She hit send and waited. And waited. The signal was bad in the bathroom. Even though the phone was secure and encrypted, it still needed a decent LTE connection to go through. She couldn't have a satellite phone on her, too suspicious if she was caught with it. This baby was a very small smartphone, beefed up by her people, all improvements under the hood. Since one of Matthew's rules was no phones, she was very careful with it.

The text still hadn't gone through.

"Come on, come on, come on."

She'd started to strip down when there was a knock on

the bathroom door. She was so hyped up she nearly dropped the phone. She called out, "I'm getting into the shower now. Three minutes and I'll be out, ready to leave."

Matthew's voice, soft and sexy, his coaxing voice: "I want to come in, Vanessa. I think it's time you and I finally had that talk."

Her heart froze. *What talk?* He was thinking about sex now? She quickly grabbed the big bar of soap from the shower, wet it, and started working the phone into it, pressing hard. Was it still showing? She kept squeezing it into the soap, praying for time. It was inside, finally, fully covered.

The doorknob jiggled. Her heart thundered in her chest.

"Come on, Vanessa, open up. I know you're mad at me, but I want to make it up to you. Now's our chance, let's—"

She had to stop this. "Now, Matthew?" She played with the bar of soap—yes, it looked harmless. She quickly set it back into the shower. "You think now's a good time because your best friend Darius isn't here to tell you not to talk to me?"

The door crashed inward. Matthew stood there, breathing hard, his eyes dark and hot. Then, fast as a blink, he smiled. "Hey, what's with locking me out? You're the one who wanted me to share, to tell you all I'm planning."

These mood swings of his were becoming more frequent. *Is it also because of Darius? He wants to talk? Now?*

No, he wants sex. Her shirt was open and she quickly buttoned it. "Come on, Matthew, not now. I thought we were in a hurry. Go away and let me shower in peace so we can get out of here."

His smile never slipped, but she knew if she looked close enough, she'd see the pulse pounding in his neck.

"I didn't come in to talk—well, not right away."

Was he for real? He knew she was angry with him, knew she'd hated all the deaths at Bayway, so what was on that genius brain of his? Did he believe pushing her for sex was the way to get her back under control? She realized what she wanted more than anything was to kick him into oblivion. She held herself steady, even smiled at him. "No, Matthew. Go away."

"Come on, Vanessa, we'll have some quick fun, we deserve it, to celebrate. You're mad at me right now, but that will change." He wasn't blind, he saw the contempt on her face, but he chose to ignore it. He added, his voice cajoling, "Hey, after, you and I can talk. You're right, it's time I told you all my plans."

Think, think. He'd tell her all his plans? She forced herself to soften her voice. "This isn't a good time, Matthew, you know that. We need to get out of here."

He ignored her, unbuttoning his shirt, never looking away from her. Then his fingers were on his belt. "We can take a shower together, save some time. It'll be fun, you'll see."

No, he can't get in the shower, he might try to use the soap, might see that something is different.

He pulled off his belt. His fingers went to the button of his jeans, paused. "Vanessa, I'm sorry, I should have told you about Darius, what we planned together. I should have told you about everything. I do trust you, and I want you by my side when I finish this."

He was playing her, she knew it. She watched him unzip his jeans, watched him step to her, didn't move when he kissed her neck.

She forced herself not to kick upward, to hold perfectly still. "Finish what, Matthew? What is there to finish?"

"You didn't think I was going to spend the rest of my life bombing small-time refineries and electrical grids, did you? Tonight was just the beginning." He pushed her up against the wall, kissed her hard, one hand holding her head still. He slid a leg between hers.

She said into his mouth, "Come on, Matthew, what are you planning? Tell me, so I can find the best way to help you."

He was kissing her face now, light feathering kisses. "Everything's in motion; Darius and I have planned out every move. You are helping me, Vanessa. All the way, baby. You and me, all the way." He kissed her hard again, whispering into her mouth, "Now it's time for us."

Why? Because Darius isn't hanging around watching you? She forced herself to kiss him back, let her hand slip inside his jeans as she whispered into his mouth, "Tell me now, Matthew. I want to know. Tell me."

He raised his head, his smile dazed, rubbed his fingers over her mouth, said between kisses, "You want to know what's next? We're going right to the top, Vanessa. No, wait, I'll fill you in on all of it later. You won't believe who we're going to kill—"

There was a loud ding from the phone wedged into the soap. The text had gone through.

13

QUEEN TAKES C4

Hodges's house
Bayonne, New Jersey

Mike didn't want to believe what she saw.

Two agents were down at the kitchen table, a poker game spread between them, and now the cards were sprayed with blood. The third agent lay on his side in the hallway leading to the bedrooms.

She didn't want to go in the master bedroom, she didn't, but she had no choice. Richard "Dicker" Hodges lay in the middle of the bed, a beautiful plaid flannel blanket covering him, a bullet hole in the center of his forehead, another to the chest. His eyes were open, staring up at the ceiling.

Everything screamed surprise attack. Whoever had gotten in was quick, clean, leaving four dead, each taken down with only two shots. They hadn't seen any brass on the floor.

Nicholas said, his voice cold as ice, "The work of a professional."

Mike turned to him, saw the pulse slamming madly in his throat, felt the fury radiating off him. Since she felt the same mad brew, she didn't bother to say anything.

She studied Mr. Hodges's peaceful face. "Whoever did this knew what he was doing. As you said, this was a professional hit."

"Have you ever seen anything similar? All four men shot once in the forehead, once in the heart?"

She looked up at the odd note in his voice.

"Executions, you mean? Yes, some Mob hits. But, Nicholas, this feels, well, cleaner. More precise. No one struggled. He shot them where they sat or stood or lay, and they didn't even raise a hand to stop him. And the method, two fast shots? Yes, very clean."

Nicholas said, "All Hodges did was speak to us, yet it was enough to send this killer over here to punish him, to erase him, and anyone with him."

"To tie up loose ends."

They left Mr. Hodges and walked back into the hallway to stand over the dead agent. Nicholas said, "What was his name?

She choked a little on the name. "Cedarson. Rex Cedarson."

"He was in the bedroom watching over Mr. Hodges, heard the shots, or heard something that alarmed him, since the assassin may have used a suppressor, and was

THE END GAME 79

moving toward the kitchen when he was shot. At least he had time to get his gun out."

Mike swallowed down grief and guilt. Rex was a good man, always up for a joke, had once even locked her in the men's room. The other men were steady, professionals all the way, good family men.

"The other two agents were Bob Ventura and Kenneth Chantler. Though I knew Cedarson the best." She didn't add he had a two-year-old daughter and an eight-year-old son, a wife he loved and didn't see enough of because he had a burning desire to move up the ladder and worked too much. The other two agents had similar lives. And they were gone, in the blink of an eye, simply gone. Their deaths were a punch to the gut. "I can't stand this, Nicholas, I really can't."

He knew this was a huge blow, knew she was on the edge and might go over if he tried to comfort her, so he said matter-of-factly, "I want to show you something, but be careful. We don't want to ruin any evidence CSI might pull from around the house." Like Mike, though, he knew it was pointless. Whoever had done this hadn't left a single trace of himself.

She followed Nicholas back into Mr. Hodges's bedroom. He was staring at the dead man, then he raised his hand and mimicked shooting.

"I'd say Mr. Hodges was asleep when the shots were fired in the kitchen and Cedarson ran out of the room."

"You think he could sleep through the shots, even suppressed?"

He didn't, but he wanted to keep her focused. "Perhaps

he took a sleeping pill. I don't think he ever knew he was going to die. So look. The assassin stood right over him and took the two shots. I'd say he's at least my height, maybe a bit taller. The ME won't find gunpowder residue on Mr. Hodges, or on the others; the wounds are all clean. The killer came in hard and fast—four shots in the kitchen, two in the hallway, two in here. Mr. Hodges was the target, of course."

"All of these men dead simply because one honest, lonely man was a good citizen and told us what he'd heard at the bar. I can't believe that level of—what would you even call this?"

Nicholas said, "Insurance. Our assassin is really careful, believes in overkill. Is he someone from COE? Until now, COE hasn't gone around killing people. And this was professional all the way. What would a professional assassin be doing hooked up to a small-beans anti-oil terrorist group? Why this elaborate killing? It wouldn't have mattered. There was nothing more Mr. Hodges could have told us."

"Remember Mr. Zachery believes someone new has been added to COE? Someone more violent? Maybe whoever this is now runs things."

"Seems to me this level of escalation pretty well nails it. A new violent addition."

They heard a siren. "Backup's nearly here. Nicholas, how did the assassin find Mr. Hodges? How did COE even know he'd spoken to us?"

Nicholas said, "I think we probably led the killer right here to Mr. Hodges's house."

"Someone followed us? From Federal Plaza?"

His mobile rang. He glanced down—one o'clock in the morning, and the number on the screen was the main number at 26 Federal Plaza.

"Drummond here."

"Nicholas," Agent Gray Wharton said, "we have a huge problem."

"Yes, Mike and I are standing in the middle of it. I'm in Bayonne, and we have four bodies, including Mr. Richard Hodges, our tipster."

Wharton swore. "He's dead? Our guys are down, too? Yes, of course they are. Give me a second here, Nicholas."

Nicholas heard him draw a deep breath, could practically see him trying to get hold of himself. "Okay, listen, on top of all that, there's more. I'm sending a file to your phone right now."

Nicholas felt the phone vibrate slightly in his hand. "It's here. Gray, what am I looking at?"

"Someone launched a major cyber-attack on all of the major oil companies. Everyone's been hit—Exxon, ConocoPhillips, Occidental, all of them. Their systems are down, and so far we haven't been able to break the encryptions. Nicholas, it's bad. It's very bad. Worse than the Shamoon virus attack on the Saudis in 2012, and with all the same hallmarks."

"Who's behind it? Russia? The Chinese?"

"I've been tracking it as best I can, but it's coming from multiple international sites. I need you. You've got to get here as soon as you can."

Gray was never an alarmist, which meant this was really bad. "I'm on my way."

Mike grabbed his arm. "What is it?"

"Major cyber-attack on the oil companies. I've got to help Gray back at Federal Plaza." He ran his hands through his hair, standing it on end. "What are the odds?"

"I had no idea COE had the expertise or the willingness to go in this direction."

"If it's them. This sounds like a very sophisticated attack. Hey, if they have a professional assassin, why not a professional hacker? Gray and I have to try and shut it down."

She shooed him with her hand. "Go. I'll stay here and handle the scene."

He lightly touched his palm to her bruised cheek. "Thank you."

"Nicholas?"

He turned at the front door. "What?"

"Be careful, okay? Whoever did this already killed three of our people. I'd be really pissed if you got yourself hurt. Again."

He flashed her a smile. "Agent Caine. Worried about me?"

"Yes, lamebrain, and I'm serious." She gestured toward the kitchen. "This isn't good."

He nodded. "I know it's not. I'll take a care. You as well, understand?"

14

PAWN TO C6

Brooklyn

Vanessa froze, but her brain didn't. She must have accidently turned off the mute when she'd shoved the phone into the soap. Had Matthew heard it, too? He was still kissing her, and now he was sucking on her ear, his hand rubbing her breast.

Distract him.

Her hand fitted over him again, caressing.

Too late, the phone dinged again. This time it signaled an incoming text.

Matthew slowly raised his head and looked down at her.

Should she kill him? She could kick him in the groin, send him to his knees, grab him and choke him or break his neck. Or grab his head and smash him into the porcelain tub. No gun, that was in her bag in the bedroom.

Her knee came up at the same moment Matthew lunged. He went for the soap, she went for his balls. He managed to turn in time and her knee struck his thigh. He grabbed her leg and jerked up, throwing her off balance, and she fell backward, three steps, into the shower. He planted his foot on her neck, grabbed the bar of soap.

"What is this?"

She tried to push off his foot, but he only pressed down harder. She couldn't breathe.

"Looks like a bar of soap, but I don't think it's just any bar of soap—maybe it's magic soap. It rings. Isn't that amazing, Vanessa? Ringing soap."

He pried the phone from the soap, wiped off the screen. He looked down at her, and she jerked at his foot to get it off her neck. "Can't breathe, Vanessa?"

He pulled his Beretta out of its holster on the back of his jeans, lifted his boot off her neck. "Who have you been talking to, Vanessa?"

Her throat was on fire. She whispered, "Not mine." She didn't know if she'd gotten the words out. She rubbed her throat as she stared at the muzzle of the Beretta. She didn't move.

He looked thoughtful, none of his manic anger she could see. "Really? What does this mean? FT or AM?" Still his voice was calm, but she could only imagine what was roiling around in that genius brain of his. She knew exactly what it meant.

Follow through or abort mission.

She never blinked. "How would I know, Matthew? I found the phone in the drawer. I was looking through it to see whose it might be. Then you came in and I was afraid you'd think it was mine and I know how you hate phones. Then this all started to happen, you were kissing me and I forgot about it—"

"So you hid it in the soap? Lucky for you it's such a big bar, otherwise you'd have hid it in your bra?" His voice was flat, emotionless. He leaned over and turned off the shower. He waved the Beretta in her face as he stepped back.

"Get out of here." She slowly rose, realized she was sopping wet, shook herself, and stepped out of the shower.

"Vanessa," he said, her name a caress, "you're lying to me."

"No, I'm not, Matthew. I'd never break your rules. Obviously the phone belongs to Ian or Andy; it sure isn't mine. You've got to believe me, Matthew. Now, let me get on my clothes and together we can show the phone to Ian and Andy, see what they have to say."

He stepped into her face, and she felt the Beretta pressing against her breast.

He whispered against her cheek, "You're lying, you traitorous bitch."

He dragged her from the bathroom, his arm around her neck, the Beretta against her temple now, and pulled her down the hall. She jerked at his arm, and he let her suck in a breath, then squeezed hard again.

She saw her uncle's face, knew he would grieve for her, and he'd know in his heart she'd screwed up. She was facing death alone. Alone. She shut her eyes, stopped struggling, and the pressure released. Matthew threw her onto the floor and she rolled, smashing into the corner of the sofa. She heard Ian shouting, heard Andy talking fast and crazy, nothing new in that.

Ian shouted, "What is going on here, Matthew? Don't hurt her, you bastard."

Matthew said nothing, merely stood over her, the Beretta aimed squarely at her heart, and tossed Ian the phone.

"What is this? I've never seen this before. Is this her phone?"

Ian paused, looked down at Vanessa, sodden, huddled in on herself. "Is this your phone, Van? Really, it's your phone?" She heard the horror in his voice, but also heard the acceptance that she was guilty.

"You think we've got a traitor here, Matthew?" Andy asked, and jerked the phone out of Ian's hand. "Let me see it, we'll know soon enough."

"Ian, Andy, it isn't mine. I already told Matthew that it wasn't, that I found it in a drawer when I was cleaning them out to pack. Is it yours, Ian? Andy? It's not mine, I swear it. But Matthew doesn't believe me. Tell him it can't be mine, Ian. Tell him."

Ian wouldn't meet her eyes. Andy was staring down at the tiny phone in his palm, ignoring all of them. "Tell me your secrets, little phone," he said, his voice almost a croon. Crazy, crazy Andy, even more twisted than Matthew was now, and that was saying something. "Where did you come from, little beauty? So tiny you are. Tell Andy your secrets."

Matthew said, "Andy, quit screwing around. Who's she been calling?"

Andy finally looked up. "Sorry, dude, there's no history, everything's been wiped."

Without a word, Matthew hauled her up and threw her into the wall. His fist moved so quickly she almost didn't see it coming. But he didn't hit her; instead, his fist slammed into the paneling behind her head, cracking the wood. He stuck the Beretta into her cheek.

Soft, his voice was so soft, cajoling. "Tell me who you really are, Vanessa. Tell me right now or I will shoot you dead." She felt the rage pouring off him, even as his face remained emotionless, as if they were talking about what to have for dinner.

"Please, Matthew," she whispered, voice shaking, a little girl's terrified voice, "please don't kill me, I didn't do anything. You've got to believe me. It was probably Andy, you know how crazy he is, haven't you always told me how nuts he is? I mean, give him a match and he'd set the world on fire, and he's always playing with that Zippo. But not me, how could it be me? You know I've wanted you, I was proving it to you in the bathroom. It isn't my phone, Matthew, really, it isn't my phone."

He grabbed her wet hair, jerked her head forward. His voice remained soft, even soothing, comforting.

"Vanessa, I will let Andy set fire to your hair if you don't start talking. Now."

Vanessa knew he was ready to kill her with his bare hands. She had to find the right words. "Listen, Matthew, you hired me to make you bombs, and I've done my job well. I've stuck with you, helped you." She raised her hand to touch his face. He froze. "Don't you know I love you, that I've loved you since the moment Ian introduced us in Belfast? Why won't you believe me?"

"How long have you been with me, Vanessa?"

Where is he going with this?

Before she could answer, he turned to Ian. "How long since you brought her to me, Ian?"

Ian was staring down at her. "Four months and, a week or so—we first met at the Duck and Deer pub in Londonderry." A look of pain crossed his face. "I thought she'd be perfect for us."

"Four and a half months. And you've been in every hour of our lives since."

Andy looked up from the phone. "I heard Darius telling you she was trouble. I thought he said that because she wouldn't sleep with him."

"Matthew, Ian, you've got to listen to me. It's not my phone. Even though there were deaths tonight at the refinery, it will be offline for weeks, and the world will listen to you, Matthew, finally listen. And look what Andy did—he took down the big oil company systems. We'll have them under our thumbs by morning. You know I feel the same way as you about how our president is cozying up to the Iranians and all those other Middle East terrorists, you know I do."

Ian said to Andy, his voice and his eyes dead cold, "Take the phone apart."

Andy plugged it into his computer and tapped on the

keyboard. There was stark silence in the living room except for the sounds of the keys and Matthew's heaving breathing.

Andy called over his shoulder, "The outgoing texts are automatically deleted, very nice custom program to do that. There's a single number in the memory, though it's deleted from the phone itself, too. The number's been called three times in the past two weeks, but the calls go different places." He looked at Vanessa. "Who are you talking to? Who's on the other side of the call?"

"Can you reverse the number?" Matthew asked, never taking his eyes off her, his gun now steady on her chest. Center mass: she'd be dead in less than a heartbeat if he pulled the trigger.

"Yeah." More tapping. "The number's cloaked, it bounces off four satellites before it goes through. Phone's encrypted, Matthew."

His voice—so soft, so deadly calm. "Where'd you get an encrypted phone, Vanessa?"

She said again, "It's not mine."

Matthew kept his eyes on her face. "I know, it belongs to Ian, it belongs to Andy. Could it belong to me as well?"

"Maybe it belongs to Darius, and he's manipulating you yet again. Maybe he isn't who you believe he is."

"Darius? Now, that's a thought." He said to Andy, "Call the number, Andy."

15

PAWN TO E4

26 Federal Plaza
New York, New York

As Nicholas drove the Crown Vic into Manhattan, he could still see the plume of fire from the refinery in his rearview, could still taste the burning oil in his mouth. It was hard to get his brain around all that had happened in such a short time. COE had murdered three FBI agents and Richard Hodges, blown up Bayway, not caring how many people died. And now, the launching of a coordinated attack on the oil companies themselves. He saw Mr. Hodges's face, the perfect circle in his forehead. He'd been a hero, he'd given them Larry Reeves, a man Nicholas was certain was as dead as all the other workers at Bayway.

The whole case had changed in an instant.

What was COE all about now? Certainly it was now

about much more than simply wanting Middle Eastern oil to stop being imported.

He parked the Crown Vic in the nearly empty underground garage at Federal Plaza, knowing the moment word was out on the shootings, the place would come alive.

Gray, as usual, looked the mad-genius part—slightly disheveled, clothes wrinkled, hair sticking up, black circles under his eyes. He was a comforting sight and had rapidly become one of Nicholas's most trusted allies. They understood each other.

Gray threw his hands up when he saw Nicholas, didn't mention the condition he was in—black face, burned hands, no sleeves on his shirt, ripped and bloody pants. No time, no time. "This is bad, Nicholas. Someone sent a Trojan horse into the oil companies' e-mail systems. A simple e-mail, designed to look internal, sent to every e-mail address on the corporate rolls, supposedly from the heads of the company themselves. And inside was a nasty worm.

"One of the staff members at ConocoPhillips opened the e-mail from home, thinking it was a note from his boss. It took control of the server from there, unspooled into the system, started wiping hard drives, and no one has been able to get back in. Their Web folks are freaking out. They called us in a panic. I've been working on it since. So far, I can't crack it. It's working like a distributed denial-of-service attack, but the attackers have put in their own firewalls. So not only can I not get in, I can't track what they're doing while they're inside. All it took was one click. One damn click. The odds were in their favor."

Nicholas's brain sparked. "Are we dealing with a DDoS, stopping outsiders from accessing the company websites, or are they taking remote control of the facilities?"

"I don't know. I can't get in far enough to tell what they're up to."

"If their goal was to blow our infrastructure, this was a good way to go about it. Is it COE who launched the attack? Have they claimed responsibility?"

"They didn't have to; their COE logo is front and center on the screen." Gray clicked his mouse a few times and the screen in front of him turned white. In the middle floated a stylish monogram with elegant, ornate letters— **COE**—atop a rotating chessboard.

Nicholas said, "We have to get in. The worm could be downloading information as well as wiping the memory off the servers. If so, they'll have access to everything from internal e-mails to finances."

"Not to mention they can turn the power off to any of the physical locations at will. So much is run by computers today—they could tell the pumps to stop working, and boom. You don't need a bomb to stop oil production in its tracks." He hit two more keys. "Look at this."

The white screen disappeared, and the Shanghai SE Composite Index came up. Numbers ran furiously along the bottom of the screen, red, red, red.

"You can see word is out that something's up—the overseas markets are already dumping oil stocks. If they continue the pace of this sell-off, we're going to be in trouble when the markets open over here. Nicholas, if you can't get in and stop it, I think we should tell Zachery he needs to try getting trading suspended and not opening the stock market this morning."

"Let me see if I can get past the firewall and limit the damage. Regardless, we need to ask Zachery to talk to the suits on Wall Street, do some spinning. The media will be wild about this, and on top of the explosion—"

"It's too late for damage control, Nicholas, since the financial markets are already reacting. We have to break COE's encryption and get the oil companies back online, pronto, or we're all going to have a very bad morning."

Nicholas sent a prayer heavenward. "Send all of this to me, Gray. I'll see what I can do. Oh, yes, you say some prayers, too."

16

KNIGHT ON B TO D7

Nicholas booted up his computer, made sure he was on the secure internal red server. If he was going to stop this attack, he had to enter the world that was alive and well and lived behind the Web. He initiated his TOR software, left the real-world Internet behind, and headed into the darknet.

He plugged in Gray's files, started probing the firewalls COE had set up.

Gray was right. The coding was good. More than good, it was solid. Seemingly unbreakable.

"No, this won't do at all," he said, and started typing, launching his own protocols to attack the worm.

Three minutes later, two layers of encryption were down. Now he was staring at a deep network of code. Whoever had written it was incredibly sophisticated, which helped narrow the suspects. He kept digging and noticed a repeated line of code. He felt a niggling sense of familiarity—it was the structure of the language. Flashy, that was it, "aren't I clever; you'll never catch me" flashy. After examining the threads for a few moments, he saw what he needed, and he smiled. This code wasn't homegrown in the United States. This had been bought from an outsider.

A few more clicks and he knew he was right. The hacker who'd written the code was more than sophisticated, he was on the highest level. And then it came to him—he knew. It was the electronic signature of a German he knew. Gunther Ansell sold hijacked server proxies to the highest bidder—making millions of dollars per proxy. Gunther had always been an egotist, and Nicholas had always known if Gunther kept showing off with his code, putting in his signature, it would be his downfall one day.

Sorry, Gunther, today isn't going to be your day. He buzzed Gray. "I've got a line in."

Gray came to his cube, laptop in hand. "How did you do it?"

"I'll show you once we've stopped their attack. Call the IT guys who are working for these companies, tell them to ready their new code now. I'm going to need you for a side attack. Upload our denial-of-service package, and I'm going to throw a little homegrown code into the mix. We have to move fast to break their stranglehold. By now they know the breach has been noticed and they'll be working to close the loop."

Gray pulled up a squeaky chair, set the laptop on it,

and knelt on the floor, brought up a screen full of code. "Ready when you are."

"Three, two, one . . . go."

Gray launched his attack, and Nicholas did as well, using his own code to snap along Gunther's, attacking, dissolving thread after thread. Gunther was good, very good, but so was Nicholas. Five minutes later the first firewall came down, and Nicholas had control of the ConocoPhillips server.

Nicholas pumped a fist in the air. "Yes! Now we're on to Occidental's mainframe."

Twenty minutes later, they'd wrested back control of all the servers and handed them off to the IT heads of each company.

Nicholas let out a big breath. The damage done by the cyber-attack would take weeks to undo, but at least they'd stopped it cold. The companies wouldn't know the depth of their issues until they had a chance to do a full security assessment. There was no doubt in his or Gray's mind the attacks would continue, and soon. But for now, they'd won.

"Gray, pray it will hold. COE's hackers will try to attack again, I'm sure."

"Still, it's a big save. Good going, Nicholas. Zachery will be very pleased, as will the CEOs of the companies we bailed out."

Nicholas looked at the clock. "It's late morning in Germany. This genius—Gunther Ansell is his name—he isn't known to frequent daylight. Chances are right now he's at home, asleep." Nicholas grabbed his cell. "If we move fast enough, we can get people in to snatch him before he wakes. We'll have them take him to a dark site, have a chat with him, get a line into who hired him to build the code and how they paid, and boom—we just might have our problem solved."

"Who are you going to call?"

Ghostbusters. "FedPol," he said, and dialed.

Pierre Menard answered on the first ring. Did the man never go on vacation? Maybe sleep late the occasional morning? "Nicholas? It is the middle of the night in New York? What are you doing working?"

Menard's thick French accent was comfortingly familiar. They'd worked together several times in the past, and Nicholas trusted Menard. He'd never let him down.

"Why do you assume I'm working, Pierre?"

A small laugh, and he pictured Menard shaking his head. "I know you, and I heard about the Bayway bombing. Now what can I do for you?"

"Do you have friends in Munich?"

"*Oui, naturellement.* I have friends everywhere."

"Good. I need someone to grab a hacker named Gunther Ansell. He lives in the Glockenbach. He should be home asleep right now. I need him taken silently, and I need him taken now."

"I believe I have heard this name recently. You said he's a hacker? One of your sort?"

"He is. Where did you hear his name?"

"Interpol sent out a Blue Notice for him last week, to gather more information about his criminal activity on the Internet. But the notice was canceled yesterday. One moment, Nicholas."

He heard papers shuffling in the background. Interpol had a variety of color-coded "notices" running the gamut from red to a mild yellow, warnings against wanted criminals, upcoming attacks, or even simply requests for more information.

Menard came back on the line. "It is as I thought. I am sorry to have to tell you this. Gunther Ansell was killed three days ago. Shot in a robbery on the street near his apartment. The police have no suspects."

17

ROOK TO D1

Brooklyn

Vanessa watched Andy hit the buttons on the phone, knew it was a matter of moments before her time was up. She gauged the distance to the door, not that it mattered, since Matthew's Beretta never wavered from her chest. She'd try one last time. Maybe Matthew would look away and she'd have a chance.

"Go ahead, Andy, make the call. I've told you already, Matthew, it's not my phone. This will prove it."

She saw Matthew smooth back his hair, a habit of his that meant he wasn't certain, maybe about her guilt? Had she gotten through to him when she'd brought up Darius?

Andy put the call on speaker. The phone rang four times, then a woman's voice answered, loud enough to be heard over the din in the background. "Green's Pizza. Can I help you?"

"Pizza?"

"Yeah, babe. That's what we do. Make a mean calzone, too, if you're interested. What'll it be? Got a fourteen-inch pie on special, pepperoni and mushroom."

"Hey, you sound pretty, well, never mind. Thank you." Andy turned off the phone. His crazy eyes shone. "How about that, a pizza place in Delaware this time. The last call, the geo-locator says the call went to a Korean BBQ joint in Arlington, Virginia. Why have you been calling restaurants, Vanessa? And why does the same number take us to different places?"

"Matthew, listen to me, I have no reason to betray you. I make bombs, I love to watch them work and work well. I'm proud to be a part of your group. It's Darius, Matthew. It's Darius."

Andy said, "Darius? That stone-cold freak killer? There's no reason for him to turn traitor. But that's good, Vanessa, you sound real sincere accusing him, but you're lying. What do you think, Ian?"

Ian looked ready to both cry and kill her where she stood. Like Matthew. "Van, you not only betrayed Matthew, you betrayed me. Me, Van. I've known something was up these past couple of weeks. I've suspected you really weren't who you said you were, but I didn't want to see it. I told myself you were for real, you'd never betray me, betray us. Did you set me up in Londonderry?"

What had she done to make him suspect? It didn't matter now. She said, "Darius has gotten into your head, too,

Ian? Don't you see? Darius tried to drive a wedge between us, has been since he came to us in Tahoe. He's the outsider; he's the one we don't know. He brought you that case full of money, blinded you, Matthew, made you accept him. You're the one to blame here, Matthew, you were the one who brought him right into the fold. He's got to be the one who's betrayed us."

Matthew stared from her to Ian, then he burst out laughing. "Darius, betray us? Now, that's rich, Vanessa. Darius isn't who you think he is, but I know, I know." He paused, his eyes flashed bright and excited. "Darius is the devil and he never betrays one of his own souls."

All over.

Vanessa pushed off the wall, kicked the Beretta out of Matthew's hand.

She grabbed an empty beer bottle from the table, cracked it, leaving jagged edges. She stood facing them. Could she get to Matthew's gun? Six feet away, she could do it. She started to move, stopped cold.

Andy was pointing her own gun at her, and said, his voice a crazy singsong. "Put the bottle down, Vanessa. You're such a pretty little liar. I kind of liked you."

She lunged at him, ripped at his face with the beer bottle. Matthew yelled, "Don't shoot, Andy, don't shoot! Get away from her, get back!"

Andy jumped back.

"Vanessa."

She slowly turned to see Matthew smiling at her. "Good-bye, Vanessa." And he raised his Beretta.

"No!" Ian lunged at Matthew and Matthew shot him

in the heart. Ian stared an instant at Vanessa, then slowly slid to the floor and slumped over onto his side.

Matthew looked down at Ian. "You fool." He looked at her now. "I think he loved you more than he did me."

He aimed the Beretta at her, smiled, and shot her.

18

KNIGHT TO B6

Back to Federal Plaza

Mike left the safe house in Bayonne a little before two in the morning, hyper, full of adrenaline from the explosion, and rage pounding through her from the murder of three of her friends.

She drove Louisa's pool car, and the sucker was fast. There was next to no traffic at this dead-night hour and she made it back to Federal Plaza in record time, and who cared if she broke a few traffic laws along the way?

As she drove down the ramp and into the silent garage, she wondered how long the adrenaline would last before she bottomed out and keeled over. No, the rage would keep her upright and alert.

She parked the car, tossed the keys to the agent stuck on night duty—Prother was his name—and he gawked at her. She'd forgotten what a mess she was. She nearly smiled, waved him quiet. She stopped the elevator at the twenty-second floor and hit the kitchen, pulling out sodas and apples from the refrigerator. Her last meal had been too long ago and there was a long night to get through.

She found Nicholas and Gray in the conference room, papers spread out on the table, both tapping furiously on their respective keyboards. She set down the sodas and apples. Nicholas didn't break stride. "Thanks. You okay?"

When the words wouldn't come out, he looked up at her.

"Mike?"

"Of course. Fill me in." She slid a Coke to Gray, opened her own.

Nicholas said, "Gray and I managed to stop the cyberattack on the oil companies. I recognized the signature of a German hacker, but Menard told me he'd been killed a few days ago."

"This has already gone international?"

"Yes."

She pushed hair out of her face, jerked it back into a ponytail. How odd, even her scalp hurt. "Someone's covering their tracks, then. You think your hacker friend was hired to do the work, then eliminated when they didn't need him anymore? But who did it, Nicholas? He was killed in Germany and COE is here."

Nicholas smiled at her. "Our question exactly."

"Tell me about this hacker."

"Gunther Ansell. His work is legendary, but he never

could resist attaching a bit of flair for others to see so they could admire his architecture. He's made a living hovering on the borders of society. But this time he trusted the wrong people. If we're right, he was killed after he provided COE with the worm."

Gray said, "One of the COE people must have flown over to Germany and killed him. In and out, fast."

Nicholas added, "These people are playing for keeps, and this plot has been under way for a while, since it takes time to build software this sophisticated, able to break through firewalls and seize control of an entire system. It required a vast amount of planning and coordination. This was not easy to pull off, nor was it the work of a single person."

"How long would it take?" Mike drank half her soda, felt the caffeine rush zing her brain.

"Weeks, even if they're really talented. An attack of this scale? To find the funding—Gunther's code is wildly expensive—develop the software, plan exactly where and when to gain entry? Plus time it to a bombing? It's possible we're looking at months of back-end work."

Mike saw a chessboard in her mind, saw chess pieces moving slowly, one space at a time, getting into the proper position. It was hard to get her brain around all the complicated and unexpected moves COE had made, all the while sticking with their penny-ante refinery explosions. "But why did they waste time killing Mr. Hodges? He did nothing, nothing. And you know Larry Reeves is most likely dead, probably buried in the rubble at Bayway."

Nicholas was stroking his hand over his chin. "What they've done, killing three agents—this group has to know we'll come after them with everything we've got."

Gray said, "Nicholas is right. They've declared war."

It didn't make sense to Nicholas, but he now knew the FBI would focus their incredible resources on this group. Did they want to go out as martyrs?

Mike finished off her soda and crushed the can. "We've got to find them before we line them all up and fire our cannon. Where are they? Who is their leader?"

Nicholas said, "We now have some light, Mike. What with the hiring of Gunther, the massive attack, we know they have ties to the hacktivist community. It changes everything. There are probably others ready and willing to help with whatever COE needs, since it appears the group has unlimited funds. Maybe even Anonymous."

Mike said. "But to date, Anonymous has held government websites hostage and stirred up trouble in places like Ferguson, whipping the populace into a frenzy. But Anonymous doesn't bomb refineries and take electric grids down and preach for people to stop importing Middle Eastern oil."

Gray looked thoughtful. "Yet."

"I know," Mike said, "yet."

19

QUEEN TO C5

Nicholas cracked open another soda. He took a sip, yawned, and stretched. "Tell me what you think."

Mike said, "My gut tells me it's got to be the new member, the person who's come on board recently and changed the group's focus, changed what they originally perceived their purpose to be—namely, to disable oil facilities that import Middle Eastern oil. It sure fits with the over-the-top cyber-attack."

Nicholas was drumming his fingers on the table, never taking his eyes off her. She had bloody good instincts, and, he admitted to himself, he believed she was right, since that's what he'd been thinking, too.

She said, "You've made the connection to this German hacker, COE launched, and you countered a massive cyber-attack. They've thrown down the gauntlet. Why, we don't know. While you guys do your fancy computer work, I'm going to pull every bit of camera footage from the area surrounding Bayway and from Bayonne and Mr. Hodges's house. Maybe someone slipped and we'll have the leader's face on film."

Zachery stepped into the conference room, dragging. He sat down hard in the chair at the head of the table. Nicholas slid a soda his way. He took it, opened it, drank half, then set the can on the table. He looked from Mike to Nicholas.

"I thought I told you two to go home," he said. "Instead, you walk in on four murders, three of them our own people, and you, Nicholas and Gray, stop a cyber-attack. The head of ConocoPhillips called to say thank you." He fiddled with the Coke can. "We lost three good men tonight. I want to know why. Tell me what you've discovered."

Nicholas ran Zachery through everything they knew or suspected, including his call to Menard and Gunther's murder, and ended with Mike's plans to gather all the video feeds from Mr. Hodges's house and the refinery.

Zachery shook his head. "Who could have guessed? I mean, cyber-attacks? Talk about shifting gears. But you pulled the plug on them, by what means I probably don't want to know. But you also know they won't stop. Not only that, it seems like they've taken one huge step from the road they were on, new game, new rules, and who knows where it's leading?"

Nicholas sat forward. "Gray and I have a line in now. I'm confident we can begin tracing the attack and have names by morning. There's a start."

Zachery massaged his forehead. "All right. Set things

up. Nicholas, write up a warrant to go after everything Gunther Ansell had on his computers, if they even exist anymore, and Gray, get Interpol to release their files to us. I want to know everything this hacker has done, thought, or planned for the past year. Mike, put in your requests for the video feeds. And then . . ." He gave them a crooked grin. "Then I want all three of you to go home. No, don't argue. All of us need some sleep."

He rose. "We'll tackle this again in the morning. You've done excellent work tonight, but it's time to shut it down." He looked at his watch. "We'll meet again at eight-thirty tomorrow—this—morning. If I see any of you a minute before, I'll make you clean all the toilets on the twenty-third floor."

Gray said, "Sir, we must get my team going so they can follow all the threads on the cyber-attack. Nicholas stopped the main event, yes, but there's no telling if they'll regroup and try again. With luck, we can protect all the systems and get the companies running normally by morning. It'll be bad news if we don't. Shanghai is reporting steady sell-offs in the oil and gas sectors. When the markets open here, there could be a huge mess."

"Very well. Call in some of your people, give them instructions, then get some sleep; you've been at it over twenty-four hours. All of you, that's an order." He paused, shook his head. "Another order."

Twenty minutes later, Mike stuck her head in Nicholas's cubicle. "Ready to get out of here?"

"I am. Gray gave his people instructions and left. I got the warrants in and sent some threads into the ether."

"And I've got in a request for the Bayway video feeds."

"I'm sure Nigel could be convinced to put together a tray if you'd like to come to the house."

"Sounds tempting, but a shower and my very own bed wins hands down. Get some sleep, Nicholas; you need it as much as I do." She touched her fingers to her bruised face. "I gotta say, though, your pretty face looks better than mine. It's going to take a gallon of makeup to make me presentable. I'll see you back here at eight-thirty." She gave him a little wave and was gone.

He watched her walk away down the hall, shoulders straight, head up, clothes ripped and black, straggly ponytail swinging. He rubbed his hand over beard stubble and his fingers came away black with soot. He was tired, sore, and frustrated. Zachery was right, things could wait until morning.

He punched a couple keys on his laptop. Most of the things, anyway.

20

BISHOP TO G4

Brooklyn

Andy yelled, "You killed Ian, dude, you killed him, your best bud, your mentor! I liked Ian; he thought I was funny." Something in Matthew's eyes stopped him in his tracks. He whispered, "Can you believe he wanted to protect her? I mean, what was that all about?"

Matthew stood stock-still in the middle of the carnage, the Beretta hanging loose in his fingers. He looked away from Andy, down at Ian, then at Vanessa, saying nothing.

"And dude, you shot her dead, too. I thought you didn't want to kill people." Andy's eyes suddenly glowed with a mad light. "Hey, way to go!"

Matthew barely registered Andy's freak show. He'd always known Andy was crazy, but now he could feel the sick excitement rolling off him in waves. It turned

Matthew's blood to ice. He couldn't stand it. He yelled, "Shut up, you idiot, or I'll shoot you, too." And he knew in that moment he meant it, anything to shut that crazy mouth, close those mad eyes forever.

Andy stared at him. The mad mania was gone; he looked ready to burst into tears. "Matthew, what are we supposed to do now? I mean, Ian did everything, he planned stuff and told us how to do things, and when to act; he always told me when I did a good job. And what about bombs, Matthew? Don't we need more bombs? Vanessa built all our bombs. Are you going to use your own bombs now . . . ?" His voice trailed off.

Yelling at Andy didn't help. Matthew had killed his friends, but the initial horror of what he'd done was gone now. It didn't matter anyway, there was no going back. He was the leader again, and the leader said, "Andy, stop your worrying, I'll see to everything. Haven't I always taken care of us all? You need to pack up everything, right now. We're leaving in three minutes, okay? Move it."

Andy was wringing his hands. "But we can't leave them here, Matthew."

"I said get everything we need, I'll take care of the rest. Two minutes, Andy. Move!"

Andy rushed to disconnect the computers and monitors while Matthew gathered the bomb bags, the suitcases, a bag of groceries from the kitchen. He was careful not to look down at Ian and Vanessa, lying drenched in their own blood.

Both men were careful to give the bodies a wide berth.

It took longer than Matthew wanted to disassemble all of Andy's equipment, and three trips to the van.

"Start the van. I'll be right back." Matthew grabbed a can of Andy's special gas, his own formula, designed to make things go up in flames in a heartbeat, and started back up the stairs.

He heard Andy's excited voice behind him: "Hey, Matthew, let me do it. Please, let me light it up."

"I told you to start the car," Matthew called back, not looking at him. "I'll be right down." No way was he going to let Andy burn down the neighborhood.

Inside, he forced himself to look down at Ian, sprawled on his back, his plaid shirt black with blood, his eyes open, staring up at Matthew. He felt a punch of pain. Andy was right, Ian had been his friend and mentor, taught him everything, but in the end he'd chosen her, not Matthew. And he couldn't forgive that, ever, and he dumped some gasoline directly on Ian, then turned to take one last look at the woman he'd wanted, but not quite trusted, not quite, but it was close. Had he loved her? Perhaps, in moments when he was desperate to have sex with her. Tonight, though, in the aftermath of their brilliant success, his blood roaring through his body, he knew he would have told her everything and she would have skipped out, dancing because she'd won.

She was dead; it was all over. She lay on her side, her white shirt covered with blood, her hair floating in it. He felt bile rise in his throat. No, no, he'd done the right thing, the only reasonable thing. She'd betrayed him.

Who was she? Some sort of spy, an agent? He didn't know, and now it didn't matter. She would burn with Ian.

Matthew turned away from her and methodically poured gasoline all over the apartment, but he didn't pour any on her. He said her name aloud, one last time, "Vanessa," and tossed the gasoline can in the corner. He threw a lighted match in the hall beside the stairs, listened to it whoosh as it caught the carpet on fire. He ran down the stairs. He never looked back.

21

BISHOP TO G5

Brooklyn

Vanessa floated.

Had she heard Matthew's voice? She wasn't sure, but her brain knew enough to keep her still and silent. There was always danger when you spent half your life undercover, and tonight she'd stepped right in it.

Being awake opened the floodgates and she was suddenly swamped in pain. She smelled her own blood, knew the pain would get worse and worse and she could die.

Matthew had shot her, after he'd shot Ian. Ian had tried to save her, despite the fact that he had to know it was her phone and she wasn't really one of them. No, she couldn't think about that now.

There was something else—she smelled smoke. Matthew had set the apartment on fire.

She didn't want to, but she touched her chest, felt all the hot sticky blood, her blood. It was bad, really bad. She managed to raise her head. She didn't see any flames, but she heard them in the hallway, whooshing along the threadbare carpet toward the living room. Smoke was creeping in; soon the room would be gray and she wouldn't be able to breathe.

If you don't get out of here now you will die. Tie up your chest and go.

Pain ripped through her when she sat up. She gritted her teeth and forced herself to move. She could barely breathe. She figured her lung had collapsed and her chest was filling with blood. The smoke was getting heavier now, the sound of the fire getting closer. She realized it was blocking the hallway to the stairs. No hope for it. She dragged herself to her feet, holding on to a chair for support. She looked down at Ian, then quickly away; there was nothing she could do for him.

She had to get to the hidden access to the roof, the only way out. It was their bolthole, one of the reasons Matthew had chosen this apartment.

The ladder to the roof was inside the closet in the master bedroom. She would make it, she had to, she had no choice. She dragged herself down the hallway, using the wall for support, to the bedroom, then into the small closet, with the ladder at the back.

She imagined she heard her dead father's voice loud and clear as she climbed that ladder, each step so hard, nearly impossible, but there he was, saying over and over,

Be glad of the pain, it means you're still alive. Now get out of there, Nessa, do you hear me? And it comforted.

His words became a mantra her mind whispered again and again as she began her climb up the ladder in the closet. When she finally crawled out onto the pebbled roof, she collapsed to the ground, coughing. Blood spattered out of her mouth and she sucked in air, but never enough. Smoke was billowing up all around her.

She crawled to the fire escape, her only chance, since the building itself was now burning.

Her father's voice kept at her, yelling now over the pain, pushing her, pushing her. She crawled to the ledge. The ground looked a mile away, but she knew it was only three stories down. *I can't make it, Dad, I can't make it.*

And again his frantic urging: *Don't you let that crazy bastard win, do you hear me, Nessa? You move, and you move now!* Vanessa felt a bolt of fury and swung her legs onto the metal tread of the fire escape.

She heard sirens. She had to get away before they got here. She couldn't be captured, it wasn't an option.

She clutched the quickly heating side bars. *Down, down, get moving.*

Something tore inside her. The pain crashed over her, a tsunami. She felt blood running down her arms. The sweater she'd bound around herself was soaked with her blood. Her father's voice died in her mind.

She was nearly down when she fainted and fell, boneless, to the hard asphalt.

22

KNIGHT TO A4

Nicholas wasn't surprised to find Nigel in the kitchen, reading a book, a lead crystal lowball of Talisker Storm, neat, sitting by his elbow.

"Waiting up for me?"

His butler raised an eyebrow, looked him up and down, and sighed. "I see you've ruined yet another pair of pants, that lovely Spanish leather jacket your father gave you for your birthday, not to mention the bespoke shirt from Gieves and Hawkes. And the shoes? My, Mr. Gunderson would weep to see them." Another sigh, a shake of the head. "They go in the trash bin as well. Barneys rejoices. And Barneys' children, since we'll be paying their college tuition for years to come."

"Ha bloody ha."

"You and Agent Caine were at the Bayway Refinery, weren't you?"

Nicholas nodded.

"And that means, then, that you two plunged into the flames and rescued workers? That explains the missing sleeves, the black face."

Nicholas saw the carnage again in his mind and nodded again, numbly.

Nigel paused for a moment, saw what a tight rein Nicholas had on himself. He lightly laid his hand on Nicholas's shoulder. "You did well. Now, what can I do?"

Nicholas snapped to. "There's really nothing, but thank you. Please go to bed, Nigel. I'm fine. I think a drink might be a good idea, though." He poured himself at least three fingers of Talisker and drained it in a single gulp. The liquor shuddered through his body, warmed him to his ruined shoes.

"Did that help?"

"Yes, yes, it did." Nicholas eased into a chair, watched Nigel pour him another.

"Would you like to talk about it?"

"No."

"Your mother called. The news of the refinery explosion already made it to England. I told her I believed you were at Lincoln Center, watching a play."

"That was well done of you, Nigel, thank you."

"I don't think she believed me for an instant, but bless her, she didn't push it. You can expect a call from your father and grandfather tomorrow. Early."

"Everything is all right back home?"

"Yes, everything is fine." Nigel studied Nicholas's face for a moment longer, then said, "You should soak up the Talisker before you go to bed. There's cold chicken and orzo in the Sub-Zero."

"No, I think I'd like to keep the bad away a while longer," Nicholas said, and he nodded at the bottle of Talisker. "This will do nicely."

Nigel didn't move.

"What is it, Nigel? Is there really something going on at home I should know about? And you're protecting me like you tried to protect my mother?"

"I've known you all our lives, Nicholas. I've seen you angry and frustrated, but not as much as you are now. I've seen you even dirtier than you are now, more banged up, seen you inches away from losing that infamous Drummond temper. But you want to know something?"

Nicholas's eyebrow shot up. "Yes?"

"You're enjoying yourself."

The Talisker spurted out of Nicholas's mouth.

"No, no, Nigel, you're wrong. All the bonkers crap that's going on? No, no, I am not enjoying myself."

Nigel merely shook his head. "I'd say you're downright giddy. I was worried about all the change, but I'm glad to say the move to New York suits you very well. Your grandfather will be pleased to hear it."

"You're dead wrong about the giddy part—well, I hope you are—and you're quite right: New York and the FBI suit me very well. It's only a pity they don't give agents clothing allowances. And stop talking to my grandfather behind my back."

Nigel grinned. "I haven't spoken to the baron. I've only spoken with *my* father. Oh, yes, he sends his very best. He said the family misses you and wonders when you might be home for a visit."

Horne, Nigel's father, was the Drummond family's butler at their home in Farrow-on-Grey, and had been a part of Nicholas's entire life just as Nigel had. A wave of homesickness hit him, or maybe it was the Talisker. He realized he missed the weekly breakfasts with his family. He missed the lime trees bordering the long drive, and the labyrinth gardens. He even missed Cook Crumbe's awful porridge.

Nigel said as he came back from the kitchen, "I'm very sorry about the tragedy tonight. But now it's time for you to get some sleep, Nicholas. Even for you, it's occasionally necessary. Good night," and Nicholas heard Nigel humming as he walked away.

Was Nigel right? Was he giddy? No, not that word, it was more that he knew he was completely and utterly involved, every single fiber in his body was sharply alive, turned on high. He'd accepted long ago that he was a predator, remembered his mother had told him he had the push-it-to-the-edge danger gene, and surely that was a good thing for the FBI. And this ridiculous COE group was still running free. But not for long. No, not for long.

And he had Michaela, and wasn't that a bit of miraculous luck? He couldn't imagine his life here without her.

Like him, she was fairly bursting with life, ready to tackle anything, always straight ahead, that was Michaela. Did she have the danger gene, too? Yes, very probably.

As he washed out his glass, he admitted to himself that he was indeed doing well here in New York. And, evidently, Barneys was doing well, too.

He took a hot shower, pulled out his first-aid kit and smeared some burn cream on his palms, then climbed into bed, his mobile next to his head.

But he couldn't sleep, too many unknown faces tracking through his mind, too many codes he had yet to untangle.

Mike was in her ancient bathrobe, eating a cold slice of pepperoni pizza, when her cell rang. She was tempted not to answer it, but of course that wasn't an option.

Nicholas. No surprise he was still working. She wished she could give him all the freedom he wanted and fewer rules, but alas, she wouldn't be that high on the FBI food chain for many years to come. And how high would Nicholas be by the time they hit forty?

Mike sat down at her small work desk, stared at the mess of papers—bills, mostly. Maybe she should dust. Or not. She swung her feet up onto the cluttered surface, put the phone on speaker. "Why aren't you asleep?"

"Why aren't you?"

She laughed. "I'm eating. Cold pizza."

"Booze is better. Mike, I'm as sure as can be there's a new player in COE."

"Talk to me."

"Remember Paris? When we chatted with a young gentleman about his future?"

He was speaking, of course, of Adam Pearce, a brilliant young hacker who'd been invaluable in stopping that madman Manfred Havelock. After an obligatory three months in jail, they'd gotten him out, and now he worked for the FBI. She understood why Nicholas hadn't used his name on an open line—the FBI were also responsible for keeping him safe until Adam's antics against foreign governments were smoothed over.

"What about our young friend?"

"I want to use him. He'd be great bait."

"So soon? He's so young and he's been through a lot. This is a major case. It may be too much too soon."

But Nicholas understood Adam Pearce, recently turned twenty years old. "He's tough, talented, and I think he'd be perfect for the role. We have to get inside the organization. Their previous help was murdered. They'll need someone new to continue the attacks. What with the cyber-attack and Bayway, I'll bet another young hacker with a grudge against the world can't wait to join the fun."

He was right.

"Will you make the call?"

She heard typing.

"Done. I've sent word. As soon as I hear something, I'll let you know."

"Do you know where he is?"

"No. Doesn't matter. What I have in mind he can do from anywhere."

"Will you be able to sleep now?"

He laughed. "Yes, I do believe I will. Sweet dreams to you, Agent Caine. Thanks for the ear, and the agreement."

Fancy that, Nicholas had acted like a real partner, called her to get her opinion before acting. She smiled as she climbed into bed. *Sweet dreams?* You bet. But short ones, given it was four something o'clock in the morning.

23

QUEEN TO A3

Chicago

Adam Pearce was staring at the brightly lit Chicago skyline when his phone beeped that an encrypted e-mail had arrived. It wasn't his personal phone, but the special cell the FBI had provided.

It was the middle of the night. Why had they chosen now to make contact? He hadn't heard from them in weeks, not since he'd been placed in this apartment and told to lie low. He was bored. He needed to work, to stretch his brain, to do something.

The e-mail was simple.

We have a job for you. Call in.

At last! His brain lit up like Christmas, his blood

roared. Even though Adam still chafed at the idea of working for the government, it was better than rotting in a federal prison or being extradited to one of the many countries he'd worked against. His call sign was no longer Eternal Patrol. Now his call sign was Dark Leaf. He'd spent the last few weeks skimming around the darknet, spying on his brethren. Carefully. If the rest of the hacker world knew he was working for the government, there'd be a contract on him by morning. There were still a lot of very powerful people in the world who would like to bury him deep.

He built in a second layer of encryption so his voice would be garbled to anyone who might be listening in and dialed the number. Paranoia had always been his watchword.

Nicholas Drummond answered the call, said immediately in his posh British accent, "Did I wake you?"

"No."

Nicholas laughed. "Ever the hacker, keeping night hours. I don't sleep much myself. How are things? You've been comfortably relocated, I trust?"

"Yeah, yeah, things are fine, but, Nicholas, I'm so bored I'm tempted to hack Director Comey's computer and tell him to give me something to do. Please tell me that's why you called."

"It is, my friend. You're aware of a group called COE?"

"Celebrants of Earth? Of course. Dorky name. They've been doing bad things, making you guys look like monkeys. Wow, I guess I'm now looking like a monkey, too, since I'm officially one of you. Are they behind the attack on the oil companies tonight?"

"You've heard about it?"

"Sure. The whole Net is buzzing. A Shamoon attack, was it?"

"No comment. Have you ever come across Gunther Ansell?"

Adam whistled. "The Blue Whale? Sure, everyone has. He does superior work, for an old guy. He's what, thirty?"

"Yes, nearly ready for the glue factory. Adam, he's dead, murdered."

There was a long moment of dead silence, then, "All right, you'd better tell me all about it."

Nicholas did. "I've got a request in for everything he was working on, maybe something's there to nail COE. But I really don't need it, I know COE. And I know they'll need someone new to keep up the cyber-attacks." He paused, waited. "Adam, you there?"

"Yeah, I'm here. I'm trying to get my brain around this. Gunther, gone, it's crazy, dude. So, Nicholas, you want me to offer my services to COE?"

"You'll need to show them you're better than their people, ah, and that you share their values and goals, which, at this moment, we're no longer sure we know. They'd been so focused, and now they've switched gears, and I'm simply not sure if their fanatical hate is at the core of it now."

"I do share some of their values, Nicholas."

"Yes, I assume they hate the government, too, which

makes you perfect for the job. Get in, Adam, and do it quickly. We need to stop them before more people are killed. We didn't know until tonight with the cyber-attacks on the oil companies that they even had a hacker on board."

"You said Gunther was killed three days ago. That means they've got to have someone already on the inside with enough smarts and know-how to implement his plan. I assume Gunther was killed because someone was afraid he'd talk?"

"Probably. Adam, you're fresh and clean in cyberspace now. We've helped you establish a whole new identity. You can get into their organization from afar."

There was a moment of silence, then Adam said, his voice formal, "I owe you my life, Agent Drummond. I'll report in when I have news."

Nicholas said, "Good, we all appreciate it. You know I can't do it, I'd be outed immediately, and besides, I simply couldn't give it enough time at this point. Adam, be sure to cover your tracks at every turn. Create a false trail, leave as much disruption behind as you can, and bread crumbs galore, so when we're done, we can blow them out of the water. I've been working a backstop to verify the information—they *will* come searching for your credentials, and I promise you they will be watertight. And, Adam? Hurry. We're running out of time."

"I hear you. I'll be in touch."

Adam hung up the phone and the e-mail dinged again—the legend Drummond created for him had arrived. It was distinctly criminal, with a number of outstanding hacks to the identity's credit. Adam memorized everything, then started sending out feelers to COE. With luck, he'd find a way in tonight. A pity Nicholas couldn't join him; it would be fun, the two of them fighting it out with the bad guys in cyberspace.

He quickly saw that every hacker with a keyboard was out and about, speculating about how COE had gotten past the oil companies' firewalls. Adam didn't see Gunther's name once, which meant Drummond had been inside the hack himself, looking for the golden thread, shutting down any ties to the Blue Whale. He was impressed; Nicholas was nearly as good a hacker as he was. Well, perhaps he was better, since he was nearly old enough for Social Security himself, at least as old as Gunther had been. Adam would miss Gunther, a great talent, but he'd been sloppy and Nicholas had caught his signature.

Adam began whistling, his fingers flying over the keyboard.

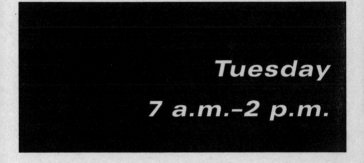

Tuesday

7 a.m.–2 p.m.

24

KNIGHT TAKES C3

Atlantic City, New Jersey

Zahir Damari—known to Matthew and his little group of ideologues, fanatics, and crazies as Darius, only Darius—drove his stolen Jeep into Atlantic City before sunrise. The ramshackle abandoned hotel where he was to meet his contact was two blocks off the main drag. There were no lights and the building was falling down. He heard rats scurrying around when his flashlight hit them.

Atlantic City was dying, and soon this whole country would collapse under greed and endless bureaucracy and people so contentious and self-interested that anything needful would never get done, no movement at all until it was too late.

It was too late now, far too late. He should know, since

it was his job to give it a big push, and when he and Matthew finished, the U.S. would buckle and collapse under the pressure.

Zahir knew there were no cameras nearby, not in this area, and no tourists, unless they were certifiable. He walked around to the back of the hotel. It was quiet, almost too quiet. He stopped walking, stood very still. He'd stayed alive this long because he always trusted his instincts. He pulled out his Walther PPK from its battered holster under his arm and began moving forward again, slower this time, his gun at the ready.

There wasn't supposed to be anyone here yet, but as he rounded the edge of the building, he saw a young man, his back to Zahir, standing very quietly. In this dying city, he was simply another shadow, of no consequence.

Wait. Was this his contact? From Colonel Rahbar? Or was he sent by the Hammer? How did this make any sense? Zahir moved, quick as a striking snake, grabbed the young man around the neck, pressed the Walther to his temple.

He whispered in the boy's ear, "Don't turn around, and don't struggle, or I'll have to shoot you, and I'm not in the mood to kill a child."

The young man stiffened. "I am not a child. I have done my job and done it well for six years now. I am here to give you a message."

Zahir loosened his hold around his neck. "Speak."

He drew in a deep breath, and when he spoke Zahir heard cool authority, realized this young man wasn't an amateur, not a simple messenger. Despite his seeming youth, he knew what he was doing, knew the stakes, knew well Zahir could kill him if wanted to, yet he'd come and he seemed calm and in control. Zahir was impressed.

The young man said, "As you can see, I did not bring the plans, I could not."

"And why do you not have my plans?"

"My asset texted me that since the explosion at Bayway Refinery and the loss of life, he is no longer safe. He thinks he is being watched. He fears that if he provides these plans to you, the FBI will find out and take him. He claims he must stop everything he is being paid well to do for us and cover his tracks. And, he told me, he is sorry to let us down." The kid snorted.

"I could not move him because he is hysterical, the weak-kneed ass, and has forgotten what he owes us. Colonel Rahbar has instructed me to tell you that you must find another way to accomplish your mission."

He leaned against the young man's ear and whispered, "Find another way when this one is so perfect? No, I don't think so. I cannot believe you are allowing this puling coward to tell you what he will and will not do, to give you orders, to give Colonel Rahbar orders."

"He refuses to act and I cannot obtain the blueprints myself. If I could I would, but I cannot. The Hammer agrees, you must find another way."

"I see, so Rahbar and the Hammer feel this fool is too valuable to threaten or kill."

"I believe so."

Again Zahir whispered against his ear. "Here is what is going to happen. I will see to it myself that your

American traitor does as he was paid to do. Paid very, very well, I assume. You will now take a message directly to him from me, from Zahir Damari. Where does this man work?"

"In Baltimore."

"Excellent. You will tell this asset of yours that if he does not bring the plans to a diner called Silver Corner in the Inner Harbor at precisely ten o'clock tomorrow morning, I will not only destroy him, I will blow up his world. Do you think he will believe me?"

The young man's voice was no longer flat, emotionless; it was filled with eagerness. "I did not agree with Colonel Rahbar or the Hammer, so I will gladly tell him. If he does not believe you, he is a fool as well as a coward and he would deserve what you will do to him."

"In case he isn't convinced, tell him I am a great fisherman and that I quite enjoy gutting fish. Now go, do not look over your shoulder. We wouldn't want you turning into a pillar of salt."

The young man drew a deep breath when Zahir lifted the gun from his temple. He turned and walked away, his footsteps sending the rats scurrying, the only sound in the quiet morning. He did not look back. Did Zahir hear him whistling? A boy after his own heart.

25

PAWN TAKES C3

One Observatory Circle
Washington, D.C.

Vice President Callan Sloane set her encrypted iPad on the coffee table. It was early, and she needed to mainline some caffeine before digging in to the PDB—President's Daily Brief. Outside the window, her assigned Secret Service agents strolled along the veranda and through the white-latticed gazebo into the gardens, enjoying the beautiful spring morning. Soon it would be hot and humid, everyone sweating, her included, a typical D.C. summer, but for now, the air was clear and cool, the flowers bloomed, and Callan was left to her own devices for another hour. She liked eating alone in the living room, with none of her people sneaking in to get a breath of air-conditioned air, or the cook bustling around preparing for the inevitable twice-weekly dinner parties.

Every day started the same for her. Rise at six; hit the treadmill; shower, feed and play with the cats; then move downstairs; grab the coffee, apple, and granola bar she preferred; and set up shop in the living room. It was clean and serene, with lush floor-to-ceiling draperies and cool, neutral beige tones, not the cluttered mess of her upstairs office or the formal severity of her two White House offices. It was much more her.

She drank her coffee from a chipped blue mug she'd brought from home when she'd moved into the vice president's mansion. The mug had once read DODGERS, a gift from her baseball-loving dad before he'd died of a sudden heart attack five years before. She treasured it, couldn't talk herself into not using it, though it would break one day and then where would she be? Up to her ears in Super Glue.

The PDB was the first thing she looked at once she settled in for breakfast. It was a daily intelligence publication that had started with President Truman, back in the late forties, to brief him on the immediate threats to the United States.

Callan set down her coffee and swiped a finger across her highly encrypted iPad. She knew what was tops on the PDB today—the bombing in New Jersey. It was being attributed to the terror group Celebrants of Earth. There'd also been a major cyber-attack on the oil sector, possibly tied to the Bayway bombing. But the biggest item would be about the current peace talks in Geneva and

Israel's balking over Iran's latest claim that they had no plans to launch any nuclear weapons ever, even in the distant future, at Israel. Like anyone would believe that, ever, except for the president. *The world's going to Hell in a handbasket,* as her grandmother used to say. Callan took some comfort from the knowledge that this was the belief of every generation, probably back to the cavemen. Truman had dealt with far worse than her boss, President Jefferson Bradley, but it was a different world back then. Today the nation's enemies no longer wore uniforms and goose-stepped to cheering crowds. Now their enemies were faceless. They attacked silently, by land, sea, air, or computer, something Truman couldn't have imagined.

Her cell rang. It was sitting on the table by her half-eaten apple. She went on alert when she saw the number. The president rarely called her directly. That meant he wanted to talk about Israel and how they were trying to destroy his precious Middle East peace talks.

"Good morning, sir."

No hello, only: "Did you read the PDB?"

"I did, yes." She said nothing more, waited.

"Callan, I need you to get the Israelis on the right side of this, and do it now. I know your relationship with Mossad; it's one of the reasons I brought you on board as my VP. We can't have anything disrupt the talks this week. When they're not ignoring each other, they're talking about this COE group's brazen cyber-attack, and needless to say all the oil-producing countries are scared after Bayway. I heard one of them claiming it was Israel's fault, that they were behind COE. Perhaps they are, I don't know. I will not allow this group to screw with my legacy. I won't have it, I simply won't." Bradley sucked in a deep breath. "The Israelis walked out last night. Call that man you know, Ari Mizrahi. Handle this, handle them, or we're going to have a very long talk when I return."

"Yes, sir." *Your Eminence.* She wasn't terribly fond of her boss, but she couldn't deny they had made an excellent political team. She'd brought California, and the female vote, which tipped the scales. Their only major disagreement was foreign policy, the Middle East in particular. She knew firsthand the dangers America, Israel, and the rest of the world faced by a saber-rattling nuclear Iran and their enforcers, Hezbollah, and the rest of the undemocratized Middle East. Bradley wanted a lasting legacy of peace in the region, and he'd made that his number-one priority when he took office. Only a year into his presidency and he'd managed to get all the parties together and actually sitting down at the same table in Geneva. That in itself was quite a coup. He'd even managed to talk Israel into letting the Taliban and the Saudis come to the party. He knew Israel wouldn't come if he invited Hezbollah, no matter what he threatened, but he managed to get the Iranian mullahs and the president, even the fanatical Colonel Vahid Rahbar, always eager and vicious in his denunciation of Israel and the West. Everyone agreed this was a miracle, and prayed.

But Callan knew it wouldn't work just as she knew the glory Bradley was seeking would very likely end up being his downfall. And the world's as well?

No hope for it; at least at this moment, he was her boss. "I'll talk to them immediately, sir."

"Do that. I'll be back Wednesday night for my speech congratulating the Yorktown facilities for moving to clean energy resources, then I'll go to Camp David for the weekend and get this peace accord written up. It will happen if you do your job, do you understand?"

"Yes, sir, I understand."

"Good. The heads of state will be in the U.S. next week to do the signing. I want your smiling face both at Yorktown and at the signing, Callan." He paused for a moment, retrenched a bit. "Look, I know you aren't on board with my approach, but I truly believe this is the right course of action. I'm showing them the right way, showing them how to save face and save their countries, their countries' futures. They will come around to reason; I will guide them."

How can you be so blind? If leaders do sign a peace accord, it's all for show, the same show that's been played in the past, to let you preen for a while, let you give them financial incentives, promises that could cripple us, before they strike. Can't you look at Colonel Rahbar and see the abiding hatred in his eyes? Are you content to ignore what he says about the West? That we're a blight, vermin, and should be exterminated?

But she couldn't tell him that, she'd fought with him enough. So he wanted her at Yorktown and at the peace accord signing next week to prove to all the Middle East leaders that the U.S. vice president had finally come to the dark side and agreed America's enemies were their friends. If it happened.

"Understood, sir." She knew she shouldn't prod the beast with a stick, but she couldn't help herself. "So, otherwise, how are the talks going?"

She knew he hated to say it, but he had no choice. "Not well, even with all my efforts, but still, it will turn around, once you get the Israelis back to the table. I have another twenty-four hours left to get them all on board. Do your job, Callan," and he hung up. Callan immediately dialed her chief of staff, Quinn Costello, her own personal gold mine, snapped up a decade earlier when Senator Willis Reed of Missouri had conveniently retired, for family reasons, now the current code word for extramarital frolicking.

"Morning, ma'am," came Quinn's bright voice. "You're on your way?"

"Not yet. Is my schedule insane today? I have some work I'd like to do from here."

"You have three meet and greets, a photo op with the dairy farmers at ten. We don't need you here until nine at the earliest. I take it Bradley is making you jump?"

"Of course. Gather the security folks. I want a full briefing on COE at ten-fifteen. I'll send word when I'm on my way."

She hesitated only a moment before dialing a number she knew by heart. When he answered, his deep voice was so familiar, and now so distant, she wanted to chuck it all and set things right between them.

"Mizrahi."

"Ari? It's Callan."

"I know. I still recognize your number." The coldness of his tone broke her heart. At least he'd answered, and that was an improvement. He wouldn't take her calls for months after she'd broken it off, had no choice when she'd joined the campaign. She'd needed him the most then, but he'd cut her off completely, seeing her as a traitor since she'd teamed up with Bradley, a man he distrusted. She understood, all too well. She'd chosen her career over him and he wouldn't get over it. She'd hoped she could break through, but after today, she knew there wouldn't be a chance. Today she had to rattle his cage.

"I'm calling on official business."

"I would expect nothing else from you."

Another stab to the heart. "Ari, please. Let's not fight. You know my situation. You know when I accepted this job I could hardly go on the campaign trail with a lover from Mossad."

He went silent, and she rested her forehead in her hand. "This is temporary, Ari. You know how I feel. That hasn't changed."

When he spoke again, his voice cool and remote, she knew their personal fight was put back in its bottle for another time. *Please be patient, Ari. Please forgive me for today.*

"What do you need, Madam Vice President?"

"I need your people, your government, back at the table in Geneva, to cooperate with President Bradley's talks."

"Our stance hasn't changed, Callan. We won't capitulate here, we can't afford to, and you of all people know exactly why we can't. Iran has their warheads pointed at us. Any concessions on our part right now will be tantamount to opening the border and letting the dogs through. They stand down, take those reactors offline permanently, then we'll talk, but you know they have no intention of doing that, not in my lifetime."

"We're working on it, Ari, I promise you we are. If you'd give us one bit of a good-faith showing—"

"I can't believe I'm hearing this, from *you* of all people. *You*, who knows firsthand what we've sacrificed, how we've continued to bend and compromise. Do you wish to ignore that we're under constant attack? That we live daily with death riding on our shoulders and blood in our coffee shops? My own innocent young daughter, slaughtered, moldering in the ground? And yet you, *you*, come to me with Bradley's message, asking my government to accept their lies?"

"I'm asking that you consider the possibility of reaching a lasting peace, Ari. Think of the possibilities, keep an open mind, that's all."

He laughed once, short and bitter. "A lasting peace. You will never see past the end of your nose. No, it's not your nose, it's his, Bradley's. He doesn't want to see that Iran has no intention of cooperating, or working toward peace, with us, Israel. They want us destroyed. They say it out loud for the world to hear. Even Colonel Rahbar, he's saying all the right things as he sits at the table, pandering to the president. These peace meetings—they're all for show."

She agreed with him, but she said, "Perhaps this time is different, perhaps—"

He cut her off. "Tell me why there's a contract out."

Her heart froze. "What? What did you say?"

"We intercepted an e-mail going to Jordan last night. In it were wire transfers to a series of accounts we've been monitoring. We believe it's the Iranians, acting with Hezbollah. We believe they belong to—"

"Don't say it," she said sharply, all personal animus forgotten. "Not on this line. Do you have any tangible proof of this?"

"He's gone. Three months ago, he flew to Mexico, through London. There was a small slaughter outside of Ciudad Juárez. A group of ISIS jihadists we've been collectively watching. A *pollero*, a local coyote, is missing as well. Official word is a pissed-off drug lord killed them, but I saw the pictures. It's his work, without doubt. He's on the move, Callan, and he's in the United States."

"And the target?"

Ari said simply, "There may be more than one target, but as yet, it's unverified. The only one we know for sure is you."

26

KNIGHT TAKES E4

Nicholas's Brownstone
East 69th Street
Upper East Side

Nicholas woke without an alarm at six. He felt good, rested, despite only a few hours of sleep. He turned on the TV as he stretched and listened to the local weather. It appeared the weather agreed with his mood, sunny and clear and warm, a perfect spring day shaping up outside. Quite different from his usual mornings in London—rain, rain, and more rain. He did miss London, but New York's weather was hard to argue with. The city was growing on him.

His good mood swept him through a shower, shaving, dressing. His ruined clothes were nowhere to be seen, which meant Nigel had been in his rooms already this morning.

He took care selecting his clothes; he needed to look shipshape and in control since there would be cameras and press and meetings with other agencies. A gray three-button suit from Barneys, a white Turnbull & Asser shirt with a hint of cream stripe, his grandfather's cuff links, polished wing tips. Yes, he would do. He started to put on a red tie, then opted for a muted purple. Zachery would be wearing red, no sense competing.

He went to the kitchen for his breakfast. Nigel was nowhere to be seen, but a surprise—he'd made oatmeal. It was much better than Cook Crumbe's bitter excuse for oatmeal at home.

While he ate, he read the headlines on his iPad. The Bayway bombing was the lead, as expected, the photos from the scene in daylight even more devastating and graphic than he remembered. He glanced at his palms. The burns weren't bad this morning, what with all the burn cream he'd used. He thought of Rex Cedarson, Bob Ventura, and Kenneth Chantler, the waste of it, and Mr. Hodges, a good man, now dead. No reason for any of it, a show of arrogance.

He drank two strong cups of Earl Grey—sent directly from Fortnum & Mason, thanks to his mum, Mitzie—had a second bowl of brown sugar–laden oatmeal while he checked his e-mail. Nothing from Adam Pearce yet, but it had been only a few hours. Give the boy a chance to make the appropriate inroads.

He got into his car, a sporty, very maneuverable BMW 335i. His new baby was sapphire black with a gray leather interior and dark burl walnut to announce the final touch of class. Though he missed his Jaguar, buying the BMW was cheaper than having the Jag shipped over from England. Well, almost. He loved the way the BMW drove. He'd named the car Freya after his first ancient Fiat from his parents when he was sixteen.

He checked traffic on his mobile, knew it would take him less than twenty minutes to get to Federal Plaza.

Mike called before he hit FDR Drive.

"Are you on your way?"

"I am. ETA ten minutes. What's happened?"

"Nothing yet," she said, "though I've only been here a few minutes. We'll sit down at the threat table as soon as you get in. The video feeds are ready, and the families have been notified. Word is out we lost three men last night. This whole place is boiling mad. It's not going to be a good day here. Ah, did you get everything worked out with our friend?"

"I did. He's up and running. He'll report in when he has entry. Is Zachery in his office?"

"I don't know, but I bet he is, all ready to rock and roll. There's a press conference scheduled for ten. No news yet on Larry Reeves—all the bodies have been recovered from Bayway, though they haven't all been identified— he's up and vanished, left his family without a word. There's a chance he's dead. Gray has something for you— important, he says, so hurry up."

When Nicholas got to his desk on the twenty-third floor, he saw Mike first thing, hunched over her computer, face close to the screen, tracing something with her finger. She took off her glasses, rubbed the bridge of her nose, then leaned back and closed her eyes. He bent down to see what she'd been looking at and was distracted by that jasmine scent of hers—alas, overlaid with a bit of smoke smell this morning. He imagined he was still on the smoky side as well.

He straightened, touched her shoulder. "Nothing yet?"

She blinked up at him. He saw her face sported a colorful array of bruises, but she still looked sharp and ready to annihilate—quite a combination. He wished he had a bad guy to throw into her cage.

"Good morning to you, Michaela. You look better this morning, though that bruise is purple and looks like Rhode Island." He lightly outlined the bruise with a fingertip. "Does it hurt?"

"Only a tiny bit." She put on her glasses and looked him up and down. "You look like James Bond, super-macho in cool clothes. Wow, even French cuffs—you look ready to play high-stakes poker and take the table. Makes me think if you took over the Bond franchise, it'd explode."

He had to laugh. "And I like that jumper. Black is your color. It sets off your hair."

"Come on, Nicholas, stop trying to jolly me up. Hey, I'm proud of Rhode Island. How are your hands?"

He shrugged. "Not bad this morning." He leaned back against the blue felt wall of Mike's cube, his arms crossed. "I've been thinking. COE needed massive amounts of money to pull off the cyber-attacks last night. Gunther's fee alone would be in the millions. Where is all this money coming from? That's what we need to find out."

Mike nodded. "Yes, of course you're right. We've also got to be certain COE is behind this."

"You know they are. Have you looked at any of the video footage yet?"

"Yes. Take a look at this, Nicholas." Mike pointed to her screen. Nicholas saw blurred dark images, barely visible. Then he saw the edge of a jaw flashing white in the moonlight, and full lips, nothing else under the brim of a baseball cap.

"Brilliant, Agent Caine. Let's find out who this woman is and track her down."

27

BISHOP TAKES E7

Mike said, "I've got more. She shows up on all three videos. She never takes off the ball cap, so all I can capture is the jaw. We'll need more for the facial recognition, since the feed itself isn't so hot." She paused for a moment. "In one of the shots she looks up toward the camera. It's like she's letting herself be seen, and what does that mean?

"There's something about her that's familiar to me, but unfortunately I can't tell you what it is yet. I have this gut feeling she could be our key. Maybe when we find out who she is, all the pieces will fit into place."

Nicholas shook his head. "I don't think the database is going anywhere with these images, but who knows? I'll start running the program immediately, see if I can't adapt the parameters to work with the angle."

Mike's phone rang. It was Zachery's secretary. "He wants both of you."

Mike hung up and stood. "It'll have to wait. It's Zachery. Showtime."

They walked down the hall to the conference room, heard Zachery call out, "Drummond, Caine, get in here."

They stepped in, faced the threat matrix board that tracked all of the ongoing and recently thwarted operations their office was working on. A quick glance showed Nicholas that they stopped attacks in Atlanta, New Jersey, California, and New York in the past twenty-four hours.

Their team usually started their workday with the threat assessment, sitting around the threat table, as they called it, going through their analysis of the threat matrix, and every single morning, the actual volume of threats astounded him. But Bayway hadn't been on the matrix as a possible action. There'd been no chatter, no threats. Nothing. How many more plots were being planned that they didn't know about?

Nicholas saw COE had moved to the immediate threat column. No wonder, after last night and fifteen deaths. No, nineteen deaths. COE was small, he knew it in his gut, probably no more than ten members, all told. He also believed COE wasn't affiliated with another group, which made them more unpredictable. They were lone wolves, and lone wolves scared him more than the large organized groups like ISIS and Al Qaeda. Groups like COE were hard to track, even with all the international cooperation.

Everyone in the room was talking: agents from the

Joint Terrorism Task Force compared notes with Homeland Security agents, NSA tap-danced with the National Intelligence Agency. Nicholas didn't recognize many of the agents, but he knew they represented an alphabet soup of agencies, all wanting to be part of this team, jockeying for who would be named lead agency and run the show.

An NSA agent raised his head, saw Nicholas and whistled, then clapped his hands. "Hey, Drummond, we already applauded Wharton, now it's your turn. Well done."

All the agents at the table clapped, but not that loudly, particularly those with other agencies. Nicholas grinned.

Zachery said, "Gray and Nicholas saved the oil companies' bacon. In addition, let me add that both he and Mike were in the middle of the explosion at the Bayway Refinery last night. They saved lives."

The claps were louder this time. This was something they all understood.

"A moment, people," Zachery said, and waved Mike and Nicholas to the hall.

He took them to his office, only a few doors down the hall.

"I have a job for you. No, no briefing, it isn't necessary. We may have another line on COE." He handed them a file. "There was a fire last night in Brooklyn. A body was found inside the building once the place had cooled down enough to check. NYPD is assuming it's the body of the owner; they're running DNA and dental records to be sure. The ME called, said the dead man had been shot in the chest. Thing is, a witness has an interesting story to tell about some people she claims were staying there.

"I want you two to go to Brooklyn and talk to her, take a look around the place. See what you can turn over."

He looked at their faces. "No, Mike, Nicholas, you're not going to Bayway for evidence recovery. I've already sent Jernigan and a team out to work with the fire department and the bomb squad to determine the point of origin."

"But the tapes, sir," Mike said. "Really, it's possible to do facial recognition on a partial face of a woman who appears in all three of them."

Zachery held up his hand. "I've got a feeling about this fire and the murdered man in Brooklyn." He waved toward the conference room. "I need you more in Brooklyn than in there. Go, find out what this all means."

Mike knew Zachery hadn't become the head of the Criminal Investigative Division in the New York Field Office because he was a good politician, which he was, a bonus. No, he was sharp, had been one of the most skilled field agents in the FBI. He knew his stuff. Mike had learned to trust his instincts.

Zachery saw Nicholas was about to argue and sighed.

"Listen, this isn't a throwaway assignment. I'm not looking to get rid of you to cut down on the distraction because of what the two of you did last night. No, this is for real. I know in my gut this is something important."

Nicholas nodded. "We're on our way, sir. We'll call in with anything we find."

"Good. Now make yourselves scarce before people start asking questions. And Agent Caine, do try to keep Agent Drummond out of trouble."

Mike went back to her desk, gathered her bag, unlocked her weapon. Nicholas was next to her, doing the same thing.

"A moment, Nicholas," Mike said, and waved down Agent Ben Houston.

"Hey, Ben, I need you to run some film footage for me."

"Sure, Mike. What do you need?"

"The video feed from the Bayway cameras shows a woman in a baseball cap. In one she's looking at the camera. Can you upload her into the NGA database, see if we get a hit?"

"I'll let you know the minute I've got something."

"Thanks, Ben. We'll be on the radio if you need us."

In the elevator, Nicholas said, "What else is on the to-do list?"

"A big-time examination of the video feeds, the bomb analysis, and figuring out who killed our agents and Mr. Hodges."

"Yet Zachery wants us in Brooklyn to interview a witness."

Mike pulled her hair out of the ponytail holder, shook it out. It was giving her a headache. "If Zachery thinks there's something here, I'll bet my best biker boots there is."

Ten minutes later they crossed the Brooklyn Bridge and Mike began winding the Crown Vic through the Brooklyn neighborhoods. When her GPS sang out, she stopped at the curb in front of a Laundromat sandwiched between a Chinese takeout and a small bodega.

Nicholas asked, "And the name of this tremendously critical witness is?"

"Mrs. Vida Antonio. She owns this Laundromat. Oh, yes, before I forget, you didn't mention Adam Pearce's assignment to Zachery, did you?"

Nicholas grinned at her. "When Adam finds a line into COE, we'll take it to Zachery immediately. If he doesn't, as you say, no harm, no foul."

As they climbed out of the Crown Vic, Mike looked him up and down. "Nicholas, I think you should Brit it up for our laundress. That posh accent of yours plus your French cuffs might make Mrs. Antonio talk more."

"If she has anything to say," he said, without much hope.

"Have some faith," Mike said, and punched his arm.

28

QUEEN TO B6

George Washington University Hospital
Washington, D.C.

Vanessa felt weightless, as if she were rising, rising into whiteness, soft, like clouds, barely touching them, passing through. She felt no pain, no discomfort at all. She was dying. Or she was already dead and this was her introduction to Heaven. Her brain turned on at the slow insistent beep beside her head. What was it? Why wouldn't it stop? She suddenly felt her breath, in and out, in and out, copying the rhythm of the beep. But where was she? She felt a sudden lick of pain, then another, more like a tsunami this time, deep and hard. Her ribs were grinding with each breath.

No, this sure wasn't Heaven, and since it wasn't, then that meant Hell. No, not Hell, either. The pain meant she was alive and she was in the hospital, not sprawled on the asphalt while the building burned around her.

"Nessa, you're awake? Yes, I see your eyelids moving. It's about time. Listen, listen, you're okay, you're safe, sweetheart. Come on, Nessa, show me your beautiful eyes."

The voice was familiar, though she couldn't place it.

She forced her eyes open. The room was swimming, as though she were underwater, and wasn't that strange? She managed to turn her head toward the voice. There was a man sitting next to her bed. Bald, for the most part, where he used to be blond. Blue eyes behind thick glasses. A funny-looking mustache. Slumped shoulders. Pale skin. Brown slacks, white shirt.

"Uncle Carl," she whispered, and saying those two words nearly hurled her into so much pain she didn't want to breathe anymore. He was holding her hand. Now he rose and bent over her.

"It's going to be all right, Nessa, I'm here. You're going to be okay, you're going to be fine. You gave us quite a scare."

"How did you find me?"

"Someone called in on your phone, several times in a row. We knew something was wrong immediately, sent a team into the GPS coordinates it broadcasted for an emergency extraction. Thank God in Heaven we did. You were shot in the chest, fell off the roof of a burning building, and thankfully survived the fall. We medevaced you to D.C. when you were stable. I didn't want to leave you anywhere near the scene, for your safety. What happened? Clearly someone found the phone, but how?"

It was so hard to talk. She managed to whisper. "Long story. Matthew heard your text come in. He shot me. He shot Ian, too."

Carl's heart stopped. He'd gotten his only niece shot, nearly gotten her killed. "Here, take a little water, it might help."

She tried to suck on the straw. "It hurts. Really bad."

"I know. You have a morphine pump. Let me give you a good dose."

He did. While they waited until the world grew hazy again and the pain pulled away, he said, "The NYPD found Ian's body. Thankfully, the bullet missed your heart by a fraction." He closed his eyes for a moment. "You were so lucky, Nessa, so very lucky. Is the pain better now?"

"Yes, I know it's there, but it's sort of standing across the room. Waiting."

He smiled at her and began to stroke her hand. "You've had surgery. It was very long and I was so scared." He paused, getting himself together. "Your blood pressure, well, it's still a worry. Do you remember falling off the roof?"

She tried to remember, but it wouldn't come.

"It's all right, don't worry about it. The fall broke a few bones. Your left tibia had a clean crack, but your radius and ulna on the right arm will need surgery when you've stabilized, probably a few screws and pins. Okay, I can see the morphine is taking you back to dreamland. Let it all go now, Nessa, let it all go. You can tell me the rest of it later. Sleep, sweetheart, sleep now."

She thought she heard him say she wasn't going to die

like her father had when he'd been undercover during the height of the Troubles in Belfast.

She whispered, "My cover is gone, and that means—"

Her uncle put a finger over her lips and shook his head. "Not now, don't worry about it."

She let her eyes close again and let the morphine take her back to float in the white clouds. She was warm, she was safe, and best of all, her uncle was here and he'd protect her. She felt him squeeze her hand. As she floated away, she thought things could be worse.

But then it hit her, she had to tell him, had to—her eyes opened. "Uncle Carl, they're going to assassinate someone, someone big."

The machines beeped faster, insistently now.

He smoothed her hair off her forehead. "Calm down, Nessa. We're going to stop them. We're on their trail already. Now I want you to get some rest."

"No, no, there's going to be another attack—and an assassination, someone important—" She was gasping for breath, fighting to stay awake.

Pain, so intense, struck her chest like lightning. She felt a strange rush bubbling inside her. Her eyes rolled back in her head. Her heart monitor went haywire.

Nurses and doctors rushed into the room, shoving him out of the way.

"What's happening?" Carl Grace yelled.

"She's coding. Sir, please, you must move out of the way."

29

BISHOP TO C4

Brooklyn

Rather than going immediately into Vida Antonio's Laundromat, they stopped to study the burned-out auto repair shop. It took up most of the opposite block. The second story had collapsed into the first, and wouldn't you know it, the broken-down cars in the lot right next to the burned-out building weren't damaged. The brick was scorched black; the glassless windows gaped onto the street. The smell of soggy insulation and burned wood still filled the air. Bits of ash were still being churned up by passing cars. A yellow strip of crime scene tape was strung across the drive to keep vehicles out of the lot.

"Nothing to do here," Nicholas said. "Let's go see Mrs. Antonio."

Vida Antonio was waiting for them behind a spotless counter in her Laundromat. She was small and round and gray and sharp-eyed, somewhere in her late sixties. She had a seen-it-all air about her, and the barest hint of an Italian accent, almost smothered by all-out Brooklynese. They were barely through the door when she said, "You the FBI?"

Nicholas nodded. Mike said, "Hello, Mrs. Antonio. I'm Agent Caine, and this is Agent Drummond. I understand you saw something of interest last night?"

Mrs. Antonio immediately held a finger to her lips and gestured for them to follow her into the back, past a dozen churning washing machines and dryers, ten or so patrons sitting in chairs reading or cruising the Internet on their tablets, or staring blank-eyed at the tumbling windows in the machines. Two young guys were folding sheets and talking. No one paid them any attention.

Once inside a small office, Mrs. Antonio breathed out a sigh of relief.

"Before I tell you anything, I need to see some ID." She held out her hand.

They gave her their creds, and Mrs. Antonio examined them closely before saying, "Anyone can see me talking to you from the street. I don't need to upset anyone, you know what I mean? Certain folk could get the wrong idea. Now, don't think I'm talking about the Mob and them seeing you and coming in to cut my throat. It's the young people, they get nervous around cops and I don't want to lose business.

"I'm pleased you took me seriously. Of course I knew you had to be FBI; the two of you are as spiffy and clean as a sunrise. Except for the bruises. What did you do, get into a catfight?"

"Yes, ma'am, and I won," Mike said. "I'm glad you called the tip line. Can you tell us what you saw across the street last night?"

"Okay, okay. Let me see, a week ago, Georgie—Georgio Panatone, he owns the repair shop—he took off for Europe. Lord knows where he got the money, business hasn't been too good this year for either of us. Before he left, he told me some friends were going to stay in his place, water his plants, keep an eye on things, so not to be worried if I saw people come and go. He gave me a spare key in case there was trouble, and took off."

She sniffed. "I don't know why he didn't ask me to care for his things, we've known each other for decades. Anyway, I'm nosy, so I watched over things, in case something happened. Friends can't always be trusted. The day he left, I saw a big black van drive up and five people got out and they had all kinds of boxes, and what looked like small TV screens. They dropped black curtains over the windows in Georgie's apartment—it's above the shop—and isn't that strange? Black curtains? Like they didn't want anyone to see what they were up to. What sort of plant-watering friends do that?"

Mike said, "I agree, ma'am, it's very strange behavior. Can you tell us what the people looked like?"

Mrs. Antonio's brows shot up. "Well, of course I can

and I was going to. I didn't bring you out here to tell you about some black curtains. You some kind of dummy?"

Nicholas and Mike both grinned. Mike said, "Ah, no, ma'am. Forgive me for interrupting. Please continue."

"Okay, then. So they didn't leave for two days, until last night. I saw them clear on the steps—four men: one was an Arab; three were white. I'd say the Arab guy was well into his forties, two were in their thirties, and a younger guy, probably late twenties, like my oldest grandchild, Nelson. And there was a pretty young woman with red hair stuffed under a ball cap. They were carrying duffel bags and backpacks.

"Last night, three of the men and the young woman piled into a beat-up Corolla Georgie had sitting on his lot. They had a lot of stuff with them in duffel bags. I don't see them come back, but every half-hour or so, the curtains twitched, so I knew for certain the young guy had stayed behind." Nicholas saw that Mike was ready to shout to the heavens.

Bless Zachery's gut.

Nicholas said, "Mrs. Antonio, I think you've missed your calling. You should have been a private investigator."

She nodded. "Not a bad idea. After five boys and thirty-two grandchildren, you bet I know how to keep my eyes on things."

"Are you certain of their races, ma'am?" Mike asked. "Could you describe these people to a sketch artist for us?"

"I have eyes in my head, Agent Caine. Yes. I am absolutely sure, and yes, I'll work with your people. Now I'm getting to the meat of the story, so hang on. I heard them drive back about two in the morning and looked out my window. There were only three of them, two white men and the redheaded woman. They were careful, quickly made sure there wasn't anybody around. The Arab man was nowhere to be seen. It wasn't more than thirty minutes later when I heard the shots."

Mike could feel Nicholas vibrate. "Tell us about the gunshots. You're sure they were gunshots? Sure there were two?"

Mrs. Antonio said, her voice patient, as if she were speaking to an idiot, "Agent Caine, I haven't lived in this swanky part of town all my life. I came from a worse area, up north. Trust me, I know what a gunshot sounds like. Yes, I'm sure. I heard two shots, but I didn't know from where, so I didn't call the police, I waited to see if there'd be anything more. Two of the men came out of the building and loaded stuff in the van. Three trips they made, then they left, fast.

"Right after I smelled smoke, I went to the window and saw Georgie's building was on fire. I called nine-one-one, told them to get someone out here right away. There wasn't anyone moving around, and I was worried, you know? I mean, what happened to the other man and the redheaded woman? Of course, I thought it had to be Georgie's where the gunshots came from. And though whoever they were and whatever they'd been doing in Georgie's apartment wasn't my business, I still didn't want someone to die.

"While I waited for the fire trucks to show, I saw a

shadow moving on the roof. It moved real slow, then it was crawling along the edge of the roof. I realized it was the woman, the one with the red hair. I saw her pull herself to the fire escape and she climbed down like she was hurt, careful and jerky, and I thought—she was the one who got shot. She was almost down when she simply fell off and dropped like a rock into the parking lot. I was about to run out when this big black Suburban drove up and two men jumped out. One of them pointed and they ran over and grabbed her up. One shoved some sort of towel in her chest, then wrapped this big white pad around her. They picked her up and carried her together. I saw them put her real gently in the back of the Suburban and one of the men got in with her, and the other one drove away. I don't think she was dead, not the way they were taking care of her. That's it, that's all I saw."

She nodded once; she was now open for questions.

Mike said, "The men who helped, the two who took the redheaded woman away, it wasn't two of the same men who moved in?"

Mrs. Antonio shook her head. "Of course not, I would have told you if they'd been the same. No, I'd never seen them before. They were very businesslike, dressed all in black, with those black wool beanies on their heads, so I couldn't tell their hair color. Both of 'em were tall, like you, Agent Drummond, taller than three of the four men who'd been there before. They moved young, though, now I think about it."

She looked over at Nicholas, who'd been taking notes. "You're a lovely big boy. You got good genes."

Nicholas gave her a blazing smile. "I agree with the good-gene part, Mrs. Antonio. Now, I'll bet you took down the license plate of the Suburban."

"Of course," she said with a grin that took years off her face. She gave Nicholas the plate number, watched him send a text to Gray. "I could never figure out how someone with big hands and fingers like yours can type on those tiny letters. You're loaded with talent, aren't you?"

"Yes, ma'am," Nicholas said, sending another text, this one to Zachery.

"Who'd they drag out of the building? There was a body bag."

"We don't know yet, ma'am," Mike said, half her attention on Nicholas's flying fingers.

"I'm hoping it wasn't Georgie. He's too nice a man to die like that. Course, I'd have known if he was back home."

Mrs. Antonio must have decided they were worthy, because she brought out a teapot and three battered mugs, poured tea before they could escape. "You're not from around here," she said, handing Nicholas a mug of tea. Now that she'd made their day, she was ready to flirt.

He took a grateful slurp. "No, ma'am. That's very good. Thank you. I'm from outside of London, in the countryside, a small town you've never heard of."

Mike accepted her own cup, nudged him on the shoulder. "Go on, Nicholas. Tell her who your mom is."

"No, no, I mean—"

"Well, come on, boy, who is your mama? I'm getting older by the minute. Who knows if I even have all day?"

"My mother is Mitzie Manders. She was a comedian, starred in *A Fish Out of Water*, a TV show back in the early eighties."

Mrs. Antonio's face lit up. "*A Fish Out of Water*—oh, my, it was one of my favorite shows. Probably my husband's very favorite, since he thought she was the cutest girl he'd ever seen, a funny Grace Kelly, that's what he called her. And she's the one responsible for making you tall and strong? How to speak such spiffy English? Did she teach you how to dress, too? Would you look at those lovely French cuffs. Very sharp. Well, I am impressed. You tell her she has a fan in Brooklyn the next time you talk to her."

When they finished their tea, both Mike and Nicholas rose. He said, "We must be going, but we may be in touch again." He handed her a card. "If you remember anything else, Mrs. Antonio, please call me straightaway."

"You'll come back and tell me what happened, won't you?"

"We'll circle back, absolutely." And to himself, he made a mental note to call his mother first chance he had. They shook Mrs. Antonio's hand, thanked her for the information and tea, and stepped out of the Laundromat in time to see a man poking around the ashes across the street. He saw them looking his way, turned on his heel, and took off running.

30

KNIGHT TAKES C3

"G o, go, go," Nicholas shouted.

Mike started after the man, her Glock in her hand. She was fast, so Nicholas knew she'd have a good chance of running him down.

Nicholas angled off at the corner even though they had no comms, no way to communicate, but he'd seen an alley across from the Chinese place when they drove up, knew he could intercept the man if he kept running straight.

He pulled out his Glock as he made a hard left on Flushing and came back out on the street in time to see their runner was trapped between them, and he knew it. Without hesitation, the guy's arm came up and he started shooting at Nicholas.

"What the bloody hell!" Nicholas shouted, and ducked back against the building. He heard Mike returning fire, yelling at the man to stop. Nicholas looked out to see the man had whirled around toward Mike, who was nearly on him. He was fast, he was going to shoot her. Nicholas took the shot, aimed for his leg.

The man stumbled, grabbed his left knee, and went down. *Got you, mate.* Now at last maybe they'd get some answers, find out who this yahoo was.

To Nicholas's surprise, the wounded knee didn't stop him, the guy was up and going again, stumbling toward a brown Honda that was screeching around a corner and coming fast. The man grabbed his knee and jumped in the passenger side and the driver gunned the engine. Nicholas got a fleeting glance—dark hair, baseball cap, probably older than Mr. Wounded Knee.

"Get the car!" Nicholas shouted, running after the Honda, trying to make out the license plate. Moments later the Crown Vic roared up to him. Nicholas jumped in. "They turned right up there."

"They're going for the bridge. We have to cut them off. Call it in." She slapped the siren on the dash and floored the gas.

Nicholas braced himself with one hand and radioed in to headquarters to get them some backup.

Mike was good, weaving in and out of traffic, ignoring curses and middle fingers and stoplights, never taking her eyes from the car in front of them, navigating to a dime.

He hung on as the Crown Vic's wheels screeched around a corner. He saw Mike was excited, focused; no doubt she was having fun. Was she giddy? Oh, yeah. God in all his goodness had blessed him with this woman as his partner.

Nicholas was shouting into the radio for some air

support. Then two NYPD cruisers joined the chase, and their cavalcade didn't slow, scattering people and other vehicles. Nicholas saw one taxi driver's face when the Crown Vic spun out at the Division and Bedford intersection. He looked like death was coming at him. Mike jerked the wheel and up they went, the wrong way, on Ninth Avenue, then she sped off to the right, toward Broadway.

"Cut them off, go back, go back. Up Bedford!"

The back street here was narrow, carved with alleys. The Crown Vic rattled and shook as it sped down the uneven pavement. Nicholas was hanging on, Mike was about to take another corner, hard. He yelled at her when he saw a large lorry pulled in front of them. Mike screeched to a halt, buzzed down her window, and yelled, "Get out of the way, get out of the way!"

The cops behind them skidded to a stop as well.

The driver wasn't a slouch. He slammed the truck into gear, shot forward, and Mike gunned the Crown Vic past him.

But the Honda was nowhere to be seen.

She said a very bad word, and Nicholas yelled into the radio, "We lost them, someone needs to pick them up."

They pulled to a stop next to an HSBC bank branch on the corner of Bedford and Third Street, the cops fishtailing to crowd in next to them.

One got out of his vehicle and approached Mike like she was a bomb about to go off. Then she saw the officer's nametag and laughed, couldn't help it—P. Friendly.

Nicholas shouted, "Officer Friendly, is NYPD on the car?"

"We were calling in air support when he slipped away, Agent, sir. I'm sorry. We've got a BOLO on the Honda, we'll nail them unless they pull into a garage."

Nicholas slammed his open palm on the top of the Crown Vic, then called Gray. "We lost them. NYPD has a BOLO out. Okay, okay, let me change gears. Tell me you got something off the license plate of the Suburban Mrs. Antonio told us about."

"I did indeed. It's registered to a Meyers Enterprises, in Chelsea. Here's the address."

Nicholas punched it into his mobile. "Good. Now back to the Honda. They dirtied up the Honda's plate so I couldn't see any numbers or letters, but the background was white and it looked like there were some sort of flowers on a branch—"

Mike knocked on the top of the car to get his attention. "Virginia. Tell him the Honda plates were from Virginia."

Gray heard her. "Brown Honda Accord, Virginia plates. Doesn't narrow it down much."

"It's all we have, Gray."

"I'll see what I can do. We're pulling CCTV footage from the area as we speak. Give me two minutes, I'll find them."

Two minutes. A lifetime.

Mike said, "We're going to need a crime scene unit sent to Brooklyn. The guy Nicholas shot in the knee was looking for something in the burned debris." She gave Gray the address, which he already knew.

"So now what?" Nicholas said. "We stand around with

our thumbs in our mouths until Gray calls back, waiting for Zachery to come take our guns and put us in front of the review board again?" He watched Mike pull her hair back into a proper ponytail. She was bruised and flushed and out of breath and looked ready to spit nails. Nicholas thought she looked pretty as a picture. He couldn't wait to meet her mom, the beauty queen.

Then she straightened, her eyes sparkled, and she gave him a sly grin. "Nicholas, we're not needed in Brooklyn. There's no way the two men are going back there, not with one of them wounded. This is a legitimate pursuit, and we think they may be headed to Chelsea to meet up with the black Suburban. So let's get ourselves to the address in Chelsea Gray gave us. We can handle the fallout later."

"Your mind is an astonishing instrument, Agent Caine. I believe you're absolutely right. I'll text Louisa, tell her about the man poking around. She and the team can check everything out, better for us to continue pursuit of the suspects. Chelsea it is."

Mike turned back onto Sixth Avenue, thinking aloud. "Those two men who loaded up the redheaded woman into that Suburban. Mrs. Antonio said they were all in black? Not COE, no, they sound like professionals of some sort. We need to find her, Nicholas. I wish Gray would call and tell us they've identified her from the video at Bayway."

Nicholas eyed her, alert to her tone, not her words. "There's more, isn't there? Something about her, Mike?"

She nodded. "I can't get over the feeling that she's familiar, that I've seen her somewhere before. Remember in the feed when she looked up at the camera? And we both wondered why she'd do that? Seems to me she wanted us to see her. We've got to find her, Nicholas, we've got to."

31

BISHOP TO C5

Eisenhower Executive Office Building
Washington, D.C.

Callan mentally replayed the conversation with Ari while her driver, Redmond, expertly threaded her limo through the heavy traffic to the White House.

"You're certain I'm the target?"

"Yes, maybe others, we don't know yet."

"And who's behind the hit?"

"We don't know that yet, either, not for sure, but probably the Iranians, Hezbollah."

"And just when were you planning on letting me know?"

Was there the slightest hesitation before he said, and she remembered his exact words, "We've only confirmed in the last hour. We've been working hard to find out where he is, and we've had eyes on you. My people, Callan. Trust me, you've never been safer."

"You should have told me immediately even though it wasn't yet confirmed."

"Contrary to popular belief, Callan, I don't owe you anything."

He'd hung up. She hadn't bothered to call him back.

She knew all about Zahir Damari, and now that world-class killing machine was after her.

Callan knew she was strong. To those who didn't like her, she was a ball-breaker, a bitch. To those who did, she was a trailblazer, a former CIA agent turned congress-woman who refused to kowtow to the good-old-boy net-work in D.C. and managed to keep her dignity and reputation intact—well, most of the time. She remembered, somewhat fondly, that ancient Southern congressman who'd slapped her hand once after a hearing and called her a bad girl. Now he was one of her biggest supporters.

A bad-girl scolding was welcome after what she'd been up against—dictators, military reconnaissance missions, and that bloody stint in the Islamabad Field Office, not to mention a decade in the U.S. Congress, probably the scariest of all. She thought she could handle anything. But Zahir Damari? After her? She didn't stand a chance and she knew it. It scared her to the bone.

He'd been on the scene for more than twenty years now, a world-renowned assassin, a freelance terrorist, a walking, talking, breathing lethal weapon. She remem-bered her time as a freshman congresswoman; she'd been assigned to the Foreign Affairs Committee. Of course she knew all about Zahir Damari, seen some of his handiwork, but this was different. She'd never forget the briefing done by a group of Mossad agents on the hunt for Damari because he'd murdered five of their brethren during a special op in Afghanistan. One of the junior agents in the delegations was a handsome, hawkeyed man named Ari Mizrahi.

Callan found herself watching the agent instead of paying attention to the briefing. He had a scar on the side of his neck, long and white, and she wondered how he'd gotten it. Shrapnel? A knife? A bullet? She knew all Israeli men and women served in the military, a mandatory three years when they turned eighteen. Knew he'd seen combat since Israel rarely saw peace.

Later, he'd told her about a sloe-eyed woman who'd gotten close to him in a coffee shop one afternoon when he was with his wife and daughter. A sloe-eyed woman wearing a suicide vest. And how it had changed him, their needless deaths.

Later, she'd traced the line down his neck with her tongue, trying, and failing, to heal them both.

The car turned onto Pennsylvania Avenue and Callan dragged herself to the present. *Damari.* What was she going to do about that madman now that her name was at the top of his kill list? Was Ari right? Had Iran and Hezbollah contracted him?

She had to assume this was tied to her resistance against the peace talks.

They drove through the security gate, parked in the

portico between the White House's West Wing and the EEOB entrance. She hesitated a second before stepping out of the car. Every minute from now until Damari was captured could be her last on this earth, and didn't that focus the brain? She took a deep breath, savored the sweet air slipping into her lungs. She had no intention of letting him kill her.

Her heels clicked against the old marble floors as she walked the winding staircase up to her office. She found herself looking at every Secret Service agent on her detail, wondering if they were working with the enemy, and that was the worst, the loss of trust.

She worked her morning, smiled and shook hands for the meet and greets, got through the dairyland photo op, and finally sat down for her security briefing on the Bay-way Refinery explosion and this maniac group COE.

All the faces in the conference room were as familiar to her as her own: the director of National Intelligence, Maureen McGuiness, sweet syrupy drawl, utterly ruthless, and held grudges; the CIA's director of intelligence, Templeton Trafford, sneaky, more devious than a snake, that was Temp; and the FBI's deputy director, Jimmy Maitland, stalwart and solid, said what he thought and shut up, lived and breathed FBI when all was said and done.

They all sat silently on the facing chairs and couch, waiting for her signal to begin. They looked serious and jumpy, all except Temp, once a CIA operative, many times on assignment with her in the field, always ready for a good brawl and a clean kill, like she'd been, she supposed, and now he ran the Intelligence Division. Temp always held information close to the vest. He was now sitting with his arm lazed over the back of his chair, his left leg crossed over the right, foot swinging.

Callan raised her hands like a conductor. "Well? Who is behind COE, and what are they really after? And this cyber-attack—are the Russians, the Chinese bankrolling them? At least we know it isn't North Korea. Jimmy, give us the rundown."

Maitland sat forward. "Until yesterday, this COE group only worked the fringes, attacking out-of-the-way oil refineries and power grids, threatening any company that worked with Middle Eastern oil. The sheer size of the bombing of Bayway, the fifteen deaths, and the subsequent cyber-attack on the oil companies, driving the oil prices into the tank, trying to get their production offline, this is bigger, they've stepped up their game on a massive scale, and, unfortunately, we don't yet know what it is."

McGuiness of National Intelligence turned to Maitland and said, her sweet drawl leaking impatience, "Jimmy, why haven't you identified the ringleader of this group yet? I thought your people had a line on them. We need answers, we need to find out who's behind this."

Maitland said easily, "We're trying to get that information right now, Maureen."

Callan said, "Good. Now, do we know the full extent of the damage yet? How long the refinery will be offline? And the hack—did they steal anything from the oil companies or was the attack merely destructive?"

Maitland said, "We'll know more once the final reports are back from the oil companies. And the damage to the Bayway Refinery was, as you all know, severe. It will be weeks before they're functioning at full capacity again."

McGuiness was shaking her head, clearly disappointed in her FBI, ready, as always, to go for the jugular. She turned to Callan and threw Maitland under the bus. "Madam Vice President, truth be told, as Mr. Maitland has unfortunately made abundantly clear, *we* have *no* idea what's happening. I fear the FBI isn't moving quickly enough to get the matter resolved."

Well, duh, Templeton Trafford thought, eyeing the group. He didn't like Maureen McGuiness, never had, thought she was a candy-coated pit bull, found her myopic, thought she never saw the big picture. Plus, he didn't like all the oversight forced down his throat by National Intelligence. A pity she had so much juice. However, he did like Callan Sloane, liked her a lot, actually, since she'd saved his ass more than once out in the field during her years in the CIA. However, he wasn't about to tell any of them what he knew. He was enjoying watching McGuiness hang herself.

Callan looked from McGuiness to Maitland. What was this blame game all about? They were all on the same team, except for Maureen McGuiness, who, Callan was convinced, wanted to become emperor of the world. She laid her palms flat on the table and spoke, her voice not at all nice. "Maureen, how is that possible? You and your team are supposed to be our highest intelligence organization. Are you saying *your* people missed this threat? Are you saying there was no chatter, no warning signs COE were about to step up their game? No clue something like this cyber-attack was going to happen? If you are still clueless, tell me now." *So I can start paving the way for your replacement.*

"No, ma'am, there was no chatter, nothing." *You power-hungry bitch.* "We have been trying to get a line into these people, particularly since the FBI in New York has dropped the ball."

Maitland took the shot, said in his mild, stolid voice, "Madam Vice President, we've assigned Agents Drummond and Caine to the case, and believe me, they've been at it nonstop. I know it's frustrating, but I assure you they'll find these people and put a stop to it."

There was a small, discreet snort from McGuiness, which everyone ignored. Callan saw that Temp was smiling behind his hand. He knew something, but what?

She said to them all, "Do we at least have confirmation COE is responsible for the bombing last night? Have they claimed responsibility?"

McGuiness beat everyone to the punch. "Yes, their signature claim showed up at CNN twenty minutes ago. So clever, aren't they? *'No more oil from terrorist countries or you will pay the price.'* We haven't been able to trace it." McGuiness added, "Yet."

Callan slapped a hand down on the table. "Come on, people. Work with me. Tell me we have something I can go out with today and give a great snappy sound bite that will calm the populace. Or at least something Costello can give *The Washington Post* on background. These people are making us—and that means you—look like incompetent morons."

Everyone at the table was pissed at her words, afraid they were true, and that they were all circling the drain.

Callan looked at all their insulted faces. "Allow me to rephrase. I want names. I want these people in custody, and I want it to happen immediately.

"You are all trusted advisers of the president. You know what's at stake. If the president were here, he'd be livid, since he'd know, as all of us do, that COE is disrupting his Middle East peace talks, focusing the public's attention on how vulnerable we are being dependent on Middle East oil, particularly since most of the oil-producing countries hate our guts and would like to see us destroyed. And if the talks get derailed, I won't want to be in any of our collective shoes. Find out who is behind this group, and do it today. Do I make myself clear?"

Nods.

"Good. Jimmy, you said Drummond and Caine are running the investigation now in New York?"

Maitland nodded. "Yes, and Milo Zachery is up to his ears in this investigation with them, and you know Milo, he's a bulldog, never gives up, plus he has an excellent brain."

McGuiness raised an eyebrow. "This Drummond is the one who stopped the micro-nuke attack a few months ago? He used to work for Scotland Yard, recently joined the FBI?"

"The very same."

"Pretty new, isn't he, for this critical an assignment?"

Maitland said, "He's not only sharp, he's fast and a genius with computers. His partner, Agent Caine, worked with him on another major case as well, recovering the Koh-i-Noor diamond when it was stolen from the Met."

McGuiness gave him a nod and a sneer. "And what about your golden boy, Dillon Savich? The wunderkind? Why isn't *he* a part of this?"

32

ROOK ON F TO E8
CHECK

Maitland didn't tell McGuiness to go shoot herself, though he did have to take a second to clear that lovely thought from his brain. He said calmly, "Agent Savich is very aware of the situation."

Callan said, "Bring him in, Jimmy, have him oversee the entire op. Hook him up directly with Agents Drummond and Caine, have him coordinate all of it.

"I'm not kidding, people, get me some movement on this. The president will be back in the States to give a great, triumphant announcement to the American people— assuming he gets all those disparate entities to sign an agreement—during his speech on Thursday afternoon at the Yorktown Oil Refinery. I want to be able to celebrate his success with news of the capture of this group."

Maitland said, "Ma'am, about the speech. The FBI believe it would be wise to postpone, or change venues. The Bayway bombing—"

Callan stood, walked to the window, then turned to face them, arms crossed. "He'll never go for it. What sort of message does it send? The president of the United States can be forced to alter his agenda by a group of terrorists?" She turned around. "Yes, I said terrorists, and that's exactly what they are, whatever their agenda, however we may sympathize with them, whatever they said about their enemies. The bottom line is after Bayway and the wanton murder of fifteen people, they are no better than the Islamic terrorists we battle every day across the planet, day in and day out. No, it won't happen. He will demand to make his big announcement Thursday, and we'll do it at Yorktown, and that's because you and your people will have solved this case. Do I make myself clear?"

There were nods, but they all knew what she was really thinking. It was no secret that Vice President Sloane was dead set against the president's peace talks in Geneva because she saw them as pure and simple capitulation to Iran. They also knew that each of them, regardless of whether or not they agreed with the president's agenda, took their oaths seriously. They would do all they could.

Callan looked at Trafford. "Temp, you've been very quiet. Do you have anything to add?"

Trafford had a low Virginia drawl that always made her think of a college boy's fraternity and too much beer at tailgates on Saturday afternoons. "No, ma'am. The CIA will do everything we can to support the FBI's and National Intelligence's efforts. All our ears are to the ground, listening, probing for information."

McGuiness rolled her eyes. Callan was hard-pressed

not to grin. Truth be told, she liked getting them into the same room together to watch the cockfight, all the one-upmanship. Who knew? Maybe the competition made them sharper. She looked around the table at each of them in turn. "There's one last thing. I've had word Zahir Damari is in the United States on a contract."

This froze everyone in their seats.

"Any word on who Damari is after?" McGuiness asked.

"According to my source, the contract was taken out on me and there could be others, as yet unidentified."

Callan wondered if she could hear a pin drop, it was so suddenly still. Then everyone talked over everyone else.

Callan held up her hand for silence, looked at Trafford and said, her voice very quiet, "Temp, would you like to explain to me exactly why you didn't know this, since you have all your CIA ears to the ground, listening and probing? And yet you've not heard a single word about Damari here to assassinate me?"

He was as shocked as the rest of them, she realized, staring at him. If he hadn't heard anything, was the threat real? Was it possible Ari was wrong?

"No," he said slowly, "your source can't be right. Our latest reports have Damari in Jordan. He supposedly has a villa there—at least there's a money trail tied to the villa, though no one's ever seen him there. We'd kill to get eyes on the man, but it hasn't happened yet."

Callan said, "Since he had his extensive cosmetic surgery, you haven't gotten a look at his new face, have you?"

Maitland sat forward, his hands clasped between his knees. "Madame Vice President, the only confirmed surgery we know is cheekbone implants, though I hardly think he stopped there. Without a new front facial baseline, we can only reconstruct so far. It's impossible to keep Damari on a watch list if no one knows what he looks like."

"Regardless," McGuiness said, "if your people have had such little luck tracking him down, Mr. Trafford, perhaps it's time to hand over the duties to National Intelligence. We'll get a bead on him, and do it fast."

Temp didn't say a word. Did he realize his people had fallen down on the job? It scared her that he hadn't known about Damari for the simple reason that it could well mean there were other critical things he'd missed. She didn't like it, and he didn't, either, she was sure of that.

Maitland said, "If your source is solid, Madam Vice President, I can only assume it's to do with the president's talks. Right, Temp?"

Temp finally said, his voice hard, "I can't explain why we hadn't already picked up on this threat, but you know I will find out. Now, no more playing around. We all know you're toeing the party line here for Bradley, that personally you're against his approach, his seeming appeasement of the Iranians, but the thing is, you're hardly the only one who disagrees with Bradley on this; there are plenty of people who don't want to see peace in the Middle East that leaves Israel hanging out to dry.

"So why you? Who took out the contract, and why target you, specifically?"

33

KING TO F1

Callan said, "It's very possible the Iranians are acting with Hezbollah. But as yet no positive verification. I've given this a lot of thought. If they're indeed behind hiring Damari to kill me, it's because they want to disrupt and cause chaos, and damn the consequences. It also sounds like ISIS, and our never-to-be-forgotten Al Qaeda, all of them willing and eager to kill all of us, reduce us to dust. One does not assassinate someone in my position and hope to survive, unless one does not have a country or care about it at all."

McGuiness said, "You're right. To assassinate you would cause immense disruption not only here at home, but all over the world, because we would react."

Maitland was shaking his head. "Therein lies the difficulty, Maureen, positively identifying the person or country behind the contract; the president would not retaliate unless he had absolute proof."

Actually, Callan wasn't sure what the president would do even with reasonable proof Iran was behind the hit and they denied it to his face.

Maitland continued: "Iran does sound like the most likely, their mullahs, their military, they are so fanatical, many of them don't care what happens to their own country, their own people, so long as we—the West—are destroyed in the process."

She nodded, told them about her conversation with Ari from the Mossad. "To remind you, there's possibly someone else in Damari's sights, and that means we need an alert to the other governments involved in the talks, just in case."

Temp said, "I'm more inclined to think it's somebody right here in the U.S., someone high up."

"Yes, I agree."

"Regardless of motive, regardless of whether it's Iran behind this contract or their Hezbollah enforcers, we will not let Damari kill you, Callan, we will not let it happen."

McGuiness said, "We will step up your security, immediately. Ma'am, I suggest you move into your West Wing office instead of the EEOB, and we can arrange for more agents to—"

Callan shook her head. "Maureen, all of you, I appreciate your concern, but you all know as well as I do that moving, or changing my schedule, wouldn't stop Damari. He's a master assassin, and with his skills and contacts, he could find out whatever he wanted to know." She shook her head at the irony of it. "If he wants me, he'll kill me.

"We must also try to find out who else he's after. Ari

was concerned. So I put my trust in all of you, that your people hunt him down before he pulls the trigger. Now you've got him on your radar."

She looked at each face. Would all the battles, all the turf wars, the endless pettiness—would they take a back burner with her life on the line?

Who knew? Perhaps they would. None of them said a word.

"That is all," she said. "Of course, you'll want to keep this to yourselves or those you involve, specifically to prevent Damari from succeeding. And, people, don't let COE bomb anything else, or it will be all our heads." She pressed the small button on her phone. Quinn Costello came quietly into the room. She stood aside as all of them filed out, and Callan heard them arguing about who should take the lead on finding Damari.

Quinn watched Callan sink into her chair, put her head down on the desk. "Hmm, how did it go?"

Callan banged her forehead three times against the ancient wood.

"That good? Well, this might cheer you up. Hmm, at least it will cheer up the president."

Callan raised her head, looked up at her chief of staff's big smile.

"Ari called. He talked the government into returning to the table in Geneva."

Callan said, "Will wonders never cease? Looks like he's trying to save my job."

"And he sent this." She handed over a slim blue file

folder. "Now, who is Zahir Damari? And why don't we like him?"

Callan sighed. "Quinn, come here and sit down. I have something to tell you."

In the hallway, Temp watched McGuiness and Maitland walk ahead, McGuiness still trying to tell Maitland what he should do, Maitland looking straight ahead, probably so he wouldn't slug her. Then, as if Maitland sensed him watching, he turned around. McGuiness waved them both off and kept walking.

Maitland said, "Anything I can do for you, Mr. Trafford?"

"I was about to ask you the same thing. Anything *I* can do?"

"Other than handing over everything you have on Damari? We need to do a full assessment on the Bayway bombing. Who's your best bomb guy? Or girl?"

Because Trafford was experienced at never showing anything, he gave Maitland a warm smile and said, "We've got some of each variety. I have a few stateside. Or do you want a whole team?"

"I want whoever you have available immediately. And I want my guys to meet with yours."

"Sure. Of course. We've got lots of possibles in our database, lots of bomb info from COE's overseas work. Anything the CIA can do to help."

Now, why don't I believe you, you little prick? But

Maitland nodded. "I'll also inform my team about Damari's confirmed contract on the vice president. Both of our groups should dig, see if we can find out exactly who's behind it." He gave Trafford a final nod, a handshake. "I'll be in touch."

Oh, yes, I'm sure you will. Trafford walked out of the EEOB to his waiting car. McGuiness had said more or less the same thing. *Yeah, like that would happen even if there was a snowstorm in Hell.*

Neither of them had any clue that Damari would get to the finish line first. He was already on the final lap.

34

BISHOP TO E6

Chelsea

Mike's cell rang. Since she was driving, Nicholas put it on speaker. "Go ahead, Louisa. You find anything?"

Louisa sounded tired. "There's nothing here helpful to us. Obviously someone was thorough when they set the fire. The second floor collapsed into the first, taking all the evidence with it. Everything's soggy. It'll take a week to go through it all. I did call the ME—Janovich got the body from the building. Said he was pretty crispy, but he could tell us the guy had been shot in the chest. Nothing else as yet. I'll tell you, Mike, they did some job on this building."

"Maybe we need to add firebugs into the profile."

"That's a good idea, Mike. Arsonists have as distinct a signature as serial killers."

Nicholas said, "Louisa, please send the chemical makeup of the accelerant into our Uniform Crime Reporting database. Though arson is wildly underreported in the UCR, perhaps we'll find a hit."

"I can do that. I'll also take a look in ViCAP, see if there are any arson fires near where our confirmed explosions have happened. Hey, I'm willing to try anything that will help us track down these murderers."

Nicholas said, "Louisa, another thought. Why not a second search with the parameters extended to violent crime in the week leading up to each explosion—homicides, especially. Who knows what sort of patterns may emerge."

"Okay, can do. I'll tell you guys, talk about finding a soggy needle hiding in a wet haystack, we're going to have to get out the metal detectors to find any bullet casings in this mess. But I'll do a rush analysis on the accelerant. Since we already know it's petrol, and we're at an auto shop, chances are it was taken from this location, but one never knows. I can probably have something for you within the hour."

"The moment you do, Louisa." He hung up, turned to Mike. "Now, as soon as we find the owner of the Suburban, hopefully we'll find the redheaded woman."

"Vida Antonio's sketches of the group staying at the body shop should come in soon," Mike said, as she swerved around a taxi. "But you know, Nicholas, there's something off here. I mean, a Middle Eastern recruit to COE?"

"It does fly in the face of everything COE stands for. Who could this man be?"

Mike hated it, but she gave in and stopped for a red light. She looked over at him, opened her mouth to say something, and what she saw made her blood freeze. She cleared her throat.

"Nicholas, you know how very elegant you looked when you came to work this morning?"

"Why are you speaking in the past tense?"

"Your beautiful suit coat has a bullet hole in it. Nigel is going to shoot you, if I don't shoot you first for getting yourself hurt. Again."

He cocked his head at her. She slapped the car into park and grabbed his arm, running her hands from his shoulder to elbow. "You lamebrain, look at this."

In the upper sleeve of his jacket, there was a small tear in the fine wool. He cursed, lots of animal body parts that made Mike laugh. The light turned green, but Mike ignored it. "You really don't feel anything?"

He shook his head. "I'm fine. Mike, we have lots of pissed-off drivers behind us. Best hit the gas." He looked back at the dozen cars, drivers waving their fists, horns honking.

Mike gunned the Crown Vic. Looked to see him shrugging out of his coat.

"Well, that's a relief."

"What?"

"No blood on my shirt. No rips. Nothing." He grinned. "Nigel will let me live another day. Maybe."

He watched her execute a daring move around two taxis, leaving them screaming in her wake. No need for her to speed, but he realized she was pissed.

Nicholas laid his hand on her thigh, felt the sleek play of muscles beneath his fingers, and quickly lifted his hand. "Really, I'm fine. I had no idea our wounded-knee guy even got close to me. You were the one I was worried about."

Mike looked straight ahead, missed a parked car by an inch. Then she looked at the impossibly handsome face next to her, saw worry—for her, not himself—and threw back her head and laughed. "Yet again, you saved my neck. Thank you, Nicholas. Sorry about your beautiful coat. You want a character witness for Nigel?"

He met her eyes, took his pinkie and put it through the hole, wiggled his finger. "Once Nigel gets a load of this I could have a dozen character witnesses, but I fear it wouldn't help. As Nigel pointed out last night, however, Barneys will rejoice."

Nicholas's mobile rang, and he pulled it from his pocket, put it on speaker. "Gray, what's happening?"

"The guy you shot in the knee? The NYPD found the brown Honda. It was abandoned at the base of the Williamsburg Bridge. Either they got into another car or they're on foot. Either way, we lost them. I've sent a team to process the car. Perhaps we'll have some luck lifting fingerprints. Or blood, that'd be good."

"I will only confirm that I shot the guy in the knee if you promise not to rat me out to Zachery. This isn't a good time for a hearing and losing my weapon."

"Yeah, yeah, I promise. You're a dweeb. As far as I know, you don't even know how to fire a weapon."

"Thanks, Gray. Ah, the knee shot? That was only because he was aiming at Mike."

"I was going to say nice shooting, Tex, but since he got away, forget it."

Mike said, "Tex? He's supposed to be James Bond, Gray, not the Lone Ranger."

Gray laughed, told some agents around him what Mike had said, and there was more laughter.

"All right, you hyena," Nicholas said, "when you calm down, let me tell you I'm calling Savich to have him plug in MAX."

Gray gave one last hiccup. "Good idea. Can't hurt."

35

BISHOP TAKES B6

Baltimore, Maryland

Zahir Damari loved nothing more than raising his face into a strong stream of hot water in a shower. Since he was staying at a nice hotel, it was piping hot and he knew it wouldn't run out, like it sometimes did in Jordan, even in his exquisite villa. He washed himself slowly, luxuriating in the loofah gliding over his skin. Everything was back on track.

Once dressed, he applied several layers of makeup and prosthetics using the photo on his current fake passport as a guide. He was always careful, always precise. After a few finishing touches to his hair, he studied the results in the mirror, nodded at his reflection. He looked good; he was ready. If the man he was meeting described him, it wouldn't matter, since he would be describing another man entirely. Zahir smiled at himself in the mirror. Actually, if the idiot did describe him to anyone at all, even his lovely wife, he wouldn't live an hour longer.

Before Zahir left for Silver Corner, he called Matthew, to make sure his part of the plan was locked in, and Matthew was ready to pull the trigger. He smiled again as he punched in Matthew's number—Matthew didn't realize it, but he was Zahir's minion, as gullible as only an ideologue could be. There were so many exactly like him on both sides, driven by hate, no real thought to the future or what could be made of the future.

He pictured the beautiful blast at Bayway, the flames that licked into the sky, and the feel of the ground shaking beneath his feet. The power of such a tiny part of that gold coin was amazing.

Matthew didn't pick up until the fourth ring, and that worried Zahir. He realized immediately something was wrong. Matthew sounded exhausted and depressed, very unlike himself.

"It is Darius. Tell me what is happening?"

"Was it you who set me up? You who betrayed me, set them against me?"

Now, this was interesting, at least for a moment. "Come, Matthew, what are you talking about?"

And it all came spilling out, his killing of both Ian and Vanessa because of their betrayal, and how he'd burned the building down around them. "But maybe it was you, Darius, who betrayed me. Was Vanessa right?"

"What do you think?" *You idiot*.

"All right, all right, so it was the only thing I could

do. I killed them, both of them. Ian tried to protect her, can you believe that?"

"Maybe he was in love with her, too."

"No, no."

Zahir listened to him ramble about a small phone hidden in a bar of soap, heard the growing hysteria in his voice. This wouldn't do. He very much needed Matthew, in case something got cocked up. It shouldn't, but you never knew, and that was the thrill of his business, the uncertainty, the wild card, like Vanessa. Sounded to him like she was an undercover agent. He didn't think she'd ever gotten a photo of him to send to her handler. He was always too careful.

"Did you learn anything from Vanessa before you killed her?"

"She kept saying it wasn't her, it was Ian, it was you. The phone messages were all deleted. Even Andy couldn't find anything."

"Very well. She is dead, no longer a threat to us. However, now we have to move quickly—whoever Vanessa was working with, or for, knows all about us." *Except me, of course.* He heard Matthew's deep, hoarse breathing. "Get hold of yourself. You did what you had to do. Now you must do your job, you must keep moving forward. All will be well."

"But does it really matter anymore, Darius? Blowing up Bayway, I realize you believed this would help our cause, but now, like you said, because of Vanessa, the Feds know who I am and will be hunting me. And all those deaths, I swore never to be like them, like those terrorists who killed my family."

What a twisted-up fool Matthew was. Who cared about the deaths at Bayway? Hadn't he just murdered both Ian and Vanessa? Zahir would never understand this genius, who seemed now like a whining, hysterical child.

Patience, patience. Pull him back in.

"Matthew, where are you? What are you doing? We need to speak more about this."

Then suddenly Matthew turned on a dime, something that always amazed Zahir. The steel was back. "I'll do my job, Darius. You do yours," and Matthew hung up.

Zahir stared at his cell phone, not wanting to believe that Matthew had actually hung up on him.

He realized he wasn't surprised that Vanessa had been some sort of undercover agent. But it was Ian—he'd protected her? Was he an agent as well? No, impossible. Ian was a true believer and loved Matthew like a brother. Yet he'd tried to protect her. Well, in the end, who cared? It didn't matter, they were both dead, it was over. Except Matthew was right, the FBI would be after him, guns blazing.

His only worry was that Matthew's brain would twist him up again and he wouldn't follow through on the assignment he and Darius had worked out. That, or he'd be caught first.

Either way, Zahir had fail-safes. He always had fail-safes.

As soon as he had the blueprints, he'd be ready to move out. In fact, he was rather looking forward to finally having his moment in the sun. His wits, his abilities, pitted against theirs. He would be tested, and he relished it.

When room service knocked with his breakfast, he shouted for them to leave the tray. When he knew he was alone again, he shrugged into a hotel robe and sat down to enjoy the big continental breakfast. He knew he needed the carbs for sustained energy, since after this he'd be surviving off granola, jerky, and water. He'd be off, into the woods, on his own to take care of the business himself.

36

BISHOP TAKES C4 CHECK

Silver Corner Diner
Baltimore Inner Harbor

When Zahir parked his rental at the Inner Harbor, he paused a moment to look at the water, covered in a light mist, vapor rising as the morning heated. He breathed in deeply, regretted it. The air smelled of algae and waste.

He walked the half-block to Silver Corner, a mom-and-pop diner he'd eaten at once three years before. It now sported a cheerful new blue-and-white-striped awning.

Unfortunately, the inside still needed a serious face-lift. He stepped inside and inhaled bacon grease and mildew.

He eased onto a brown cracked vinyl seat in one of the six booths. He ordered black coffee—that surely couldn't poison him—from a middle-aged waitress with a towering beehive of brassy red hair. Over her left oversized breast her nametag read, fittingly, Red. That made him smile.

"Getcha anything else, hon?"

What planet was she from?

"No, the coffee will be fine." He turned to look out the window and saw his contact on the street outside, wearing, of all things, a tan trench coat and a slouchy hat pulled down over his forehead. *Well, hello, Mr. Subtle. You're pretending to be the spy who came in from the cold?*

His young handler in Atlantic City had evidently convinced him that Zahir always followed through, so he had come. Mr. Subtle was looking around furtively, as if he was afraid someone would jump out and slap handcuffs on him.

Kill you, maybe, but no handcuffs. Mr. Subtle slithered into the diner, saw Zahir nod at him, and slinked over, slid into the booth. He looked scared and wary. "I'm here."

"Of course you are."

Mr. Subtle slid down in the booth, as if it would hide him and his paunchy belly. Zahir flicked a hand toward the waitress, mouthed *Coffee.*

Woody Reading looked at the man opposite him, the beaked nose, dark hair and eyebrows, not a handsome man, mid-thirties, the man his handler, Aziri, had said would not kill him easily and fast if he didn't bring him the blueprints, he would gut him like a fish, then he would destroy his reputation and his family. He knew Aziri believed it to his soul, and so did Woody.

Zahir was amused and pleased that the man was

looking as if Zahir would strike like a snake if he said the wrong thing. *Good.* A frightened man tended to do what he was told.

The coffee was delivered. The waitress didn't linger. She wasn't stupid; she could smell the fear roiling off the man in his silly trench coat—and the other man, the dark one who looked sexy until she'd looked into his eyes and felt her flesh crawl. *Dead eyes. Dead eyes.*

"Aziri told me to bring you the blueprints or you would kill me."

Zahir only smiled, nodded. "At the very least. So you have them under your trench coat?"

Mr. Subtle leaned forward to whisper, "Yes, but please, won't you reconsider? I know what you're planning, but believe me when I tell you that the FBI is closing in. I don't want to be caught."

"After what you've already done, you're only now considering you could be caught?"

"Look, I gave the Bishop the plans for the plane, even backup plans for Bayway. But now it's getting too hot. People aren't stupid. My company will be targeted soon, then they'll fix on me. Won't you reconsider? I could still return the blueprints, no one the wiser. Do you really need them?"

Ah, Matthew and his ridiculous moniker—the Bishop, bestowed by Ian several years before like a crown on his head. Zahir laughed low, and Woody jerked back, nearly upending his coffee. "That is none of your concern. You are well paid. You need know nothing more. Give me the blueprints."

Unspoken, but quite clear, was: *Give me the blueprints right now or I'll slit your throat and walk away before the first drop of blood splashes in your coffee cup.*

"Listen," Woody said, desperate now, "surely you realize everyone's on edge after Bayway. I thought the explosion was only supposed to disable the refinery. I didn't know you were going to kill a dozen workers. Since the Bishop has always told me he didn't believe in collateral damage, it was you, wasn't it, who pushed the button, not the Bishop?" He stopped himself, looked over his shoulder. No one had heard, but it didn't lessen his fear. He leaned across the table. "My superiors are asking questions. There was a security briefing this morning, about COE. I don't know how much longer I can stay off their radar."

Zahir took a sip of his coffee. "You never had to accept the first payment made to you, did you? You never had to buy that rather flamboyant house on the cliffs in Saint Bart's. You never had to give your mistress diamonds. And you've continued to steal and lie and savor the money given to you.

"So, Mr. Reading, this is not a negotiation, nor do I owe you any explanations. Give me the blueprints. Now. Or we're finished, and you won't ever see me again until late one night when you are sound asleep with your arm around your mistress and the knife slips between your ribs."

Zahir began to stand, and in his hand was a small stiletto. He felt the tube nudge his leg under the table. He pulled it up and clipped it inside his jacket.

"Smart decision." Zahir threw a ten-dollar bill on the table, smiled, noting the sweat on Mr. Subtle's face as he slid an envelope across to him. "The amount agreed upon. Do you know, Mr. Reading, I've never been a patient man, and you surely tried my patience this morning. Never go against me again or you won't enjoy what happens. Nor will your whore or your wife or your three children. Your cushy job will go up in smoke and everything you hold dear will burn around you."

He rose. "We do thank you for your cooperation."

Zahir left Silver Corner to the sound of an envelope being ripped open. As he walked away, he tapped the tube to his leg, pleased.

37

KING TO G1

Interstate 95

Matthew couldn't shake the vision of her, on her side, legs drawn up. He saw the blood flowing into her hair, the strands turning black.

She was dead. Ian was dead and he'd chosen Vanessa over him. His friends, his only friends, so close to him, like family. Yet Vanessa was a lie. Who had she been working for? Some government agency, the CIA maybe, since she'd first hooked up with him in Ireland. And that meant they knew who he was, who all of them were, yet they hadn't come after COE.

Why hadn't she simply walked him into a police station at gunpoint? Obvious answer—whoever she worked for had heard talk about his gold-coin bombs, and they wanted his technology so much they were willing to let him continue his bombings. No doubt they'd tasked Vanessa to get the coins, having her infiltrate COE as a bomber. But he'd never let her near the coins, always kept them hidden, after that first time in Belfast he'd shown them to her, to impress her. Well, before he'd had to kill her, she knew how powerful his bombs were, realized in that moment before death that she'd failed.

He wondered what would have happened if he had shared the coins with her. Well, he hadn't been that stupid.

She was nothing more than a traitorous bitch. She wouldn't get them now, and neither would her bosses.

Andy started to moan again.

It was too much. "Shut up, Andy! The bullet only grazed your leg, went right through, didn't bust it up. I put an antibiotic on it and taped it. I even gave you the last of the pain meds. So stop your infernal whining. I've got to think through how we're going to deal with Yorktown."

Still Andy moaned, like he were dying. "We shouldn't have gone back to the apartment, Matthew. It was a huge mistake."

"Yeah, like it's my fault you forgot the bag of memory sticks with the counter-codes. And all we got for our efforts was your leg shot through by that agent's bullet."

"I didn't think we should go back, I told you that. I mean, who cares if we can't stop anything now? You're planning on following through on that deal you made with Darius, right?"

"It was insurance," Matthew said, as he pulled in behind a big eighteen-wheeler. "The counter-codes were my bargaining chips with the Feds if everything suddenly went into the crapper. I told you that. Stop whining."

Andy moaned again, kept ragging on him, blaming him, not letting up.

Matthew said very politely, never taking his eyes off the road, "If you don't shut up, Andy, I'm going to shoot you, kill you dead. You deserve it for being so stupid."

Shocked silence, but it didn't last. "You rattled me, man. I mean, you killed Ian and Vanessa and then you ordered us out of there." He added, in a sulky little boy's voice, "You used my own gasoline mixture but you didn't even let me torch the place."

Matthew remembered thinking if he'd given Andy the gasoline can he'd lose it and burn down the neighborhood. It had been a stupid decision on his part to go back. In all that wet rubble, how had he ever expected Andy to find the memory sticks? Still, there was a possibility. It was rotten luck that had those FBI agents come waltzing out of that old lady's Laundromat. No one could have foreseen that. Bad luck, mistakes. He knew he couldn't afford any more.

It hit him again like a fist to the gut. Ian was dead, by his hand. He blocked out Andy's moans, and saw in his mind that first time he'd met Ian, his oldest friend, his only friend, really, after his family had been murdered by those terrorists in 2005. He saw himself again in that little bar near the Ponte Vecchio. He'd felt lost and alone, so filled with rage and impotence he'd wanted to kill himself. And then this beefy Irishman had swaggered in and started a monologue about the football on the bar TV he was looking at, but not watching, he was too miserable. He remembered it was Manchester versus Italy.

"You rooting for our Manchester boys, not those Italian pussies, right?" Matthew didn't give a crap, but he checked the score, saw Manchester was losing, said, "I am, sadly."

"Well, glory hallelujah, a man with a brain, and the good Lord behold, he's a bleeding American to boot."

The Irishman was a man somewhere in his thirties with sandy brown hair sticking out in all directions, a sunburned nose ready to peel, and wearing a Manchester United jersey.

COE—Celebrants of Earth, the name had been Ian's brainstorm, he'd believed it sounded highfalutin and righteous, and all of it had started by sharing a pint in an Italian pub with a blue-eyed fanatic Irishman who'd shared Matthew's hate of radical Islam, whipped him up since his own hatred ran deep as well.

Seven years and a lifetime later, it had ended in a stinking apartment in Brooklyn. It still seemed like a mad dream—Ian dead, burned up, Matthew the one who'd killed him. And Vanessa, lying dead not two feet from him.

No, he would have no guilt, no regrets; he'd done what he had to do. They betrayed him, they deserved death. So why didn't he feel cleansed, whole again, since he'd meted out the proper justice, done the only thing he could? He felt nothing. All he knew was he was alone again, except for bleeding, whining, crazy Andy next to him, and Darius, and only God knew where Darius was. All Matthew knew was what Darius had told him—he was getting the final pieces together for his part in their big score.

Of course Darius wasn't his real name. Matthew had no idea who he really was, but like Ian, he'd looked at the vast amounts of cash Darius had brought to him and listened for hours to him speak fluently in his upper-class British accent about how the world had to change, and how Matthew would be the one to do it. He'd given Matthew renewed focus, given him greater purpose, showed him a wider vision of the world, and he'd demonstrated with Bayway what it would take for Matthew to truly make himself the world's savior, how he could truly avenge his murdered family and rid the world of the vermin that threatened to take it over.

He thought about his family, dead, too, a decade now, not enough of them to bury after the bombs blew them apart.

Ian and Vanessa, their bodies burned beyond recognition. What he was doing, buying into Darius's plans—was it worth it? He thought of the codes Darius had helped them buy from that German hacker, the codes that were in his control, the codes he couldn't now undo because of the memory sticks lying sodden in the ruins of the burned apartment.

Screw insurance. It was his final big act. He was ready.

"Yes," he said aloud, "I'm ready, more than ready. No going back now."

Andy turned at his voice. "Going back? Why would we do that?"

Matthew laughed.

38

KNIGHT TO E2
CHECK

Washington, D.C.

Carl Grace climbed into his car in the hospital parking lot, pressed his forehead to the steering wheel, and cried. Nessa could die, and for what? It would mean he'd let down his brother and not kept her safe. Who would have ever believed Vanessa would want to follow in her father's footsteps so literally, getting herself shot while undercover? And now she might die, just as her father had died.

Nothing was worth her life, nothing. Certainly not those stupid gold-coin bombs Matthew Spenser has created. He should have pulled the plug, pulled her out, but he hadn't. His boss, Temp, had been adamant that Vanessa stay active in COE until she could get her hands on the bombs. Now she could die and all he knew was

Spenser had disappeared and there was an assassination coming. *Who?*

And it was his text that had broken her cover. He'd never forgive himself if she died because he'd decided to screw Temp and he was trying to warn her to leave.

He swiped at the tears, straightened, and looked blindly around him at the staff pouring out of the hospital. Shift change. No, Nessa couldn't die, she couldn't. He simply couldn't imagine what he would do if he lost her. She'd been going above and beyond the call of duty for two years now, working undercover in Europe, then the UK with the IRA, now infiltrating that mad group, Celebrants of Earth—COE. He hadn't slept decently for weeks, constantly worried about her, and the stress was beginning to take its toll.

He didn't want to leave her, but he had had no choice. He had to stop Matthew Spenser, put an end to COE.

His phone rang as he pulled out of the parking lot. "Yes?"

A female voice said, "The DI wants to see you now."

"Good, I want to see him, too. I've got vital information he needs. Tell him I'll be there in fifteen, Gladys. I'm off-campus."

"Hurry. When he got back from a meeting at Tango Two's place, he was on the warpath. I've never seen Temp like this. It's something big, Carl, really big."

"So is my news."

He knew about Trafford's meeting with the other muckety-mucks and the vice president, not surprised Callan Sloane was now loaded for bear, given the explosion at Bayway.

Ten minutes later he parked in the orange lot on the CIA campus and hurried toward the new headquarters building, not even glancing at Kryptos—Jim Sanborn's encrypted, elusive cypher-sculpture. When he passed the wall of stars, all he could think about was seeing Nessa's name on that wall, a single star to show her worth to the Agency. Like her father's star.

When he stood in front of Gladys, with her double strand of pearls and gray silk blouse and ladylike pumps, he smiled. All the analysts liked her; she was always in their corner. She said immediately, "Is Vanessa all right?"

It hurt to say the words. "It's still uncertain" was all he could manage.

"All of us are praying for her. Now go in, Carl." As he walked past, she handed him a folder. "I don't know what it's all about, but like I told you, it's big. Good luck."

Director of Intelligence Templeton "Temp" Trafford stood in the window overlooking the CIA campus. A light rain had begun to fall, and the window was misting. Trafford was always impeccably dressed, but this morning, meeting with the VP, he was more formal than usual. Carl recognized the silk tie and polished presidential-seal cuff links Trafford kept in his lower drawer, next to the Grey Goose vodka.

Trafford turned. "Is Vanessa okay?"

Stiff back, stiff voice. "She's back in surgery. Her doctors—they don't know, or won't say."

"How did Spenser find out she was a spy?"

"A text from me. Spenser heard the phone ding. He

lost it, shot her. Look, Temp, she managed to tell me about an assassination attempt before she coded, but not the target, or targets, not the where. Do you know anything about this?"

Trafford said, "Yes, partly. We've received word of a major assassination threat, so maybe it's the same one, I'm not certain."

"Who?"

"The vice president, Callan Sloane. Possibly others as well, still unidentified."

Carl couldn't believe it.

Trafford drew in a deep breath. "I imagine her buddy in the Mossad tipped her off. It gets worse. The assassin is Zahir Damari."

Carl whistled. "Damari. Who put out the contract?"

Trafford said, "Mossad believes it's Iran, so that means it's probably Hezbollah, since they've been threatened by her from the beginning—a vice president of the United States dead set against them and all they preach, and a woman to boot?

"As for Hezbollah, they're particularly dangerous, since they have no desire for a peaceful world, only chaos and destruction and anarchy in the West, well, and the world, if they could pull it off, and the takeover of Shia.

"Callan has always preached no nukes in Iran, so obviously they would want deniability. Her ties to Israel aside, all the terrorist states also are well aware of her disagreement with the president on the peace talks. To have her eliminated, they'd cheer."

Carl said, "But if it's proved they paid to have her assassinated, don't they understand the president would be forced to retaliate? Big-time?"

"But retaliate against whom, exactly? Don't forget, Carl, Hezbollah gives them plausible deniability. So the president hits Lebanon, so what? Tehran gets off scot-free and without their biggest roadblock.

"In addition, we're nearly certain now that the man calling himself Darius is Zahir Damari. The photos Vanessa took of him match body type, height, and skin tone, plus the timing's right. Did he change his face when he went to Matthew Spenser? We don't know, so that makes the facial parameters sketchy. And as you know, Damari is a quick-change artist."

Carl said, "Well, if Darius is indeed Damari and he managed to get himself embedded in COE, the FBI can nail him with this recent photo. Their guys Savich and Drummond have been working on a supplement to the NGA database."

Temp said, "Before Bayway, Spenser never killed anyone. Why the sudden change? I think Damari changed it, somehow spurred Spenser to more violent, more dramatic action, using one of his own coin bombs, or perhaps only a small portion of it, if all the hype as to its power is true. There's more. Unverified from the Mossad is that it's not only Callan who's targeted by Damari, maybe even someone more important."

"The only person more important than Callan Sloane is the president." Carl was frankly disbelieving. "No state would dare assassinate a president of the United States. The fallout would be catastrophic."

Temp said, "You know as well as I do, Carl, that many terrorist organizations, like ISIS and Al Qaeda and Hezbollah, would like to bomb the world back to the Stone Age and reduce civilization to rubble. Their only goal is to be the last ones standing. Question: can Spenser's bomb accomplish this for them?"

Carl paused. Given Bayway, and positing that only a very small portion of one of Spenser's small bombs was used, then yes.

"Temp, this is very scary."

"At least now we have a visual on Damari, Carl, and with that we can stop him, hopefully before he can steal one of Spenser's bombs and get it to Iran and Hezbollah." A pause, then, "You think we can catch him, Carl? In time?"

"With all our agencies focused on Damari, I'm hopeful."

Temp looked decidedly happier. "Yes, of course you're right. We stop Damari, we get our hands on Spenser's gold-coin bombs, and you know what? No one will care that we had a CIA operative undercover on U.S. soil."

Carl knew his boss very well indeed. A master of justification and strategy. He said, "Yes, we must accomplish both those things. And you're right, if we do, all our sins will be forgiven. And we might save the world while we're at it."

Temp didn't laugh, he was too deep in plots, reeling out scenarios in his mind. "But here's the thing, Carl, the vice president wants names in this organization by tonight, or heads will roll. And that means confessing we know all the players because we had Vanessa embedded with them.

"I like this job, and that means if I have a chance of keeping it, when Vanessa is out of surgery we've got to find out everything she knows. You know there's more, there's always more. When she is able, you need to find out what these fanatics are planning to do next. Knowing who they are doesn't help us anymore. We've got to find out about their next hit, and Vanessa has to know about that. If only we knew where they were, we could pull them in right now, Damari with them."

Carl said, "When Matthew Spenser and Zahir Damari find out Vanessa's still alive, you know they're going to want to kill her."

"Of course, of course. I'll send agents over now to cover her. Carl, you know once this all shakes out I'll have to testify in front of Congress and they will want names. It could come out that she designed the COE bombs, all for a good reason, of course, getting the technology behind those gold-coin bombs, and that might make them back off a bit, but I hate to take the chance. On the plus, she did confirm COE is planning an assassination, and hopefully she will give us much more, so we could still come out whole-hide.

"Now you've got to get back to Vanessa, give me more to work with. Surely she knows where they're headed, their next target, and how Damari is going to kill the vice president. And ears to the ground—is he indeed targeting someone else?"

Carl splayed his hands on the desktop, leaned in close. "Listen, Temp, Vanessa might die, that's how badly wounded she is." He felt tears burn his eyes. "Don't you understand? I don't give a rat's ass if Sloane finds out we've been operating on American soil if Vanessa dies."

"I understand, Carl." Then Trafford paused for a moment, and Carl realized he was seeing a brilliant mind come up with a solution. He waited.

Temp said slowly, "I think I know how to save our asses and keep those idiots in Congress from censoring us. You will quietly give all the needful information to Maitland at the FBI. If they manage to find these people and bring them down, we'll stand back, out of the limelight, and let him and his team take the credit. Nicholas Drummond and Mike Caine are the leads on COE, both smart and focused. Maitland has put Dillon Savich on the case—they've worked with him in the past. Yes, they'll fit right in. And if they manage to stop Damari, then no one need ever know the CIA was involved here."

"I see a big hole," Carl said. "If Vanessa survives surgery, the FBI will insist on speaking to her. There's no way, if you're forced in front of Congress, that I'll allow Vanessa to be thrown to the wolves, Temp."

"No, no, of course not. Carl, I can massage that. This is our play: we'll dump it off on the FBI, let them run with it. They can have all the glory and keep us out of it. Vanessa isn't dirty. She was trying her best to keep us all safe. They'll understand and we'll cover for her. I promise, it will all work out." And he beamed at Carl and added, "I want you to meet with Drummond and Caine personally and give them anything they want to help them find Matthew Spenser and Zahir Damari. Many lives are at stake, Carl, not the least of which is Callan's. You must find out what Vanessa knows about COE's plans, when and where, before the FBI grills her. Then we can move toward neutralizing this assassination threat against Callan, because the last thing we want is her dead. You're on board, right?"

"Of course."

When Carl Grace left him, Trafford sat down at his desk, laced his fingers behind his head. He'd been tired, but now, if everything went right, if Maitland's wunderkinds proved themselves as great as their rep, then he would keep his job and the CIA wouldn't get a black eye.

Carl's cell phone rang as he left Trafford's office. It was the hospital. His heart hammered in his ears; his mouth went dry. "Any news?"

The nurse said, "Mr. Grace, your niece started bleeding internally again and that bottomed out her blood pressure. The doctors are still working on her. I'm afraid it's rather dire, sir."

39

KING TO F1

George Washington University Hospital

Vanessa wasn't floating this time. She knew immediately she was in the hospital, knew she was in bed, tethered to more needles than she wanted to think about, all of them helping her stay alive. Yes, she was still alive.

She couldn't open her eyes, nor could she really think, so she let herself drift. Back, back to Londonderry, Ireland. Was it four months ago that it all started? She remembered being undercover in Northern Ireland, working her way ever closer and closer until finally Ian McGuire had talked in a lowered voice about the Bishop, patting her hand, telling her how he was the one she needed to join up with, given her amazing talent at building bombs.

The Bishop this, the Bishop that; Ian had a serious love

affair going on with the man who was her target. He and Ian had been together seven years, Ian told her finally, they'd met up in a bar in Italy, of all places, found they were like-minded, and they'd traveled all over Europe, a bit of destruction here, a bit of havoc there, and the Bishop had finally surpassed Ian, he freely admitted it, sounding for the world like a proud papa.

No one had heard of the Bishop before a year ago, when he burst onto the scene with a bombing at an oil depot in France, no deaths, and that was a surprise, but the CIA was on it immediately. He had no face, no name, except the Bishop, and she'd been sent to Ireland because he was a known associate of Ian McGuire's. And then came the chatter about his advanced nanochip gold-coin bombs, undetectable to the normal scans and powerful in their destructive capabilities. The CIA wanted the coins, wanted them badly, and they wanted the recipe, if possible.

And she'd had a chance to get close to him.

Ian had permission to invite her to a meeting, eyes shining with excitement. Again, the proud papa. "The Bishop's comin', Van, at last you'll get to meet him. I'll tell you, I've been singing your praises to him for long enough. He's your kind of bloke, so smart it's scary, and he knows how to hate. And who to hate, for that matter. And I know he needs a good bomb maker, and you're the best. Throw you a brick of Semtex and you could blow up the moon, that's what I told him."

Vanessa wondered why he needed a bomb maker if he'd created the ultimate tiny undetectable bomb, but since she wasn't supposed to know about the coins, she couldn't ask Ian. She supposed the Bishop hadn't perfected them yet.

Vanessa felt a spike of pain deep inside her chest. She heard the beeping, but the pain began to ease, then it drifted away, and her brain could wander back again.

Ian and the Bishop shared the same single, overarching desire—getting rid of the followers of radical Islam swarming all over Europe and the UK, before their terrorists killed everyone in their quest to destroy the Western devils, and the Bishop determined the best way to do this was to destroy oil refineries to make their owners stop buying Middle East oil.

She saw Ian chucking her under the chin, felt the affection he had for her. "The Bishop believes it's time to mete out justice at home. His home, your home. So what do you think? You want to see the Bishop? Perhaps throw in your lot with him, head to America? That's where what we do will really count. I'm in, Van, how about you?"

Vanessa felt wetness on her cheek. She realized it was tears. Tears for Ian, shot down simply because he'd tried to protect her.

She also realized she couldn't die.

40

KNIGHT TAKES D4 CHECK

Criminal Apprehension Unit
Hoover Building

Maitland found Savich and Sherlock together in Savich's office. Like every other agent in the FBI, they were talking about the Bayway explosion and COE.

"No, don't get up, you two," he said, and closed the door, knowing that everyone in the CAU was staring, wondering if there'd been a break, what was happening.

Maitland pulled up a chair. "I just came back from a meeting with McGuiness of National Intelligence; Templeton Trafford, CIA; and the vice president." And he told them what had happened.

When he finished, he sat back, shaking his head. "We all know everyone wants to protect his own turf, but I tell you, where McGuiness would spew it all out if she thought it would make her look good, and take full credit for knowing it, Temp Trafford has more secrets than the Sphinx. I'll bet under that titanium vest of his lies answers to most of our questions, and he ain't about to share, no matter what he says, no matter how critical the situation.

"The only thing I'm positive about is that Trafford didn't know about Damari, and the threat of assassination of Callan Sloane and possibly others, but COE—you bet. And how, I wonder?"

Sherlock said, "The CIA always has a reason. But finding out what it is?"

Maitland said, "Trafford isn't about to let anyone stick their nose under his tent."

Sherlock said, "All of us understand the tremendous pressure the CIA is under to protect the U.S. from any foreign threat, but Trafford—why doesn't he realize it's time for him to cough up everything he knows? I mean, lives are on the line here, and everyone knows Bayway signaled that COE is stepping up their game, that another probably larger refinery has already been targeted."

"You'd think." Maitland sighed. "Why I'm really here, Savich, is to assign you to work with Drummond and Caine, coordinate on this end, since all the push is coming from the vice president and she's laid this in our laps. Starting now. I'll barbecue you the best corn on the cob if you bring COE in and stop Damari. Oh, yes, I've cleared this with Milo in New York. He's on board." He rose. "Mossad believes it's Iran and Hezbollah behind the contract on the vice president. We need to stop them."

When Maitland disappeared from Savich's office,

Sherlock grinned at him, punched his arm. "For you, Big Dog, it's obviously only a small assignment. Why, you can whip out the answers in a matter of minutes."

As for Savich, he felt pleased at the huge vote of confidence and worried he couldn't pull it together and the vice president could be shot. *No, not going to happen.* Who had hired Damari wasn't his concern, Damari was. So first things first.

Sherlock rose. "You know what I'd like to do? Wrap my hands around Trafford's throat and shake him until he gives up everything he knows. And you and Nicholas and Mike are supposed to uncover everything in one day?"

"Looks like it." Savich laughed, picked up his cell to call Nicholas to give him the good news that he was now coordinating his investigation, whatever that really meant, in addition to his boss, Zachery.

Savich's cell blasted out Blondie's "Call Me." Speak of the devil. "Nicholas, I was about to call you. There's a lot—"

Nicholas overrode him. "Listen, this is crucial, Savich. We think we've found the last knowns of COE. We have a witness who claims there was a group of four people staying in an apartment in Brooklyn. Last night, the place burned down. Here's the kicker—one of the men staying at the apartment looked Middle Eastern. Which leads to the question—if this guy really is Middle Eastern, then what the bloody hell is he doing hooked up with a bunch of fanatical terrorist haters who want the West to stop importing oil from terrorist countries, which includes just about all of them?

"Our witness said when the original group returned late last night—we're assuming from the Bayway bombing—the Middle Eastern man wasn't with them. Like I said, we need to find out who he is. We've got a sketch artist working with the witness, and—"

"Nicholas, stop a moment. Send me the sketch when it's finished and I'll see if I can't find out who this guy is. Now, are you and Mike familiar with Zahir Damari?"

"Yes, of course," Mike said in the background. "Über-assassin, arguably the most deadly in the world. He's a really bad dude, on everyone's most-wanted list. Why, what's up, Dillon?"

"We found out a couple of hours ago that he's here in the United States. The Mossad believes he's going to try to assassinate the vice president. Maybe others, still un-verified. Probably Iran and Hezbollah behind it. Yes, yes, I know, the peace talks."

Stunned silence, then Mike's voice in the background: "And I thought our problems topped the list. You're not putting us on, are you, Dillon?"

"Wish I were. Let me tell you all of it." After Savich had briefed them, he said, "Sherlock says not to worry, that I'll be a great coordinator, and look at the bright side, it's only a day or two before we get this wrapped up. Now tell me about the fire in Brooklyn, your witness, and whatever else I need to know."

Once they'd told him about the shooting, the fire, and the black Suburban that carried away an unconscious woman lying beside the burning building, Savich said,

"It's all coming together; we simply need more and we need it fast. I fear there's another terrorist attack coming and we have to stop it. Find that Suburban and find that woman. We've got to know who pulled her out of the fire."

"She's the key, I know it," Mike said.

"Could be. Keep me posted. Nicholas, give me the description your witness gave you of the Middle Eastern man, then send me the sketch the moment you get it."

41

KING TO G1

The black Suburban was registered to an address in the middle of the block of 30th Street. It was a brown brick high-rise, recently redone. The long, narrow lobby was clearly visible through the big front windows. They saw a doorman inside, another man behind a counter. Tenant mailboxes filled the wall opposite the doors.

Mike pulled the Crown Vic up in a no-parking zone, put her FBI card in the window.

"Gray said fifteenth floor," Nicholas said. "At the very end of the east hallway, 1507."

They breezed by the doorman and the young guy behind the counter, their creds held high. "FBI, we'll talk to you later," Mike said. The elevator was fast, with no tenants getting on to slow them down. Mike knocked on the bright red door of 1507, waited, knocked again.

Then, "Coming!"

They knew they were being studied through the peephole, so Mike held up her creds.

"FBI. We'd like to talk to you."

They heard chains falling, a dead bolt twisting, and then the door was pulled open by a pretty young woman sitting squarely in her mid-twenties. She had long, straight black hair and wore stylish black glasses, a short plaid skirt, and Doc Martens on her small feet. A perfect advertisement for Ms. New York Hip.

"Goodness, FBI?" She splayed her hands in front of her. "Listen, I haven't done anything, I mean, I couldn't have even if I wanted to since I've been here all morning. Oh, I'm sorry, come in, come in."

She waved them toward the living room, but Mike shook her head. "Agents Caine and Drummond, FBI. And you are?"

"Melody Finder."

"Ms. Finder, do you own a black Suburban?"

Ms. Hip laughed. "Not a chance. I'm a lifelong New Yorker. I have a driver's license only for ID."

Nicholas showed her the screen of his phone. "Ms. Finder, we show a black 2009 Chevy Suburban registered to this address. In the name Melody Finder and that's you."

"Well, yes, you already know I'm Melody Finder, but I think I'd know if I had a car." A gray tabby poked its head from beneath a green-and-white-striped sofa, then ambled over to ribbon between Melody's feet. "Tigger, not now, you're going to make me fall on my face. Oh, dear, get back, no, you can't run out!" She grabbed the cat. "Sorry about that, I really need to close the door or my critters will make a break for it. Please, come in and tell me why you think I own this car. There's got to be a mistake."

The space was a small loft with floor-to-ceiling windows and lots of natural light. Not much furniture, only the sofa and three chairs, all in shades of green and white, a couple end tables loaded with magazines. A big silver tabby lay on its back in the middle of the sofa, smack in the center of a shaft of sunlight.

"That's Pooh."

At the sound of his name, the cat cracked an eye, gave them a stare, then promptly fell back to sleep.

"I don't think Pooh is all that ready to run free," Mike said.

"He had a huge lunch he's sleeping off. Please, sit down, both of you."

Mike and Nicholas sat on the sofa, on each side of the cat. Mike leaned forward. "Ms. Finder, we really don't have much time. We—" Pooh opened her eyes, eyed Mike, and stretched out a paw to touch her on the knee. Mike automatically rubbed his ears. In the next moment the cat was curled on Mike's lap. If the situation weren't so dire, Nicholas knew he'd be hard-pressed not to laugh, particularly since Ms. Finder was staring at Mike in amazement.

"Pooh hates strangers."

"I suppose even a cat has to respect the FBI," Nicholas said. "Now, Ms. Finder, do you know anyone in the building who might have a Suburban? It seems the records were listed improperly."

"Not that I'm aware of, but it's a big building, a huge garage. Like I said, I don't own one. I'm a writer—a blogger, I mean—and most of what I do is either food- or wine-related."

"Excuse me," Nicholas said, and stepped away to call Gray.

Mike scratched Pooh's ears and asked, "What's the blog?"

Ms. New York Hip sat forward, so excited she couldn't sit still. "TheWineVixen.com. I search towns for the best wine buys, then pair the bottle with a recipe. I've been running it since 2009, since I turned twenty-one. I have lots of celebrity guest chefs and stuff."

Nicholas held up his hand. "Ms. Finder, not only is the Suburban registered to this address, it's also registered in your name. I believe you need to rethink ownership and tell us the truth." His voice had lowered, and sure enough, Ms. Finder looked alarmed.

"No, no, it's not mine. Really, it's got to be a mistake. I mean, who would do that?"

"Let's back up," Mike said. "Perhaps you have a friend, someone who needed a landing spot for their vehicle? You have a garage space, don't you?"

"Yes, all the tenants do, it comes with the apartment."

"Maybe someone is using your spot and you don't want to report it to the building managers?"

"That's not a bad idea, Agent Drummond. I could rake in the bucks letting other tenants park their second cars there." She grinned at them.

Mike didn't grin back. Like Nicholas, it was time for her to intimidate. "Ms. Finder, the Suburban we're looking for was identified at a crime scene in Brooklyn last night. Please tell us where you were yesterday from five o'clock on."

Ms. New York Hip drew back, more than simply alarmed now. Mike could see the fear.

"I don't understand. You think I had something to do with a crime that happened in Brooklyn? I don't even know what you're talking about. You're asking me to give you an alibi? Look, I haven't been in Brooklyn in two weeks, not since I had drinks at Cow and Clover and reviewed them for the blog. The entry went up yesterday. I was here, working on it." She jumped up and ran to the chair by the window, grabbed her open MacBook Air. Both cats stared at her but didn't move.

"See? I posted the piece at six-thirty last night, perfect timing for people getting ready to go out for the evening and looking for the coolest places to eat. Then I ate dinner, drafted five more blogs, and went to bed. I watched two episodes of *The Walking Dead* before I fell asleep. Had bad dreams, too. My Netflix queue would be able to verify the times, wouldn't it?"

She started tapping on the computer, pulling up the website.

"I would assume it's geocoded to both my account and my television. You can contact them, see where the account was being accessed and when."

Nicholas took the computer from her. Nothing like the young computer geeks to speak the right lingo. He looked at the screen. *The Walking Dead* was indeed listed under "recently watched." She was telling the truth.

Mike picked up one of the pictures sitting on the table by the sofa, held it up. "Ms. Finder, is this your boyfriend?"

"Yes, yes, that's Craig. He's in Paris right now. He's training at Le Cordon Bleu. When he graduates, we're going to open a restaurant. And before you ask, no, he doesn't have a Suburban. Really, I don't know what this could be about. It's got to be a mistake."

In the 5x7, Melody Finder and Craig were wearing hiking shorts and boots, standing in front of a mess of trees Mike didn't recognize, wide grins on their faces.

"We ziplined in Costa Rica. We did it maybe half a dozen times."

Mike lifted the cat off her lap, rose, and set him back down. He gave her the stink eye, then fell back asleep. "Thank you for your help, Ms. Finder. We'll be in touch."

"But why? I mean, you see now it's all a mistake, right?" Melody was practically running after them to the front door, her Doc Martens hitting the floor hard.

Nicholas said, "We'll let you know if we need anything else."

"Well, okay, I guess. Hey, stop by my blog sometimes. You look like you'd enjoy a good Chianti. I have a lot of recommendations there." And she gave them both a big smile, showing lots of white teeth.

When the door closed behind them, Mike said, "Property management company, now. Since it appears Ms. Finder doesn't know anything, that means someone probably registered the car in her name. Let's see if they're using the garage, too."

42

KNIGHT TO E2 CHECK

The on-property agent for the property management company was short, heavy, and annoyed, but willing to let them scout the garage for anything helpful. He rose from his comfortable leather desk chair to show them the way down.

"I don't know if any of the tenants have a black Suburban. Then again, I don't spend a lot of time in the garage. If someone buys a new car, they're supposed to tell us what it is, but half the time they don't. Melody's space would be coded to her apartment, 1507, but she doesn't use the garage, so I rented it to 1202 instead. He has a Prius and a Jaguar. Can you imagine, having two cars in this city? But he's some Wall Street jockey who likes to go to the Hamptons on the weekends."

This monologue took them to the elevator and down into the garage, where he handed off two Maglites.

"Have a time," he said. "I'll be back upstairs, checking with the management company to see if they have anyone with a Suburban." He left them, the elevator doors closing with a whisper in the dark.

The lights were on motion detectors to save energy. A step forward and the whole quadrant lit up but left large swatches of dark. There were more than a hundred spaces on three underground levels to explore.

The slot for 1507 was on the top floor. It was empty.

Nicholas said, "Too much to hope for. Let's split up. You take this floor, I'll go down to the bottom. We'll meet in the middle." He checked his mobile—three bars. "I have service, so call me if you find something."

Mike nodded. "Last time I was in a Manhattan garage with you—my very own apartment's garage, I might add—we ended up in a shootout." She touched the bullet hole in his jacket. "Let's not do that today." She stepped into the darkness, the flashlight beam skittering in front of her.

Nicholas took the elevator down two levels, stepped out, and started the search, looking systematically left to right. He was glad of the flashlight. The motion-detectors were slow because the lights were CFL to save energy; they needed to warm up to give maximum light, and that took a while. If it was busy, there'd be plenty of light, but in the midday with only two of then, all the shadows, the sounds of their footsteps, the dankness of the air, it was downright creepy.

It didn't make sense, someone squatting his car registration on Melody Finder. Whoever did it must have known she didn't have a car, so didn't use her space, probably rented another tenant's. Or she was right and it was all a mistake.

Ten minutes later, they'd searched the whole garage. Nothing. Nicholas saw the cameras as he walked back toward the elevator. They were tucked away, all but impossible to see. He pointed them out.

Mike shook her head. "That putz property manager could have mentioned they have video feed. Let's go grab it for the past forty-eight hours, see if there's anything worth seeing."

The property manager was on the phone with the management company when they got back to his apartment. Nicholas asked to speak to them. With a few brief sentences, they happily agreed to let the FBI look at their feed, housed off-site. They promised to send the tapes to 26 Federal Plaza immediately.

For the moment, they were at a dead end.

Mike said, "This is getting frustrating. We keep having these great breaks that don't pan out."

"The bright side," Nicholas said, "Mrs. Antonio might wrap this up for us, give us the faces of everyone in COE."

She nodded, dialed Ted "Bud" Anders, in her opinion their best sketch artist. Between him and his laptop, if there was a chance to come through with a good likeness of the four individuals, he'd find it. They'd asked him to do the Middle Eastern man first.

Nicholas heard Bud's enthusiasm. "Mrs. Antonio has great visual memory, so it won't take too long, Mike. I'll send the Middle Eastern guy's sketch to your cell as soon as I have something."

When she punched off, Mike said, "No way to nail Bud on how long it'll take, so I guess we now have to focus on the Honda with Mr. Wounded Knee and his buddy, whoever that was. You know they were probably two of the four people staying in that apartment."

"And Mr. Wounded Knee was looking for something. But what?"

She threw up her hands. "Nicholas, we need more agents and another twenty hours in the day. And I'm hungry. Let's head back to the office, pick up some pastrami on rye on the way."

"I heard your stomach talking, but I was too polite to say anything. Pastrami on rye? I could go for that, maybe a double."

They jaywalked, got into the Crown Vic. Nicholas had just turned over the engine and started to pull from the curb when Mike suddenly grabbed his arm.

"Nicholas. I don't believe it. Look, a black Suburban, coming up the street."

He braked, the car half out into traffic. "Are they going into the garage? Bloody hell, they are. It's about time a little luck flowed our way. Can you see who's driving?"

"No, but I can get the plate. It's New York." She read off the rest of the numbers.

"Yep, it's our car." Nicholas reversed the Crown Vic back into the spot while Mike kept her eye on the Suburban, idling in the garage drive, waiting for the door to go up.

She said, "The driver is young, white, wearing sunglasses and a Boston Red Sox cap. I think I see blond hair, and it's long. I can't see his face. We need to get in there, Nicholas, before he parks and goes upstairs to wherever he lives. I'm calling for backup."

Nicholas was already halfway out of his seat. "I'm going to follow him down the ramp. I'll text you what floor he goes to." He took off at a run, weaving in and out of traffic, ignoring curses and loud horns. She saw him bend double to slip under the garage door before it closed again.

Mike called Zachery as she jogged in and out between cars to get across the street. "Sir, we need backup at West Thirtieth and Sixth, in the Meadow Arms apartment building garage. We've identified a black Suburban involved in the possible abduction of the woman from the burned repair shop in Brooklyn last night."

She heard Zachery shout in the background, "Get agents to West Thirtieth and Sixth, and alert NYPD, they'll be closer." He came back on with her. "I love it when a talking gut pans out. People are on their way. Get the Suburban, Mike, and be careful. Where's Drummond?"

"Nicholas is already in the garage following the guy to see where he parks. I'm going in now."

Her text dinged.

B3

Zachery laughed. "Why am I not surprised? Keep in touch. And, Michaela? No more shootings."

Crap, so he knew about Brooklyn and Mr. Wounded Knee. Mike punched off and started running.

Their black Suburban was all the way down on the third level. The elevator was her best bet. She waved her creds by the young guy at the front desk again and kept running.

He stepped from behind the desk this time, alarm on his face. "Hey, is everything okay?"

She whirled around. "Can you shut down the garage door, so no one can get in or out?"

"I can, but I don't think the management company would be happy—"

"Do it. Do it now. We have more agents on the way. Tell them there are agents on level B-three, looking to talk to a suspect in a black Suburban."

The elevator took only three seconds to rumble to the basement garage. She prayed it wouldn't alert the Suburban driver.

43

KING TO F1

Nicholas leaned against the gray concrete wall. The ramp down into the basement was circular; he'd jogged behind the Suburban, careful to stay out of sight.

The driver hadn't seen him, another bit of good luck. The big SUV went to the very back row, the farthest from the elevator. It gave Nicholas time to get down to the third floor and take up a defensive position. Mike had been only half joking when she'd made the earlier crack about the other garage shootout. That had been a close one.

Nicholas didn't want a repeat performance. This time it was the Suburban guy who would be taken by surprise, not them.

He pulled his Glock out of the clip at his waist, heard the elevator ding a soft single note—good, no way would their Suburban guy hear it.

And out came Mike, bent at the knees, looking, looking, hand on the snap of her holster. He laid a finger to his lips when she saw him, and gestured for her to come to him. He pulled her behind a blue MINI Cooper. Not much in the way of protection, but at least it was parked next to a wall space, completely away from the line of sight to the Suburban. He hoped whoever was in the Suburban didn't have bat ears and hear the elevator ding.

He whispered against her temple, "He parked back there. No sign of anyone yet. And no talking, so he's probably alone."

Mike whispered back, "Backup's on the way. Since this is the only way out, he'll have to pass us to get onto the elevator or walk back up. If the doorman did what I told him to, the garage door is now closed. Your call, Nicholas, wait here or storm the trenches."

"Let's wait, let him come to us." But no one came. After twenty very slow seconds there was still no movement.

Mike whispered, "What could he be doing? Fixing his hair? A bit of makeup? Nicholas, I can't stand it any longer. Let's go see what he's up to."

Music to his ears. Nicholas grinned like a bandit. "Let's do it. Careful, Mike." They started down the row of cars, one at a time. Still, they heard nothing from the end of the row. What was he doing?

When they were two cars away, they heard a door open. Mike, in front, stopped, raised a fist. Nicholas closed in behind her.

They heard whistling, then the back lid of the Suburban opened with a clunk.

Nicholas held up three fingers. *Three. Two. One.*

They came in hard and fast, one on each side. Nicholas shouted, his voice echoing hard and low off the walls, "Stop, right there. FBI. Hands where I can see them."

The man's hands shot up. "Hey, hey, relax."

Mike was looking in the back of the truck.

"Holy crap! Nicholas, he has an arsenal in here—weapons, grenades, radios. All right, buddy, what are you planning, some sort of siege?"

"Listen, let me explain—"

Nicholas said, "Turn around, slowly, right now, and put your hands on the car. Now!"

The guy did have long hair, looked bleached, like an L.A. surfer. He was still wearing a baseball cap and sunglasses. Nicholas couldn't see his eyes, couldn't see what he was thinking. He said, "What are you, some kind of surfer-dude terrorist?"

"Hey, it's her majesty's secret service, talking right to me. No, mate, I'm no terrorist. Trust me, this is all a big misunderstanding. If you'd give me a chance to put down my hands and explain—"

"Hands, *mate*. On the truck. Do it. Now."

Surfer Dude didn't move.

Nicholas aimed his Glock right at his face. "Are you deaf? I told you to put your hands on the roof."

Mike kept her distance, blocking Surfer Dude if he made the poor decision to make a run for it. She kept one eye on the elevator, a good fifty feet away; they should have backup here any minute. Surfer Dude turned, raised his hands, palms up, to plant them on the roof. Then, at the last instant, he whipped around, dove at Nicholas, sent his fist hard into his jaw, and was off and running.

Nicholas whipped around and grabbed his shoulder before he'd taken two steps, threw him backward. Surfer Dude landed hard against the Suburban's bumper, bounced off, and went down to the concrete floor. Amazingly, he rolled, came up in a crouch.

"So you want to play, do you?" Nicholas said, and Mike would swear she saw joy in his eyes. She realized soon enough that Surfer Dude was a seasoned fighter. She could see his eyes assessing for weak spots since his sunglasses had gone flying. *Good luck to you, sir,* she thought, and called out, "Take the moron down, Nicholas."

Nicholas feinted to the left, turned fast, and kicked out at Surfer Dude's knee. He got only the side of his leg, barely grazed him, Surfer Dude was that fast.

He narrowed his eyes, came at Nicholas, punches no longer wild but now fast and controlled, arms moving in a blur, all of it textbook moves, lethal, designed for maximum impact.

Trained, Mike thought. *He's been trained.* She smiled. No matter, he wasn't Nicholas. In fact, she saw herself taking the clown down and sitting on his back, maybe smacking his head as she cuffed him.

Nicholas had a height advantage and he used it, punching Surfer Dude's neck, landing a hard kidney shot, stomping his arch. It was a relief Surfer Dude didn't have a knife. Both Mike and Nicholas hated knives, far too dangerous. She watched Nicholas kick Surfer Dude's belly.

Surfer Dude backed up fast, wheezing. He spat out blood. "Hey, mate, you aren't all that bad, for an FBI pussy," and he sprang to the side, whirled around, and came at Nicholas with a flurry of kicks and punches.

"And you're a right pain in the arse," Nicholas said, and landed a massive uppercut that sent Surfer Dude stumbling backward, still grinning, even with a line of blood coming from a cut above his left eye. *Who is he? What's going on here?*

Mike didn't interfere. All the lethal weapons were in the Suburban, and Nicholas was the better fighter. And the big plus? He was having fun. Why deny him? Mike only wished she could be the one doing the pounding, relieve some of her frustration. She checked her watch. "Sorry, Nicholas, time's a passin', finish him off. If you do it within the next ten seconds, I'll take you to the gym myself, let you go a round with me."

Nicholas hit him hard in the nose and blood spurted out. She saw visions of the media claiming brutality, and called out, "Okay, that's enough."

Nicholas reined in immediately, gave her a quick grin, started to put him in a half nelson, but Surfer Dude managed to break free and took off running.

Mike rolled her eyes. The idiot. "My turn," she said, and bolted after him. She caught him quickly, tackled him from behind, drove him down into the concrete floor as the elevator doors opened and Ben Houston ran out with five agents on his heels.

Nicholas lifted Mike off his back and hauled Surfer Dude to his feet one-handed, threw him back against a car, got into his face. He jerked off his baseball cap, then grabbed his shirt and shook him like a dog.

Mike yelled, "Nicholas, hold him still. Good grief, does he look familiar to you?"

Nicholas hauled him up close. "Bloody hell, even with the bloody face, you're that guy in the photo, Melody Finder's boyfriend. You're supposed to be in Paris, studying how to chop onions and debone chickens."

Surfer Dude was panting hard, but he still managed a grin, even with the dribble of blood coming out of his nose. "I tried to tell you before you started pounding my face in. I know who you are, too, you big bastard." He stuck out a hand sporting bloody knuckles. "Craig Swanson, CIA."

44

KNIGHT TO C3 CHECK

"CIA—bloody bollocks, I should have known. You're a bloody spook." Nicholas wanted to punch him a couple more times, but he heard Ben and the other agents laughing behind him. He backed off. "All right, you bleater, show us some ID."

"I'm all the identification you're going to get, pal. I don't carry creds like you *federales*. They call it being undercover for a reason."

True enough, Mike had to give him that. Mike waved to all the weapons. "I suppose this traveling armory is part of your *undercover* job?"

"We're not supposed to use our personal vehicles, but it was a bona fide, true-blue emergency. I loaded up and made it a tactical vehicle, had no clue if it would be needed. No choice, I had to hurry."

"Mike," Ben called out, "I imagine the NYPD are outside the garage as we speak, wondering what to do. Tell you what, since you're having so much fun with our CIA brother, we'll go upstairs and handle things for you."

"Ben, you stay here," Mike said. "Tommy, Lynn, could you go upstairs and deal with the NYPD?"

The agents disappeared back into the elevator.

Nicholas said to Swanson, "You registered the car in your girlfriend's name? Kinda dumb, dude."

"Hey, I'm not picking on your methods."

"Your girlfriend thinks you're in Paris and doesn't know you have a Suburban."

"No, I didn't tell her that, she didn't need to know. She's part of my cover."

Mike's eyebrow went up. "Does she know about the weapons stashed down here?"

"Certainly not; it would scare the crap out of her. But she is part of my world and she's good. I'll bet she convinced you guys she was as straight as an arrow, all cute swagger in those Doc Martens of hers."

Mike said, "Yes, she sure did."

"Let me wipe the blood off my nose." Craig snagged a rag out of the back of the Suburban and pressed it to his nose. "It doesn't feel broken, that's good. Having Melody, it's one of the perks of working for the Agency, you get to tell the people you love what you do. She knows to tell anyone who comes asking that I'm a chef, studying the restaurant business. Helps for when I need to make overseas runs. And I am an excellent cook, no lie there."

Mike said, "Like I told you, she was good, believable; she lied right to our faces, smiling all the while. Hmmm, I think I might go back upstairs and pound on her."

For the first time, Swanson looked alarmed. "Nah, please don't, she's a sweetie, bought into the whole deal, plus she thinks I'm very cool. However, this time it doesn't appear she did a good enough job, since you're here poking around, looking for me."

"No, she's a very good liar," Nicholas said. "We saw you pull the Suburban into the garage. You didn't even bother to check your surroundings before you led the FBI right to your doorstep. Now, enough fun and games. What were you doing in Brooklyn last night? Who's the redheaded woman you took away? Where is she? We know she's involved with COE, so that means you aided and abetted a terrorist, and you better believe I will light you up like a Christmas tree in two seconds flat if you even try to lie to me."

Swanson stopped cold, held his hands palms out in front of his face. "Listen, you want more, you gotta talk to my boss. I've said all I can. Trust me, mate, we're on the same side."

Nicholas turned to Ben. "His girlfriend is up in 1507. Go arrest her on obstruction."

He turned back to Swanson. "You got something to say to me before we arrest Melody?"

Swanson said, "No, no, don't arrest her, she didn't do anything. Seriously, that's a low blow. Leave Melody out of this. All right, I'll talk to my boss."

"And who might your boss be?"

"Let me use my phone and I'll call him. He can debrief you from here. Please, don't arrest Melody."

"Not a chance in Hell, mate. You give me names, I run a background to make sure you aren't lying, then you can talk to him."

Swanson pulled the cloth away from his nose, saw no new blood, and managed a sneer. "And here I thought all you FBI types were nerds and wing tips. But not you, you're a real tough guy." He touched his fingers to his nose. "I gotta say, you have a mean right hook."

"The contact, now, or you'll see my left jab, and trust me, you won't like it."

Swanson spit blood onto the garage floor. "All right, all right. Lighten up. My boss is going to rip *you* a new one, not me." He read off a number.

Ben typed it in on his tablet. "It's legit. Goes to Langley."

Mike said, "Call it, Ben."

Ben dialed the number from his own phone. It connected and he put it on speaker.

A male voice said, "Craig? Everything okay?"

"Yeah, there's—"

Nicholas spoke over him. "This is Special Agent Nicholas Drummond, FBI. Please identify yourself."

There was a brief pause. "Carlton Grace. CIA."

Ben started tapping away, looking for the name. A few moments later, an eyebrow raised, he nodded.

"Agent Grace, we have your subordinate Craig Swanson in custody. He was—"

"Drummond?" They heard a whistle. "Well, how's that

for luck. I already spoke to your boss, Milo Zachery. You and Mike Caine need to come down to Langley to meet with me right away."

"You never know, do you?" Craig Swanson said, grinning.

Nicholas managed to resist smacking him again. His spook boss had already cleared it with Zachery? What was going on?

Nicholas said, "We're not going anywhere unless you tell us right this minute what this is all about."

Carlton Grace laughed low and quick. "What's wrong with you? You know I can't tell you a thing, not on this open line. Agents Savich and Sherlock will be here as well. It's time. Oh, and Drummond? Bring Swanson with you. He needs a few lessons in subterfuge, apparently."

The line went dead. Swanson was still grinning.

"Ain't that a kick?" Ben said.

Nicholas looked at Mike. "What in the bloody hell is going on here?"

She was playing with her ponytail, staring off at nothing in particular.

"Mike?"

"Nicholas. Remember I told you the redhead was familiar to me? Well, I remember who she is."

"How do you know? Facial recognition hasn't come through; we don't even have Mrs. Antonio's sketch of her."

"Everything clicked into place. Her name is Vanessa Grace, the same name as Craig's boss. Is she related, Craig?"

"Yes, he's her uncle."

"I went to Yale with her. Nicholas, she's got to be CIA, too."

Nicholas's eyebrows went up a good inch. "You're telling me COE has a CIA agent inside?"

"Had," Swanson called out. "Not any longer."

Nicholas turned on him. "Bugger off, Swanson. You people, you're as bad as the Foreign Office. You had someone inside and you didn't bother to let us know? Particularly after Bayway—why weren't we informed?"

"Hey, man, that decision is way above my pay grade."

All Nicholas could think of was how many lives could have been saved if the CIA had only told them about their undercover agent. He wasn't surprised, this sort of interagency secrecy was one of the reasons he'd left MI6.

"Mike, please call Zachery and verify this. I'm calling Savich."

45

KING TO G1

Before Nicholas had a chance to call Savich, his cell phone blasted out one of Sousa's marches. *Nigel*, he thought, and when had he programmed that bouncy hit in?

No, not Nigel. Adam Pearce. At last.

He nodded at Mike and stepped away.

"Adam, what do you have for me?"

"Enough news I hope you've got a computer in front of you to type it all."

"I'm in a basement garage in Chelsea with FBI agents and a moronic CIA undercover, so please keep it simple. I'll call back for the rest."

"Understood. You know that body you're running DNA on? The one burned in the fire in Brooklyn? Did you hear who it matches?"

"I have not. And I must ask, how do you know before I've been notified?"

"You asked me to do all I could to find a way into COE. Since I work for you, it's not like I hacked into any databases, not technically. And I do have a way in, if you're interested."

Nicholas said, "Adam. Let me say I'm very glad you're working for the FBI and not against them. And you're entirely correct: technically, you can do what's needed to help solve this case. Tell me, who is the dead guy?"

"Ian McGuire. He's an IRA bomber—well, he was until he got shot, then burned. He was the head of the Londonderry branch. We're talking a guy who has a sheet the length of my arm."

"Do you know when he came to the U.S.?"

"Good news and bad news. McGuire's been here for several months, with his whole crew of fanatic nutcases, maybe eight of them, all long-timers. They came through different airports on different days, under known aliases."

"How did we miss this? They're on the watch list, aren't they?"

"A lot of people are on the watch list, Nicholas. I believe I was on it for a while myself. It doesn't take any great brainpower; people cross the borders all the time."

"I trust you know where they've been, what they've been doing?"

"As much as I can reconstruct. I don't know where his team is, but I think it's safe to assume they allied themselves with COE. Speaking of which, let me skip ahead. I found the communications between COE and Gunther Ansell, the whiz in Germany. They paid old Gunther ten million for his proxy servers, then manipulated the code to insert the worm into the oil companies. All it took was a single click on an e-mail and the whole network got infected. Easy."

"And then someone killed Gunther. So where are they, Adam?"

Adam sighed. "That's the bad news, Nicholas. Until twelve hours ago, they were in Brooklyn. But now? I don't know. They're offline. There hasn't been a peep on any of their IPs, not since the cyber-attack began. I've been sending feelers everywhere I know, but so are half the hackers in the U.S., looking to party along. COE went dark after the attack, and there's nothing else I can do until they come back online, so I can't get in if they're not answering the door.

"But I do have something you'll like. I found an e-mail generated out of one of their known IP addresses to a guy at a brokerage firm on Wall Street by the name of Porter Wallace. Wallace runs a couple of major hedge funds and is young, really young, to have so much power. He's even been written up in *The Wall Street Journal* a few times. I can't get into his system without an epic hack, and I'm juggling five searches as it is. I've sent you all the information I've found. You have a lot of manpower there. If your onsite team can start taking apart the data—"

"I will set them to it immediately."

"Good, because there's a possibility we can find a trace from earlier to tell us where they were headed next. Right now I can find no rhyme or reason to their targets."

"What about the targets themselves? There must be a

reason COE attacked the places they did. It takes too much time and effort and coordination to set the bombs, like getting plant plans to know where to set the bombs, like at Bayway, with this guy Larry Reeves. There has to be a tie-in. Find it for me, Adam."

"I'm working as fast as I can. I'll keep you updated." And he was gone.

46

PAWN TAKES B6

Mike said in a friendly voice to Craig Swanson, "You move one step and I'll flatten you."

"I'm not budging," Swanson said. "Hey, maybe you want to talk about this, maybe—"

Mike turned her back to him, said to Ben, "Whatever Adam's telling Nicholas, it's making him glow, so that means we're getting some needed answers." She shot a look at Swanson, who was very gently wiping the blood off his teeth, pushing them to see if they were loose. "And now we've got the CIA involved. I've got to call Mr. Zachery, see if he knows what this is all about."

Ben looked over at Swanson. "Seems to me you're safe from the CIA bozo, so I'll head back to the office and see what's happening. Work with Gray. The code he and Nicholas wrote to stop the cyber-attack last night was impressive. Gray's got his team following up on it, patching all the remaining holes and working with the IT guys at the companies hit to get them back up and running. From what I heard, the damage could have been exceptionally severe, though I don't think they're letting the news out yet. If he and Nicholas hadn't stepped in, we'd be facing a whole different issue. See you later."

Once Ben had climbed into the elevator and was off, Mike looked over at Swanson again. He was sitting on the ground next to his Suburban, his arms clasped around his knees. He looked up. "Can I have my cell? I need to call Melody."

"No. Well, maybe, if you tell me why you were planning on leaving a tactical vehicle full of weapons in an unsecured garage. This is SOP for the CIA?"

"No. I was going to unload shortly. I came to say hello to Melody."

"Love life before work, then?"

Swanson shook his head at her. "You Feebs are so uptight. Surely you think those Doc Martens of hers are hot."

"If I were your boss, Mr. Swanson, I'd pound your head with those Doc Martens."

"Can I use my cell now?"

"No. Tell me how well you know Vanessa Grace."

Swanson shrugged. "Like I told you, she's the boss's niece. I've met her a couple of times, but I don't know her all that well. It's not like we have undercover asset mixers. CIA's not a sorority."

"According to a witness, she was injured last night. What happened? Why were you sent in to retrieve her?"

"My boss called and asked me to grab her up. I did as he requested."

"But you didn't take her to the hospital, and she was badly injured. Why?"

"I follow orders even when I don't agree. I was a combat medic in a past life. She was hurt bad, a bullet to her chest, broken bones, but Grace wanted her back in D.C. So I patched her up and put her on a CIA medevac chopper home. Did she make it? I don't know."

Mike gave him the fish eye. "Of course you're lying."

He had the gall to grin. "Nah, not about this. Far as I know, this ain't classified. Can I have my cell now, to call Melody? No one else, I promise."

Mike said, "No," and she turned away and called Zachery.

"Agent Caine, is everything all right? Ben went tearing out of here, his hair on fire. And Louisa told me Nicholas has a bullet hole in his jacket sleeve."

"We're fine, sir," she said, and she briefed him on the situation. "Did you agree that Nicholas and I should leave immediately for Langley to meet with a CIA agent named Carl Grace?"

"Yes. You and Agent Drummond have been asked to make an appearance at Langley to get a full debrief on COE and the Bayway bombing. I assume Dillon Savich has already called you, told you of our new interface with D.C.?"

"Yes, sir."

"Speaking of Bayway, we've got the analysis of the bomb. It's not exactly what we were expecting."

"Tell me."

"Problem was, there wasn't much to find, which means it was small, Mike, very small."

"But the load was huge."

"Yes. We've got very small pieces of carbon-fiber casing, but the internal mechanism was blown to smithereens. It seems there was some sort of timer inside we haven't seen before. Putting together what we found, I'd say the whole bomb was no bigger than a watch battery."

This wasn't good. But then again, after actually being in the middle of the havoc that bomb had created, she wasn't all that surprised. "So we're talking some sort of advanced technology?"

"Very advanced nanotechnology, and that word gives us all chills after Manfred Havelock and his micro-nukes.

"It's a very different bomb from the others COE have used—plain old Semtex. So what's this all about? Where did COE get this marvel? And what are their plans now? That's what the CIA better tell us.

"Oh, yes," Zachery continued, "we finally identified a badly burned body in the blast center—it's your drunk barfly, Larry Reeves."

"I guess I'm not surprised. The man made a very poor decision."

"Ben's been taking apart his financials. We'll find the thread."

"Sir, there's something else. This meeting with the CIA—they're going to tell us about how they had an undercover agent in the group. Her name is Vanessa Grace, she's the redheaded woman, and her uncle is her handler. He's the one who wants to meet with us."

Silence, then, "Her uncle? When Carl Grace called me, needless to say, he didn't tell me about his niece. Talk about tough—can you imagine? Well, now, this meeting with Grace at Langley, I imagine the CIA finally understands they can't keep us in the dark any longer spouting their party line—protect state secrets, jeopardize national security, blah, blah, blah."

"Sir, I know her, I know Vanessa Grace, or I did. We were at Yale together, in the same undergrad psych program."

Zachery whistled. "Tell me about her."

"I remember she was smart, very steady, capable, but it's been eight years since I saw her last. It looks like she was the female victim from the Brooklyn fire, and also we'll find her on the videotapes from Bayway. I saw her this morning on one of the feeds before we left for Brooklyn. I didn't recognize her then, but I knew the woman seemed familiar. Ben was running the tapes for me."

"No idea if she's still alive?"

"No, sir. But you know what this means—the CIA had an agent operating undercover on American soil. Big no-no."

"Indeed," Zachery said, and she could practically hear him mentally sorting through everything.

She said, "Is there anything new on the Hodges crime scene in Bayonne, sir?"

"Nothing good, Mike. Ballistics are back. Our three agents were shot with a nine-millimeter. The bullet fragments were recovered, but the rifling hasn't matched anything in our databases. All we know is the gun wasn't used in any other crimes. There aren't any extraneous latent fingerprints, no DNA to speak of outside our agents' and Mr. Hodges's. Whoever did this was clean and thorough, and we have very little to go on. The families, Mike, the notifications, some of the toughest I've ever had to do." He was silent for a moment, then, "You and Drummond get down to Langley, have this meeting, find out how this is all going to work with Savich, and brief me immediately on what's happening. There's a chopper waiting for you at the heliport. I've sent an agent with your go-bags."

"Thank you, sir, I appreciate knowing I'll have my toothbrush, although I don't think those sharks at the CIA deserve a nice fresh breath."

"Stay in touch, Mike. And be careful. There are still too many unknowns, too many secrets. You know as well as I do there's something a lot bigger going down. I'll do my best to find out what's happening from my end, too." He hung up.

Nicholas joined her. "Adam Pearce is a miracle worker."

"A miracle hacker, you mean. What'd he find for us?"

"Maybe a trail of bread crumbs leading to the money. We need to have a talk with a Wall Street broker named Porter Wallace. Though by the look on your face I assume we have new marching orders yet again."

"Yes. We're to take a helicopter to Langley. Kick some CIA butt. Think you're up for that?"

Nicholas looked over at Swanson. He flexed his bruised hand and smiled. "Yes, oh, yes, Agent Caine."

47

QUEEN TO B4

George Washington University Hospital

When Carl Grace raced to the nurses' counter, he was told there was nothing new on Vanessa. He sucked in a breath. That meant she was still alive.

He calmed himself; he had work to do. He found an empty conference room, closed the door, and sat down. He put on his headphones and started to dissect the past four months of data Vanessa had sent him to prep for his meeting with the FBI.

He found himself not really seeing the words, but rather remembering. It seemed like only yesterday when he'd gotten word in 1995 that his brother, Paul Grace, had been killed in Northern Ireland, leaving an orphaned daughter, Vanessa. The very next week, the aunt who was taking care of Vanessa was killed in an auto accident. Carl had immediately asked to be brought back to Langley, and adopted Vanessa. He remembered clearly when she was ten, Vanessa had found one of her father's diaries and brought it to him, saying in an unwavering, overly adult voice, "Uncle Carl, I want to do what my dad did and what you do," and that had been that. She'd never wavered from her goal, though Carl had done his best to tell her how fragile, how fragmented such a life could be, how it made children into orphans, as she knew firsthand. It had made no difference, Vanessa was committed. He remembered how she begged for the undercover case in Northern Ireland, where her father had died, and look where it had led.

She could be dying now, and like then, there was nothing he could do about it. Even though Spenser had shot her, Carl had put the weapon in his hand when he'd sent that ill-timed text.

He shook his head, refocused on Vanessa's transcripts, trying to control the guilt. He wanted to find Matthew Spenser and COE and put a stop to them once and for all. He really wanted to put a bullet into the man's brain himself.

He pictured her pale slack face again and wanted to cry, but he had to hold it together; time was running out.

He started with the most recent conversation, two weeks earlier. She'd managed a secure video feed at a café in South Lake Tahoe near where the COE stayed off the grid, hunkered down in a mountain retreat.

I don't have much time. We're going to be on the move again soon. I have more photos. I've uploaded them to the server. Finally caught scary Darius on camera. I hope you can find out who he is because now I'm certain he came specifically to hook up with Matthew, but not to further COE's goals. I'm thinking he might be after Matthew's incredible invention of the tiny undetectable bombs—his special gold coins, he calls them—just like I am. It's like Darius is weaving a spell around Matthew, encouraging him to think bigger, think about what he could do when he's perfected the bombs, the power he would have to actually stop the terrorists who killed Matthew's family.

My feeling is that this man who calls himself Darius is something else entirely, something evil, something soulless. I know he has a definite purpose in mind, and whatever it is, it isn't good for Matthew or any of us. I know this all sounds melodramatic, but he scares me deep down where monsters live.

I'm sure now that Matthew trusts him more than he does me, because he's closed me out. Darius's doing? Probably so. Matthew's mood swings are more pronounced and happen often now, and that, too, is frightening, but nothing like Darius. No, nothing like Darius.

Now, something critical: I overheard Matthew and Andy talking about the oil companies and accessing their databases, but when I came in, they clammed up. Does Darius know about this as well? Is this also one of his ideas, and if so, what are they up to? You must identify

Darius, as soon as possible. I'm really afraid of him. Believe me, he is dangerous, very dangerous.

Vanessa, I've got the photo. Great job. I'm on it. Now, accessing oil company databases, that is worrisome. I'll start digging. See if you can't get Matthew to open up about this, okay?

As I said, Matthew's closed me out. Now he only tells me what he thinks I need to know for the placement of my Semtex bombs, that's all. All Matthew's told me is we're going to head to San Francisco next week.

What's the target?

I'm pretty sure it will be the Rodeo San Francisco plant.

I'll make sure the security is aware.

Good. Let me know when you have the ID on Darius. Uncle Carl, he scares me, he really scares me.

And she was gone.

Grace had run the photos but drawn a blank. He'd run them against every known database in the U.S. arsenal. Nothing.

It wasn't until this morning after the meeting with the vice president, when Temp had told him about the assassination, that he knew in his heart, without a doubt, that Vanessa's Darius had to be Zahir Damari.

He'd let the FBI run the two photographs using their extremely sensitive facial-recognition system. Maybe they'd be able to give them one hundred percent confirmation, but he didn't need the proof. He knew.

If Vanessa's instincts were right, not only had Zahir Damari been hired to steal Matthew Spenser's new technology, he also planned to assassinate the vice president. If Hezbollah and therefore Iran managed to get their hands on the small gold-coin bombs, Carl feared for the safety of the world. Imagine having those small undetectable bombs in a world of chaos and anarchy. You'd be at the top of the food chain.

He read several of Vanessa's recent e-mails. She'd found out from Crazy Andy—that's what she called him—that they'd bought some cyber-software to attack the computer systems of a company. Thanks to the FBI in New York, that particular cyber-attack had been shut down.

He called up other videos, stared at her beloved face, so like her father's, a beautiful face, his eyes, but she had her mother's, Isabella's, glorious red hair. Poor Isabella, dead at thirty-three of a brain tumor. She'd never truly known her daughter, the woman she'd become.

Vanessa wouldn't die, she simply couldn't.

"Mr. Grace?"

He came slowly to his feet, staring at the nurse who stood in the doorway. He was more afraid than he'd ever been in his life.

Then the nurse smiled. "She made it through surgery."

"Will she be all right?"

"The surgeon will be along shortly. He's—"

"No, don't put me off. Is she all right?"

"She's not out of the woods yet. She's on a ventilator and they're going to keep her in an induced coma for a little while. The damage was worse than they first thought. Like I said, the surgeon will be here shortly to explain everything." She came to him, lightly laid her hand on his arm. "I know this is incredibly difficult, Mr. Grace, but you must keep faith. She's still with us, and I for one will do my best to see she stays with us."

48

ROOK TO A4

Maryland

Zahir drove toward Frederick, Maryland. He was calm and relaxed, and felt really good. Everything was coming together. He had twenty-four hours, a long day's hike, to get into position. Having the security layout and blueprints of the target made it easier to decide where to set up his base camp. He admitted he was a bit worried about the dogs; he'd be stupid not to be, since the K9 security teams were in place as well. Their schedule was set so he should be able to avoid them. He had deer scent in his bag; he planned to bathe in it to mask his own human smell.

He reached the entrance of the Catoctin Mountain Park at three in the afternoon. He left the car in a campground, hoisted the pack to his shoulders, and set off.

There was no one around to see him, a good thing since he really didn't want to leave a trail of dead bodies. He wanted to get in, get the job done, get himself back up through New York into Canada, and eventually find his way back to Jordan, to the warmth of his estate. The future looked very pleasant.

The forest was quiet, only the sounds of animals scurrying about, the birds overhead occasionally squawking, but no people. It was nice to be able to think clearly. Being around so many people for so long made him crazy.

He thought back to those months of training by the British Special Forces, and wasn't that irony for you? But it was an American who'd paid him to kill the first time. To a young man not yet twenty, the ten thousand dollars was a vast amount of money, and that made him smile. The client had sent Zahir to Saint Petersburg to kill a man who worked in the oil business. To this day Zahir had no idea why. He'd enjoyed spending that vast amount of money, and in those days, what he'd been paid had gone a long way. Then, of course, the money ran out and he wanted more. By the fourth kill, Zahir realized he'd found his calling.

He traveled all over the world for his clients, learning, always learning, never repeating a mistake, always silent and deadly. He was the best of the best—a chameleon unhampered by a conscience, shrewd, never giving up. He loved each challenge and discovered along the way he also enjoyed the dramatic. To kill flamboyantly, more than most of his targets deserved, probably, but it pleased something in him. And he made his hits more and more dramatic because he wanted the world to know it was he who was responsible, and to fear and praise him in hushed voices. He wanted to build his legend. When the client wanted the deaths to be undetectable, Zahir was disappointed.

A sociopath, his father once called him, which was rich, coming from the mouth of that old hypocrite. With every kill, he supposed now he was sending the old man a message, telling him clearly that perhaps one of these days he might see his son for the last time. His father's last time.

He enjoyed reading speculation about himself in the newspaper, particularly the comparisons to Carlos the Jackal, that covetous madman who wasn't in his league. He'd even done a few off-book killings, suitably complex, to keep the blood flowing through his veins, to keep his brain razor sharp, his reflexes fast and lethal.

He liked to think of himself as a maestro of killing, always unexpected, always successful.

Hands down, this was the biggest job he'd ever accepted. The splashiest. The one that would make his name go down in history. There were so many variables, so many unknowns, and more than any of his other jobs, this one held a high risk of failure.

No, he wouldn't fail. He never failed. He smiled up at the sky, careful not to draw attention to himself in case anyone was nearby. He had a better chance of living through this operation than he had of leaving any battlefield in his father's homeland alive.

He stopped by a small mountain brook to fill his canteen, looked up through the thick canopy of branches. It was still early.

At this rate, he'd be in place by moonrise.

Twenty-four hours—so much he'd had to accomplish, and he'd done it all, no problem. Once he'd placed the small portion of one of Matthew's coin bombs at Bayway in the sweet spot pointed out by Reeves, he'd run unseen to the car he'd left half a mile away, driven straight to Bayonne, dealt with the four men there—three of them FBI agents—in three minutes flat, eight shots—four chest, four forehead, no time for flourishes—then headed south.

And now he was here, tramping along the forest trails. Maybe he'd meet up with a wolf or a bear. He spent some time considering various ways to kill, then reminded himself to stay focused, to review once again each step of what was to happen.

**Tuesday
2 p.m.–6 p.m.**

49

QUEEN TAKES B6

New York Heliport

Nicholas and Mike buckled into the MD 530 Little Bird's hard seats, put on headsets and sunglasses. Craig Swanson was slumped across from them, eyes closed, looking the worse for wear after his couple rounds with Nicholas. Mike found it curious that Swanson seemed to harbor no ill will, maybe a token of respect, professional to professional. He'd gotten in a couple good shots— Nicholas's jaw was a delicate shade of eggplant beneath the stubble of his beard. Mike could only imagine what they were going to look like trooping into Langley—the three of them banged up. She could hide her shiner with sunglasses, but no, she was proud of her battle wounds.

At least they'd dropped by Katz's Deli, grabbed thick pastrami-on-rye sandwiches, chips, and sodas, and eaten as they drove to the helipad. She'd even had time to call her folks, tell them as far as she knew, Timmy, her younger brother, was gainfully employed in an off-Broadway show, and not in jail. Always good news. Her father, of course, knew all about Bayway, knew she was up to her eyebrows in the case. His last words, always, were: "You take care of my girl or I'll bust your chops." As for her mother, the Gorgeous Rebecca, she'd said only that she had a new lipstick shade for Mike to try, and then she'd laughed, hiccupped, and said she'd do more than bust her chops if she let anything happen to her, she'd cut off her beautiful hair. And she'd heard her father laughing in the background.

Charlie, their pilot, hyper with too much coffee, this his sixth run of the day, had them lifted off in the gray New York skies in no time, no muss, no bother.

Nicholas tapped her shoulder, put up four fingers. She moved the dial on her headset to channel four and nodded. Staying off the main frequency so they could have a private conversation was a good idea.

He punched his mike. "Tell me about Vanessa Grace."

Mike crossed her legs, put her heels in the empty bucket seat across from them. Swanson was staring out the window, but Mike would bet he was listening for all he was worth. She wondered how he was going to explain his absence and bruises to Melody Finder.

She said low into her mike, "Vanessa was in my dorm at Yale freshman year. I don't want to say I knew her well— we would say hi if we saw each other, had some friends in common. I was already gearing up for law enforcement, wanted to be a cop like my dad. I would have been happy going straight into the Academy, but he insisted I get out of Nebraska, apply to Ivy League schools, see a bit of the world, make sure I really wanted this life. Yale was as far away from Nebraska as I could get, in mileage and ideology, and, wonder of wonders, I was accepted, and so I humored him and flew to New Haven."

"Nebraska meets the Ivy League—it boggles the mind."

"I didn't exactly fit in at the beginning. I mean, some kids thought I was a hayseed, others thought I was dangerous because I went to the gun range every weekend."

"What did your roommates think when you cleaned your gun in the room?"

"I was smart enough never to do that. Can you begin to imagine the rep I'd get? It took the whole first semester for them to be comfortable with me and for me to be comfortable with them. So much drinking and partying—just like home.

"Enough of my history. Let me tell you more about Vanessa Grace. When I first met her, I thought she was a princess. She was gorgeous, masses of red hair almost to her butt, guys falling all over themselves to ask her out. It seemed to me she played one against the other, and I thought she was a jerk until I realized she was very shy and didn't have a lot of social skills. She had no clue how to deal with guys. One of our mutual friends told me she'd lived all over the world with her uncle and had been homeschooled for the most part. She'd been in a few American schools, but she was shy and had trouble fitting in.

"We finally did have a class together, Cognitive Science of Good and Evil. She'd come out of her shell by that time, even had a boyfriend who was on the rugby team. We talked about what we were planning to do when we graduated; I told her I wanted to be a cop. She said she wanted to take the Foreign Service exam and go to work for State. Her dad was a diplomat and he'd died, as had her mother. She was raised by her uncle, who also worked in the Foreign Service. We all know what it really means."

"Spies."

Mike nodded. "I wondered about her mother, but she never talked about her, said only she'd died of cancer, real young. She wanted to be like her dad and her uncle.

"Then we graduated and I went off to grad school at John Jay, and haven't thought of her since."

She gave him an arched eyebrow. "I don't suppose you ever had any adjusting to do, not like I did at Yale?" A pause, then she shook her head. "Of course you didn't. Eton, Cambridge, the Foreign Office. You fit in perfectly the whole way. And now the FBI, where you've been welcomed with open arms. Oh, yes, I like your scruffy beard."

He grinned at her, touched his fingers to his bruised jaw. "Like my mom and her TV show, and you, at first I was a fish out of water, but this strange and wondrous city is becoming home. I'm enjoying it here. Good food, good peers. Everyone wants the same thing—catch the bad guys, keep terrorists from blowing anything up, and if they do, nail their asses to the floor." He shrugged. "Do you know, I even like going to Barneys with Nigel. Do you think I'm giddy?"

"What? Giddy? About what?"

He looked embarrassed. "It was just something Nigel said to me last night when I came in half dead, clothes ready for the dustbin. He said I was giddy here in New York."

Mike realized that, yes, Nigel was right. "Well, I do know you enjoy kicking butt," she said, and she sent a look in Craig Swanson's direction.

He didn't tell her that if indeed he was giddy, she was right there with him.

The helicopter lurched to the side, then straightened again. Charlie said over the intercom, "Just making sure you guys are awake. All's okay."

Nicholas said, "We surely appreciate that, Charlie. Now, Mike, let me check my e-mail, see if Gray has sent me a dossier on Carl Grace, her uncle. Yes, here it is."

"Tell me."

"Apparently Vanessa's dad, Paul Grace, is rather legendary in the intelligence community. He was an undercover agent in the eighties and nineties, working deep cover with the IRA in Northern Ireland. He nailed a faction of IRA bombers, then was shot dead by a wife of one of the men in the group."

Nicholas closed the cover of the tablet. "As for his younger brother, Carl Grace, he came out of the field after he adopted Vanessa. This has got to be unusual—he became her handler after she joined the CIA."

Mike said, "And now she's been shot. I don't want her to die, Nicholas, I really don't."

"I don't, either. We'll soon see."

Charlie said, "Nearly there, folks, and only one little bump to keep you alert. I've been asked to patch through a call from Special Agent Savich. Please switch to channel two."

Nicholas flipped the channel, as did Mike. "Savich? What's wrong?"

"I just got a call from Dominion Virginia Power. They're having trouble with their electrical grid powering Richmond. Get here as quickly as you can, Nicholas. I'm afraid an external attack is coming."

50

KNIGHT TAKES D1

There were two cars waiting at the heliport, one FBI, the other CIA. Swanson gave them a small wave and went to join his compadres. "I hope they tear him a new one," Nicholas said, and Mike spurted out a laugh at the Americanism.

"I have a feeling Ms. Finder might do some of the tearing, too, once she gets her hands on him again," Mike said. "I know I'm not at all sad to see the last of him."

They got into the back of a black SUV. Special Agent Dover, their driver, said, "Seat belts, folks. I've got to get you to the Hoover Building in ten minutes."

As Dover ducked and dodged through the insane

traffic, Nicholas said to Mike, "Sounds to me like you'd like to join Ms. Finder."

"You bet. That jerk said I was uptight." She turned to face him. "I am not uptight. I'm not, am I, Nicholas? I'm the furthest thing from uptight I can think of, right? I mean, I know how to party, I know how to let my hair down and hang out. Shut your mouth. If you laugh at me, I'm going to belt you."

He swallowed the laugh. "No, Agent Caine, *uptight* isn't ever something I'd ever say about you."

"Yeah, and what would you say about me?"

"Hmmm, how about fast off the mark without a lot of thought—"

"Me, fast off the mark? What about you and Craig Swanson? You couldn't wait to pound him. You didn't even give it a second's thought, did you?"

"You wanted to jump him, too. I was simply closer."

Well, now, that was the truth. "Stop trying to make me laugh."

Three horns honked off to their right, and Dover raised his middle finger. "Out-of-towners," he said, and sped through a yellow light, whipping to the left to avoid a taxi.

Nicholas slid against her. He didn't move, closed his eyes for a moment.

Mike was looking out the window. "Everything's ready to burst into summer. Cherry blossoms are long gone."

Nicholas moved back to his side of the SUV. "I wonder what's happening to the power grid in Richmond."

"No word from Savich—that's got to be good news. Maybe it was a false alarm."

"Like that ever happens," Nicholas said.

Agent Dover pulled up outside the Hoover Building. "Go in this entrance. Nine minutes on the dot. Have fun with Savich, but be careful he doesn't take you to the gym and tie your legs around your necks." He gave them a small salute, and they went into the cavernous marble lobby to see Savich waiting for them.

"Nicholas, Mike. Great to see you. Come on, we'll get you signed in and official, then we can go upstairs and get started. Nothing definitive from Richmond yet. False alarm? We could get lucky, I suppose."

Mike hadn't spent much time with Savich herself, but she knew he was very worried. About the power grid in Richmond, sure, but something more.

They signed in, clipped visitor badges to their jackets, went through the metal detectors, then the elevator to the third floor.

Nicholas had been here before, during his training at Quantico, when Savich had needed some English background on a case. Mike hadn't ever visited the CAU, but it immediately felt like home. Every agent in the large room stared after them, knowing something was up, something major, alert and ready to move, the lot of them, just like New York. She nodded to a couple of agents she'd worked with on other assignments. And she wondered how many of these agents had worked with the agents murdered in Bayonne at Mr. Hodges's house.

She saw Sherlock through the huge glass window in Savich's office. She was reading something on a tablet, her curly red hair veiling her profile. Sherlock rose and hugged both Mike and Nicholas. "It's so good to see you two. I'm very sorry, all of us are, about the agents we lost in Bayonne."

Savich said, "Sit down, both of you. We hope that our meeting with Mr. Grace will make us believe the CIA is finally ready to fess up, unburden their souls, and tell us everything they know about COE. But don't count on it."

Sherlock turned to face them. "Before we get down to business, you're both coming to dinner tonight. And glory be, it's lasagna night, Dillon's specialty. Since we have plenty of room, you'll also stay at the Savich Hotel, limitless hot water and towels aplenty.

"When I told Sean he would see you, Nicholas, he was yelling how he was going to take you down to your underwear with his new *Captain Mook* video game."

"You got him the strip version of the *Captain Mook* game?"

Sherlock laughed. "That's his newest slang. He wanted to say boxers, but Dillon assured him that underwear was cooler."

Mike said, "Does the hotel also provide Cheerios?"

"Sean's favorite," Savich said. "Okay, then, you're staying."

"Thank you," Mike said. "Oh, yes, I believe Nicholas loves oatmeal. Instant would be great for him."

Smiles, a crack of laughter, then Savich said, "You'll find info in your e-mails." He handed them two manila folders. "In here you'll see the breakdown of Richmond's security systems. Thankfully, they did a risk assessment only three months ago. Juno did the work, and they're one of the best cyber-firms in the U.S."

"I'm familiar with them," Nicholas said.

Mike nodded.

Savich said, "They beefed everything up. However, I'm thinking if there's an attack under way, perhaps there was a worm already inside the system, put in before they made the changes."

Nicholas frowned. "That would mean Juno didn't do a thorough job. If the worm was already inside, then their security measures should have picked up an anomaly."

He flipped through the information while Savich continued to explain to Mike and Sherlock, "No matter how or when, if the bug was introduced into their systems, we won't have long to stop the attack. You're better at this than I am, Nicholas, and you've already stopped them once. That makes you better equipped to deal with this than our people. So get out your laptop."

Not two minutes later, The Who belted out "Won't Get Fooled Again." Savich listened, punched off. "Official confirmation, the power grid's down in Richmond. Nicholas, go."

Nicholas quickly accessed the servers at Dominion Virginia Power and hit a solid firewall. "Okay, so far, Juno does know their stuff." He looked up, grinned, flexed his fingers, and started to code.

Within moments he'd tuned the rest of the room out completely. The code he was bumping up against was not only sophisticated, it was familiar. He found a back door to the server, something the original company that had developed the security system had given themselves to try and stop exactly the kind of attack they were experiencing.

"Ah," he said aloud, "here we have a line of self-written code, and wouldn't you know it—there's Gunther's signature. At least I know how to disable it." Nicholas uploaded his own worm to disengage the attack, then sat back and let it run. "That's the best I can do by myself."

Savich said, "First, Nicholas, tell me how Gunther did it, then I'll call our tech team."

Nicholas said, "This attack is a DDoS, which as you know means distributed denial-of-service, which normally only disables the company's website and replaces it with a message, and people can't log in. But this one, it's very advanced. The attack vector has taken down their security grid by installing malware to allow remote control of the power system. Malware, according to the signature, purchased from our buddy Gunther Ansell. The positive here, and you can tell your tech team this, is that I didn't see any excessive activity, a good thing. If they were trying to shut everything down, there would be more movement, the code shifting, being rewritten in an attempt to eliminate my uploads to stop it.

"They may think Gunther's code is enough to disable the power grids, or they could be waiting for the attack to crawl through everything before they play with the lights. I put up some firewalls, hopefully to stop them before they do."

Savich nodded. "Okay, good, let me call the team, tell them what you said."

Sherlock said, "Nicholas, you talked to FedPol about Ansell's death?"

"Yes. Our friend Pierre Menard was going to take over the investigation, but we haven't heard from him in several hours." He glanced at his screen, made a few adjustments to his code. "This isn't exactly the same type of attack as the oil companies—it's not downloading financial and intellectual information, but it is similar. With Gunther's signature again, I'd say it's probably COE."

"Of course it's got to be COE," Sherlock said. "Who else could it be?"

51

PAWN TO H3

Mike looked at each of them in turn. "Yes, it's COE. After Bayway, who knows what they're after? They are trying to take down the Richmond grid for a reason. It's up to us to figure out what that reason is."

She picked up a paperweight off Savich's desk, passed it from hand to hand. "What I find amazing with this escalation is that COE has lost two important members in that fire in Brooklyn—Ian McGuire, the IRA bomber, and Vanessa Grace, bomb builder and undercover CIA. And don't forget the Middle Eastern man working with them. Who is he and what is his expertise? What is his purpose being with them? With the losses, it's amazing they've continued, much less escalated."

An agent appeared in the doorway, a manic grin on his face.

"Good news, Davis?" Sherlock asked him.

Savich said, "Agent Davis Sullivan, meet Agent Mike Caine, and you already met Nicholas Drummond. Why are you grinning like a fool?"

"Our firebug in Brooklyn. Louisa Barry identified his ass. Smart girl, she put the accelerant signature into the databases. After lots of integration and inputting data into ViCAP, she identified our firebug as one Andrew Tate, twenty-seven, first convicted of setting a string of fires around a high-end housing development under construction outside Seattle when he was only thirteen. Caused millions in damage. He went to juvie for four years, got out, then quickly went back in when some cars along a 'peaceful protest' route ended up on fire.

"And catch this, guys, while Tate was behind bars, he took several computer classes. The teacher marked in his record that he was amazing, a natural, outstripped him—the teacher—in weeks.

"Too bad, but this doesn't tell us where he is now. His last known is a Seattle halfway house. He bolted on his parole in 2010, has been off the books since. I'm afraid that's as far as I've gotten."

"This is great, Davis," Nicholas said, "and it explains a whole lot. I think you and Louisa not only found our firebug, we also found COE's hacker."

Davis tried not to look too pleased with himself, shrugged. "I gotta say, it was Agent Barry who did the heavy lifting. All I did was grab the report off the printer and look up a couple of cases."

"Yeah, right," Sherlock said.

"Davis," Savich said, "I want you to get photos of our

firebug out everywhere, particularly near Richmond. And again, good job." Savich looked at each of them. "There's something more, guys."

"You have all our attention now, Savich," Nicholas said. "Out with it."

"Mike, Nicholas, have you both gotten up to speed on Zahir Damari?"

"Yes," Mike said. "He's right up there with Carlos the Jackal, possibly even more deadly, will kill anyone for the right price. And the biggie: no one's ever seen his real face."

Nicholas added, "In England, we spoke of his chameleonlike ability to alter his looks, using plastic surgery and plugs and implants to change his face, allowing him to easily cross borders under false papers."

Mike said, "I know that Interpol had an Orange Notice on his movements a few years back, thought he was gearing up for an attack in Paris. Everyone knew he'd murdered Benar Bhuttino in Qatar in 2010. Eliminating Bhuttino allowed the Arab Spring to take hold since he was no longer alive to fight against it. But again, he couldn't be identified, so how could he be found?"

"Better question," Nicholas said. "Who hired Damari to assassinate the vice president?" He trailed a hand over the top edge of his laptop, glanced at the screen. All was running as planned, his patch was holding. But who knew for how long? He was thankful the IT team was keeping a sharp eye on the situation.

"We have to figure that out," Savich said.

"He's crazy to even try," Mike said. "I mean, she's covered from here to Sunday and sideways with security;

he'll never succeed." Mike was sitting forward as if she wanted to pull the information out of Savich's mouth.

"The Israelis had been closing in on him, watching some bank accounts he supposedly has," Sherlock said. "They say he flew from Jordan to London to Mexico City three months ago, then probably went north and over the border into the U.S."

Sherlock went on, "Callan Sloane is lucky she has friends in Mossad, and they alerted her immediately that Damari was hired to kill her, and others as well, as yet unidentified.

"No matter how well she's covered, guys, you all know Damari's rep. He never fails, so this is a very serious threat indeed."

Savich said, "When we meet with Carl Grace, we'll soon see if the CIA truly intend to be up front with everything they know not only about COE, but also about Damari."

"Well," Nicholas said, sitting back, "that certainly tops what we have to tell you and Sherlock, but"—he nodded to Mike—"tell them, Mike."

She gave them a fat grin. "I went to school with Vanessa Grace. Carl Grace is her uncle, evidently her handler. She was shot in Brooklyn, picked up by the CIA, stabilized, and medevaced down here. I hope Uncle Carl will tell us if she's alive or dead."

52

ROOK TAKES A2

Nicholas's laptop beeped.

Mike leaned in to look. "Is it the breach? You didn't get it contained?"

Nicholas said, "It's being difficult."

"Is that a Brit understatement?" Mike asked.

Savich came around his desk, looked over Nicholas's shoulder. "No, I don't think so, Mike. It looks like the threat assessment from Dominion's security servers ran us through multiple failure scenarios—are you going to be able to contain this breach, or do I call in the IT cavalry?"

Nicholas was watching his worm chew through Gunther's code. "So far, so good, and I know your IT guys are looking at the same thing, and they haven't yelled out. But you know, I don't like the feel of this. What do you think, Savich?"

Savich called his IT department. "Martin, I'm putting you on speaker. What are you guys seeing?"

A man's very calm, very soothing voice said in a dead monotone, "People, this is an incredible DDoS attack and it's managed to access the DERMS—the Distributed Energy Resource Management System—which controls the grid itself." They heard him draw a deep breath. "Sorry, the power is now shutting off, quadrant by quadrant."

"A moment, Martin. Nicholas, do you see it?"

"Oh, yes, I see it. He's right, we're going down."

There was a beep from Nicholas's laptop, then a series of three in a row, fast and steady, an alarm going off. "Oh, no. Oh, bugger me!" He started typing frantically. "The bloody worm isn't working now, Gunther's code kicked it out and accelerated the grid collapse. The DDoS attack is spreading instead of halting. Exactly what I was afraid of."

"I copy that, Drummond," Martin said.

Sherlock asked, "How many homes are without power? How far has it spread?"

"It's happening really fast. Right now, millions are without power, all over Virginia. Even more widespread power and voltage fluctuations, too. If we can't get it back online, we may start seeing larger failures across the board. Once one system is overloaded and goes offline, it's a domino effect. If we're not careful, the whole eastern seaboard could go down. You did a good patching job, Drummond, but COE's hackers did a superb number on us. There's no stopping this now. You with me?"

Sherlock's cell rang, and she listened, punched off. "Can you hear me, Martin?"

"Yo, what now?"

"That was the head of security at Dominion. They've put a call in to their contacts at Juno to see if they can step in and help shut this down. He said this attack is so specialized, so perfectly timed, it makes him very suspicious of the assessment Juno did on their systems."

"Bloody well right they should be suspicious. Someone in their operation screwed up big-time. It's spreading too fast for us to contain it."

And the lights went out.

Dead silence, then shouts from the outer office, chairs squeaking on the floor as agents pushed back from their desks. Then a deep grinding noise filled the office, as the Hoover Building's many generators kicked on and the emergency lighting came on.

Martin's calm voice came out loud and clear, "Nicholas, look at the grid of lines crisscrossing the eastern seaboard—like arteries into a heart."

They all stared down at Nicholas's laptop. One by one, the lines disappeared.

"It's the worst-case scenario," Nicholas said. "The grids have gotten out of balance, the peak load is too much, so they're systematically shutting down. The bastards have managed it. They've overloaded the grids."

Sherlock asked, "Can we get them back up and online, Nicholas? Martin?"

Nicholas said, "I can't, not alone, anyway. Martin, we need to get together and reverse-engineer the code. They have remote control of the grids, and they've managed to use it." He stared at the screen. "Outages are being reported from North Carolina to New York." He looked up at Savich. "If the vice president is a potential target, this could signal the beginning of an attack."

Sherlock was already punching in numbers on her cell. "I'll alert the Secret Service."

Mike was scrolling down her cell phone. "The media is already having a field day. Twitter has exploded with speculation."

Nicholas said, "Martin, I'm on my way; get your team ready to reverse-engineer. Mike, can you get a SitRep on the outage for me?"

"On it."

Savich said, "Nicholas, let's get down to IT and stop this thing. Martin, get ahold of Juno, we need to work with their protocols."

Nicholas said, "I want to bring in Adam Pearce, too. We have to move fast." Savich nodded and Nicholas dialed as they walked.

Adam sounded exhausted and harried. "I know, I know, Nicholas, COE pulled a doomsday on you. I'm working on it."

"Work faster. I'm in D.C. and I'm about to work with the IT team here at the Hoover. Can you trace where the signal is coming from?"

"I'm looking. It's south of you. They're popping online then getting off as quickly as the IP addresses register. The last signal came from near Richmond. I'll call you back."

Savich and Nicholas broke into a run, down the long hallway and into the mainframe server room. There were a dozen men and women scrambling around, making sure the backups were safe. A man with short black hair, aviator glasses, and a small mustache walked up to them. He said in a voice so calm, so soothing, Nicholas felt his heart rate slow, fought the urge to yawn: "You Drummond?"

At Nicholas's nod, Martin said, "Come this way."

Savich knew he wasn't needed. He stood there and watched the room of people shift into a complex ballet, people switching stations, screens glowing, keyboards clattering, all under the oddly green-tinged lights of the emergency backup generators.

Mike came up, tugged on his sleeve. "Air traffic control is rerouting all planes in the area. The Capitol power plant is offline, so the Capitol police are enacting emergency measures as if there's an imminent attack coming on their locale. Sherlock spoke to the Secret Service, and Vice President Sloane is being moved to a secure location. All the nuclear plants up and down the eastern seaboard are executing emergency measures. The Metro and the trains into and out of D.C. are all offline. We're going to have massive gridlock, and fast. We need to control this, make sure we don't have a panic on our hands. What else can we do?"

"Honestly?" Savich replied. "We see how good our team is."

53

KING TO H2

The White House

The power went out without so much as a whisper. Callan was reading an up-to-the-minute brief on the Geneva talks. "They're falling apart," she said aloud. "Not a surprise now we think Iran and Hezbollah were trying to undermine the talks."

Quinn rushed into her office, hair flying. "Secret Service are coming to move you to the bunker."

"Because the power's out? Isn't that a bit of an overreaction?"

"The Richmond power grid's been attacked, and there's a rolling blackout making its way up the eastern seaboard. The FBI feels an attack on you could be imminent and this could be the start. We've got to go."

Damari, Callan thought, her heart leaping into her throat. *Ari, you were right. Thank you, thank you.*

Her heart was kettledrumming in her chest, but she wasn't about to freak Quinn out.

Callan was well trained in the emergency protocols; they'd been drummed into her from the moment she accepted the nomination of vice president and was suddenly surrounded by men bristling with weapons concerned solely for her safety. She'd also helped improve them when she'd been in the CIA. She grabbed her jacket from the chair back, got her heels on. Quinn had her secure laptop and her briefcase.

Callan's lead Secret Service agent, Tony Scarlatti, appeared in the doorway. "Good, you're all packed up. Ready, ma'am?"

"Yes, I am." As they walked briskly toward the West Wing, Tony said into his wrist mike, "Cardinal's on the move." He gave Callan a big smile. "You're going to be just fine, ma'am. No worries."

And she no longer wanted to break into a run. If Tony wasn't concerned, then she wouldn't be, either.

He said very matter-of-factly, his voice as comforting as warm syrup, "Ma'am, we've got planes in the skies and no good way to track them, except the old-fashioned way, by hand. Any one of them could deviate off course and try to fly into us. Communications and transportation are down all over the city, the Capitol is being evacuated. We aren't going to take any chances with you."

Is that all? How about a meteor heading our way? "What else do you know, Tony?"

"Just a moment, ma'am," he said, and turned away to speak into his comms. When he turned back, his voice remained calm and reassuring. "I'm to bring you to the Situation Room. I don't know what's happening."

The stairwell in the West Wing was lit in ghostly green. Down one level was the Situation Room, and Callan saw a flurry of activity inside.

Callan pushed into the room, Tony and Quinn on her heels.

Several military staffers stood in the center of the small space, watching huge monitors, above which time clocks from all over the world ran. They stood at attention when she entered.

"Madam Vice President, we're relieved you're here."

"Commander Zarvick, tell me what's happening."

Commander Zarvick was the senior staffer attached to the JSOC—Joint Special Operations Command. "Ma'am, we have eyes on a nuclear facility in Iran that's gone live. One of the ones they're refusing to let the UN inspectors near."

Her blood chilled. "Tell me what you mean—it's gone live?"

"We're not entirely sure exactly what they're doing. Thirty minutes ago, activity started at the Bushehr facility. The heat signatures showed multiple forces moving into a defensive position, and their medium-range ballistic missile batteries are lit up, too."

"Which missiles?"

"Sejjls and Ashouras. Two-thousand-kilometer range. They may only be executing maneuvers, that would be par for the course, their ritual thumbing their noses at us, just to rile everyone, the good Lord knows they've done it enough in the past. But this time, I've got to admit it surprises me that they'd do it now, what with the president and all their leaders at the table supposedly talking peace. And that's why I wanted you to know, ma'am."

Commander Zarvick was perfectly right. The Iranians loved to shove provocative behavior in their faces, then claim only testing, but now? Callan clicked off in her head: Bayway blowing up, the electrical grid attacked, Zahir Damari gunning for her, and now Iran pulling their usual crap, using the exact methods they were pledging to stop in order to cooperate. Well, nothing new.

Was this not simple saber rattling? Was this show the ultimate screw-you? The Iranians using the peace talks as a cover, knowing the United States wouldn't take their actions seriously? Did they want an all-out war? Well, of course some of them did, but they had to know they'd be wiped off the face of the earth. What was going on here?

Callan said, "Do we have anyone on the ground who can confirm the movements, or are we relying on the drones?"

Zarvick held up a finger. "One moment, ma'am." He picked up the phone, and she heard him asking the question, assumed he was talking to the regional team leader at JSOC command. He hung up. "Ma'am, there is a SEAL recon team two hours away. We'd have to give them a mission parameter and get them humping asap."

"Covert assets?"

He shook his head. "It will take a day to get word to this area. I can't simply send an e-mail, you understand."

She did. The men and women on the ground in Iran and other Middle East hot spots weren't tied into the system. They had prearranged meetings and movements already being coordinated. Operating in the Middle East was difficult enough, operating in Iran's backyard was more than dangerous.

This is too well-coordinated to be anything but the precursor to a legitimate attack.

"Get the president on the line immediately. Pull him out of his meetings. Now, Commander. He needs to know the Iranians are talking out both sides of their mouths—again— but this time, they've got their reactors all lit up and glowing. Get Mossad on the phone—Ari Mizrahi. If these idiots are about to attack Israel, we need to let them know. What am I thinking? Of course they already know. Ari might be in a better position to give us some information."

The air was electric, but everyone knew what to do and they did it, calmly and efficiently. She watched views of the screens constantly changing, calls being made, computer keys typing fast and furious. Commander Zarvick handed her a secure phone. "Ma'am, here is President Bradley's secure phone."

"Callan? What is this? What is going on?"

"Iran's facility in Bushehr is lit up like a Christmas tree. I know, I know, it could be that Iran's simply saber-rattling again, but this time I've got to think they're gearing up for something." And she updated him about Bayway, told him about the power grids just going down, and the threat from COE to take out all the lights on the eastern seaboard. "Sir, I really don't like the feel of this."

Commander Zarvick said, "Arak is online now, too, ma'am."

"Did you hear that, sir? Two facilities online now. They're moving missile batteries. No troop movement as yet, but I wouldn't be surprised if it didn't happen soon."

The president sounded impatient. "Of course they're putting on their usual dog and pony show, for their own people, for their enemies and neighbors, to show they're not being ground under by the U.S. It doesn't mean anything. We're close, only inches from a comprehensive nuclear deal, Callan. Inspections and total cooperation with the UN."

"And what do we give in return?"

He paused a moment, then: "We lift all sanctions. Acknowledge them as a player."

She sat down hard. "As a nuclear state? Sir, have you lost your mind?"

"We're talking a historic moment in time, but you won't accept that, will you? Don't you see? We could put our differences aside, become allies. They want to be a part of the world stage. They're not about to compromise this opportunity; it's all simple face-saving."

Face-saving? That's how he sees it? "And Israel? How would they like that result? The headlines will scream 'U.S. and Iran BFFs, Israel Left Out in the Cold.' That's not going to go over well in Tel Aviv."

"They're here at the table, too, Callan. They're a part of this, they're participating. The two sides are talking, for the first time in years, really talking. We can bring about a serious brokered peace, one that could last decades, centuries, even."

She heard the denial of reality that marked his views toward the issue. What was really happening there that he refused to see? *Keep calm, keep calm.* "Jefferson, you've always wanted peace in the world and that's an admirable goal, a goal all of us would love to achieve. But now you must face facts. The Iranians are playing you. Hezbollah isn't there in the negotiations, and nothing will be final without their express approval. You know they aren't interested in a brokered peace, you know their stated goal is to annihilate Israel, annihilate the world, anyone who isn't Shia.

"Iran already is a nuclear state, far more advanced in their program than they've ever let on. All our briefs show this. You're talking about giving them the keys to the kingdom, and us an ocean away. You must take a step back away and think clearly—I've told you what's happening, what they're doing. You must at the very least inform the Israelis what's happening. Let them make their own decisions."

She could tell he wanted to curse her, call her hysterical, but he managed to hold his voice level. "Here's what I do know, Madam Vice President. If we walk away now, the chances of Iran's sending nukes to Israel is overwhelming. I can't let that happen. We will not have World War Three on my watch. Do you understand me? We may not achieve a lasting peace, I'll grant you that, but we will slow everything down. Let them say 'Death to America' while they're vowing they want peace, let them light up their nuclear plants to prove to the world they're the ones in control, not us. It's all mere posturing, something they do all the time and do well.

"Listen to me, this is simply the way they behave, always provocatively. They are sitting here at the peace table. They are not stupid enough to believe our shields are down during these talks."

Callan wished she could think of a *Star Trek* reference to toss back to him, but all she could think of was their nacelle cells were dead, and that wouldn't work. She forged ahead. "Sir, we're looking at a screen that says this has gone too far for their usual crap posturing. CIA and Mossad have confirmed that there's a contract out on me, and word is they believe it's come from Iran, and that means Hezbollah, of course.

"You know Hezbollah wants war, so do many of the power players in Tehran. They want to blow up the world. I told you we're already under attack here with the Bayway bombing, and at this moment we have a multistate electrical-grid issue.

"Sir, the time has come to face them down and demand to know why they're doing this, what their intentions are." *And you will see the lies flowing from their mouths.* "We can't let them get away with this. I strongly recommend you give the go-ahead to use our new cyber-attack. It's geared up and ready to go, and you know that it makes Stuxnet look like child's play. Let us unleash it, take them back offline before they do something stupid."

An alarm sounded behind her, its klaxon wail making her skin crawl. Another reactor online, more movement.

Callan felt her heart freeze. "I think they'll be taking the decision out of your hands, sir."

She heard him curse, heard some anger. *Good.* He said, "What are these yahoos playing at? I need to speak to the Israelis immediately, make sure they don't launch a preemptive counterattack. I'll get back to you, Callan, let you know if I feel we need to move to the DEFCON level or if they're really only prancing about to show how mighty they are," and he was gone.

At least he was thinking clearly now, she hoped. What would the Israelis do? She imagined they knew as well as she did what was happening and would be gearing up to defend themselves, as they always did. Would they listen to Bradley?

She hoped they would. Just in case, she called Ari.

54

KNIGHT TAKES F2

Yorktown, Virginia

Andy tapped the computer screen, cursed, yelled, "Matthew, someone's into our code. We have to hurry."

"Don't worry, we'll get it done in time."

Matthew always knew they'd have a short time frame to get the bomb into place. His bomb, not Vanessa's. He was going to turn the heat up higher, make the refinery light up the world. Turning off the lights was only the first step. Now they had to get the truck into the facility. Matthew knew it wouldn't be a problem—they were dropping off a load of tungsten for the plant, a scheduled delivery. With a lovely surprise inside.

He'd spent days working on the ID cards. The black-coded magnetic strip wouldn't work, but it didn't have to. Since the power was down there would be no way to double-check.

But they needed more than ID cards to get into the facility.

He stripped the other unconscious body of his gear and stepped into the blue coveralls. He slapped a new patch on his breast to match the name on his ID.

Andy stood, watching, already in the other worker's uniform. He'd wanted to kill them, safer that way, but Matthew said no. And why? He'd already killed at Bayway, not to mention Ian and Vanessa. Whatever. So they'd taken the time to tie them well and hide them in the woods.

Matthew looked over at Andy. He was moving his fingers, mentally writing code. He could easily imagine what Andy was thinking, probably how lovely it would be to blow up the world—all those flames shooting up into the sky—he knew him that well. He also knew Andy didn't have a clue that things could be unraveling, though Matthew felt to his gut something was wrong, the wheels were coming off. But Andy knew only what was dancing in his mad brain.

And yet again, Matthew saw Ian's face, Vanessa's face, and wondered for an instant if Darius was right, if this was the way to bring down the terrorist nations. To bring such havoc that the United States would have to act. But President Bradley—Matthew believed he'd kill his own mother before he'd make a move toward the terrorist nations. Matthew smiled. Soon it wouldn't matter if everything got screwed up. He'd still have time to deliver the ultimate blow.

One big surprise, though. He hadn't expected any of the computer agents to be on par with Andy and Gunther. It made it interesting, gave him brief periods of excitement to cover the pain and rage at Vanessa and Ian. Would things play out as he and Darius had originally planned? He didn't know about Darius, but his part would play out perfectly. He was ready, eager. Darius had promised him it was all set up, only a matter of time.

He said to Andy, "Come on. Get in the truck. We have to hurry."

Matthew drove, Andy navigated. Within five minutes they pulled into the drive that led to the entrance of the plant.

With the power down, every check would be by hand. As expected, there were two guards stationed at the entrance. They looked alarmed, as well they should, since the news was out that the power was down all over Virginia and no one knew why. One of the men stepped forward, stretched out his hand.

Matthew braked the truck and rolled down the window. The guard said, "I can't believe you still came considering what's happening. Where do you need to go?"

Matthew unclipped his ID from his shirt pocket, handed it out the window, and checked his manifest. "South Four-G. Got a shipment of tungsten to drop off."

"With all the power out, it might be a while before they can open the bay doors." He handed the ID back. He'd barely glanced at it. "This is a pisser. You got any idea what's going on? Did you see any trucks working on the lines on your way in?"

"Nope, I don't have a clue what's going on, been driving forever."

"Well, keep to the lanes, watch for the Secret Service guys. They're crawling all over the place getting ready for the president's big speech here tomorrow. If it happens, that is, and sure it won't unless they fix this power mess."

"Got it." Matthew rolled up the window and reminded himself to breathe.

Andy was flushed with pride. "Imagine, Matthew, everyone's afraid, isn't that great? They're afraid because of me. I like that, I really do. Don't you think this plant would make a fine burn?"

"Yeah, everyone's afraid because of you, Andy. Now, keep an eye out. How goes the outage?"

Andy pulled his laptop from back under the seat. "It's all the way to the Pennsylvania Turnpike. It's slowing down, though. Whoever is into the back doors is good, but we have time. Even if they counteract it now, it would take at least a few hours to get the grids reset and the power back on. Am I good, or what?"

"You and Gunther. Make sure it's down long enough so we can place the bomb."

"I'm doing my job. You do yours," Andy said. "More me than Gunther; you think about it. Hey, everything would be perfect if you hadn't gotten me shot."

Patience, patience. "Right," Matthew said, "and you're the idiot who left the memory sticks behind, you're the one who ran when the FBI saw you. If you'd played it cool, you would have been fine. But you panicked and got *yourself* shot." How many times had he said this already? His hand fisted on the steering wheel to keep from punching Andy, maybe knocking him out of the truck and running over him, the idiot.

The little idiot pouted, no other word for it.

"Matthew, you're going to have to place the bomb yourself. I can't limp in there, now, can I? I'd draw attention. The police aren't stupid; you know they're looking for us. This place is crawling with Secret Service, too. I'm staying in the truck."

"Grow a pair, Andy. We're in this together." He sounded calm, in control. Wasn't he the Bishop?

"I don't know you anymore. I mean, lots of girls screw guys. So Vanessa played you, Matthew. She played all of us. She was really good and she hurt your feelings. You shot her, killed her dead, paid her back, so don't take it out on me."

Matthew saw the blood flowing into her hair, turning it stiff and black. He couldn't help it, couldn't stop it this time. He struck out with his right fist and punched Andy in the jaw. Andy's head snapped against the window with a crack.

Andy yelled, "You bastard, you hit me, you hurt me. Without me, you'd be back in Belfast jerking around with Ian." He began to rock back and forth as he held his jaw.

Matthew whispered through clenched teeth, "Listen to me, you moron. You will do as I say or I will cut out your tongue and leave you bleeding next to the bombs with a sign nailed to your chest saying you planned the whole thing. Then I will drive to your mother's house and do the same to her. Do you understand?"

Andy didn't say a word. He turned to stare out the window. Matthew thought he might be crying.

"Answer me," Matthew repeated quietly. "Do you understand?"

Andy put up his hands to ward off another blow, drew his legs up to his chest. "Yes, yes, of course. I'll do it. Stop threatening me."

"Then stop trying my patience, Andy. Stop your whining, your mouthing off. There's too much at stake. We've got to focus."

He pulled the truck to a stop. A man in a black suit hurried over. "Don't screw it up," Matthew whispered between clenched teeth. He got out of the cab and said, in a thick Virginian accent, "Hiya."

"Papers, please. We'll need to check the truck, too."

"No worries." He handed over the clipboard with the bill of lading on it. "Droppin' the load off." Matthew cocked his head a bit so the baseball cap hid his face.

I'm a good old boy doing my job. Don't make me kill you.

The agent was thorough. After five minutes, though, he waved them through.

Matthew got back into the rig, slammed the door, and slapped the rig in gear. He drove toward their spot, careful not to pop the air brakes as they went down a slight hill.

Andy said, "I'm setting the timer, Matthew. I'll be ready to drop the code."

55

ROOK TO E1

The attack was deep, moving fast, overloading the grids as they watched, threatening to take down even more power. Nicholas had five guys working on each leg of the code, but no one was making any progress.

Martin said, "We're not getting it done. Do you have any more ideas how to stop the code from spreading, Nicholas?"

Think. Think. Be the code.

The code was everything. Gunther was the architect. He'd built something new, so new Nicholas had never seen it before, but there was a key to unlock every code. He simply needed to find the way in. *Think, think.* And then an idea sparked. "I need to get into Gunther's server, look at his code from the inside out."

Savich said, "Nicholas, doesn't Menard have Gunther's computers? You can access them remotely."

"Savich, you've nailed it. That's it. Mike, get me Menard. Right now."

Mike was fast. "It's on speaker. What else can I do?"

"You can cross all your fingers."

Menard said, "Nicholas, I have no more news for you. I—"

"Pierre, forgive me for interrupting. I need access to Gunther Ansell's computers. Can you get me in?"

He blew out a breath and Nicholas could picture his Gallic shrug. "I can try, but it will be *trés difficile*. Give me some time."

"We have no time, Pierre. I need in there, right now. Who can I speak to locally? Who's working the case?"

"Hold a moment, I will conference you in."

The phone went silent. Martin said from behind him, "What are you thinking?"

"Gunther always wrote a special key to his code. It's something we all do, in case of catastrophe. If I can hijack his system I might be able to find the key. Without it, we can't stop the attack quickly enough. It continues to grow, the power outages are spreading. The power could be out for days at this rate, and with no one prepared, the results could be devastating."

Menard said, "Nicholas, I have on the line the head of Munich's police technology intervention unit, Lieutenant Elsie Splatz. She is the one who has been working on compiling the information requested in the warrant you provided. She can help you."

A woman's voice came clear on the line, accented, but her English was excellent. "Special Agent Drummond, I have the hard drives of Gunther Ansell's computers in my office. We have been searching them, but his security is very good. We have not been able to get back his second layer of firewalls."

"Give me access to your servers, I'll look myself."

"I am sorry, Agent Drummond, but that will not be possible. Your warrants have not cleared."

Mike rolled her eyes at him, and he smiled for the first time in an hour. He said, "We certainly wouldn't want a little thing like errant paperwork to get in the way of an international cyber-attack."

"Your sarcasm is duly noted. What would you like me to do?"

"Look for a file called 'Roman.' It will be in the subfolders of an encrypted drive called 'Fever.'"

A few taps. "Yes, I see it here. As you say, it is encrypted. We have not been able to get through this firewall."

"Stop trying. Every bit of code you throw at it is making it tighten down more instead of less. I can access it. Send it to me."

"You do not know what is in this file. It could launch another virus, another attack."

Nicholas said, his voice calm, "Lieutenant, it's Gunther's key file. Trust me. I know how he works. I know how to get into the drive, into the files, through the encryption, but I need it in front of me to do so. It's too complex to walk you through over the phone. We're losing time. Please, send it along now."

Menard said, "I will take responsibility, Lieutenant, and FedPol will send the appropriate paperwork as soon as possible. Give him what he wants."

"Yes, sir. I have sent it through our secure network. You will have it momentarily."

Nicholas's laptop dinged. "I have it now. Thank you. Please stay on the line for a moment in case this doesn't work."

Nicholas clicked on the file, put a fresh thumb drive in, and executed the commands. Everyone in the room watched as the code unspooled, the drive whirring. The screen went black, then began shattering incrementally, breaking in half, then into fourths, then eighths, then sixteenths, then suddenly spiraling into a 3-D cornucopia-shaped web of complex numbers and letters. It was incredible and baffling, and not for the first time, Mike regretted that her background was in psychology, not computer science.

"This blows my mind," Martin said, and was there a bit of excitement in that calm voice?

Savich grinned. "Mine, too."

"I'm in," Nicholas said. "I'm past the firewall."

The numbers swirled around, spinning so quickly Mike had no idea how he could follow them. Nicholas suddenly slapped the screen. "There you are, you little bugger." He clicked his mouse and every screen in the room mimicked his.

He said, "Martin, this is the code we need to disrupt to stop the attack. Here's the protocol that should take it down."

Martin shouted, "People, go!"

The room began to hum. Nicholas leaned back in the chair and gave Mike a huge upside-down grin.

Savich slapped him on the back. "Good job, Nicholas, Martin, all of you. Let's hope it works."

Pierre shouted, "You have it, Nicholas?"

"Yes, we've nailed it. We have the code and we're stopping the attack as we speak. Thank you, Pierre, thank you, Lieutenant, for all your help. Pierre, I'll send the paperwork along as soon as I'm able."

Menard gave a charming snort. "Paperwork, from you? I will believe it when I see it. There is still paperwork missing from the Koh-i-Noor case."

"Not so loud, Pierre. Savich might hear you."

Menard laugh. "Hello, Agent Savich. Good luck, Nicholas. Michaela, I hope we will see you again very soon. *Au revoir.*"

Nicholas stared at the screen in front of him. As his finger traced a length of code along the screen, he felt Mike's hand on his shoulder, felt her lean in, and her hair brushed against his face. *Jasmine,* he thought. *Jasmine.*

"It's beautiful," she said, her breath on his cheek.

Yes, beautiful. Nicholas cleared his throat. He said, "Gunther was an artist. I will miss him."

Mike smacked his shoulder. "Get a grip, Nicholas, this maniac caused billions of dollars in damage, and nearly gave all of us a heart attack, and you're admiring his art?"

Savich laughed. "I suppose I will, too. Sorry, Mike."

Nicholas said, "You have to respect the enemy, first rule of warfare."

"You're both nuts."

Sherlock stepped into the room. "If all is peachy keen again, then why aren't the lights on?"

Martin called out, "That will take a while. Once we kick the intruders out of the system, the power companies will have to turn the grids back on gradually so they don't overload the system again."

Nicholas stood up and stretched. He felt good. It was a major save. He shook Martin's hand, yelled his thanks to everyone in the room, and let Savich pull them both out of the IT room.

"Listen up. Mr. Maitland called. Iran's nuclear facilities are online, and Vice President Sloane is, needless to say, closely monitoring everything. We may be called upon to help launch a cyber-attack."

Nicholas said, "What? What's this? Aren't they all in peace talks in Geneva?"

"The talks have been suspended. The president is coming home early. And listen to this. POTUS's schedule has him and the vice president giving a speech at the former Yorktown Refinery tomorrow."

Mike cocked her head to one side, said slowly, "The president's speech tomorrow at Yorktown—it's all about clean energy, energy independence, probably more, but that's the gist and that's why we took Yorktown off our COE threat matrix after they announced they were changing from refining to being simply a depot. The move is in answer to the president's green-initiative program. It was bought by a private investor who is bringing all the facilities up to current environmental standards. It's what he's announcing tomorrow, and I'll bet he was going to announce success with the peace accords, too."

"Probably, though it sounds like that's off the table. What are you getting at, Mike?"

Nicholas was watching her. He recognized the look on her face—focused inward, brain sorting through scenarios at the speed of light—it was mental leap time. She said, "A lot of people in the oil industry would be invited to this event, correct? The people from ConocoPhillips and the other companies who were part of the cyber-attack last night would be invited?"

Savich said, "You think the cyber-attack was more than sowing chaos in the oil companies, don't you?"

"Yes. The fact is that COE downloaded a ton of stuff off the servers. They could easily know exactly who's going to be at Yorktown. They'd also know the president's exact schedule, and very possibly the vice president's schedule as well. But you know, I bet what they really wanted was the plant plans.

"If they bombed Yorktown, not only could they take out the oil company leaders, they could take out the president and vice president. Yorktown is their target."

She grinned maniacally. "And now try this on for size. I think it makes sense—that third unidentified Middle Eastern man seen at the apartment in Brooklyn could very well be the assassin Zahir Damari. I think he'll be at Yorktown to make sure the vice president is blown to bits, and if she isn't, he'll assassinate her himself. Maybe the president as well."

Nicholas knew she was right. He loved her brain.

Savich said, "Mike, it's the first question we'll ask at Langley. Come on, let's go. The CIA is ready for us."

"I have a feeling," Mike said as she double-stepped to keep up, "that the CIA already knows this and now they have to admit to us that Damari was part of COE. The bastards."

56

ROOK TAKES E1

Catoctin Mountain

There'd been rain recently, and that was good luck for him. A thick layer of wet leaves mulched the trail and kept his steps quiet and obscured. Zahir had walked for half a day without seeing another human being, but now, as twilight began to creep in around him, the guards appeared, silent as wraiths, walking alongside him in concert, weapons at the ready, the dogs tight on their leads, one hundred yards away. Separated by space, and a large electrified fence.

He followed the path of the fence, listening to the static hum, like a hive of bees off in the distance. It made his teeth hurt and his jaw clench. He shook his head, trying to get the aggravating sound out of his ears, but he needed it as a guide, needed the buzz to tell him when to move.

He inched closer and closer to the fence, staggering each step forward to coincide with the steps of the guards. He'd covered himself in deer scent, thought he actually smelled like a goat, but these dogs were trained to the scent of man, not beast, so wouldn't alert unless they saw him moving. He was hungry, but food would have to wait.

He checked his watch and settled against the trunk of a tree. He was ahead of schedule; the walk in had gone easier than planned. He double-checked his GPS, and yes, he was in the right place.

Since he was a control freak, he had to admit he didn't like having to rely on Matthew and Andy to fulfill their end of the bargain, but he was philosophical, everything was out of his hands for the moment.

I told you to do that but you didn't!

His father's voice, sounding now in his head, as it did sometimes over the years. When he'd heard the old man had collapsed of a fatal stroke five years before, he'd rejoiced and gone to his favorite pub in London and bought everyone there pints of Guinness.

Zahir had always been different, unique, that's what his mother always told him, touching him, kissing him, praising him while his father looked on, disgust on his face.

He remembered he'd done his best to impress the old man, with his gray beard and mustache, his heavy jowls and his gap-toothed smile that wasn't a smile at all, more a smirk, recognition that he was the only one in this household that was important, the only one with the power and that was because he had money, lots of it, and he ruled. "My darling, you are unique, you will do great things." His mother, his beautiful fragile mother, who'd died when he was only eight years old.

Since he was the fourth son, he always knew he was worth less than spit to his father. And when he was eighteen, he realized his mother had been right. He was unique. He was chosen. God had given him a gift. He was clever, more clever and shrewd than his crude, peasant elder brothers, more cunning and more sly than his weak, whimpering sisters. Certainly more brilliant than his venal, grasping father, with his love of money and custom planes. Was he more astute than even his quiet, beautiful British mother, who'd given up her world to come live in the pit of Hell? He didn't know. Sometimes he'd suspected she could have ruled the world, if only she'd been given the chance. He found himself thanking her again, as he had so many times throughout his life. She'd taught him perfect English, since he was, after all, an English citizen, and taught him pride and freedom. He'd joined the coalition forces, knowing, somehow, it was where he belonged. They trained him, they taught him to kill, to blow up people, to shoot from a distance. With his gift, they soon made him a perfect killing machine.

He was unique, and now he knew what it all meant.

It didn't take long to develop a reputation. And with it came the money.

It never ceased to amaze him how many people wanted other people dead. And how rich he could get taking care of their problems for them.

And now this, surely the pinnacle of his life's work. He had to admit he was still amazed at the complexity of Rahbar and Hadawi's plan. So many moving parts, all the pieces having to dovetail at exactly the right time. He wondered how many more men in Iran wanted to lay waste to the world, consequences be damned. Centuries-deep hatred made them blind and deaf to all but death to their enemies.

That nutter Iranian colonel Rahbar had texted him that the gold coin Zahir had sent the month before had been turned over to his hand-picked scientist, brilliant and trustworthy. He was loyal to Rahbar. The Iranian scientist was in awe of Matthew's genius, the way he'd combined certain elements, deleted and adjusting others to produce a payload to cause extraordinary damage. And the formula was really quite simple, but his genius in imagining this work of art had left him in awe.

And the colonel had laughed, said the stage was set and the Americans were doubtless scrambling around, unsure what to do, everyone on edge and just wait. Just wait. And the timing was perfect. As planned, the president of the United States had left Geneva in a huff aboard *Air Force One* to return to Washington.

Everything was on track and Zahir could see the colonel rubbing his hands.

Zahir found it delicious that the brilliant ideologue Matthew Spenser, hate-filled, yet so very naïve, would be the lynchpin. He'd given Zahir—Darius—a coin bomb for a souvenir, now being disassembled in Iran, and Zahir had stolen a second one, currently residing in his pocket.

Even though the coin he'd sent to Rahbar hadn't as yet been tested, Zahir had known to his soul it would work, and he'd made doubly sure at Bayway, and when he'd texted colonel Rahbar with the result, he'd been elated.

Zahir fingered the coin in his pocket, smiled, and thought of Matthew's finger pressing the button that would signal the beginning of the end of the earth as anyone knew it.

Yes, all his bases were covered, all contingencies dealt with, as the Americans said, and because the FBI could close in on Matthew before he could act, Zahir had his backup plan firmly in place. In fact, he rather hoped he would have to use it. More drama, more impact, the killing blow.

He sat back against an oak tree and closed his eyes, listening to the guards' footsteps, their low voices, the dogs. Not much longer to wait.

He heard a dull thwap, then the buzzing stopped. Matthew had succeeded. The fence was down.

Shouts from the guards, movement all around. Now was the time. He had to move.

He knew their protocols: the guards would leave the fence in this quadrant. The left flank guard would cover the area of two while the guard closest to the camp turned on the generators. He watched him walk away, gun cradled in his arms, the dog following, tail wagging, liking the change of pace.

Three steps, two, one.

The guard was one hundred feet away now, the dog lunging toward the path.

Zahir ran out of the woods, went up and over the fence.

He lost his footing, landed hard on the other side, scrambled away as quietly as possible. He'd knocked out his breath, but the guard hadn't seen him.

He was inside the perimeter.

When he could breathe easily again, he moved carefully, slowly, always out of sight. When he got close to the farthermost cabin, he put the earwig in, and sure enough, as Matthew had promised, the voices came through clear as a bell.

The door was unlocked, and he eased inside. No one would be out this far, they'd already done a sweep earlier. According to the notes he had, this area was checked only twice a day. He adjusted the earwig. He'd have plenty of time to move, since he could hear them coming now.

He reset his watch, started the timer.

Forty-eight hours and counting.

Tuesday
6 p.m.–Midnight

57

QUEEN TO D8 CHECK

Washington, D.C.

Driving through the city without power was eerie. Police were out in force, helping people try to get home. Savich navigated through the intersections carefully in Sherlock's stalwart Volvo. Mike rode up front; Nicholas was in back with a laptop in his lap, monitoring the situation in Richmond.

"We've arrested the attack. I have a note here from Adam Pearce. He's working on the threat assessment with Juno. I—"

Savich looked in the rearview. "What is it, Nicholas? You have something?"

"The risk assessment is bothering me. As you know, Dominion Virginia Power recently had one. They put in new firewalls, new safeguards, so an attack like this shouldn't be able to happen. Yet it did, and it quickly became worst-case. You know Juno is very respected in the cyber-world. I don't understand how they could have screwed up this badly."

"You said yourself Gunther Ansell's coding was world-class," Mike said.

"I did, Mike, and it was. But to exploit a flaw and get the code in to begin with, you must get into a back door, whether one you create, or one left for emergency access—should something like this ever happen. We mentioned it and now I'm wondering if Juno's programmers left a back door for their assessment and Andy Tate was smart enough to use it."

He went quiet again.

It took Savich a few more minutes to navigate the overrun streets to George Washington University Hospital. No Metro, no trains, so the lines at the bus stops were hundreds deep, people standing in the street because the sidewalks were full. A nightmare security risk.

With the electricity off, the hospital looked strangely deserted. Savich parked and put his FBI placard on the dash. As they walked to the front doors, Mike suddenly stopped, turned, whispered to Nicholas, "We're being watched."

"Well, yes," Nicholas said. "I make two cameras on the second and third floors, and a car two rows over in the handicap spot."

"No trust from our CIA compadres," Savich said. "It never fails to amaze me."

"Maybe they're afraid someone might be coming after Vanessa," Mike said.

"That's the more optimistic view," Savich said.

Vanessa's uncle, Carlton Grace, waited for them in the lobby. Mike saw the look of Vanessa in his face, the long nose, square jaw, family traits. Where Vanessa was beautiful, though, Grace was homely. Comfortable, sort of wrinkled. A guy you wouldn't give a second look to walking by on the street. He disappeared.

The perfect look for a spy. Had Vanessa's father looked the same way?

He introduced himself, shook hands with all three of them. "Thank you for coming. Please don't ask any questions until we're inside. The room is clean so we can speak freely."

Nicholas said, "Why do you have so many eyes on us?"

Grace smiled. "I wasn't spying on you, Agent Drummond. It's Matthew Spenser, the man who tried to murder Vanessa. If he found out she's alive, he could try to finish the job. I have no intention of letting that happen. There is more, of course. Come with me."

Savich thought that was good to hear, but he didn't know whether or not to believe him.

Grace led them through oddly lit halls. The generators were running fine; the power didn't flicker.

They turned a corner and there was Craig Swanson lounging against a wall, arms crossed. His face was bruised and his nose was bridged with white tape. When he saw Nicholas he straightened like a shot.

Nicholas grinned at him like a bandit. *So to add insult to injury, you got a real dressing down, didn't you, mate?*

He would swear Mike growled as she passed by.

Swanson called out, "Hey, Agent Caine. Good to see you again so soon. No warm hellos for me?"

"Yeah, big hello, Craig. I'd like to belt you, but it looks like you really can't take much more."

He automatically touched his fingers to the white tape, then looked at Nicholas once more. "You broke my nose, you flippin' Brit bastard."

Nicholas shrugged. "I told you to stop fighting me, mate, gave you lots of chances to back off. It's your own fault."

"That's enough," Carl Grace said. "Status, Craig?"

The aggression switch flipped off instantly. "Sir, Vanessa is awake and hurting, but holding it together. No one's come near her who shouldn't."

Grace nodded and Swanson knocked once, then opened the door.

Vanessa saw Mike Caine first, blond hair pulled back from her face in a fat ponytail, black biker boots, black pants and jacket, and a nice black eye. From Craig? He'd told her he'd gotten into it with a couple of FBI pussies in New York. But his nose, she'd asked him? Two against one, he'd said. But now she didn't believe him. Mike Caine could wipe the floor with Craig. And only two days before she'd looked as alive, her stride as confident, ready to take on the world.

"Michaela." She realized she hadn't said her name aloud, only thought it—soft sounding, that name. She remembered she'd initially thought Mike Caine was a country bumpkin, but that hadn't lasted long. What she was, Vanessa had realized, was fierce, committed, and focused. She remembered meeting Mike's parents, her father a big solid cop with crinkly blue eyes, high up in the Omaha Police Department, and her mom, the Gorgeous Rebecca, Mike had told her she'd always been called. Wow, what a knockout, and Mike was a young version of her. She'd been funny, too, making jokes about how old everything was at Yale, how the bathrooms needed a major overhaul. Odd she'd remember that now.

Mike didn't appear to have changed at all since Vanessa had seen her last—what was it? Yes, eight years ago at Yale.

Two big men followed her in—one she recognized from Bayway, Nicholas Drummond; the other she'd never seen before. He looked hard as nails and tough, a man who understood his world and controlled it, a man you didn't cross, if your brain was working.

As for Drummond, she could feel the pull of him, feel the intensity pouring off him, feel his powerful focus on her, no one else in the room. He looked like he'd never back down, and she knew he'd never stop. Look what he'd done to Craig, and Craig was no pushover.

Their faces blurred and she blinked double time until they cleared. She hated the meds but knew without them she'd be whimpering in the fetal position. She had to be strong, she had to focus as much as Drummond, she had to get through this. She wanted to tell them everything, because only then could she let go and rest.

Her uncle closed the door quietly, walked up to her bed, gently took her hand in his. "Nessa, these are the

FBI agents I told you were coming. I've told them you would try to answer all their questions, but if you can't go on at any point, we'll stop immediately, all right?"

She nodded, only a slight movement, but he smiled.

Carl Grace introduced the three of them.

"Special Agent Savich, he's the head of the CAU—that's Criminal Apprehension Unit—here in D.C. This gentleman is Special Agent Nicholas Drummond and his partner Special Agent Mike Caine, both of the New York office."

Vanessa tried to smile at them, but her mouth didn't want to move. She managed a whisper. "Agent Drummond, I've heard of you. As for Mike, hello. How are you?"

"I'm good, Vanessa." Mike stepped up and took her other hand, gave it a very light squeeze. A thin sheet was pulled up to Vanessa's neck, but the thick bandage around her chest was a grim reminder of what had happened to her. She looked bruised, Mike thought, through and through, as if her body were still wondering whether or not to keep going. And she looked so very tired, her face nearly as pale as the hospital sheets. Her beautiful red hair was lank around her head. Mike knew the meds were keeping her with them, but only barely.

"So you've heard of my partner, have you?"

Vanessa tried for a smile and managed a small one. "I gotta say, Mike, the guy is too hot for his own good. And that cleft in the chin, I've always been a sucker for those." She didn't say he looked like the predator he was, hard, no-nonsense, probably ate nails for breakfast, like Savich.

"It's a pleasure, Agent Grace," Nicholas said. "Mike's

told me a lot about you. As for the hole in my chin, it does make shaving a bother. Are you up for some questions?"

"Yes, there's so much. Then I'm going to sleep for a month, well, maybe two months." She closed her eyes for a moment. She hadn't realized it would hurt so much to talk. Who cared? It was nothing compared to the Mack truck squatting on her chest. She could do this, she had to do this.

58

BISHOP TO F8

Savich pulled a chair up close, took her hand in his. "I know you very nearly died, Agent Grace. I know it's a miracle you're still with us. All of us are very pleased that you are. Your uncle is right, if you can't go on, you simply tell us, and we'll let you rest." He paused for a moment, gauging how cogent she was. *Enough,* he thought. "Thank you for agreeing to answer our questions." Savich then stood and backed away.

Nicholas came a bit closer, looked down at the woman who should by rights be dead twice over, what with the bullet to the chest and the fall from the burning building.

"Agent Grace told us you've been undercover in COE for the past four months. Can you tell us exactly what your mission was?"

"It all started with the chatter about a special new bomb under development, said to be undetectable by any of our scanners. The genius making this bomb, we found out, is Matthew Spenser, also known as the Bishop. He was operating out of Belfast at that time.

"I posed as a bomb expert, which I am, and an IRA bomber I worked with, Ian McGuire, introduced me to Spenser and I joined his group, COE. My mission was to steal the specs once Matthew perfected the bomb. He showed it to me, told me how it would be undetectable, and so small, you can't believe how small they are. Gold coins, the size of a fifty-cent piece.

"But Matthew was very secretive, very careful, with everyone. He only told each person in the group what they needed to know to pull off the next bombing."

"Undetectable bombs," Mike repeated quietly. "I can't imagine how that's even possible."

"I know they're made of gold and tungsten, with carbon-fiber hulls, which wouldn't ever set off the scanners. You could walk onto a plane with one in your pocket, leave it in the magazine pocket, and walk away, and bring the whole thing down, or you could leave it in a coffee shop, or a police station or a stadium. But they were theoretical only, until now. There are, of course, other components I couldn't find out about. And then he perfected it."

Savich leaned forward. "Bayway was a test?"

"Yes. I'd built a bomb as well, and that was the second blast, designed to destroy, not kill." Her breathing hitched. "I didn't know, didn't know. How many workers were killed?"

Mike said, "Fifteen people, and the blast destroyed the refinery. I'd say Spenser's bomb is ready for market."

Savich asked, "How did Matthew Spenser find out you were an undercover agent?"

Vanessa whispered, "When we got back to the apartment in Brooklyn, I knew I had to tell Uncle Carl immediately what was happening. I was in the bathroom, sending him a text, and Matthew came in to bully me. When Uncle Carl's message came back, he heard the ding on my phone. I tried to talk my way out of it—the message was ambiguous—but it didn't work. Ian tried to protect me, and Matthew killed him, then he killed me, or he thought he had. Then he set the apartment on fire with Andy's special gasoline mixes. I managed to get out but fell off the fire escape. And that's all I remember until I woke up here."

She lay pale and silent now, staring up at Savich. She licked her dry lips, drank a bit more water. Finally, she whispered, "When he looked at me, I knew it was the end. His eyes were dead. I guess it was the only way he could deal with the ultimate betrayal, both Ian and me."

Vanessa couldn't get spit in her mouth. She nodded again toward the water carafe. Why did her mouth feel like a desert?

Grace immediately placed the straw against her lips.

He looked down at Vanessa, his niece, his brother's only child, then up at the agents. "We need to stop here for a moment. Nessa, while you were in surgery, we realized Darius is actually Zahir Damari, the assassin hired to kill the vice president."

Savich nodded to Mike. "She figured this out already. My question is why you people at the CIA didn't think this information was important enough to pass it along to us?"

Grace shot a look of approval to Mike, splayed his hands in front of him. "Please understand, everything has been moving so fast, we only just made the connection ourselves, plus I wanted to tell you in person. We knew about Zahir Damari, but we had no idea he was the same man as this Darius who joined up with COE. This wasn't a matter for phones, you see."

For a moment Vanessa couldn't get a breath, couldn't think her way through it, then said, "Darius, he's really Zahir Damari? I knew Darius wasn't his real name, but I didn't expect this."

Nicholas said, "How did he hook up with Spenser and your group?"

"He showed up at our camp in South Tahoe, a million in cash, and he told us his name was Darius Coles, and he went to Oxford, which was one of the reasons Matthew talked to him in the first place. Matthew went to Oxford, too. But the way he hooked Matthew was that he claimed he'd lost friends in the July 2005 London terrorist bombing. He appeared to be genuinely surprised to learn that Matthew had lost his family. All a ploy, of course."

Grace said, "Based on Vanessa's information, we ran Darius Coles through every known database, and a few off-book ones. It was a false identity."

Mike said slowly, "Now all the pins are lined up. Zahir came to COE, to Spenser, because, like you, he wanted the bomb for his clients."

"The clients would be Iran and Hezbollah," Carl Grace said. "This chatter about the amazing new bomb the CIA heard about has been heard elsewhere, obviously.

But now we believe Zahir's mission was two-pronged: to get Spenser's bomb and kill the vice president."

Nicholas said, "May I have a crack at the photo and the identity? Savich and I have designed a new update for the NGA database utilizing a different method for identifying underlying bone structure. Perhaps we'll be able to find something that will allow us to identify him."

Grace nodded. "We were hoping you could help. I'll have it for you when we're done here."

Vanessa said, "But how can that be right? Zahir was hired to assassinate the vice president? Because she's so against the peace talks? Why would Iran and Hezbollah care? I mean, the president is in charge, he's the one who insisted on the peace talks, he's the one who believes if he can make them happy, they won't continue to threaten Israel and the West."

Savich looked at her pale face, her eyes losing focus, and knew she couldn't hang on for much longer. "All sound points, Agent Grace, but think about who these people are, what they are. Now, one more question and then we'll leave you in peace. Where is Matthew Spenser now? And Andy Tate? And the rest of the members of the COE?"

"With Ian dead, I think all the other COE members have already run for cover. None of them is stupid, most are online, anyway. So that would leave only Matthew and Andy."

Savich continued, "If Spenser hadn't shot you, what would you be doing today?"

"Working with Andy to comb through the data they stole from the cyber-attack on the oil companies—verify the schedules for Yorktown, the president's, the vice president's, find out all the visiting oil company representatives coming, itineraries, hotels, everything. But most important was getting the Yorktown plant blueprints."

Mike had nailed it.

Savich said, "So Matthew plans to blow up Yorktown when all these people are there, using his new bomb?"

Vanessa closed her eyes, swallowed. "I don't know. Maybe. If he does, it will be worse than Bayway. I think he only used a small part of one of his bombs there. With the plans, Matthew and Andy will know how to get into Yorktown and plant one of his bombs. You have to find him, stop him." She tried to press Mike's hand, but didn't have the strength.

A low, angry male voice sounded behind them. "You will all leave now. As you can see, Ms. Grace is gravely injured. All of you, out, now."

It was Dr. Pruitt, her surgeon. They stepped back to watch him lean over her, listen to her heart, take her pulse, then fiddle with the IV. In the next moment she was asleep. Pruitt turned on them. "If she is well enough, you may see her tomorrow, but not until then. Do I make myself clear?"

He left the room without waiting for an answer, Craig Swanson following him out. Carl Grace said, his voice lowered, "I know you have more questions, need more information to make sense of all this. I brought some recordings Vanessa has sent me over the past four months. We'll go in the corner, keep our voices down, and listen until you're satisfied you've got the full picture."

But first Savich called the Secret Service to warn the detail searching Yorktown.

59

KNIGHT TAKES E1

Grace hit play on his tablet, and they heard Vanessa's voice, calm and strong.

Darius came to COE with a bag of money and the Devil's tongue. Don't get me wrong, Darius wasn't a hammer, he was subtle about it, slow, easy, methodical. It took me a while to realize that he was poisoning Matthew, convincing him to stop targeting oil refiners because it did no good. He needed to target people. And he needed to finish creating his magic gold coins—his bombs—and do it quickly. It was time to strike.

She paused a moment, then:

How to describe him so you'll understand, Uncle Carl? Matthew Spenser was an idealist, a genius, a man with a bright future, until the terrorist bomb that killed his family in London on July 7, 2005, changed everything. He became committed to destroying all our ties to terrorist nations and to him that meant stopping all Middle East oil imports into the West. His plan was to destroy infrastructure because without funding from oil wealth, big organized terrorist groups couldn't continue. Then Darius came and he changed.

Darius talked to Matthew day and night about how he could leave his mark, how he could attack the terrorists by taking out the people who wanted to protect them, fund them, empathize with them. Darius convinced him the Americans, our own president, wanted to make peace with them, and yet our president, instead of doing his job, protecting the American people, protecting our allies, is at a supposed peace table in Geneva, drinking tea with these soulless maniacs, and working on diplomatic solutions, ridiculous, all of it.

Matthew works well into the night on his bomb, but he won't tell me how close he is to perfecting it, won't even tell Ian, his very best friend.

Carl Grace hit stop, loaded in another recording.

I overheard Darius and Matthew talking. Darius was supposed to meet someone, get a package. They never discussed what it was. I listened and knew the pickup had fallen through and now he had another,

*at a diner in Baltimore, the Silver Corner. I saw his
contact once when he delivered some information
about the grids to Darius, but I couldn't find out
his name. I took photos of him. I hope you can
identify him.*

Carl Grace punched off the recording. "We do have
his photos and have been running them, but we've come
up empty so far. I'll get his photos to you, see what you
can find. The secondary pickup for the diner was for
yesterday. We're getting the video feeds as I speak."

He turned the recording back on. "This is three days
before Bayway."

*Uncle Carl, last week, Matthew was going on about
how we must change the course of history, that
political discourse is now absurd because the
Iranians are about to eliminate half the world with
their nukes, ISIS is on the move, Al Qaeda, the
Taliban, the worst of the worst, want to kill us all.
He spoke of Israel, their people living in constant
danger and conflict.*

*He said over and over that these people had been
killing each other for centuries and they weren't
about to stop now, it was hardwired in their DNA.
They still lived in the Middle Ages, not the modern
world. Talk was worth nothing to them. The only
thing they understood was violence, and force. And
then he pounded the table and said again, "violence
and force." The way he said it, it scared me to my*

toes. And then he said, "I have to be the agent of change so we can save our culture, our people, our lives."

Uncle Carl, Darius has changed him utterly. He's different. I don't know what he's capable of anymore. Remember I told you before my first test with Matthew at Grangemouth in Scotland, he emphasized that no one could be hurt. No one. But now? I don't know.

In a couple of days, we hit Bayway. I've got my bomb ready, but I have this feeling that Matthew has perfected his bomb and this is where he wants to test it, a bigger explosion, a bigger statement. Our contact is a night supervisor named Larry Reeves. Matthew paid him a ton of money to give us the plans. It's how he's always worked, as you know— pay off someone close to the site to get the blueprints, and find the best places to plant bombs for maximum damage. Sometimes he gets access online, sometimes they bring physical prints.

Nicholas raised a hand and Carl turned off the recorder.

"I can't believe you didn't warn us Bayway was coming."

Grace said, "It wasn't my decision. We stepped up their security. No one was supposed to get hurt."

Mike wanted to stomp him, stomp all of those who'd made such a stupid decision. "Save us from our own law enforcement. Fifteen dead, Agent Grace, and even the one who sold out, Larry Reeves, is dead, killed in the very blast he helped facilitate. I know you heard three FBI agents were murdered as well, in an informant's house. His name was Mr. Richard Hodges, a very nice man who overheard Reeves mouthing off in a bar about how much money he was coming into, and he called us, and died with the agents protecting him. His wife had died three years before of cancer. He ate bacon sandwiches for dinner. And the three FBI agents, all of them married with children. And now all those kids have no fathers. And you people let the whole thing happen. You stepped up security? And that's all you've got to say about it?"

Carl Grace said, "There are no simple answers, Agent Caine, you know that. Compromises must be made, to gain the greater good, sacrifices must be made." He saw she would explode and raised a hand. "I'm very sorry for that decision, the whole series of decisions, including leaving Vanessa in place.

"Now, I believe it was Zahir Damari who murdered the informant and the three FBI agents."

Nicholas said, "It makes sense. He was tying up loose ends."

Savich said, "We will sort out who's to blame later. Please keep going, Agent Grace."

Carl turned the recording back on.

Uncle Carl, it's coming down to the wire. I believe Matthew when he laughs and says his bomb will be so much bigger, more powerful than anything I'd ever put together with my pathetic Semtex. When, not if, he perfects them, he could sell the formula,

and any country could use it against us in
unimaginable ways. I must get my hands on his
notebooks, I must.

Carl turned off the recorder. "That's the last I heard from her until the emergency text she sent to me after Bayway. I told her to get out, but it was already too late. And then he tried to kill her." His voice was flat, steady, but his eyes were hard with pain and hate. He said after a moment, "Do you know, not an hour after Vanessa came out of recovery, she was telling me to announce she was still alive and let her play bait. She knew he'd want to come back and finish her off, he was that enraged at her betrayal. She could barely talk and she was begging me to let her get it right."

His cell phone buzzed. When he punched off, he said, "The video feeds from that diner in Baltimore and the photo of Zahir are ready for you."

Mike took Nicholas's sleeve. "Dillon, Nicholas and I will be with you in a moment."

When they'd left, she whispered, "Listen, Nicholas, what Vanessa said, it's a good idea. Vanessa can't do it, but I can, I can be bait. I'll get a red wig, crawl in bed with my Glock, yes, we can do it. Fast, we have to do it fast."

Nicholas grabbed her arm and jerked her around to face him, pulled her up close.

"You want to be bait? You want to take Vanessa's place in that bed with a red wig?" He shook her. "Listen to me, I am your partner. Absolutely, one hundred percent, no. We'll find another way to get him. I forbid it. Do you understand me? I am not putting you at risk. I don't care if I were lying on top of you, covering every inch of you and—"

He stiffened, his eyes went hot.

Mike felt strangely calm, no urge at all to smack him for what he'd said, for shaking her. His anger came from fear for her. She looked at his eyes, stark, dangerous, and his face was hard, no give. She didn't say anything, simply raised her hand and touched his cheek, traced the bruise on his jaw.

Nicholas didn't move as her fingers lightly passed over his face. He closed his eyes when her fingers were smoothing down his hair.

He felt her fingers now resting on his mouth, opened his eyes, met hers. His control, his anger, all his fear for her came together, and he knew it was all over for him.

Mike cupped his cheek, pressed her lips to his cheek. "Nicholas," she said. Nothing more, and it was enough, it was too much.

Nicholas pulled her tight against him, felt her heart pound against his, and kissed her, all his fear and the deep well of feelings for her, burst out, and his mouth was hard and urgent. When she leaned up and kissed him back, he went wild, but it didn't matter because she did, too, gripping his arms, his neck, then his face, her fingers touching him, and the kiss deepened and she opened her mouth. He lifted her off her feet and pushed her against the wall, pulling her against him, never once breaking contact. His hands moved down to the small of her back, over her hips, traced around her thighs, pressed her legs open.

His beard scraped her face and Mike could feel every bruise on her body, and who cared? She wanted more, she wanted everything. The taste of him, of Nicholas, the hardness, the power of him, and she tried to press closer, wanting all of him, and she moaned into his mouth.

There was a groan from the bed, six feet away from them.

His mouth, hot and fierce the instant before, stilled. Then he jerked back as if he'd been shot. He looked at her mouth like he wanted to weep, and very slowly, Nicholas eased her back down, his hands on her waist, holding her steady. The feel of her—no, he stepped back, and his eyes were nearly black.

"I'm sorry, I'm sorry, I shouldn't have done that, it was a mistake. I know we have to talk, but—" He shot a look over at Vanessa, quiet now, and he was out the door like a man running from a firing squad.

60

BISHOP TO D5

He was a clod, he'd practically attacked her. It didn't matter that she was all over him, too, he was embarrassed and he didn't know what to do.

"Nicholas Drummond!"

He whirled around at her ear-shattering yell to see Mike standing, outside Vanessa's door, her blouse pulled out from the waist of her pants, her ponytail straggling over one ear, and how had that happened? If he wasn't mistaken, her eyes were still glazed, and that was nice, but—

Her hands were on her hips, then she actually shook a teacher's finger at him. She was now standing not two feet from the crowded nurses' counter, surrounded by techs, doctors, nurses, and there was an orderly standing in the doorway of a room, holding a bedpan. No one was moving, every eye on them. Craig Swanson stood behind her, and the bastard was smirking.

Time stopped.

She took one step toward him, drew up, shook her finger at him again. "How dare you say you're sorry, that it shouldn't have happened, that it was a mistake, and then you bolt?" She shook her finger again at him and yelled, "Bad dog!"

The silence was deafening.

No, she hadn't said that, she couldn't have. He cleared his throat. "Bad dog? I'm a bad dog?"

"You're worse than a bad dog, but that's not the point. Now you're all sorry you smashed me against the wall? Sorry you had your hands all over me? You regret turning into a wild man? You want to *talk*? *Talk*? Well, forget that, Special Agent Drummond, because that will not happen. I will never talk about this, do you hear me? I will pull my own tonsils out through my ears if I'm ever even tempted to talk about this. Do you understand me?"

"You're yelling, of course I understand you."

"Good. So that must mean your brain is functioning again." She looked neither to the right nor to the left, marched right up to him, saw him open his mouth, and shoved him back. "No, you keep your mouth shut. We need to get downstairs. I believe Dillon will be there, although I don't exactly remember what we're going to do with him, but it will come to me."

She smacked her hand again against his chest. He started to grab her wrist, but didn't. Nicholas stared at her furious face, saw the pounding pulse in her throat, the snap and fire in her eyes, and couldn't help himself. He laughed, then cleared his throat and called out to all the staring hospital staff, at all their now-blooming smiles, the stirrings of laughter, "As you were! No charge for the show," and he punched the elevator button and they waited, silent, side by side. Nicholas heard Craig Swanson hoot with laughter, and others joining him, talking, laughing, a couple of them even shouting suggestions to the Bad Dog. He even heard a bark and a woof.

When the doors opened, a nurse stepped out, humming the theme from *Frozen*, "Let It Go." She took one look at them and said, "Whoa," and hurried off.

"What!" Mike yelled after her. "We have our clothes on! What's wrong with you?"

As the doors closed, they heard more rolling shouts of laughter. A couple more barks.

He opened his mouth.

"Be quiet unless you can verify that Dillon is meeting us in the lobby."

"I believe so. It's about the video feeds from that diner in Baltimore. I think. Then we're going home with him to have lasagna for dinner. But I suppose that could have changed, what with no power. I'm not really one for cold lasagna, are you?"

"No."

"Would you like me to call Savich? Verify?"

She shook her head, kept staring at the slow-moving numbers. The elevator stopped on the second floor, the doors opened, and there stood two white-coated doctors talking about nausea. One look, and by mutual unspoken agreement they turned and walked quickly away.

When the bell dinged and the doors opened onto the

lobby, he watched Mike march out of the elevator, head high, never looking at him, not looking at any of the dozens of people in the lobby. She spotted Dillon, waved, and continued her march toward him.

She had to stop when three teenagers, one of them with his arm in a brand-new cast that was already covered with lewd drawings and scrawls, blocked her way. She couldn't knock the kid out of the way, he was hurt and drug-addled.

"Wait," Nicholas said, and she ignored him, then reluctantly slowed.

Mike could smell him, that fine Nicholas scent that was his and his alone, but more than that, she felt him, felt him drawing closer to her. She knew he was leaning in, felt his warm breath on her cheek.

"No, not a word, do you hear me? No pathetic excuses, no going on about what a mistake that was."

"Okay. Shall I?"

"Shall you what?"

"Tell you to fix your ponytail? It's rather lopsided."

Mike grabbed her hair and pulled it back into place and slipped the band back on.

"I guess your shirt needs to be tucked in again, too."

She shoved her shirt back into her trousers, called out, "Dillon, we're coming," and she stalked away from him, going around the teenagers, leaving him to listen to the boy with the broken arm laugh like a hyena since he was happily floating on pain meds.

61

KNIGHT TO F3

The White House

Callan had spent half the evening on the phone—talking either to the president or to Ari, or the head of the Iranian security services, who swore up and down his government had nothing to do with the reactors turning on. She wanted to tell him he was a lying moron, but of course she didn't. It drove her mad, but denial was woven into their brains, par for the course. Then who did know about the reactors? But he didn't have an answer to that.

A big muckety-muck had ordered someone to push the button and keep pushing. The Israelis had taken one look at the Iranian landscape lit up like a series of way stations across the desert and started planning a preemptive offensive, launching drones and preparing their battlements, which made the Iranians move more troops into place, shuffling their missile batteries around for the best offensive. How long would the Iron Dome last under a true barrage of nuclear warheads? Not long, and the collapse would be immediate around the entire region.

It was all happening lightning-quick, too, a match set to a fuse, flaring to life and settling in to burn fast and hot. If they didn't nip it in the bud right here, right now, too many people to count would be dead.

The talks had fallen apart, no great surprise there, considering one of the parties was lying big-time. What had started as Bradley's hopeful road to lasting peace was fast turning into a fistfight to see who would kill the other first. Again.

The president had ended up stalking out. He was now flying back to the United States on *Air Force One*, expected to land by ten in the morning. She hoped his blood pressure hadn't spiked too high. She assumed she'd get a royal ass-chewing simply because she was handy, and given her opinions on the Middle East talks were diametrically opposed to his, that would make him even more pissed off to have her proven right. And then he'd have a nice long ride to lay into her on their way to the Yorktown event. Given he was the president of the United States, she couldn't slug him.

She stayed in the Situation Room, her cup of strong black tea at her elbow, watching the movements across the region. The domino effect of the nuclear facilities coming online was a wonder to behold. Every country who'd been at the table in Geneva—from Saudi Arabia to Russia to Israel—was scrambling for position. The reports had been filtering in for the past few hours—major movement in Lebanon, Syria, Yemen. The ISIS media machine had been on Twitter promising attacks. Hezbollah and the Palestinians were openly calling for the Israelis' immediate surrender, threatening attacks on the Gaza Strip, threatening to bomb Tel Aviv. Israel wouldn't hold back for very long.

And, of course, this was what Iran was waiting for. Provocation. Why had they pushed it now? She knew they didn't yet have a nuclear weapon, so why?

She had to fix this. She had to stop it. And she had no idea how she was going to pull it off.

Callan picked up the phone and called Trafford.

"Temp, tell me you have news for me. The media is all over us, trying to find out what's going on, and believe me when I say *'the president is unhappy'* is a gross understatement. He is adamant he doesn't want to cancel the event at Yorktown, won't be seen as knuckling under to a terrorist threat, et cetera. All I'm concerned with is making sure he gets to Yorktown, that we aren't going to have to do something stupid, like stop a war instead."

"We're working on it, Callan. FBI's been officially briefed, we're all on the same page and moving forward. Again, I strongly recommend the president cancel Yorktown. This man, Matthew Spenser, is completely unpredictable. We don't know what he plans to do now and we haven't found him yet. But our agent is certain he plans an attack, probably at Yorktown."

"I'll keep working on Bradley."

"Good. A few minutes ago, Agent Savich, FBI, sent us

over an enhanced photo of Zahir Damari. I'm hoping that since we now know what he looks like, we can keep him from getting anywhere near you.

"Even better, we have a video feed of two males; one of them is very likely Damari, although he doesn't look like the enhanced photo the FBI sent us back. He's probably wearing cheek implants, makeup, maybe a wig, really an excellent disguise. He's lasted so long in his business because he appears to be very careful, no matter the situation."

"Who was he meeting with?"

"As yet unidentified. The video shows them meeting in a diner in Baltimore. The unidentified male passed Zahir something in a tube. Plans of some kind, the waitress said. They were arguing, but talking low, and she tried to stay out of the way. As soon as we have more, I'll let you know."

"You're sure it's Zahir? Tell me, Temp, where are you getting all your information?"

He was quiet for a moment. "Callan, you know sometimes it's better not to know all the details."

"Would you say that to the president?"

"In this case? Actually, yes, I would."

That gave her pause. She wasn't used to being kept out of the loop on top-secret covert actions. "Temp, we've known each other a long time. If you're trying to save me from a possible political hit down the road, I appreciate it, but to be honest, I think it would be best for me to know the whole story, as soon as possible. I have a bad feeling about all of this. A very bad feeling. Now, tell me, where are you getting your information?"

He sighed. "You asked for it. We've had a deep under-cover agent in with COE for the past four months."

She was shocked into silence, then came to life with a roar. "What were you thinking? You should have briefed me immediately, the president, too, at the very least—"

"Callan, when we sent in an undercover asset, it was because we heard this man, Matthew Spenser, was developing a new undetectable bomb with a huge payload. When he suddenly brought his band back to the U.S., what could we do? The asset had to wait until he perfected the bomb before she could steal the final plans and get them back to us. We couldn't very well pull her out."

"She? It was a female agent?"

Temp chuckled. "What is this? You're surprised? You, the first female vice president?"

"It's not that, Temp, and you know it. Where is the agent now? I want a briefing, I want her in front of me right away."

"You can't have her. She's in the hospital. Unfortunately, Matthew Spenser discovered she was working for us and shot her, left her for dead in a burning building."

"Will she live?"

"Yes. She was very brave, Callan. It's amazing she survived. Spenser still believes she's dead."

"Who is this agent? What's her name?"

"I'm not at liberty to say."

Callan slapped her hand onto the desk, the sound sharp as a gunshot. "Templeton Trafford, do not play games with me. I want her name, now."

"Vanessa Grace."

Callan said, "Is she related to Carlton Grace, by chance?"

"Yes, she's his niece. You remember her father, also an undercover expert. He was killed when she was a girl."

"Yes, I remember Paul and I remember mourning him."

"Well, her uncle Carl raised her. She's been with the agency six years. She's very good, might even prove to be better than her old man one of these days, maybe even better than her uncle, and he was incredible in the bad old days."

As Callan listened, she walked to the window and looked out at her city. Since the power went down, it had quickly emptied. It looked surreal, a painting of a city without movement, without people. A dead city. She'd nearly forgotten there was a blackout, being inside the White House, where everything still ran smoothly.

"Temp, does anyone other than the FBI know about this?"

"No, only the FBI. Carl Grace told me Savich, Drummond, and Caine were speaking this afternoon with Vanessa. Small world, turns out Vanessa knows Agent Caine from school. Carl said it went well. They won't speak to the press, if that's what you're worried about."

"And Spenser believes she's dead?"

"Yes, no way for him to know she's not. We've kept it all very quiet."

Callan said, "Do you think he would be upset were he to find out she's still alive?"

"I'd say so, after shooting her in the chest and leaving her in the fire, along with his own BFF, Ian McGuire, a minor IRA bad guy he's been working with for a very long time. McGuire tried to protect her. It was a major betrayal, Callan. You know how some people feel very strongly about betrayal."

"Who else from the group have we identified?"

"Other than Zahir Damari, the only other major player is a computer guy named Andrew Tate. As for the rest of the group, Vanessa thinks they're very likely gone from the country by now. So we have Matthew Spenser, Andy Tate, and Zahir Damari on the loose. Yorktown, Callan, that's got to be the target, and you, of course. Will Zahir Damari try to take you there? It sounds plausible."

Callan looked at her watch. It was a few minutes past nine o'clock. "Call up someone you trust in the media. If we hurry, we can make the eleven p.m. news. We've got to draw Matthew Spenser out as soon as possible. Don't worry, Vanessa Grace won't be in that hospital room. Assign another of your people to play her. Get it on the news, Temp, get it on the news right away. Vanessa Grace is now officially bait."

A pause, then: "Callan, it's good to know you haven't lost your chops."

62

KNIGHT TO E4

Sherlock passed the lasagna to Mike. "A good thing the power came back on as you guys pulled into the driveway. It's Dillon's special sauce, which I have to say, being the recipient for lo these many years, is well nigh the best ever made."

Savich said, "It's my grandmother's recipe, actually, with only a few additions."

Nicholas said, "Savich, could I give Cook Crumbe your recipe?"

"Cook Crumbe runs the kitchen at Old Farrow Hall," Mike said to Savich, who'd cocked his head. "This ancient shack where Nicholas was born."

"That's good, Mike. How many bedrooms, Nicholas?"

He thought about that, then said, "I really don't know. Now, about the sauce, I think my mother would love it.

As for my grandfather? You've met him, Mike, you never know. But it's worth a try."

"Papa didn't make the garlic bread," Sean said, "Mama did. She's good at garlic bread, and she likes me to tell everyone."

Laughter, and it felt good.

When dinner was finished, Nicholas played four rounds of *Super Spaceman Spiff* with Sean, and lost every round.

Sean studied his face. "You aren't losing on purpose, are you, Uncle Nicholas? I mean, I beat you fair and square, right?"

"Yes," Nicholas said, "I did lose on purpose. I'm trying to be nice."

Sean said, "You will not lose on purpose this time. Do you promise?"

"Yes, I promise."

Sean beat him. Then he pulled an excited, tail-wagging Astro onto his lap, leaned back against the sofa cushions, and frowned at Nicholas. "You weren't telling the truth. I really beat you all those rounds, didn't I?"

"All right, you caught me. I was trying to spare my ego." He said to Savich, "He's too smart, he saw right through me."

Sherlock nodded. "I'm the only one he can't beat, right, Sean?"

"Well, Mama, maybe not this week."

Sherlock grabbed both him and Astro up and swung them around and around, making Sean shout with laughter and Astro bark madly. She gave him a big smacking kiss. "No, no kiss for you, Astro. All right, my boy, it's time for bed. You've humiliated Nicholas enough for one night. Astro, it's time for your evening walkabout."

"Good night, Uncle Nicholas. Good night, Aunt Mike."

Mike shook his hand. "A pleasure to watch you trounce my partner. He occasionally needs trouncing. A lot of trouncing." And even though she'd meant to keep her voice light, hey, all a joke, both Savich and Sherlock gave her a look that said everything.

They know there's something going on. Mike looked over at Nicholas. His face was stone vacant and he was staring at his shoes as if the soft Italian leather held all the answers.

Savich looked from one to the other. "Whatever's wrong, you two need to fix it."

"There is absolutely nothing wrong, Dillon," Mike said, jumping to her feet. "There's absolutely nothing at all going on, not a single thing. Besides, I don't want to talk about it. Nicholas, isn't it about time you checked in with Ben?"

Nicholas nodded, punched in Ben's cell number. Ben answered immediately. "You're not going to believe this, Nicholas. We found trackers on both your personal cars and five of the vehicles you've used from the pool in the past month. Nice Beemer, by the way, you have to let me drive it sometime. The trackers are small, very small, state-of-the-art, placed in the engine block instead of the wheel well. It took some looking to find them. Someone has definitely been keeping track of your—our—whereabouts. From what we can tell, the trackers send a GPS signal strong enough that the person who's following can watch your movements on a laptop, remotely, up to fifty miles away. Very sophisticated." He paused, then, "And that's how they found Mr. Hodges and our three guys."

"Any chance you can reverse-engineer the data, see where it broadcasted to?"

"We're working on it, but it's a moot point, really. They've been turned off now. We've taken them all to the lab to be worked over for any DNA or fingerprints."

"Unnecessary. We know who placed them."

"Who?"

"Someone in COE, probably Andy Tate—he's their computer whiz. Or Zahir Damari, aka Darius. It sounds more like him.

"Any movement on Gray's end, on the nanotriggers Spenser engineered for his bombs?"

"He's right here, hold on. Let me put this on speaker."

There was a click, then Gray came on the line. "The triggers were definitely Havelock technology. Good catch, Nicholas. The only issue is they are on the market, being used by a number of people, legitimately. We'll have to get a warrant to see who they've sold them to, and it will take time."

Mike said, "Gray, anything on the money trail?"

"Now, here I have more for you. We ran a forensic accounting on the guy Adam Pearce found, name of Porter Wallace. He's definitely managing a few portfolios on the side. I found a link between him and Larry Reeves—the insider at Bayway. The money was moved into Reeves's account from an offshore account in the Caymans. It's closed now, totally untraceable. But Wallace went to Grand Cayman three weeks ago. Stands to reason he opened the account, put the money in, moved it when he was given the go-ahead, then closed the account. We're going to pick him up in the morning, have a nice long chat, start taking apart his entire world. The warrant was issued an hour ago. We're planning a five a.m. knock at his house. From what I can tell, he's been a very bad boy."

"Any ties to organized crime you can find? We could make a nice RICO case against him."

"On the surface, it looks like he's only been working with COE. I'll keep digging into his background."

Mike leaned over the phone. "Gray, who is this guy, anyway, this Porter Wallace? How does a Wall Street broker get hooked up with Matthew Spenser?"

"It's a small world. Wallace is from Hartford, Connecticut, went to Avon Old Farms, a swanky private boys' school—"

Nicholas interrupted him. "Gray, you found the link. Matthew Spenser went to Avon. They must have known each other in school. Whether he's helping out of the goodness of his own heart or he believes Spenser's ideology or he's being threatened—either way, we have a direct tie to Spenser. Well done."

Mike was grinning. This was huge. "This is great, Gray. Thank you. Next time we're at the Feathers, your beer's on me."

"I'll take the beer gladly, but I've got to point out that Adam Pearce really got everything we needed. I simply followed the trail. I'm very glad you talked him away from the dark side, Nicholas."

Nicholas said, "Let us know how the knock goes on Porter Wallace. Just so you know, I have Adam working on a few more things."

"We'll keep running the trackers, see if we can find where they may be broadcasting to. Otherwise, it's the usual craziness associated with crime scenes. I notice you're not here to do any of the paperwork."

Mike laughed as she looked at Nicholas and gave him the first real smile since, well, best not to revisit that. "He does manage to escape the paperwork, doesn't he?"

When Savich was showing her the guest bedroom, Mike said, "Dillon, do you think they'll cancel the Yorktown speech? I mean, it would be stupid to carry on as if nothing has happened."

He shrugged. "I've long given up trying to determine what a politician will do in any situation. It's the president's decision. We'll find out in the morning."

Nicholas said, "Maybe everything will be handled before it's crunch time. The place has to be crawling with advance people, and now even more Secret Service. How in the world would Spenser get in to plant one of his bombs?"

Mike said, "Maybe the bomb or bombs were planted before the Secret Service got there. I give up. My brain is fried. I'm going to sleep." She laid her hand on Savich's arm. "Thank you for letting us stay."

She was setting her go-bag on the bed when Sherlock called out, "Wait, guys, you'd better see this."

On the small television in the kitchen was a still shot of George Washington University Hospital.

"Your informant's on the local eleven o'clock news."

They all watched as the reporter fed the information to the anchor, who seemed pleased as punch to announce that a government agent, believed dead in a Brooklyn fire, was very much alive and being treated for gunshot wounds.

Mike looked Nicholas straight in the face. "At least they didn't use her name. But you know Spenser will come after her if he hears this. Who in the world leaked the story? I mean, if we were setting it all up and I were taking her place, that would be different—"

"Well, no matter," Nicholas said, "since you're not."

Savich was already dialing his cell. "I'll see what I can find out."

Nicholas's phone rang. "Savich, hold on a minute. It's Carl Grace."

He put it on speaker. "Agent Grace?"

Grace was shouting, nearly incoherent with rage. "What are you people playing at, exposing my niece like this?"

Savich said, "We don't know anything about it, Carl. We haven't talked to anyone. We told you we wouldn't."

But Carl was too furious to listen. "The FBI leaks like a sieve, always has, and you wonder why we don't take you into our confidence? And you're trying to pretend you had nothing to do with this? Don't bother coming back to the hospital, I will see you banned from the grounds." He hung up.

"I think he's a bit upset," Nicholas said.

Savich said, "Hold on," and made a call. He was frowning when he punched off. "Mr. Maitland has no idea where this came from. He imagines the CIA will have extra agents watching Vanessa tonight. Or moving her, that would be better."

Mike straightened her shoulders and said to Nicholas, "You know if Spenser sees that broadcast, he'll come for her immediately. It's not too late—I can take her place."

"No, you will not." Nicholas turned on his heel and walked out of the kitchen.

63

QUEEN TO B8

Off I-95, near Lorton, Virginia

The motel room smelled like wet dog and burned coffee, and the tatty bedspread was a nasty orange. But Matthew knew it wouldn't be smart to stop at a better place. He and Andy would make do. If only Andy would shut his mouth.

At least the grid attack had worked well, so well that when the lights came on ten minutes before, both he and Andy were startled.

Now Matthew was pacing the length of the stingy room, back and forth, thinking, worrying. Had Darius managed to get through the fence when the electricity shut down? Stop worrying, sure he had, Darius was that good. He glanced at his watch. Yes, Darius was in place by now.

At least today everything had gone according to plan,

but still, he felt itchy, his brain looping in and out, and nothing seemed right. Matthew knew he was ready, knew he going to pull it off, even though Darius was making other plans in case he failed or lost his nerve. But he didn't feel pumped with the familiar manic excitement, didn't feel hot blood whipping through his body. And he knew why. *I killed my best friend and Vanessa.* He'd murdered her and even now he wasn't sure what she'd been to him. But no longer hearing her voice joking with Ian or one of the other men, listening to her hum as she built one of her small Semtex bombs, watching her eat a hamburger, mustard, not ketchup—she'd been a part of his life and look what she'd done—she'd forced his hand because she'd betrayed him. She'd played him and here he'd always thought he could judge people so well. She'd blindsided him, and then she'd turned Ian against him, too.

She'd only wanted his bombs. She'd forced him to act against her, not his fault. Back and forth, his brain kept looking from guilt and pain to justification.

Matthew finally threw himself down in the single chair in the room. He looked over at Andy, sprawled on the bed, headphones in, listening to one of his frenetic hard-metal excuses for music, eating red licorice from the bag, probably hacking God knew what or watching porn on his laptop. Matthew had cleaned and bandaged his knee and given him two Vicodin, both now swimming happily in his bloodstream. At least it had stopped his infernal whining, stopped his questions about why Matthew was doing this, doing that, something he did more and more.

Andy sat up suddenly and turned the laptop around.

"Matthew, you're not going to believe this. Hurry, look."

Matthew leaned over the laptop and stared at the shot of downtown D.C., nothing he really recognized. It was no longer dark and empty since the power had come back on.

"What is it?"

"George Washington University Hospital."

"So what?"

"Matthew, listen, Vanessa's alive. She's alive!"

Matthew shook his head. "No, impossible, I shot her in the heart and burned the building down around her. With Ian. What are you talking about?"

"They're talking about Vanessa. Listen."

Andy pointed to the laptop screen, turned up the volume. A reporter—long smooth blond hair, perfect makeup—stood, mike in hand, in front of a hospital.

"Turn it up, Andy."

". . . The explosion at Bayway Refinery in Elizabeth, New Jersey, continues to be under investigation. We can now confirm the reports that a federal agent tied to the investigation was also recovered Monday evening from a burning building in Brooklyn. The agent, thought to be undercover, was transported to George Washington University Hospital. I have been told she is in serious but stable condition in the ICU."

Andy was shaking his head back and forth. "That's gotta be a lie, I mean, I saw her with my own eyes. Like you said, you shot her dead, and she was on the floor, bleeding all over the place, and she wasn't moving. They've got to be making that up."

Matthew felt strangely detached from himself at that moment. Andy was right, it was a lie, had to be. Vanessa was dead. True, he hadn't seen her sightless eyes staring up at him as he had Ian, he hadn't leaned down to feel for a pulse, but he'd never doubted that she was dead. Obviously they were trying to set up a trap to get him to the hospital. The idiots. He wasn't that great a fool.

His brain looped back. But what if she'd really survived? Vanessa was smart, he knew that. He didn't doubt she was a hotshot agent, always thinking, always on red alert, always knowing what to do.

The reporter continued: "The Federal Bureau of Investigation has been tasked with finding her assailants. It is not known how she is attached to this investigation, nor what her role was. We'll have more on this story at the top of the hour. Back to you in the studio . . ."

Matthew sank back into the chair, covered his eyes with his hand. No, he didn't think it was a lie, not now. Vanessa was that smart. She'd played dead until he was gone. How had she not burned up with Ian? *The hidden exit to the roof*—that must have been how she'd managed to get out.

"She's alive," he heard Andy repeat again. Andy seemed a mile away, his bewildered kid's voice like a loud echo. Matthew scarcely heard him. He was utterly unimportant at the moment.

Andy's voice broke in on him, louder now, "Hey, Matthew, she's a federal agent. Can you beat that?" Andy started slapping his hands against his head and his voice rose to the familiar whine Matthew hated. "Man, we are screwed. Totally and completely screwed. What do we do now? She's going to tell them all about us. Wait, she's already told them about us, they already know who we are.

"And how did she survive? Why didn't you make sure she was dead? But you didn't, you just ordered me around and wouldn't even let me set the fire, and here it was my own special mix, and look what happened."

Matthew looked toward the grating voice. He didn't really see Andy. He saw failure, and it was bright and hard and burned deep, making rage grow, roil around, twisting, bending his mind, taking over.

Andy shouted, "And Ian named you the Bishop? Because you're such a genius, like a great chess player who can figure out twenty moves ahead? Well, you sure blew this one, didn't you? Talk about failure, this is the biggie, Matthew. They're going to find us and if they don't kill us dead, they're gonna put us in prison forever or fry us. You've killed us both!"

Matthew stood slowly, looked to where Andy's voice simply wouldn't stop, and said, "Why not get it over with now, Andy?" And Matthew raised his gun and shot Andy in the forehead.

Andy fell back without a sound, his head striking the cheap backboard, flipping him onto his side, away from Matthew.

Matthew sat down again, laid the gun on his thigh, and listened to the golden silence.

Andy was probably right, the whining little puke, so best hit the button now. He picked up the blood-splattered laptop, set it on his knees, opened the program.

He had to admit, it was a beautiful program. Andy had done well. He smiled as he hit the button, launched the attack. The countdown clock started in the window.

His beautiful bomb would show the world power beyond belief. There was no stopping it now, and no stopping him. He was set, he was ready to go, ready to change the world, locked and loaded.

He was whistling as he shoved the gun in his waistband, grabbed his bag. He was only forty minutes from downtown D.C. This time he would do it right. This time he would look into her sightless eyes and know she was finally dead.

If it was a trap, he'd still make it happen, and who cared if he bit the big one? Maybe he didn't care, he was no longer sure about it.

As he closed the door to the motel, hung up the flimsy DO NOT DISTURB sign, he wondered how long it would be before someone went into that room.

Good-bye, Andy.

He was still whistling as he walked to the car.

64

PAWN TO B5

Georgetown

Mike stuck her face in the shower stream of the hot water. She was angry, but she knew it was no use getting into another fight with Nicholas. In the morning she'd present her case to Dillon, maybe Mr. Maitland, that she would be the best at playing Vanessa. It wasn't like she was helpless—no, she'd have her Glock. She was fast and smart. She was a professional.

She fumed and fretted as she towel-dried her hair, combed it out, and pushed it off her face, hooking it behind her ears. She pulled a pair of yoga pants and a T-shirt out of her go-bag.

The bed looked nice and firm, the way she liked it. She had to admit she was dog-tired, and the bruises were singing out loud and clear. She cursed Nicholas one last time and pulled back the covers.

There was a knock at her door.

"Yes?"

Nicholas opened the door, closed it behind him.

"We need to talk."

She eased out of bed and stood facing him, hands on her hips. "There is absolutely nothing to talk about, unless you're ready to stop being such a lamebrain about me taking Vanessa's place. I am a professional, Nicholas, I've played bait before, not a problem. I'll be armed, not helpless, like Vanessa. And I'd—"

He waved his hand in front of her. "Pay attention, Caine. This is a CIA op. Bait will be a CIA operative. Hang it up."

That stopped her mid-rant. She should have come to that obvious conclusion, which went to prove how tired she was, even her brain was operating at twenty watts. It hurt to say it, but she did. "Very well, I suppose you're right. It's too bad, their mistake. What did you want to talk about?"

"About what didn't happen today, between us. I think we should, don't you?"

She took a step back. "There is nothing to talk about, since nothing happened. How many times do I have to tell you that? You're like a dog with a bone. And isn't that fitting? No talk, do you hear me?"

"Is a dog with a bone better than a bad dog? Never mind. Since you're shouting again, of course I can hear you. I like those pants and that shirt—what does it say?"

She looked down at her chest. It was one of her favorites: FEEL SAFE, SLEEP WITH A COP.

"So you can read. Bravo."

He grinned. "Yes, okay, I want to feel safe."

She stared at him. He was wearing pajama bottoms that came low on his hips and a T-shirt, black and snug, and she kept staring.

In the next instant, she ran those six feet across the room and he grabbed her up in his arms, brought her long legs around his waist, and pulled her tight against him.

"Mike—Michaela." The words sounded magic in her mouth and in her brain, and she was kissing him like there was nothing else in the world but the two of them.

Her hands were in his hair, pulling his face to hers so she could kiss his nose, his cheeks, his forehead, but it wasn't enough. She yanked and pulled on his T-shirt as his hands went under her bottom, stroking up her back beneath her shirt, feeling the soft flesh, smelling the jasmine in her damp hair. She carried her shampoo in her go-bag? Of course she did. He was losing his mind and didn't care. He butted her head back to kiss her neck, felt her tighten her legs around his waist. His hands found the smooth, stretchy band at her waist, and he wanted to jerk them down even as he moved to the bed.

"Uncle Nicholas?"

They froze.

"Uncle Nicholas? I woke up when you left our bedroom. Is Aunt Mike okay?"

He touched his forehead to hers, managed to grab a

breath. "Sean, sure, Aunt Mike is fine." Was that his voice, all deep and gravelly, like he was in pain?

He felt her heart pounding, cleared his throat, gave her a final fast kiss, then felt her legs loosen at his waist. He lowered her feet to the floor but didn't let her go. He wanted to cry, maybe howl. He called out, "Sean, I always have to say good night to her or she doesn't sleep well. And I forgot."

"Are you telling her a story? Do you want me to sing to her? I know lots of words to Papa's songs."

Mike cleared her throat. "Thank you, Sean, but that's okay. I'm really tired and Nicholas already sang me 'Soft Kitty'; it's one of my favorites."

"Mine, too," Sean said, and both of them pictured his small hand on the doorknob.

Nicholas took a fast step back. "Good night, Mike, sleep well. What's 'Soft Kitty'? I don't know that one."

She waved him away. He was nearly back to the door. She saw his pajama bottoms were riding even lower and his lovely tight black T-shirt was ripped. How had that happened? Surely she should remember. She stood perfectly straight.

"Good night, Nicholas. I will sleep well, as will you. We will have nothing to speak about tomorrow. This did not happen, do you hear me? This. Did. Not. Happen."

He gave her a grin and was out the door in the next second. "Hey, Sean, let's go back to bed."

"Sean, Nicholas?"

All he needed. Slowly, Nicholas turned to see Savich

standing in the doorway of his and Sherlock's bedroom. Unlike Nicholas, he wasn't wearing a T-shirt, only pajama bottoms.

"Papa, everything's okay. Uncle Nicholas had to sing Aunt Mike a song, like you do me, so she could go to sleep."

"I see," Savich said, and Nicholas knew he saw very well, particularly the tear in his T-shirt. "Both of you sleep well. Sean, don't keep Nicholas up. He's had a very long day."

You don't know the half of it.

Wednesday
6 a.m.–Noon

65

PAWN TO H4

Mike woke to a quiet knocking at her door. She rolled over to see Nicholas standing in the doorway, already dressed in one of his crisp handmade white button-down shirts, and, oddly, a pair of jeans. Tight jeans. He looked like a prep school boy gone rogue. It was on the tip of her tongue to tell him she liked him better in the low-slung pjs, but she didn't. But it was close.

He was all business. "Get dressed. We leave for a briefing in ten minutes with Vice President Sloane."

"You're wearing jeans to the White House?"

"We're heading to her place. And they've requested we dress down."

"What in the world is going on?"

"I don't know, but you need to hurry. I'll see you downstairs."

Five minutes later, Mike presented herself in the Savich kitchen, her hair in a ponytail, dressed in jeans and motorcycle boots, a short lightweight black leather jacket over a boatneck black-and-white-striped shirt. Without a word, Nicholas handed her a cup of coffee.

Savich was sitting at the kitchen table, two laptops open in front of him. She recognized magic MAX, wondered what in the world was happening.

He looked up from one of his computers. "Good morning, Mike. You slept well?"

"Yes, yes, thank you." *Was there something in his voice?* Nah, she was imagining it. She had to stop it.

She took a sip of her coffee and sighed. A dollop of milk, nothing else.

"The lord and master of the coffee universe made it," Sherlock said, and smiled. "Enjoy."

"Five minutes," Savich said, "and we'll need to hit the road." He glanced at Sherlock. "I'm sorry, sweetheart, but with Gabriella down with a cold, you're elected to take Sean to school."

"Yeah, yeah, curses on all of you," Sherlock said. "Good luck to you guys." And she immediately left the kitchen when Sean's voice came loud and clear from upstairs: "Mama, where's my special Batman shirt?"

Mike said, "Do I need to know anything in particular?"

Savich packed up MAX. "The vice president set a plan in motion last night and has decided to bring us in."

Mike stared at him. "So the vice president is behind the leak about Vanessa? I guess it makes sense, after all, she was in the CIA."

Savich nodded. "Yes, a planned leak. If you're all set, we can go." He called out as they went out the front door, "See you later, Sherlock. Sean, have a good day."

They piled into Sherlock's sturdy Volvo and headed toward the Naval Observatory. Mike knew the vice president's mansion was on the grounds, and it must be close to Savich's home in Georgetown. She was right.

Savich drove straight up Wisconsin, turned right onto Observatory Lane. They were checked through a tall gate, then wound around the circle to park in front of an impressive white Victorian mansion. She wished she weren't so nervous, so on edge, to fully appreciate it. The vice president's house, and wasn't that something, Mike from Omaha visiting the VP? She tightened her ponytail, then checked herself to make sure she was put together.

But still, meeting the vice president of the United States wearing jeans and biker boots and no makeup, it would make her mom cringe. So unlike Nicholas, curse him, who looked very cool, she felt like she should be going to a bar to drink beer and line dance.

She said to Nicholas, "Savich didn't tell you what was going on?"

He shook his head. "I think this is a command performance. He woke me, I threw on some clothes and grabbed you."

She saw half a dozen Secret Service agents patrolling the house, each of them focused, each of them ready for anything, and she wondered how they could keep up the edge day after day. A tall, fit gray-haired man who looked like he'd never taken crap from anyone in his life came down the steps to greet them.

"I'm Tony Scarlatti, no relation to the dude who wrote all that cool music for the harpsichord back in the day. I'm the vice president's lead agent. Thanks for coming to us this morning. Come meet Vice President Sloane."

They all shook hands, introduced themselves, then trailed after Tony into the house. Mike immediately wanted to whisper, it was so quiet inside. It was also more modern than she'd expected, all cool grays and creams with a few sprinkles of pale green. There wasn't much time to admire the house; Tony herded them through the round entrance foyer toward the back of the house.

Vice President Callan Sloane was in a large modern kitchen overlooking the gardens, sitting at a Carrera marble countertop, a large cup of tea in front of her, *The Washington Post* in her hands. She looked completely relaxed, at ease, as if she was used to a bunch of FBI agents interrupting her breakfast every day.

"Thank you, Tony. Hello, come in." Introductions, handshakes, then, "May I get you coffee? Tea? Tony, could you ask Maisie to bring the trays into the dining room? And I'm sure you can smell the cinnamon buns, they'll be out of the oven in a couple of minutes. Follow me, we'll talk in there."

The few times Nicholas had seen the vice president on

TV, he'd thought her impressive, an in-charge type, probably scary competent. In person, though, he realized not only did she look like the ruler of her world, she was also a stunner—pale skin, blond hair without a single strand of gray, and a stubborn chin. Nicholas knew she was fifty-seven, but she didn't look it. Unlike them, she was wearing black silk slacks and a cream blouse with small mother-of-pearl buttons down the front, and a choker of graduated pearls around her neck.

She looked expensive and completely in charge, ready to greet the leader of a country or three FBI agents. For a moment, she reminded Nicholas of his ex-wife, Pamela Carruthers, always together, always ready to stride out on the stage, ready for any situation. He remembered the card Pam had sent him upon his graduating from the FBI Academy. Showed a dog with a wagging tail, enthusiastically digging a deep hole. She'd signed it "Your Pam," whatever that meant—well, he knew what it meant, particularly after the dinner they'd shared in New York. He shook his head, paid attention.

They followed Vice President Sloane into the dining room, wallpapered in the same creams and grays, with draperies that nearly touched the ceiling above the windows, making the room seem taller than it was. Nicholas knew his mom would really like the rosewood table, large enough to seat twelve people, without extra leaves.

Mike sat down, wondered who else had sat in this exact chair, looked over at Nicholas. He looked like he belonged, like he assumed a servant would quietly appear at his elbow and pour him a glass of wine. And Savich, his face showing nothing but polite interest, taking in his surroundings with a professional's eye.

Once they were served, the vice president got right to it.

"Thank you for coming on such short notice. I decided last night to let the media know Vanessa Grace is alive. I did not use her real name, but obviously Matthew Spenser will know it's her.

"It's imperative we draw him out as quickly as possible. I'm counting on his seeing the media's announcement, and believing that the woman he believed he'd murdered had miraculously escaped. I am personally amazed she survived."

She turned to Mike. "Agent Caine? Agent Savich tells me you wanted to be bait, but the CIA will be using one of their own agents. Do you believe as I do that Matthew Spenser will come to the hospital to try to kill her again?"

"Yes, ma'am," Mike said. "Given what we heard Vanessa saying on the videotapes, Matthew Spenser felt something for her, at the very least he believed to his soul she was there for him, sharing his goals, sharing his missions. Her betrayal hit him very hard, sent him over the edge enough to kill his best friend, Ian McGuire, and believe he'd killed her. So yes, I think he'll come and he'll see killing her as righteous.

"Also, Vanessa told us Spenser is a news junkie, so if he's anywhere near a screen, he will see the announcement, and then he will make plans."

"Her uncle Carl Grace agrees," Callan said. "Anything else?"

Mike said, "Ma'am, we also believe you need to talk the president into canceling the Yorktown event."

"Already done. Neither of us will be there. We will announce the cancellation at noon today. The president is not happy about it, but we can't take any chances with his life, and that is an understatement. And I'd just as soon keep my own hide intact as well. What else, Agent Caine?"

Mike hadn't expected humor, and smiled. She said, "Ma'am, we don't know that Zahir Damari was planning to kill you at Yorktown. We don't even know where he is and that means we have to keep on red alert, as well as you and your protection team. Damari is a consummate professional. As you probably know, we have a photo of him at a diner in Baltimore. He looked nothing like the photo Vanessa managed to send from COE, which means he makes it a habit of altering his looks, which is why we haven't been able to identify him. He never gives up and from what we've heard and read, he always has redundancies built in."

"So he's never at a loss," Callan said, and nodded. "He'd make a good politician. Now, trust me, none of my people are letting down their guard. I was told it was possible he was also here to kill another, still unverified, target. Do you agree, Agent Savich?"

Savich nodded. "Unfortunately, we're not certain as yet who this other person is. Mossad still doesn't know?"

"Not yet. Take a guess, Agent Savich."

"The president of the United States."

66

PAWN TO H5

Callan tipped her head to the side and nodded slowly. "I agree. As of twenty minutes ago, Mossad had traced money from Iran to accounts Damari is known to use. Is Iran running the show? Mossad believes it's one of their high-up military, and more than likely they have the active assistance and involvement of Hezbollah." She said to Nicholas, "Your PM once described the Hezbollah thugs to me as the Nazi SS of Iran." She paused a moment, then, "Of course, logically, it wouldn't seem to make sense to want to kill the president, since he is very pro-peace in the region, at almost any cost, and that means incredible concessions to Iran. So why cut off the hand that is eager to feed you?

"But the truth is, as we all know, Hezbollah, as well as ISIS, Al Qaeda, and elements in Iran, would like nothing more than to see the world completely destabilized, a delightful euphemism for destroy every human being that isn't Shia. What didn't make sense to me is the fact they have to know they can't win since we have superior weaponry. They'd be crushed.

"Then I was told about Spenser's tiny undetectable bombs with a huge payload—witness Bayway—and it all became clear. They believe they can obliterate us without huge casualties on their side. They send their soldiers out far and wide and go. If the payload is as massive as advertised, if the bombs are indeed undetectable, there would be so many casualties, it boggles the mind.

"Now, do you agree with this assessment, Agent Savich?"

"It makes terrifying sense, ma'am, particularly if Zahir got one of the coin bombs to Iran, which I have to believe he did. After all, he was with Spenser for months. I imagine he got one of the coin bombs back to his masters in Iran before it was even tested at Bayway. He'd have had to so they would have time to dismantle it, figure out how to make it, then mass-produce it. Yes, they're ready and eager. The supposed peace talks were a stall."

"So it's all been orchestrated. It's not a bad plan, all in all, but still, a lot of ifs and maybes. And the keys are the assassinations and the bombs.

"People, trust me, the CIA is on this. Now, tell me how you think Damari will kill the president. Kill me."

Nicholas said, "Given what Vanessa Grace told us, it's very possible Spenser and Damari planned a two-pronged attack—Damari killing you and Spenser blowing up the president at Yorktown. Killing both the president and vice president of the United States during Middle East peace talks would send a loud message to the world—the Great Satan is a fool, led around by the nose, and now he's a dead fool. As you said, ma'am, to destabilize the world is something we know many factions want to happen. With the tiny bombs—"

Callan nodded. "Yes, it is difficult to take in.

"Now, people, back to Spenser. He's our key. Please remember our goal is to capture him, and we will trust the CIA to turn Spenser against Damari, find out not only when and where he plans on killing me, but what he eats for breakfast. Does Spenser know Damari has his bombs and what he did with them? Maybe, maybe not. I don't know.

"Meanwhile, the CIA is concentrating on verifying if indeed Damari delivered the bomb to Iran and if indeed they have figured out how to make them, and have already begun."

She turned to Nicholas, smiled. "I met your father once, at Ten Downing Street. I remember it was a lovely party. And I waltzed with him. Please send him my best."

"I will, ma'am."

"If all this comes down to the wire, I do hope you live up to your reputation."

Nicholas merely inclined his head, wondering what she expected him to say. *Yes, ma'am, I'll save the world single-handed? Would ma'am like another happy pill?*

Callan said, "Vanessa Grace is safe; she is no longer in residence at George Washington University Hospital. CIA agent Carrie Munson, armed not only with her Glock and red hair, but with a fast and sharp brain, is currently in her room, in her bed.

"As of five minutes ago, no sightings yet of Spenser, which is why I asked you to dress down. I want you all to go immediately to the hospital, look at everything with professional eyes, stake it out. Remember, he is our only link to Damari. We're making sure the news story is spread far and wide so he'll see it."

Mike said, "Ma'am, I have only one concern. Is Spenser crazy enough to believe this isn't a trap?"

"From what I've personally seen over the years, an ideologue whose closest allies betray him loses it big-time. I believe Spenser will implode, for want of a better word, that he'll be pushed to kill her, for real this time. I've read the profilers' reports on him and this is the picture they paint of the man.

"So yes, when Matthew Spenser finds out this betraying bitch somehow survived, he will certainly consider it's a trap, but it won't matter, he'll have to come, he'll have to see her alive with his own eyes, then he'll try his best to get up close and personal and kill her."

Savich nodded. "Agreed. Whatever Spenser felt for her, it morphed into instant killing hate the moment he found out what and who she really was."

Nicholas said to the vice president, "You've seen a great many killers like this?"

Callan burst out laughing. "Killers? Well, yes, we all have, but you know what? I was actually thinking of politicians. Like Spenser, politicians want complete and ultimate control, they want destiny in their hands, and no one better get in their way. The TV series *House of Cards?* More right-on than not, only they're not, thankfully, as brilliant as Kevin Spacey's scriptwriters for Frank Underwood."

She stood. They all did as well.

"Spenser's history shows he isn't known for collateral damage, but after Bayway, we have to assume Spenser and Damari are more alike now than they ever were, and you know as well as I do that Damari is one of the most dangerous assassins in history. Remember, he didn't hesitate to murder three FBI agents in Bayonne; oh, yes, I'm sure it was him. It fits his profile, despite the fact there was no good reason to kill anyone in that house.

"The three of you are going to face one of the monsters. I want all of you to be extraordinarily careful."

Savich shook her hand. "Believe me, ma'am, we're hardwired to be careful. We'll coordinate with your people. And be in touch."

"Excellent." Callan handed each of them a card. "This is my personal cell phone. If you need anything, call me directly. Please, be careful."

And they were dismissed.

As they drove away, Tony came to stand by Callan's side, both of them staring after the Volvo.

"Think they can bring down Spenser?"

"Yes."

"And Zahir Damari?"

Callan watched the car disappear around the circular

drive, then turned. "I wish I knew, Tony. How to find him? I don't know if Spenser even knows what Zahir is up to or where he's at. But I do know one thing for sure: Damari is the most dangerous individual on the planet."

She laid her hand on his arm. "Let's brief the president about Damari and about those bombs."

67

KNIGHT TO E5

George Washington University Hospital

Matthew wasn't stupid. He knew the TV report on Vanessa had been leaked on purpose. The whole place had to be crawling with Feds, he could practically feel them, waiting, guns ready.

But it didn't matter. If she was alive, he wanted to finish the job, he had to finish it. She'd betrayed him, she didn't deserve to live, and this time he would make sure her eyes were vacant and her heart didn't beat. He laughed, thought maybe he'd burn down the freaking hospital while he was at it, give a final salute to Andy.

He'd found a good vantage point in the garage across from the back entrance to the hospital. He'd sat in the darkness, waiting for three hours now, getting a sense of the ebb and flow of the area.

Hospital staff parked here. The right person would come, sooner or later. He was patient, something he'd had to learn during his years with Ian.

Hospital employees walked in and out of the garage, wearing scrubs and clogs, some in white coats, carrying messenger bags and backpacks. A few biked to work, then changed their shoes. Some left, more came.

There was a shift change at six in the morning. Nurses began flooding the garage. He stepped from the car, into the meager sunrise, watched for someone his size and hair color. It didn't take long.

There he was. He rode a bike; it was chained up twenty feet from where Matthew silently waited. He took off his white coat—a doctor, then, or an intern, not a nurse—folded it carefully, and put it in his messenger bag. Matthew waited for him to get on his bike and start down the ramp. He got back in the car and drove, careful not to be seen by the cameras, turning his head away at the right moments. The plates would be visible; no matter, he intended to ditch the car the moment he had the ID anyway.

The doctor took a right out of the garage, began pedaling down New Hampshire Avenue toward the Potomac. Matthew followed, slowly now, making sure he kept him in sight. A bike meant he lived close by.

Within minutes, they were at the entrance of the Watergate Apartments. The doctor stopped at the Watergate Café. Matthew followed him in, watched him standing in line. He got coffee and a roll, tucked in right there like he was starved.

When he came out of the café, a second coffee in his hand, he walked his bike toward the Watergate garage.

Matthew took him from behind, jerked him back into the bushes, slapping his hand over his mouth. It was risky since there were a couple of people not twenty feet away, but he found, oddly, that he didn't care. It didn't take him more than a moment to decide—he slipped his knife into the doctor's heart, and the man dropped like a stone.

Matthew stripped him of his badge and the white jacket he'd stashed in his messenger bag, plus his wallet, in case they needed two forms of ID. His name was—had been—Aaron Tasker. He left him there in the bushes and didn't look back. He realized he didn't feel a thing. Not a single bit of fear or remorse, nothing. He was a man on a mission, and he knew he had to win this time. But what if he didn't win? *Focus,* he thought, *it's time to focus.*

Matthew took the bike and rode back to the hospital.

As he pedaled, he found himself remembering how he'd felt the moment he'd heard he was a Rhodes scholar and was on his way to Oxford. He remembered how he'd been acknowledged as a genius in the scientific field, remembered the stark happiness, the pride his parents felt, and how he'd basked in the honors flowing over him.

And then the bombings happened, his family blown apart simply because they were in the wrong place at the wrong time. And he remembered clearly that day he'd become a different man with a different future.

In a blink of an eye, he'd lost everything, and his rage festered and grew. And he'd met Ian McGuire in that pub in Italy, and they'd hooked up. He remembered Ian praising him endlessly, calling him a genius, so proud of him as he developed his new bomb, one smaller than the usual, and he'd figured out how to make it light and portable, and best of all, undetectable. His invention, his genius, and the rest of the world was still working with DIME bombs, Semtex, C4. He'd created something new. Powerful. And useful.

Matthew had discovered all he had to do was attach a nanotrigger to a small piece of his new metal, and boom. He felt like a god, gloried in what he'd created. Then he saw his mother's face and knew she wouldn't be praising his genius. *Revenge, Mom, really, all revenge, for you and Dad and my sister, but I'm not going to murder, not like they do. I'm going to cut them off at the knees, let them drown in their oil.* And he'd believed it, believed it to his soul. Then.

When Ian had brought Vanessa into his life, and she'd wanted to join him, he was convinced she shared in his beliefs, his goals. But now, in hindsight, he realized she hadn't shared a thing with him. All she'd wanted was his new bomb.

But he'd been smart, careful; he'd never told her all of it. And then Darius had tested it at Bayway without telling him and he'd been furious until he realized how amazing it had been.

And now Ian was dead, burned to a cinder, and the lying bitch was still breathing his air, but not for long.

Matthew rode the bike into the garage, chained it to the rack, and walked across the pedestrian bridge into the building, swiped Aaron's card through the reader, and walked right in the door. No one gave him a second glance. He belonged.

Now he needed to find Vanessa.

GW had multiple ICUs, multiple floors. He couldn't afford to waste time wandering the halls looking for agents in their dark suits guarding a hospital door. He needed to access the computer system and look her up. He felt the bloody knife move in his pocket as he walked.

68

KING TO G7

Mike stood behind the door where she couldn't be seen from either the hallway or the windows. Nicholas was in the bathroom, sitting on the counter. There was so much glass in the place, so many open lines of sight to help the nurses keep eyes on their patients, they'd had a hard time finding the perfect places to lie in wait.

Agent Carrie Munson, CIA, was a good ten years older than Vanessa and Mike, a seasoned agent who looked hard as nails. "I'm into krav maga," she'd told Mike and Nicholas. "Don't worry about me, I can handle myself. Plus I have this." She showed them a tidy Glock 17, stashed under her pillow. Mike didn't doubt Carrie could handle herself, but if Matthew came in gun first, words later, who knew what could happen?

They decided it was better to let Spenser get close,

move all the way into Vanessa's room before they brought him down.

Agents dressed as nurses and orderlies worked alongside the regular staff. They all had photos of Matthew Spenser, not the face you'd think looked like a murderer or a terrorist, maybe a madman, rather the face of a handsome man, serious and thoughtful, one of the first photos of him Vanessa had sent to her uncle.

After an hour on high alert, they all began to tire, to lose focus. Mike was tense. Her shoulders started to ache.

After two hours, Nicholas and Mike switched places.

Nicholas said, "I might consider giving up trying to talk to you if I could have a cup of coffee."

"Even if there was something to talk about, which there isn't and never will be, you still couldn't have any coffee. We need to keep hands free to handle weapons." As if he didn't know that.

"I guess tea is out, too?"

Both their earpiece comms units suddenly came to life.

A voice she didn't recognize, CIA, she assumed, said, "We have him. He's gotten off the west elevator, moving toward the room. He's dressed as a doctor, looks like he belongs. He's not hesitating and that's smart, so you guys need to be ready."

A doctor, Mike thought, adrenaline spiking, and wondered what had happened to the man whose white coat he'd stolen.

"He's reaching into his back pocket, wait, I saw a flash, not sure if it's a blade or a gun."

The bathroom door was cracked. Nicholas looked at

Mike through the small gap. She nodded. He signaled to Carrie, who rolled a bit onto her side, away from the door, making sure her red hair was showing. He looked back at Mike, saw her hands on her Glock, double grip, loose and ready.

Nicholas hoped Spenser was carrying a gun. No one liked close quarters and a knife.

"He's twenty feet away now. Ten. Five."

Come on, come on, come on, you bugger.

"He's stopped. He's turning. Oh, crap!"

Nicholas's earpiece exploded into a cacophony of curses. He heard shoving, a thud against the wall, shouts. "What the bloody hell has happened?" he whispered into his wrist unit.

"He's taken a nurse. He has a knife to her throat. It's already bloody, but not from her. If you get a clear shot, take it."

"No, we can't shoot him. We need him alive."

Another man's voice in his ear: "Why don't you come out and see what's happening for yourself, Special Agent? I know you're in there."

Mike heard Spenser loud and clear, telling Nicholas to come out of the room. He'd gotten onto their comms channel. He was here, less than ten feet away, and here she was stuck in the bathroom. Unless Spenser came into the room, all she could do was wait, and be ready. She kept looking through the crack in the bathroom door into the hospital room. Nicholas motioned to her. He had a pen out and was writing on his hand. He held up his palm toward her.

I'm going out. He thinks there's only one of us in here.

She shook her head, pointing to Carrie, to the door, then swiping her hand in front of her throat in a cutting motion.

Matthew's voice came over the comms again. "Come out, Agent, don't be afraid of what I'll do. I only want to talk to her. I only want to say I'm sorry."

Nicholas wrote *Plan B* on his hand.

What was Plan B?

But she knew, of course. Nicholas was going cowboy.

Spenser's voice was soft and persuasive over the comms: "If you don't let me come in and talk to Vanessa, I'll cut this lady's lovely throat."

Mike watched, helpless, as Nicholas disappeared from view. If he survived this, she fully intended to kill him.

Nicholas took it all in in a millisecond—Cindy Carlisle was a pretty nurse with short, spiky blond hair and a wonderful smile she'd given him when they'd stepped onto the floor to set up the op. Spenser was holding her tight against him, his arm around her throat, a bloody knife against her flesh. She was the perfect shield.

Nicholas had supposed if he ever saw Spenser up close, he'd see madness in his eyes, but it wasn't true. Hate had twisted Spenser, but it didn't show on the outside. He was handsome, his face smooth, his eyes intelligent, clear, focused on Nicholas's face. He looked calm, as if he were in a college seminar, not in a death dance. With the doctor's white coat, he fit right in, except for the bloody knife at Cindy's throat, digging in slightly, drawing a drop of blood, to show he was serious. Cindy wasn't moving, was barely breathing.

Four agents stood around him, weapons drawn. One false twitch, and Spenser would be dead, the nurse, too. They couldn't risk it.

Nicholas held his gun in his palm, finger off the trigger, nose pointing skyward, his other hand up, too. Open. Vulnerable.

"Drop the knife, Mr. Spenser. You can come in and talk to Vanessa, but I'm covering you every second. You try anything and I will shoot you, understand?"

"You're Drummond. It's nice to meet you. I'm the Bishop."

"No, you're Matthew Spenser. The other name, it's nonsense and you know it."

Matthew stared at the big man, heard the Brit accent and wondered at it. "I'm telling you the truth. I want to speak to Vanessa, tell her I'm sorry. Will she live? The hospital records said she was critical. She survived two surgeries?"

Matthew took a step toward him, shoving Cindy in front of him. Cindy didn't make a sound, but Nicholas knew she was petrified. She was staring at him, her eyes wide, pupils dilated.

Nicholas said, "She's going to make it. Amazing for a woman who'd been shot in the chest and left for dead in a burning building, don't you think? Did you or Andy Tate set the fire?"

"Andy wanted to, but as I told him, I didn't want to burn down the whole block."

"Like I said, you can speak to her out here, not in the room."

"Is Vanessa really in there or is it one of your agents?"

"You let Cindy go and you can come over here and see her. Red hair and all. You're in luck, she's awake right now."

"Have her call out to me to prove it's really Vanessa and this isn't a trick."

On cue, they all heard Vanessa's voice come from the room—weak, sounding a bit blurred with drugs, and angry. "It's me, Matthew. I didn't believe them when they said you'd come back to try to kill me again. I didn't think you were such an idiot. But here you are. Well, what are you waiting for?"

Spenser went white. His hand holding the knife at Cindy's throat began to tremble. Not good. He began shaking his head back and forth. What did he think? Vanessa's voice was coming from the grave?

Nicholas studied Spenser's face. He watched him lose more control with each passing second. His arm began to fall. Cindy, smart girl, dove to the floor and rolled against the nurses' station into the fetal position, covering her head with her arms. She didn't move.

Spenser exploded into action. He ran toward the door, shoving Nicholas out of his way, screaming, "You bitch! You should be dead! You deserve to be dead—look what you did to me!"

Nicholas shouted, "Mike, now!"

Spenser came racing through the door as Mike stepped out of the bathroom and shouted, "Stop!"

But he didn't.

Carrie rose up, her Glock in her hand, as he sprang toward the bed, arm in a wide arc, the blade flashing red as it slashed down. He screamed, "You're not Vanessa!"

And the knife kept coming.

Mike pulled the trigger three times, quick succession. Spenser spun around to face her, eyes wild, jaw working. She'd clipped him twice in the hand and once in his arm. He hugged his arm to his body, and moaned with the pain, but somehow he still clutched the knife. He stared at her, then turned slowly to look at Carrie. "I don't understand. You're not Vanessa, I know you're not, but I heard her voice."

Carrie turned on the recorder. Vanessa's voice sounded. "Hello, Matthew. Won't you come in and talk to me?"

He stood quietly, holding his arm, staring at Mike, then Carrie, and the pain was making him weave where he stood.

"That was really smart. A recording," and he hugged his arm tighter against him, then, amazingly, he began to laugh.

"You tricked me good, didn't you? She really is dead, isn't she? What, this is her dying message?"

"Oh no," Nicholas said from behind him. "She was happy to record this for us. She only wished she could be here to speak to you in person."

Mike said, "She recorded more for you, Spenser, if you would like to hear it." And she pressed the button.

Vanessa's voice, weak but steady: "Matthew, you need to tell them everything, where you planted the bomb in Yorktown, where Darius is, what he plans.

"He wasn't ever who you believed he was, Matthew. We believe now that Iran and Hezbollah hired him, the very people you hate. He's been using you. They've been using you.

"Please cooperate with Drummond and Caine. They'll make sure you're treated fairly."

Vanessa's voice stopped. The only sound in the room was Matthew's hoarse breathing.

Mike kept her Glock trained on him as she took a step toward him. "Vanessa told you the truth, Mr. Spenser. We will treat you fairly, but you must help us, you must tell us where Darius is. Did you know his real name is Zahir Damari? He's an assassin, not a comrade in arms.

He used you, simple as that. Does he intend to kill the vice president? Or the president? Did he manage to get one of your bombs to Tehran?"

Matthew began to laugh again, and Mike edged a little closer, her weapon steady.

Matthew looked from Nicholas in the doorway, to the three agents crowded in behind him, to the woman who shot him, to the woman with the red hair. The pain in his arm and hand was immense, thudding and pounding, making him want to scream, but he didn't. When he spoke, his voice was steady, firm. "Darius, or Damari, whatever, I don't care, what he's going to do is just, it's righteous, no matter his motives. You're lying about Iran and Hezbollah, Darius was English, and like me, he understood loss and pain. As for the bombs, he doesn't have any." He stopped cold, then slowly shook his head.

So Damari had stolen one.

Spenser looked from her to Nicholas and down at Carrie. "You people don't understand. Vanessa never understood. I know there isn't a single person in this world who thinks clearly when it comes to the terrorists. They aren't one country, one group, they're an entire section of the world stuck in the Middle Ages, and their sole purpose is to kill us. Our current administration believes we can work with them, show them how we respect their beliefs, their religions, regardless of their sects.

"We're told we should be tolerant, we should excuse what they do to women, do to anyone who disagrees with them, and then, if we do, we're assured they'll stop hating us and wanting to kill us. What a joke that is.

"Our own president wants to placate them, appease them, give them endless concessions, drop sanctions, let them come and go as they please. And the minute we agree to do these things, they will smile at the peace table and drink a toast to peace with us, then parade in and slit our throats, chop off our heads, burn us to death.

"They hate us, they hate everything we stand for. We are a pestilence to them, nothing more.

"They must be stopped, to be shown once and for all that we will stand up for ourselves, that we will not let them murder us. I'm taking the first step. I'm killing that idiot who would hand us over to the terrorists on a silver platter." His voice rose to a yell. "No more appeasement!"

He smiled at each of them in turn, a triumphant smile, one that scared Mike to her toes. His hand came away from his wounded arm. He was holding a cell phone.

He paused only a brief instant, then, "I'm the beginning!"

He pressed a button on the cell phone an instant before Mike pulled the trigger.

Spenser went down hard. The phone spun away out of his hand, hit the floor, and rolled out into the hall.

Everyone dove for cover, bracing for the explosion.

It didn't happen.

Nicholas was out the door, scooped up the phone, and began to frantically search. Mike stood at his elbow, leaving Carrie to see to Spenser.

"No bomb," Carrie called out.

"Nicholas, what's on there?"

"I don't know yet. It has to be some sort of trigger.

There's a countdown going. We better clear out of here in case he dropped something in a trash can on his way in."

The agent who'd spoken to them over their comms shouted, "I didn't see him put anything anywhere. He walked in, didn't stop, didn't toss anything. He never took his hands out of his pocket except to pull out the knife, so I think we're okay."

A huge relief, Mike thought, since clearing an ICU would be a nightmare.

Nicholas pulled out his laptop, set it on the counter. "I'm going to plug it in, see if I can override the program."

The phone was an Android and he had a cord for it in his bag. It didn't look like it could do much, yet the countdown was still going on.

He plugged it in, set his code to override the countdown and break into the phone's software.

After a few minutes, he said, "I'm in. Phone was encrypted, but I have it now."

"Where's the bomb?" Mike asked.

Nicholas was staring at the screen of his laptop.

"Nicholas, what is it?"

He turned the screen. She saw silver metal, a complicated control system, half-moons in blacks and oranges, blues and greens. An altimeter, a horizon, engine loads.

"It's a plane. Spenser planted a bomb on a plane."

"It's not just any plane," Nicholas said. "See the insignia in the middle top? It's bloody *Air Force One*."

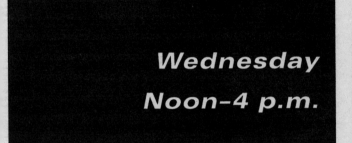

Wednesday

Noon–4 p.m.

70

BISHOP TO C5 CHECK

Air Force One
Over the North Atlantic

President Jefferson Bradley was alone, finally, in his private office in the upstairs of *Air Force One*. They'd gotten a late start, a threat there was a sniper on a building near *Air Force One*, and wasn't that just par for the course? Everyone was on edge until they took off.

Now, six hours later, he was nursing a lovely single-barrel Blanton's bourbon and all his aides were elsewhere, either talking about the aborted peace talks, or maybe about what they were going to do Saturday night, who knew? At least he no longer had to deal with those treacherous two-faced fools who'd supposedly come to talk peace. He consigned the lot of them to the deepest pit of Hell.

He sighed. Those small undetectable bombs Callan had told him about. Were they real? If so, that was a worry. What was going on?

Calm, he wanted calm, and distraction. He picked up a new biography of Churchill, wished it was a thriller instead, something to distract him, and had flipped a page when alarms began to sound. He slapped at the conference button on his speakerphone. "What's happening?"

The pilot—Air Force colonel Simon Moore—came over the speaker. "Sir, we're experiencing some computer issues down here. We'll be fixed up in a moment, we're waiting for an upload from Command."

"Turn off the alarm, then. No sense freaking out the whole plane."

"Yes, sir."

There was buzzing behind the alarm. For the briefest of moments, he could hear the faraway squelch of the copilot on the radio speaking to their air recon planes, telling them they'd lost an electrical port, then the alarm turned off and the pilot released the speaker button.

It was suddenly deathly quiet. Bradley shrugged it off, set down the book on the table in front of him. He closed his eyes, and there they were, all pomp and circumstance—the Iranian negotiators, and look what they'd done. At crunch time, they'd thrown it all away, with smug smiles, and lies pouring out of their mouths. The reactors lit up? Soldiers massing? All a misunderstanding, only their normal scheduled tests.

He felt unutterably depressed. All his hopes, his plans for his legacy, nothing now. What was wrong with these people? Was Callan right? Was this all meant to play him along until they'd stolen the bombs? Until they had copied them? Tiny undetectable bombs, as small as gold coins? He didn't know if he even believed it.

When Callan had told him Iran had moved several of their missile batteries, turned on their blasted refineries, he'd believed it their usual posturing, their usual middle finger to the West. But now he supposed he had to believe it was more, like Callan said, given the unguarded last look he'd seen on the lead negotiator's face in a mirror the man wasn't aware of. He'd looked—pleased. Excited. And then he'd known it was no use.

Bradley felt rage building. All their petty arguing, fighting over an inch of land, a camel here and an oil derrick there, whose God was more important. They couldn't agree where the sun rose, hadn't since the dawn of time. Fighting and killing, and watching with hatred and distrust a world that had moved on without them. It was exhausting. He said to his glass of Blanton's, "If only they could see a future that embraced other beliefs, other races, not death, always death." And he sighed. He doubted they ever would change, their boundless hatred seemed hard-wired over more than a thousand years. He remembered telling Callan they were like children, all they needed was a firm hand to guide them, *his hand*, but he hadn't said that aloud, and she'd laughed.

"No, you're wrong there, Jeff. They're like drunk teenagers ready to run away from home after burning their parents to death."

He tried to pound his hopes and beliefs back into place.

Surely Callan was wrong, the CIA was wrong, the military was wrong. It was Iran's leadership at fault, he had to believe that, crushing their people under the weight of intolerance and ancient rules and commandments. He'd desperately wanted to give the next generation a chance. They were the only hope.

But no amount of pounding would do it. Iran had tossed it all in the fire, rejoicing as they did so. He realized now he'd never met Iran's lead negotiator before these talks. Was Colonel Vahid Rahbar the one behind this insanity? Along with his Hezbollah bullies?

And now Yorktown was canceled. For heaven's sake, he was used to threats—he was the leader of the free world, they happened daily. Still, Callan had been adamant the threat was real, and Mossad, the FBI, and the CIA agreed. He may not like the woman, but he did respect her. She wasn't reactionary; she'd been out in the real, dirty, nasty world, and no agency was more real, dirtier, or nastier than the CIA. He knew her bringing him California in the election had really turned the tide in his favor. It rankled, particularly if she turned out to be right.

He took a deep drink of the bourbon, feeling the fire burn all the way to his belly.

He set the glass back on the table, glanced over at the flight map. They were closing in on land, coming in above Maine. The flight tracker said he'd be back in D.C. within two hours. When he landed, the very first thing he was going to do—

The plane jolted. His bourbon started to slide. Bradley grabbed it.

A shudder ran the long line of the plane, then it banked suddenly, hard left, like a fighter jet coming about. Bradley knew the feeling—he'd flown F-16s in the war. The Boeing 747-200B wasn't capable of making such a sharp turn.

They went slightly sideways, and a small frisson of panic went through him.

Colonel Moore came over the intercom. His voice was remarkably calm—not a surprise, since Moore had been a fighter pilot for years before taking on this position.

"Sir, we have a problem. Someone has hacked into our flight computer. They have taken over the controls and engaged the autoland."

"Well, take it back from them."

"I can't, sir. There's a bug in the system of some kind. When we uploaded the new software for the electrical issues, we also uploaded a worm embedded inside the software. I don't know how it happened, but we can't get into it to change course, heading, altitude, nothing. Someone outside is flying the plane now. Sir, I'm sorry."

The plane executed another hard turn. Bradley could hear people running. The door from the communications room burst open, smashing back into the wall and hurling his chief of staff, Ellen Star, nearly into his lap. She grabbed his arms. "Sir, we're being attacked! We're under attack!"

Bradley steadied her. "It will be all right, Ellen." The plane rattled and heaved and he pulled her to his side and held her tight. "We'll be just fine, you'll see."

And he said into the intercom, "Get this plane under control immediately, Colonel Moore. That's an order."

The down angle of the plane's nose shifted suddenly, and they began to lose altitude. Star screamed. He heard shouts, calls, screams throughout the plane, and then thumps and bangs as luggage fell and people toppled.

Moore said, his voice still calm, "Sir, I regret to tell you that we have no control of the plane. Repeat, we have no control. You're going to want to put on your life vest, sir. We're going down."

71

KING TO F1

George Washington University Hospital

Nicholas watched, helpless. The glide slope of the plane had changed dramatically. The horizon shifted hard, and he realized what was happening. No, he couldn't let the plane go down, couldn't. He had to do something. Adrenaline burst through him, and there was Mike beside him, asking, "So it was Matthew's job to assassinate the president. What exactly is happening, Nicholas?"

"Someone has control of the autoland. I don't know if they're trying to land the plane somewhere, or crash it into the ocean. We need to find a way to override the system, but this bastard has shut down all the electronic controls. I don't know how to stop it."

She said, all calm certainty, "Yes, you do, Nicholas. What do you need to do first?"

He looked up at Mike. "I need to find a route in through their wireless system before the plane lands or crashes. From the heading, it's the latter, and I have about two minutes before it's in the water."

She cleared the space, waving people back, then came back, hunkered down beside him, saw the fierce concentration. "Tell me what you need."

And it hit him. "I need secure comms with the plane. Get me through, Mike. Now. They'll need to be ready to take over if I can dismantle the attack."

He closed his eyes in a brief prayer. Seventy-eight souls were in the palm of his hand.

Mike didn't hesitate, she pulled out the private card and called the vice president directly.

Callan answered, "Agent Caine, what's going on there—"

"Ma'am, we need immediate access to *Air Force One*. It's being attacked. Audio, cell, radio. Anything we can get, and we need it right now."

Callan said, "Hold." The phone went quiet. Ten long seconds later, she came back on. "You're being patched through."

Mike put the phone on speaker, set it by Nicholas's left hand.

"This is Special Operations Command, Captain Reynolds here. Who am I talking to?"

"Agent Nicholas Drummond, FBI. *Air Force One* has been compromised. I need to overtake their flight controls."

"Can't be done."

"Someone already has done it, mate. Did you alter the software for the controls in the last thirty days?"

Silence, the man disappeared for a minute. "Come on, come on," Nicholas said under his breath, typing hard and fast on the computer. Mike watched code stream from his fingers onto the screen like he was something from the Matrix.

Captain Reynolds came back. "Yes, about ten minutes ago, in flight. They had an electrical issue, we pushed an update to get them back online."

"We need to push a new update. The one they pushed in was compromised."

"Can't do it, the controls are down. Wait, wait, the readings are offline. Drummond, the plane is going down!"

"I know this, Captain Reynolds. We have less than a minute left. Lift the firewall. I can break through it, but we can't waste any more time. I'll take it from there."

"This is Vice President Sloane. Captain, do as he asks. Right now. That is a direct order."

"Yes, ma'am."

The screen in front of Nicholas changed. Mike saw him take a deep breath and she gripped his shoulder. "Go, Nicholas."

"Captain Reynolds, listen carefully. I'm going to create a new wireless network, and we're going to log off *Air Force One* and put the plane's communications onto the new network. Then you'll push a fresh update. Backdate to the one prior to the one you sent."

Reynolds said, "Are you crazy? I don't have enough time—"

"Do it," Nicholas said. "I've already founded the new wireless and I'm ready to override the attack." And to Mike, "What's my countdown?"

"You have forty-five seconds."

He clicked on his other screen and the plane's cockpit came up. The altimeter read eighteen thousand feet. They were going down fast.

"Are you ready?" he said to Captain Reynolds.

Reynolds stressed voice, "I need thirty more seconds."

"This is over in twenty. Get the bloody firewall down now! Crash the system, don't be nice to it. Force it!"

A pause. "It's down, it's down. Go!"

Nicholas started to type fast, strings of numbers. Everyone in the immediate area was creeping close again to watch. It was so quiet, Mike could hear herself breathe. She watched the clock over Nicholas's shoulder, and she prayed.

"Nicholas, twenty seconds," she said.

"I know, I know."

The code was done. The altimeter still spun crazily downward. "I need the pilot now, please," he said, more calmly than he felt. If he'd missed one letter, one number, one iota of code, the plane and all the people inside were dead.

"This is Colonel Moore. You're the one trying to fix this?" The man's voice was steady as a rock.

"Yes. When I say now, I want you to take the plane back, execute all evasive maneuvers. Three, two, one, now!"

He typed EXE and hit return. Stopped. Didn't move an inch.

There was nothing more he could do.

The code fed directly into the plane's database. In a perfect world, it would take fifteen seconds to take over the computers. They had five.

Four.

Three.

There was complete silence on the line.

He'd failed. The plane had hit the water, ripped apart, and now it was sinking and everyone was dead. His closed his eyes. *Please, forgive me.*

He didn't see the altimeter stop moving and level out at thirteen hundred feet.

Mike leaned down, hugged him tight. "Nicholas. Look! You did it!"

He opened his eyes as Colonel Moore's voice came over the phone's tinny speaker. "I have control of the plane. Repeat, I have the plane. Climbing to ten thousand feet. That was rather close. I thank you, Drummond, my wife thanks you, everyone on board thanks you. The president especially."

72

KNIGHT TO G3
CHECK

Nicholas heard the cheering but shut it off, too much more to do. "Colonel Moore? I don't know how long the patch will hold. You need to land, right now."

"We're in contact with the TRACON in Halifax, Nova Scotia, will be on the ground in less than ten. Can't wait to shake your hand, young man. Drinks are on me, dinner's on my wife. Thank you. This is Moore, out."

The vice president's voice came over the line. "Special Agent Drummond? I see you do live up to your reputation. Good job. How did this happen?"

"It was Spenser, ma'am. Mike was forced to shoot him, but not before he started the countdown to blow up *Air Force One*. As he pressed the button, he yelled, 'I'm the beginning!' There must be more coming. All I can think is that Spenser was to kill the president, which means Damari is still out there, gunning for you."

A brief pause, then, "I understand. I will speak to you soon."

Then Savich was at his side. "Everything is stable now, Nicholas?"

Nicholas turned to look at Savich. "Yes. Thankfully, the plane will be landing shortly. Now I have Matthew Spenser's phone. I'll continue decrypting it and find if he was also involved in killing the vice president. We do know this was his goal, and, hopefully, his finale."

"You had to kill him, Mike?"

"Yes, I did, but he still had time to press the button on his phone."

Savich watched Nicholas rise and take her arms in his hands. "Listen to me, you did what you had to do and you did it in the right order. I'm very proud of you." He paused, then, "Thank you for helping me, Mike."

Carrie came out of the hospital room. "Hey, guys, look what I found sewn in the cuff of Spenser's trousers." She held up two gold coins. "Are these his undetectable bombs, the ones that blew up Bayway?"

"Yes," Mike said, staring at those harmless-looking gold coins, so small, so innocent-looking. "Hold them gently, Carrie."

"You can bet your sweet patoot on that," Carrie said.

Savich cleared both Nicholas and Mike through, saying quietly, "You and Nicholas need to get on out of here, let the crime scene unit come in and do their jobs. Go to the Hoover Building. Sherlock will meet you and take you to the command center with all the cameras on Yorktown. Questions later."

Nicholas nodded. "We have no idea what's going to happen, but if what Vanessa said is correct and Spenser did have the opportunity to plant bombs on-site, we've got to find them. We can't let anyone else get hurt."

"Already done," Savich said, and ushered them onto the elevator. "They have two bomb units there searching, but they've been coming up dry. Since the bombs are meant to be undetectable, they've evacuated everyone anyway."

Before they parted company Mike handed her gun over, procedure, watched an agent slip it into an evidence bag, and wanted to cry. At least she had a small snub-nosed Glock in an ankle holster in her motorcycle boot. It would do.

Savich gripped Nicholas's shoulder. "You did great, both of you," he said, and headed back into the fray.

Nicholas felt a bolt of pleasure at Savich's words, then shook his head. No time to bask. He turned back to Mike, saw myriad feelings play across her face. He didn't blame her.

"Let's get out of here, Agent Caine. I think we both could use a nice cup of hot tea."

She didn't know where it came from, but she laughed. She let him take her hand.

"If you're a good girl, I might even add a dollop of whiskey."

She felt the depression begin to lift. "You know, that might be a good idea."

"And maybe that'll make you want to talk."

"Not a chance."

———

They stopped at a coffee shop near the State Department and got the tea, but alas, no whiskey, plus bagels hot and ready to be smeared thick with cream cheese. She hadn't realized she was hungry, but when she took that first bite, her taste buds started a stampede.

When she finished, she sat back, laced her fingers over her stomach, and looked over at Nicholas.

"Better, Agent Caine?"

"Much. You did good, Nicholas, really good. I mean, you saved the president's freaking life, not to mention all those people on the plane. Plus the captain's wife will now make you dinner."

He wanted to tell her without her quick thinking, calling the vice president, hooking him up with the pilot, he couldn't have saved them, but knew she'd only shrug, dismiss it. He said only, "You know what I think? You should frame the vice president's card."

That was good, she thought, but it didn't quite lift the cloud of doom. "About Spenser, Nicholas, I really wished I hadn't had to kill him."

Nicholas shrugged. "I don't think he ever planned to walk away from the hospital. He knew it was the end of the line. Blowing up the president's plane? Killing the leader he saw as giving in to terrorists? I'll bet Damari didn't have to do too much convincing." He shrugged again, took another sip of his tea. "I don't guess we'll ever know."

He was right, or close enough. "And now we have to

wonder if that other countdown on his phone means he's going to blow up Yorktown."

"Not a doubt in my mind, unfortunately." Someone had turned up the volume on the television and they both watched the breaking news about a shooting at George Washington University Hospital. The anchor said, "No details, and the hospital is no longer on lockdown, we'll have more news on this during the noon broadcast."

Mike said, "Everything boils down to a news bite." She raised her face, and he saw pain there and regret and hated it. "He was fast, so fast. When he pressed the button I thought we were all dead, boom, gone up in smoke. All I could think was I failed, I failed everyone. And I thought about my mom, and my dad, and how upset they would be at me getting myself killed because I wasn't fast enough." She leaned forward, balanced her chin on her hands. "I made the wrong decision, Nicholas. I shouldn't ever have let him press the button on that phone."

He wanted to tell her she'd stopped a killer, saved innumerable lives, but knew she'd kiss that off, as the Americans said. He said only, "So tell me, what did you do wrong exactly?"

Instead, she surprised him. "I'd like you to meet my folks sometime, Nicholas. You'd like them. You'll start panting when you meet my mom, the Gorgeous Rebecca."

This was interesting. "Yes," he said, never looking away from her. "I'd like to meet them."

"Spenser is dead and we still don't know where Damari is or what he's planning. My folks come to New York regularly. Maybe we can all have dinner. No, no, lunch would be better."

He laughed. "We can discuss it."

"All right, yes, we can talk about my parents, and lunch, that'd be okay."

"Time to pack away all the second-guessing, Agent Caine. You made exactly the right call, and I would have done the same if I'd been in your position. Don't forget, he made it past me, too. If anyone's to blame, it's me. And no one is."

She waved that away, as he expected she would.

"I wonder if the president will invite you to the White House, give you the keys to the Lincoln Bedroom? But I've heard the bed is really short, too short for you."

He glanced at his Breitling. "Seventy minutes until the speech at Yorktown was supposed to happen. No doubt in my mind there'll be an explosion and we'll be treated to another display of the bomb's power."

"And still it won't be over." Mike banged her fist on the table. "Where is Damari?"

73

KING TO E1

Hoover Building

Sherlock met them in the lobby, hugged them both. "Andy Tate's body was found an hour ago in a motel in Lorton, Virginia. He was shot through the forehead. There were some electronics lying around, but no laptops, no phones. Only Spenser and Tate went into the room, so it wasn't Damari, unless he was wearing Potter's invisibility cloak."

"Yes," Nicholas said. "Matthew Spenser, no doubt."

Mike frowned. "Why did he kill Tate? He was one of his core group, his right hand—the computer guy who implemented the cyber-attack."

Sherlock said, "Dillon believes Spenser had simply gone over the edge at that point. His only focus became killing Vanessa and blowing up the president. He knew he was going to die, accepted it.

"Dillon just called me, told me to tell you he'd spoken to both Carl Grace and Vanessa, told them what had happened. He wanted to assure you that Vanessa was going to be okay, and she sends her thanks for helping wrap things up, glad what she recorded for Spenser worked. But like the rest of us, she's terrified Damari got Matthew's coin to Iran.

"Still—you saved the president of the United States, and that makes everything, for the moment, at least, okay. I've already heard from at least six agents that you guys were amazing. Nicholas, what does it feel like to have the president of the United States owe you big-time?" And she laughed, punched him in the arm. "My advice is to call the IRS, make a deal. I bet those dual taxes are crippling. Now follow me, guys, not much time now until Yorktown. And no one wants to guess what will happen."

Sherlock took them to the fifth floor, to a large conference room that had been turned into a sophisticated command center, similar to the command and control room in the New York Field Office. Four large flat-screen televisions showed four different aerial shots of the Yorktown refinery and surrounding area. There were light-green labels on the waterways—Back Creek, York River.

There were a dozen or so FBI agents sitting around the large center table, drinking coffee, speaking in low voices to one another, always one eye scanning the television screens.

Sherlock introduced Mike and Nicholas. There were so many new names, Mike knew it would be impossible to remember everybody, except Director Comey, of course, who rose and shook their hands. He looked closely at Nicholas. "Ah, our very own Brit. Didn't I just graduate you from the Academy thirty minutes ago? And already you've managed to save the president's life?"

Everyone laughed.

"Talk about hitting the ground running. The vice president wanted me to thank you, Agent Caine, for your quick thinking, and you, Agent Drummond, for your remarkable demonstration on the computer. I must say, I am very grateful both of you were at the hospital." He paused a moment, then shook his head. "I read Matthew Spenser's dossier and I'm left feeling it was all a tremendous waste. It was as if Spenser became the very person he'd started his crusade to fight against, a killer who eliminated everyone who got in his way or betrayed him."

He looked toward the map of Yorktown, slowly shook his head. "So many people in this world filled with hate, so many people who see violence as the only solution, who see murdering other people with dissimilar views as the right thing to do, as the only thing to do. Ah, well, that's why we all have jobs.

"Enough of that. Agent Sherlock, explain to Caine and Drummond exactly what they're seeing on the screens."

"Yes, sir. We have drones and a satellite sitting over Yorktown, waiting. The bomb teams and K9s will continue searching until three-thirty p.m., in exactly three minutes, then everyone's out. No matter what happens, no one will be in or near the facility at four. Though I have to tell you, the bomb squad doesn't think there's anything to worry about. They've seen nothing out of place, no violence toward any of the workers, no sign of any of Spenser's undetectable bombs, and if you know the K9s, you know they're thorough. We're all hoping the attack on *Air Force One* was Spenser's real target and the threat of Yorktown blowing up was simply a misdirection."

Nicholas didn't think so, but he only nodded.

He didn't think any of the agents in the room, including the director, believed that, either.

Sherlock pointed to the middle screen. "The Yorktown Seaport runs out into the Atlantic Ocean. It's the main reason they're turning it into a depot, and storing gas and petroleum and metal there. Those huge freighter ships have easy access. They've already begun the transition." She pointed to the far side of the screen. "See, you can make out the Chesapeake Bay in the background, there. Amazing the detail we can get with these shots. We'll have a bird's-eye view if the place blows. And look at this angle."

She pressed a remote, and the view shifted, almost like they were on a ship out to sea, coming in to land. It was now clear enough they could see the stripes of the red-and-white-painted smokestack, looking almost like a quaint lighthouse, reaching a hundred feet into the sky.

Mike imagined the smokestack would be a welcome sight after a long journey, and the cheerful candy-cane stripe in the sky could be seen far out to sea. They would have the best seats in the house.

As everyone settled in again to watch Yorktown on the screens, Mike leaned over to Nicholas. "We have to check in with Zachery, see if Ben Houston and Gray Wharton have dug anything up."

74

BISHOP TO B4 CHECK

M ike called Milo Zachery first, put him on speakerphone so Nicholas could hear, and filled him in on
what had happened, her voice matter-of-fact, emotionless.
He didn't interrupt. When she finished, Zachery said,
"Thank the good Lord you were able to stop the attack,
Drummond. I hear you created a wild new hack to get
into the flight control on *Air Force One*."

"Yes, sir," Mike said, "he did. He was amazing."

"But you, Mike, I hear you were on the phone to the
vice president making it all possible."

"Well, okay, I'll take credit for that one."

"Nicholas, what did you do exactly? That's Gray who
wants to know."

"Tell Gray I need to review it once we have the time.
But tell him now that I'm not entirely sure what the code

read, other than 'Please God don't let the plane crash' in ones and zeroes."

Zachery laughed. "Gray will like that and you can count on teaching our cyber-team how to do it. You two get back up here tomorrow. I'll even go so far to say a round of drinks on your boss might happen."

There was still Damari unaccounted for, and finding out if he'd gotten Spenser's bombs to Iran, but he said, "We'll try, sir."

"Mike? The investigative board will meet in the morning to discuss the Spenser shooting, but don't lose any sleep over it. You'll have your gun back by noon tomorrow."

After they'd rung off, Nicholas said, "Now we need to catch up with Gray and Ben," and he dialed them. He said without preamble, "Ben, tell me what you've got."

"You guys are going to like this. Our knock this morning was a treat. Like all our surprise early-morning visits to unsuspecting criminals, Porter Wallace heard us pounding on his front door, yelling 'FBI, open up,' stumbled out of bed and tried to run, the idiot. He didn't even have slippers on. His wife was yelling at him through it all, demanding what was going on."

Gray said, "In the end, though, Wallace proved to be quite cooperative. We barely needed to nudge him, he started singing like a canary when we showed him the statements Adam Pearce dug up for us. Let's hear it for the kid, he's good, Nicholas."

Nicholas said, "He's got great criminal instincts for someone so young. So Matthew Spenser and his Celebrants of Earth had their very own stockbroker. Who would have believed it?"

"Porter Wallace confirmed he and Matthew Spenser knew each other in school. Spenser showed up on his doorstep a year ago with a massive amount of cash and a need to invest it quietly. According to Wallace, he was forced into the scheme, which, I must say, is absolutely ingenious. When you get back, I'll give you all the details and numbers in our secure documents. From what Wallace said, he's been parlaying information from the backroom chat sessions he was having with his fellow brokers. They all get on a chat once a week and talk about what they're going to be buying in the upcoming session. After the chat, Wallace makes all of his buys for his legit clients, and a few buys for his not so legit clients."

"Two sets of books."

"Exactly. High-stakes, too. The last numbers I saw give COE a bank account in the ten million range. This number grows and shrinks based on the market, but Wallace is a shrewd investor, and has done well for them."

"Where did they get the money to invest in the first place? We've known they were well-financed from the beginning, but we haven't been able to find the trail. Who's behind this?"

"They were initially self-funded—Matthew Spenser's quite large trust fund was more than enough to get them started. Then, three months ago, COE shows up with a massive influx of cash."

Mike said, "That was when Zahir Damari showed up, with the money from Iran."

"Exactly," Gray said. "I started back tracing all the IP addresses they've used for the past month. Their computer expert is—was—first rate."

"But you're better."

"I'm skilled in a different way. Last known IP address came from a motel in Lorton, Virginia. I heard they found the computer guy's body—Andy Tate?"

"Right. They purchased DDoS attacks from Gunther Ansell, Tate loaded his own code next to it, and launched it into the systems. Ingenious plan."

"Lot of moving parts," Gray said. "But we've got them now."

Nicholas said, "It does sound like we have nearly everything we need to wrap up this part of the investigation. Great work, thanks to both of you."

Ben said, "Come on home, guys. We miss you. Mike, give the big Brit a smooch for me."

Ben and Gray both laughed like loons, and Mike looked like she'd been shot. She punched off the cell.

"You want to talk about it?" Nicholas asked.

"No, there's nothing to talk about, you know that. As for those two, they're idiots."

"No big smooch?"

"No more in this lifetime."

"We'll see. Now, how much time before the bomb at Yorktown?"

"Seventeen minutes, and there's nothing to see."

"Good, enough time to speak to Adam about a theory I have about how Spenser managed to break into the electrical grid and upload the worm to *Air Force One*'s flight computers." He punched in Adam's number.

Adam answered immediately. "I've been waiting for your call. Wow, that was some really gnarly coding, Nicholas. I've never seen anything like it. You two okay?"

Nicholas laughed. "Yes, we're fine. Now tell me, how exactly did you see my code?"

"Dude, you're an instant freaking legend! The entire hacker community knows what happened. They're calling it the Swoop, and calling you Superman. Go into the darknet, check it out when you get a chance. It's totally awesome. They are bowing at your feet. Reddit blew up with requests to join your forces of good—you now officially have minions."

Nicholas cleared his throat. "Thank you for passing that along, Adam." He decided having minions couldn't hurt. "If you're through, I need your help again. It shouldn't be too much trouble."

"Go for it, Superman, Sir Superman."

"Shove it. Let's see how clever you are. Is there anything *Air Force One* might have in common with Dominion Virginia Power and the attacked oil companies, ConocoPhillips, Occidental, etcetera?"

"Well—yeah, software, I suppose."

"Exactly. And what do we do with software used for national security?"

"We run risk assessments constantly, like any other software, though at a much higher level, to make sure there are no breaches. It's part of what I did when I was—ah, before. Break in, then show them the faults. For a price."

"And is there a particular company who might be responsible for these risk assessments?"

There was a sharp intake of breath. "Holy crap, Nicholas. Juno. It has to be, but you already figured that out, since Juno caters to all the high-end military and government installations, and has a number of private-sector contracts. They are the leader in the field of cyber-security."

"Good, you agree with me. Here's what I think. It's not about Juno's incompetence, no, I believe someone who worked the risk-assessment teams for all of the companies planted the bad code during the assessments. All Andy Tate had to do was upload Gunther Ansell's code COE had purchased, and they were in."

Adam whistled, long and low. "So someone left them keys to the back door. It makes sense."

"Find out who it was for me, Adam. Look at all of Juno's male employees thirty-five to fifty years old. I'm sending you a photo right now for comparison. Tear apart their financials. We'll take care of the warrant on this end, but we need to find out who this man is, and find out now."

"How did you get a photo of the man?"

"We have video from a café in Baltimore. Zahir Damari was meeting with him, and the man was passing him a tube that possibly had plans for Yorktown refinery inside, or plans for something else, we don't know for sure. I'm willing to bet this is our guy and he works for Juno."

"Got it."

"Run the photo through their employee profile, Facebook page, everything. Cross-check against the risk assessment teams. Find out who this is."

"Give me five minutes. You want to stay on the phone?"

Nicholas smiled at Mike. "I'm timing you. Go."

It took Adam three minutes.

"Got him. His name is Woody Reading, works risk assessment out of the D.C. office. Sending you his particulars now."

Mike watched Nicholas's computer screen light up. "This has to be our mole," she said. "You're fast, Adam."

Windows continued opening on the screen. Adam said, "Would you look at this—what an idiot. Guy has two houses, in Bethesda, no less, but only has enough money coming in from Juno to afford one of them. His financials are suspicious, Nicholas. You have everything I do now."

"I see it all. This is great work, Adam. I'll be in touch soon."

"This was fun. And I am glad it's all shaking out for us. Hey, am I your head minion? Direct all the other minions?"

"Go for it." Nicholas hung up, grinned at Mike. She said, "You could have done that as fast as Adam."

"Maybe, but my brain has been otherwise occupied. How much time until zero hour?"

"Four minutes. We've got our mole. Now all we have to do is tie the money to COE, which in turn ties to Zahir, and the Iranians and Hezbollah. Hard proof of their contract to assassinate the vice president. But we still don't have Damari and we still don't know about those bombs."

"One problem at a time, Agent Caine. Now, since

Woody Reading is local, we'll have Sherlock send a team to grab him up, get him arrested and brought in. Zahir seems to like eliminating people he works with. We might be able to save this guy's life."

Mike shrugged. "Hopefully he'll think being alive is better than being charged with high treason."

Nicholas said, "Good point. When his world begins to unravel, he might not want his life saved."

"Nicholas, we need to find what was in that tube Woody Reading gave to Zahir Damari, and fast. If it wasn't plans for Yorktown, and I don't think it was since Vanessa said they could get that information when COE took down the oil companies' computers, then whatever the plans were, it can't be good for us."

"No, it can't be good for us."

In unison, they both looked at the countdown clock. Two minutes to go.

Wednesday
4 p.m.–Midnight

75

KING TO D1

They had a bird's-eye view from the satellite images over Yorktown. One of the screens now showed strategic areas around the plant and stress points, and listed the names of the various buildings, too. There was no movement. It looked deserted.

When they told Sherlock about what Adam Pearce had discovered, she rubbed her hands together. "Well done, Adam. We'll send a team to grab Mr. Woody Reading as soon as the ink's dry on the warrant."

Nicholas said, "I'm beginning to think of Adam as our secret weapon."

All eyes in the conference room were watching the countdown clock draw closer to four zeroes.

With every tick of the clock, more agents filed into the room. All the agents from the CAU came in, Jimmy Maitland with them. He said to Sherlock, "Savich called, said to keep him informed. He can't get back in time." He said aloud to the room, "No surprise, the media is going wild on the story of the president's plane. They've only been told there was a mechanical problem, and they were forced to land in Nova Scotia. The press secretary's statement assured the president is fine and resuming his schedule as soon as he's back in D.C. However, apparently it's all over the Internet what Superman here pulled off. They won't be able to deny the truth of the attack much longer."

Director Comey asked, "How did the media take the news about the cancellation of Yorktown?"

"Not a problem, sir," Maitland said. "The president is being praised up and down, primarily for not backing down in the face of Iran's provocation and walking out of the peace talks, and almost as important, for proving he's not stupid for canceling Yorktown. Not in those exact words, of course. I believe the word more used was the president was prudent."

Sherlock said, "It's nearly four o'clock."

Mike flashed on a memory of the high school principal gathering all the students in the gym to watch the Space Shuttle *Columbia* take off. She remembered clearly the heart-pounding excitement, wondering what it was like to be inside, a real live astronaut. And then, two weeks later, watching the shuttle return to earth, and with no warning, it exploded. Dead, all dead. *Please, please,* she prayed, staring at the countdown clock. *Please.*

The countdown ended.

The drone and satellite views drew closer to the facility.

Everyone was holding their breath.

Her prayer wasn't answered.

It started in the western edge, a small plume of smoke, and then every screen flashed a blinding white, with yellow edges. A ball of fire consumed the plant entirely.

It was Bayway all over, only bigger, huge in fact, which meant Spenser used a larger portion of one of his bombs. What would a whole one do? Two of them? But this time she and Nicholas weren't running through the flames, feeling the heat burn their lungs, singe their flesh, hearing screams, knowing people were dying, already dead, and the fear, the gut-wrenching fear.

She said aloud, "But where was the bomb?"

Nicholas said, "The smoke plume came from South Four-G. We need to find out what was stored there."

Sherlock unrolled the plans for the plant. "Here's Four-G. It's a metal depot. They keep tungsten there, among other things."

Director Comey said, "So that's where Spenser put his bomb? In a mess of tungsten?"

"Yes, sir," Nicholas said. "I imagine Spenser and probably Tate managed to deliver it in a shipment of metal—maybe even tungsten. It would be totally disguised. The agent undercover with COE told us the new bombs had tungsten components, and would be near on impossible to distinguish it from the rest of the metal." And Nicholas would bet Nigel's best bottle of Scotch Spenser had done it during the blackout when everything was down, all the cameras, everything, security precautions heightened but handicapped.

Mike read his mind, more likely their brains were

running on the same track. "I'm betting Spenser and Tate took down the power grid so they could have easier access to the plant."

Nicholas said to Mike, "And some very creative coding by Woody Reading at Juno that made the blackout spread so quickly. Hard to control an overload of outages like we had."

Sherlock said, "We'll start tracking all the tungsten shipments over the past week."

Stunned silence continued in the conference room. The sheer enormity of the explosion, the complete destruction, it was hard to take in.

Mike said, "Matthew Spenser's final roar and no one was hurt. That's got to be a win for us."

All the phones in the room began to ring.

Ten minutes after the annihilation of Yorktown, Vice President Sloane called Mike. She said only, "Thank you both for what you did today."

The vice president was actually thanking them, live, on Mike's own cell phone? Her heart speeded up. What an amazing feeling. "You're welcome, ma'am," and that sounded stupid, but she couldn't think of anything else to say.

"Do you have any further word on the whereabouts of Zahir Damari?"

"I'm sorry, no, ma'am."

"We have Homeland on the lookout for him. About half my advisers and half the CIA believe Damari will pack it up since it would be suicide for him to try and attack me now, with the entire world watching. However, I plan to be on the side of the other half who tell me he simply never gives up, not in his DNA. You can bet all my staff are on alert until he's caught. Which assessment do you agree with, Agent Caine?"

"I come down with the side that says let's take extreme care. Damari is the type of killer who has backups for his backups. Yes, he's out there, somewhere, and he's got a plan."

"Thank you. Now, actually, I'm also calling you two to tell you the president would like to thank you himself for saving his life. He, and I, of course, would like you to join us at Camp David this evening. We're having a small dinner, cocktails prior. It will be casual, only staff, a few people from the Hill. The president was planning on being at Camp David this weekend to, ah, recover from the peace talks. We've simply moved his schedule around to get him there a day early. Given what we know about Spenser and his group breaking into the POTUS scheduling, the prevailing wisdom says if we change our plans, there's no way Zahir Damari can surprise us."

Mike said, "But, ma'am, I didn't think the president and vice president were allowed to be at Camp David at the same time."

Callan laughed. "Well, what the public doesn't know won't hurt them. Tony Scarlatti, you remember him, my head of security? He felt it would be smart to keep me on a different schedule, too. Since it's not protocol, we think it will be the safest place for me to be. Secret Service will pick you up—some of Tony's guys—and we'll chopper you in. Trust me, you don't want to spend the afternoon hours driving up there, not in our traffic. This is much more efficient. You're at the Hoover Building?"

"Yes, ma'am. Thank you so much for the invitation and the transportation."

"The car will be there in thirty minutes. And, Agent Caine? Thank you again. What you and Agent Drummond managed to do today, it will not go unrewarded."

Could she mean a tax break? No, probably not.

Nicholas was watching her, an eyebrow raised. Mike slipped her cell into the back pocket of her jeans. "Well, that was the vice president."

"Yes, I gathered. Why are you grinning like a loon?"

"I was just thinking about my taxes. Hey, you want to go to a party?"

76

BISHOP TO B3 CHECK

Catoctin Mountain

Over the past twenty-four hours, Zahir learned that Secret Service agents gossiped like hens. They spoke freely of myriad operational movements, schedules, and the people involved. Unwittingly they gave him an excellent understanding of everything going on in Washington. And he heard talk about himself. These guys evidently weren't afraid of him, but it seemed everybody else was. He smiled. *Just wait, boys, just you wait.*

He learned that Matthew Spenser had been shot to death trying to kill Vanessa Grace. Andy Tate was dead, probably killed by Matthew, Ian McGuire was dead, and Vanessa was still alive. He had to admire her surviving not only a gunshot to the chest, but falling off that building. Except she was a CIA undercover agent and that rather pissed him off. Maybe as soon as he was done here, he'd head south to the hospital and get rid of her.

And the president's plane hadn't gone down in the Atlantic when Matthew had pressed the trigger. They wouldn't shut up about a Brit FBI agent who'd managed computer magic, and saved the plane.

A failure, but when it came down to it, Zahir wasn't all that disappointed.

Sorry, Matthew, you did try.

He had Plan B ready to put in motion. The only question he'd had, the only worry, was answered only minutes before. Both of them would be here. *Both of them.*

He had to move up the schedule based on the flurry of activity he'd heard, but he couldn't be more pleased.

Zahir locked the bathroom door, an unnecessary security measure, but he hadn't reached this ripe old age being stupid, and reached into the bag.

After nearly an hour of painstaking detail and concentration, he was done. He smiled at the face in the mirror. He looked again at the photograph, and nodded. Perfection.

He was ready.

He sat on the couch in the small cabin, and waited for the party to begin.

77

KING TO C1

Andrews Air Force Base
Outside Washington, D.C.

The Sea King, only known as *Marine One* or *Marine Two* if the president or vice president was aboard, was a luxury liner compared to the Little Bird that had flown them down to Washington, D.C. Once strapped in, Mike ran her hand over the soft leather, pulled back the blue drapers to look outside. "I could get used to this."

"You enjoy being treated like the queen—whisked around from car to chopper, do you?"

"Better a chopper than a Gulfstream. I'll never fly easy in one of those again."

Nicholas remembered all too well the gut-wrenching fear. "I'm with you."

The chopper's liftoff was smooth, and a moment later they were heading northwest toward Camp David.

Mike watched Nicholas pull an orange file out of his laptop case. "What is that? And who was that man who gave it to you?"

"That was George Hempton from the British embassy. I'm very glad he caught us before we left the Hoover Building. My father sent it to me, said it was urgent. Let's see what it has to say." He pulled out a sheaf of papers and read aloud:

> *Nicholas,*
>
> *Be very careful hunting Zahir Damari. He's extremely intelligent, skilled with guns and knives, primarily, and has the disguise skills of a master Hollywood makeup technician, which you probably already know. But he's better than you think, so be alert. Attached are a series of potential photographs. You'll at least get a sense for his build, his movements.*
>
> *This is a copy, burn this when you're through.*
> *Come home soon. We miss you.*

It was signed simply, *HD*.

Nicholas moved to sit beside Mike. He opened the dossier, and the two of them began to read.

Damari was a chameleon. He managed to elude capture mostly because no one knew what he really looked like. The photographs included in the file showed a tall man, estimated height between one ninety and one ninety-three centimeters, which fit with what Nicholas knew about the Bayonne shootings. The man was about Nicholas's height. There was a photo of him from twenty years earlier, a shot of a young man in green soldier's garb, holding a worn Kalashnikov rifle.

Mike lightly touched her fingers to the photo. "Isn't that strange? He's young and he should look innocent, but he doesn't."

"I doubt he looks anything remotely like this now, except maybe for the eyes."

They read the various physical descriptions. Mike pulled out the photo of him that Vanessa had taken, and the photo of the man who'd met Woody Reading at the diner in Baltimore. They all looked like different men. "I knew he must be good," Mike said, "but your dad's right. This is incredible."

His kill list stretched for pages. Damari had been involved in or solely responsible for several major assassinations, and many more minor ones. He was charged with unseating governments in Chile and Uganda through pinpoint strikes against certain players, taking out a DA in Argentina, a member of the Saudi royal family who'd gotten too full of himself. Page after page, a long, storied career for an assassin. And these were only the confirmed kills. Who knew how many others there were, off the radar?

Mike elbowed him, showed him a text on her phone. It was from Gray.

Border patrol stopped man fitting
Damari's last known description in
Texas. Will let you know more when we
have it, not that it matters all that much
now that we already know he's here, in
our backyard. Have fun partying w/ big
dogs. Bring us presidential M&Ms.

Nicholas stared out the window at the lush green landscape below, at the sprawling towns, wanting to feel excited, but he didn't. There was something that wasn't right and he didn't know what it was. It was driving him nuts.

78

KNIGHT TO E2
CHECK

Camp David
Catoctin Mountain

We'll be landing shortly at Camp David," Captain Willis said over the intercom. "Naval Support Facility Thurmont is a full-time naval base tucked high on Catoctin Mountain here in northwestern Maryland. It's one of the most secure places in the world. I hope you had a pleasant flight and enjoyed our brief tourist spiel. Do give our best to the president. Agent Drummond, he knows he's a very lucky man, thanks to your being right on the spot."

When the green-and-white Sea King touched down and the rotors stopped, they climbed out, shook the pilots' hands. Mike shivered; it was at least fifteen degrees cooler in the mountains, and she was glad she'd packed a sweater.

Two rows of sailors, one on either side of the concrete path, waited to greet them. She knew the Navy and Marine personnel who worked on NSF Thurmont had high-level security clearance. It was a coveted position in the military. They were standing at attention. It felt incredible to be at the center of the amazing pomp and circumstance.

Vice President Sloane was at the end of the line of white-uniformed men and women, standing between the U.S. flag and another flag with the presidential seal on a blue background. She was smiling at them.

"Yes, I could get used to this," Mike said to Nicholas, who gave her a distracted smile. What was this? What was he thinking about?

Callan shook their hands. "Welcome, welcome. We're so glad to see you. Thank you for everything."

Mike saw the sailors who'd greeted them tip their caps. She felt touched, a bit overwhelmed, and managed a wobbly smile.

Nicholas said, "I am very grateful things turned out well."

"They did indeed, thanks to you," Callan said. "Tonight we celebrate. Tomorrow we'll worry about the bombs and Damari. Come."

Mike had never imagined herself being here, at Camp David, of all places, in conversation with the vice president and soon enough, the president himself. Her father was going to love it, want every detail about security, and her mom would want to know about everything from food to clothes to who said what to whom, particularly who had admired and praised her daughter. Oh, yes, and what did she wear?

Nicholas said, "You honor us, ma'am. Thank you." He appreciated the respect they were showing. He committed it all to memory for his mom and Nigel. He sent a prayer heavenward, so grateful the code had worked.

Callan waved for them to follow, began moving toward two waiting golf carts. "We'll ride to the cabins," she said. "Hop in."

Nicholas was looking around, searching the area, alert, not at all relaxed, taking careful measure of exactly where they were, where the Secret Service and military personnel were stationed, points of ingress and egress. It made Mike more alert, too. Something was definitely up with him.

Callan said, "We've put you in Dogwood, where we're headed right now. It has a storied history—Brezhnev, Sadat, Medvedev, why, Nixon's secretary typed up the Watergate notes in the lounge. But no ghosts, so don't worry about that. I'm over there, in Birch. We're flaunting protocol, but not too much. It's a quick walk up to Aspen; Mike, if you're in heels we can easily leave you the cart, but you'll have to buzz around to the front entrance, though. Cocktails start in twenty minutes, you have exactly enough time to freshen up. We're business casual tonight, though whatever you have with you is completely fine."

Mike said, "Nicholas always has the right clothes. I think I can muster something out of my bag as well. No heels, though."

The golf cart stopped at a green painted cabin with redwood steps leading up to a porch. To the right of the door, the rustic brown wood placard read DOGWOOD in white lettering. Flowers bloomed, the heady evening scent of night-blooming jasmine was heavy in the air around them. Mike could tell they were meticulously cared for, even in the growing dusk.

The vice president gave them a wave. "I'm sure you'll have everything you need, I'll see you in twenty minutes." She got into the cart that had been following them, and buzzed away.

The door was open, and they went inside. It smelled woodsy, like lingering fires and evergreen and the sharp scent of starched sheets. They were very casual here, Mike saw. The whole setup screamed "Kick back and eat chips and dip," and that suited her perfectly.

The cabin had two bedrooms with updated en-suite baths, a lounge room with tall fireplace, a table with four chairs. Bookshelves lined the walls, with a section near the floor full of cards and poker chips and board games. It was cozy, and the two bedrooms afforded individual privacy. Mike didn't want to think about what sleeping under the same roof as Nicholas meant, but on the other hand, this cabin had more privacy than some of the hotel rooms they'd shared in Paris and London. Ah, but that was before—no, she wasn't about to think about that, not now when she would be meeting the president of the United States in fifteen minutes.

"I'll take left, you take right?" Nicholas said. "Okay with you?"

"Fine. Please don't tell me you don't have white tie and tails in your go-bag. If you do, prepare to die."

"No, not quite tails. Come, now, I know you, you have something black and a little slinky in there, right?"

"Yep. After our last trip to Paris, I thought something showing more leg than bloody, ripped jeans might come in handy."

"Mike, we need to talk."

She held up her hand, palm out. "No way. There's nothing to talk about. How many times do I have to tell you? Forget it, Nicholas, forget everything."

He looked startled, then grinned. "No, I wasn't going to talk about what didn't happen between us. This is something else entirely."

"Oh. Well, I knew something was wrong," she said, as she set down her go-bag and headed to the small kitchenette. "You want a Diet Coke?"

"No, nothing." But he grabbed a bottle of water and took a swig.

"You've been distracted since before we landed. You're worried about Damari, aren't you?"

He took another drink of water, then faced her. "After reading how my father emphasized what a chameleon he is, how he can fit into any situation, uses makeup and prosthetics to alter his looks regularly, I think I'd be remiss not to worry. Could he somehow be here? Yeah, I know, that sounds crazy, but still, I can't shake it off. If he is, could he have one of Spenser's bombs and plans to set it off?"

She'd never seen him quite like this. She felt her heart begin to pound. "Nicholas, we know he hasn't had time to have plastic surgery since Vanessa took his photo at Tahoe. So we're not completely in the dark." Well, that was a lie. "With what your father told us, maybe it's enough of a baseline."

He tipped his water bottle in salute. "Every photo of him we looked at on our flight here, he didn't look anything like the photo Vanessa sent in. So, a baseline? Oh, no." He raised his hand, swiped it through his hair. "I'm still hyper, ignore me." He stared around the cabin. "It's just a bad feeling I can't seem to shake."

"The vice president is safe here, Nicholas. Camp David's security is legendary. I mean, this is a working naval base. Even if Damari had been able to track us, or the vice president, this place is crawling with military. Did you see the men with dogs walking the perimeter? They had HK416s, you know, that's the updated M4 the SEAL teams like to carry now. I don't know what their security measures are here on a usual basis, but they've clearly stepped things up." She walked to him and laid her hand on his arm. "It will be all right. Like the vice president said, tonight we celebrate."

He nodded, everything she'd said was true, but still . . . He finished the water, sent the bottle in a looping arc toward the trash can, where it slipped in without touching the sides.

"Nice shot. Not quite a three-pointer, but close."

He put his hand over hers. "Humor me, Mike. Promise me you'll keep your eyes open. Just in case."

79

KING TO B1

The president of the United States met them at the door of the Aspen Lodge. Up close and personal, Mike thought Jefferson Bradley looked pretty impressive. He was sixty-four, in excellent shape. He had gleaming silver hair, dark eyebrows, a chiseled jaw, and, best of all, he was tall with a commanding presence, seemingly a must to win an election in the United States. He looked the part of fighter pilot turned politician, still had the cocky walk.

When he folded his hands around hers, they were warm and smooth, a long time since he'd been the wild-hair pilot back in the day.

He leaned close. "A pleasure, Agent Caine. Thank you for all your help today. I hear your father's in law enforcement, too. Pretty impressive pedigree you have."

"Thank you. Both my father and I love what we do.

He tells me I'm very lucky to be working for you, sir." Not quite the truth, but it would do.

He laughed. "Yes, I am your boss, aren't I?" He turned to Nicholas, took his hand, and simply looked at him silently for a long moment.

"I owe you my life," he said simply. "Without your intervention, I'd be fish food right now, as well as my staff and all the people aboard the plane. I owe you a debt of gratitude which can never be repaid."

Nicholas felt the pull of the man's power, and he felt the emotion in his words.

"I am very grateful everything worked, sir."

"I won't forget, Agent Drummond." He stepped back, smiled at both Mike and Nicholas. "Now, welcome to Camp David. I can't tell you how much I appreciate you two making the journey on such short notice. Come on in, I want you to meet some people."

Mike thought it was a lovely room; the ceiling had brown rafters and a cozy fire was burning. She could see the lights gleaming off the flagstone back terrace, and the lit pool beyond.

So the party was an *intimate* affair, if you considered forty or so people in the living room intimate. She saw everyone was buffed and polished and so very happy to meet her and Nicholas. She recognized congressmen and -women, some military bigwigs, and was that a justice of the Supreme Court? She was glad she had stashed a little black dress rolled in the bottom of her go-bag. No heels, as she'd told the vice president. She wore her motorcycle boots, better than the sneakers, Nicholas had told her.

Chic and funky, he'd said. And he'd watched her as she'd twisted her hair into a chignon and set her black-framed glasses on her nose.

He'd looked her up and down, nodded. "Yes, you are armored up and ready to go, Agent Caine."

She could only shake her head and feel like a bag lady next to Nicholas, who, naturally, was dressed impeccably in gray worsted-wool slacks, a light-blue button-down open at the collar, and a dark purple suede jacket, all of it screaming Savile Row, she'd told him.

"No, like I told you, Nigel has found Barneys and fallen in love. I think our days on Savile Row are now in the past. Except for shirts, of course."

"Of course." Handmade for him—of course. "Aren't we a pair?" She looked down at herself, then over at him.

He'd stared at her, and slowly nodded. "Yes, we are quite a pair." He'd said nothing more and they'd walked to Aspen, side by side, silent, Nicholas watching, always watching.

She looked over at him now, speaking with someone whose name she couldn't remember. He hadn't shaved, but he didn't look scruffy or unkempt. He looked like a well-dressed bad boy, walking around the room, completely at ease. And always, he'd turn to her and take her hand, but there were too many people who wanted to speak to them individually, so he couldn't keep her with him.

Callan was introducing her to her chief of staff, Quinn Costello, a firecracker in a nice suit. She looked over to see Nicholas speaking with Tony Scarlatti, Callan's Secret Service lead. He was still worried, and now, she was certain he was warning Tony. Surely he'd relax a bit now. Tony was frowning, and nodding. His crew were the watchmen now.

Mike accepted a glass of champagne, clicked her glass to Callan's. Callan nodded over her shoulder. "Nicholas Drummond, he's a lot like his father, I think, and I quickly recognized that man as the complete package."

"Yes, he is," Mike said simply. "A lot like his father, I mean. Did you meet his mother, Mitzie, too?"

"Alas, no. But I remember her TV show. She's quite as remarkable as his father."

"She solves local village mysteries, you know," Mike said. "Nicholas tells me that's where he gets his love of puzzles."

"Speaking of solving mysteries," Callan said thoughtfully, eyeing Mike up and down, "it seems to me the two of you fit together well. I suppose you could say you're perfectly attuned to each other, each of you needs the other. An amazing partnership. You each have your strengths, and they're complementary."

"You mean like I'm the wallflower and Nicholas is the outgoing charmer?"

Callan said very precisely, "Do not do that. You are an intelligent woman, Agent Caine. You know very well what I mean." She looked again toward Nicholas. "And, I might add, speaking as the voice of ancient experience, don't waste your opportunities."

Mike wished she didn't know what that meant, but of course she did. She also realized it was a long-standing habit, downplaying what she could do, turning away compliments, a habit she should break, but growing up with a mom like the Gorgeous Rebecca, it was tough to be cocky and self-assured.

Callan Sloane tapped her champagne glass to Mike's. "If you ever decide you want another life, give me a call. I could use someone like you on my team. I see that Nicholas and Tony were in close conversation earlier. About Zahir Damari?"

"Yes, he's still on the loose. Nicholas is concerned."

"Don't worry, everyone's on the lookout for him. So relax, Mike. It's a party and you're the guest of honor. Like I said, tomorrow we'll face the next enemy.

"I sent Tony to grab us some Beluga from the pantry. He was in the kitchen earlier with the chef, stealing blinis, I'm sure. The chef said he was making them especially for you and Nicholas. You do like caviar, yes?"

"Certainly," Mike said. "Caviar is very popular in Omaha."

Callan laughed. "If you don't like it, you can hide it under the crème fraîche. Now, let's go introduce you to some more people who are dying to meet you."

When Callan pulled Mike away, the president took over Nicholas and kept him at his side. They moved around the room from person to person, Nicholas patiently smiling and shaking hands and accepting praise and compliments, most of them sincere. It was an honor and he was grateful, but he'd rather be eating pizza with Savich and Sherlock, maybe playing a video game with Sean, or with Mike, maybe even pulling those pins out of her hair, slipping those glasses off her nose, telling her they needed to talk.

He saw Mike laughing with the vice president; the two looked like they were sharing a secret, and that made him smile. He was beginning to relax—Mike was right, the security was extraordinary, and it would take an act of God to attack the president in the middle of all these people. Tony had actually patted his hand like a kid he was trying to reassure.

He took another glass of Veuve Clicquot from the table, shook the hand of yet another staffer to the president. He saw the vice president bringing Mike over now. Mike was smiling, but no matter how incredibly hot she looked in her little black dress and her biker boots, he could tell she was tired.

Callan said, "Nicholas Drummond. How is it you find yourself on our shores, working for the FBI? You can tell me the truth, you're some sort of spy for her Majesty, keeping an eye on our intelligence services?"

He opened his mouth to tell her about his stint in MI6, the Brit equivalent to the CIA, when his mobile vibrated in his pocket. He held it up. "Excuse me a moment, ma'am."

"Certainly. Take it to the kitchen. The reception in here is piss-poor. If you lose the signal, find Tony, he's in there bossing the chef around, getting caviar for Agent Caine, who tells me it's a favorite in Omaha. He'll get you a house phone."

80

KNIGHT TO C3
CHECK

The vice president was right, the reception was piss-poor. Nicholas crossed the room, accepted pats on the shoulder and well-wishes as he did. When he reached the surprisingly empty kitchen, he took a deep breath and glanced down at the screen. It was a text, from Adam Pearce.

> 911. I've tried to call, phones down.
> Plans Damari received in Baltimore
> were for Camp David. Be on alert. The
> cavalry is on its way.

He'd known, somehow he'd known to his bones, something wasn't right. His heart began to pound. Damari was here, close, he had to be.

He tried to call Adam, but there was no cell service. He hurried deeper into the kitchen, wondering where all the staff were, looking for a landline. He spotted one, put it to his ear. The line was dead. He had to warn everyone, get the president and vice president to safety. He spun on his heel, and his foot slipped. He nearly went down but managed to catch himself with the edge of the granite counter.

And he saw the blood on the floor.

There was a closed door opposite him, blood seeping out. He pushed it open, met with resistance. He gave it a shove with his shoulder.

There were two people inside, both unconscious, both bleeding. One was the chef, his white hat beside his head on the floor, and the other was Tony Scarlatti.

Nicholas felt for a pulse in each man's throat. Both were thready, but both were still alive.

Nicholas ran to the kitchen door and looked out. He knew the guards were all outside the lodge, patrolling. He'd have to get across the large living room crowded with laughing, chatting men and women, and open the door to alert them.

First the president. The brief his father sent flashed in his head as he moved quickly back into the living room.

Master makeup artist.

Tony down in the pantry.

And of course he knew.

His eyes roved the room to search out the president and vice president. Mike saw him, her eyes fixed on his face. Then she looked over her shoulder as if Damari would be right there.

Which he was, across the room, laughing with the

president and vice president, hovering at her right hand where he always was. And that was surely impossible, since Tony was bleeding in the pantry.

Nicholas started toward them, dodging people who were trying to intercept him then moving out of his way, still speaking to him, but he was focused, moving as quickly as he could.

He never took his eyes off Zahir Damari, a part of him amazed at the transformation, a part of him counting the seconds, praying Damari wouldn't pull a gun or a knife, and it would be all over. No, no gun or knife, he'd never get out alive. Then what?

He was still ten feet away when he saw Tony—Damari— coming up on the far side of the president. It took a moment for his mind to register—*the champagne.* He'd handed them glasses of champagne for a toast, and the president was raising his glass, clicking it against Callan's and the two of them lifted their glasses to their lips.

Nicholas shouted, "Don't, don't!" but someone had turned up the music and it drowned out his words, or maybe it didn't, but they didn't register, or they didn't hear enough to understand.

Nicholas was shoving people out of the way, screaming now, "Don't drink the champagne!" People were grabbing at him, asking him what was wrong, becoming alarmed. No one knew what was happening, but they kept getting in his way. He saw the Secret Service agents had heard him yelling, and were looking through the windows at him, and then they were inside, now charging across the room toward him, as if he were the threat.

"Don't drink it, don't drink it, it's Damari!"

Callan heard him, finally, and she looked up, saw him racing toward her, yelling, and her glass was halfway to her mouth, her head cocked to one side, puzzled, but the president, the president.

"Stop him, stop him!" It was one of the Secret Service and he grabbed at Nicholas. Still five feet away, Nicholas dove in the air like he was after a football, eyes focused only on the glasses. His arm swept across their bodies, slapping the glass right out of Callan's hand. He caught the bottom edge of the president's glass, but he'd already tipped his head back before Nicholas had begun his charge across the room; the champagne was in his mouth.

"Don't swallow!" he shouted, then crashed hard against the fireplace beside the president. Glass shattered, people started to scream. The president grabbed at his throat, fell to his knees. The Secret Service were on Nicholas, pinning him to the floor, and the soldiers flooded the room.

No more than five seconds had passed.

Nicholas struggled to get to his feet, pulling two Secret Service agents with him, a small cut on the forehead trickling blood into his left eye. He pointed, shouted to Mike, "It's Damari, it's Damari, he's made up to look like Tony Scarlatti, he poisoned the champagne!"

There was a long moment, the space between a heartbeat, when Damari turned and made eye contact with Nicholas. His face looked so much like Tony it was eerie, but his hairpiece had been knocked askew.

In that second, Mike understood, pulled her Glock out of her boot holster, and yelled, "Stop!"

But Damari ignored her, moving fast toward the glass door to the back terrace. His hand was outstretched to grab the door handle when Mike pulled the trigger three times without hesitation, and he was slammed against the glass, his head cracking it, smearing it with his blood as he collapsed.

81

KING TO C1

The security team circled Mike in a heartbeat, and she stood there, not moving, seeing the lights, hearing shouts and screams coming from all corners of the room. And over the chaos, she heard the rotors of a helicopter drawing closer.

Mike held out her ankle gun, butt first, her arm outstretched, then she tossed it to the floor and put her hands on the top of her head. She dropped to her knees, knowing if she didn't the guards and agents would throw her down.

She heard Nicholas shouting, but couldn't understand his words over the yells and commands from the security team. Then she heard him. "It's Damari. She shot Damari, Tony is in the pantry, he's been stabbed. We need medics, we need medics, the president is down!"

Secret Service was already swarmed around the president; Nicholas was being held to the side, struggling against the agents holding him back from Mike.

One agent wrenched Mike's shooting arm behind her back. "Stay on your knees, don't you move, keep your hands on your head!" She didn't resist, it would be suicide to do anything other than what they were telling her right now. She felt the cold steel of an agent's weapon pressing into the base of her neck, heard a woman's voice, clear and strong. "The president's down. Where is the medic?"

The vice president? Yes, Callan was okay.

A young naval officer with a huge medical kit in a red bag burst into the living room, yelling, "Here, ma'am! What happened? Was the president shot?"

"He's been poisoned. It was in the champagne. It smelled somehow off to me, I hadn't had any yet but he got some in his mouth before Agent Drummond knocked it from our hands. It was a fast one, given the speed at which the president had grabbed his throat and fell to the floor."

Mike stayed on her knees, her heart pounding, and she prayed the president would be all right. She looked over to the blood-smeared glass door, at Damari's body in the fetal position against the door. So much blood. He was dead. She'd shot him. It was over, but strangely, she couldn't get her brain around it, couldn't accept it yet. A measure of shock, she supposed, and knew it would pass.

How like Tony he'd looked, but not now. She'd shot him in the back and in the head. Staring at him, she felt huge relief. *Now you're dead, you monster.* She drew a deep breath and waited. If she hadn't had her ankle gun, who knew if they would have stopped him escaping. No, surely the Secret Service would have grabbed him. Though they'd only seen their guy—their agent—not Damari. Now that he was dead, she could give him the credit for coming up with a remarkable plan.

She sucked in a deep breath and smiled up at the soldier with his gun trained on her face. Another soldier spoke to him and he pulled his gun away, holstered it. He was young, not older than she was and he was pale, adrenaline raging through him. He flicked a gaze toward Damari. "You killed him dead. Excellent shooting on the move like that."

"Yes, thankfully, yes. It's not Tony, it's Zahir Damari."

"You did good," another soldier said, and pulled her to her feet and formally handed her back her small Glock.

Then Nicholas was there and he stood beside her and together they watched two soldiers roll Damari over and stare down at a man who looked like Tony's double. But not in death. No, not in death. The prosthetic nose was inches off-center, knocked sideways when he'd slid down the glass. An agent pulled the wig off as he felt for a pulse. When he shook his head, Mike's heart slowed.

An agent pulled a wrist mike from Damari's suit jacket cuff, lifted it to his ear, and said, "It's live. This is a frigging live comms unit. He could hear everything we did, every move we made since he managed to sneak into Camp David."

They turned from the ruin of the man to see the medic working on the president. He already had an IV started, and was pumping in something from a syringe.

"Nicholas, you said it was poison. How can they treat if they don't know what the poison is?"

"They can't. I imagine they're most likely giving him Narcan. I don't know if it will work on whatever this poison is, but it generally reverses the effects of an opioid overdose. They have to try something."

Mike heard the medic say, "He's not responding to the naloxone, continue chest compressions. I'm going to push flumazenil."

Nicholas looked on, not moving, except he took her hand. "Damari succeeded, Mike. I was a second too late."

Mike said matter-of-factly, "If you hadn't knocked the glasses away, he'd surely be dead already, Callan, too. They have to figure out what was he given. It worked fast, so fast, he went down almost immediately."

Nicholas suddenly jerked her after him. "Let's get to the kitchen, maybe Damari left something behind."

They found nothing except more chaos, more soldiers, pulling Tony and the chef from the pantry, a medic tending them.

Callan rushed into the room, knelt at Tony's side as they worked on him.

"Will he make it?" Mike heard the awful deadening fear in her voice. She knew too well what Damari was capable of. She wondered idly why Damari hadn't simply killed them.

"We're doing our best, ma'am," the medic said, not looking up. "He's lost a lot of blood, but he's still with us. Chef's gonna be okay, he's knocked out is all. Medevac is on the way, we'll get them to the hospital, get them patched up." He finally looked up at the vice president's face. "The president, ma'am, will he live?"

Callan swallowed. "I don't know."

She looked over at Mike and Nicholas leaning against the counter, the cut on Nicholas's forehead still trickling blood down the side of his face and onto the collar of his shirt from his collision with the fireplace. Callan walked to them, ignored the blood and embraced them both. They felt her shaking. Then she raised her head and smiled at them.

"Now I owe you my life, too." She grabbed a towel from the kitchen counter and wiped the blood from Nicholas's face. "The president will pull through this. He will." And she raised her head at the sound of the Medevac helicopter landing on the back lawn. "And Tony will live."

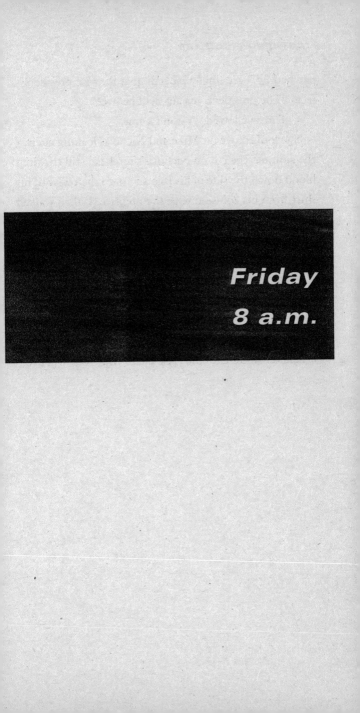

Friday

8 a.m.

82

ROOK TO C2 CHECKMATE

The White House Pressroom

Chief of staff to the vice president of the United States Quinn Costello gave her boss one last hair fluff, handed her a ChapStick, waited for her to smooth it on, then, "Are you ready, Madam Vice President?"

Callan was dressed to kill in a cream suit, heels. She was ready, more than ready. She handed the ChapStick back to Quinn. "I am. Let's do it."

The pressroom was packed full, easy to do considering how small it was. Callan had been shocked the first time she saw it—the iconic views were angled beautifully, didn't show the foreshortened wall in the back of the room, the angle of the seats, the slope of the eastern and western walls. Everyone was smashed in like sardines, every D.C. reporter in their seats already, the room humming, all anxiously awaiting her.

There was no announcement. Callan simply walked in and stepped in front of the lectern. There was a brief moment of shuffling, as every person facing her leaned forward slightly.

She took a breath and said without preamble, "At five o'clock this morning, coalition forces launched air strikes against Iran's key nuclear sites Arak, Isfahan, Qom, Natanz, and Bushehr, as well as research reactors in Bonab, Ramsar, Tehran, and Parchin. Simultaneously, military sites and identified hideouts of known Hezbollah leaders in Iran, Syria, and Lebanon were struck as well.

"These coordinated strikes are in direct retaliation for Iran's attempted assassination of President Jefferson Bradley and myself at Camp David.

"I am proud to say our Middle Eastern partners in this action come from all sectors of the region. As you know, President Bradley was in talks in Geneva this past week with representatives of all the countries in the Middle East, trying to find a way to address Iran's nuclear efforts and to bring peace to this long war-torn region. It was his greatest wish to find a path to the future for those living in the past."

She looked at the cameras in the back of the room, and away from the reporters, who sat in various states of shock.

And now she spoke directly to those who'd paid Zahir Damari to kill both her and the president, assuming, she thought, any of them had survived the attacks.

"All of you out there who wish us ill, who wish to kill

us, make no mistake. We will no longer sit idly by while you plot against us. The strikes this morning are simply a first step toward eradicating the hatred and destruction you spawn throughout the region.

"There will be no more negotiations, no more concessions, no more compromises that are always from our side. We have sent you our first message. If need be, there will be more. You cannot hide. You cannot run. We are coming for you. We are doing all we can to minimize collateral damage in these attacks, unlike you, our enemies."

She took a sip of water, looked from face to face. You could hear a pin drop in the room.

"Iran's movement against us was an open declaration of war. To that end, I say, yes, this is a war. It will be swift, and it will be just, and at its conclusion, perhaps, then, we can make peace.

"As you have already heard, President Bradley was gravely injured in the assassination attempt. He continues to be treated in an undisclosed location, for his safety. He is in a medically induced coma while the doctors endeavor to save his life. I am happy to report he is showing signs of improvement this morning, and I have no reason to feel he will not make a full recovery.

"For the moment, though, he is unable to discharge the duties of his office. I am following the steps set forth in our Constitution under the twenty-fifth amendment to lead this country in its time of need. When the president is capable of returning to active duty, I will return to my role as vice president.

"In the meantime, I will execute the duties of the

office, and continue to punish those who dared attack us on our own soil.

"May God watch over our coalition forces in this endeavor. Thank you, God bless you, and God bless America."

The room exploded with shouted questions as Callan stepped away from the lectern. Quinn gave her a smile and a thumbs-up, and the press secretary took the stand to handle the questions.

Nicholas and Mike were waiting outside the pressroom, watching Callan on the monitors in the small hallway. They heard a reporter yell after Callan, "Madam Vice President, what happened to the person who tried to kill you?"

They watched her turn, raise her hand, and instantly there was silence. She said in a loud, clear voice, "He was shot and killed." And then she came out of the room and was walking quickly toward them. "Walk with me," she said, not pausing, and they followed her to the Cabinet Room. The long table was full. On the backs of the chairs, discreet brass placards with the names of the president's cabinet identified those Mike didn't recognize.

The room erupted into applause as they entered. Every cabinet member got to their feet.

Callan brought Mike and Nicholas to the head of the table, a hand on each back.

"Ladies and gentlemen, I want to introduce you to the people who saved the life of President Bradley—not once, but twice—and saved me, as well. Special Agents Nicholas Drummond and Michaela Caine are shining examples of the heroes this country is honored to employ in our law enforcement services. We owe them both a debt of gratitude, and when the president is back on his feet, I will be recommending them for the Medal of Honor for their intelligence and their incredible bravery."

More applause, shouts, and whistles, decorum completely lost after Callan's words.

Callan raised her hand. "Let me add that Agent Caine was the one who shot the assassin, Zahir Damari, while he was trying to escape."

More applause.

Callan again raised a hand. "I want to assure all of you that I wasn't spinning a tale for the media. The president is doing better. The poison Damari used in the champagne was midazolam—you might know it as Versed, a drug they give you before surgery. It was a fatal dose. Without Agent Drummond moving so fast, without the medic really knowing his stuff well enough, the president would be dead. Now he will live."

Mike felt goose bumps rise on her arms. She was trying to memorize every word the vice president said, everyone's reaction—and there was the secretary of state, clapping wildly, for her and Nicholas—so much, too much, and she couldn't wait to tell her parents. She knew she would hold this close to her for as long as she lived. There was no doubt in her mind that patriotism was still very much alive and well in the halls of the White House.

She felt Nicholas's hand close around hers. Strong, steady, that was Nicholas, honorable to his core, not to mention a wild man. *A moment in time,* she thought, she'd just lived through a moment in history that would last her forever.

Nicholas tightened his hold on Mike's hand. When Callan turned and winked at him, he very nearly laughed. He was very grateful they weren't expected to say anything. His mind was perfectly blank.

Callan said, "I would like to tell you that I received word from Mossad that they'd captured both Colonel Vahid Rahbar and his Hezbollah cohort, Hasan Hadawi, known, I'm told, as the Hammer, along with the scientist who'd reproduced Spenser's coin bomb. They were headed for Israel's border.

"Evidently, both the colonel and the Hammer wanted to witness what the bombs could do with their own eyes.

"As to any bombs found with them, I formally requested that the Israeli government return them to us, which they will do. I fully expect the count to be on the short side." And she thought of Ari's jubilant shouts, and smiled.

There were huge sighs of relief around the room, more applause.

"So all's right with the world."

"Until tomorrow," a general remarked, and laughter and groans followed them from the room. They followed the vice president into the Oval Office, also small, so much less than Mike had always imagined it.

Callan waved them to one of the sofas, sat opposite them. "Tony sends you his best, Nicholas, Mike, and his thanks, between curses, since he naturally feels he failed me."

Nicholas said, "I'd be royally pissed off as well, even though I'd eventually come to accept that it wasn't my fault that madman Damari stole my face. Tony's a good man. He'll be back to himself soon enough."

Mike asked, "We found out too late that Damari had the plans to Camp David. Has there been any word on how he managed to get in? How he managed to break into the Secret Service's communications?"

"The prevailing theory is he crossed the fence during the power outage, then hid in one of the outlying cabins. They found evidence of him there. Since he could hear everything happening, he was able to dodge the Secret Service and the dogs. This was a very sophisticated attack, lots of planning, lots of moving parts. He did it with the help of Matthew Spenser, of course."

Mike said, "Isn't it ironic that, in the end, Matthew Spenser got what he wanted—we're at war with his enemies. His goals are now our goals."

"My hope is our war will be brief. Between the air strikes and the cyber-attacks, we're neutralizing them for a long time to come. Perhaps in the future, wiser heads will prevail and peace talks could become a reality." She rose and they did as well.

"Now, I have to leave you in Quinn's very capable hands. We've arranged for transport back to New York for you."

She grew serious. "I hate to say good-bye, but I have a few things on my schedule today. I want you to know you both have an open line to this administration. If there's ever anything you need, you pick up the phone and call."

She took both of their hands, held them tightly for a moment, then said again, "Thank you."

Nicholas said quietly, "Ma'am, it's been an honor."

Quinn Costello waited for them in the antechamber, a grin on her face.

With a last nod, Callan headed back across the hall to the cabinet room, and Quinn gestured for them to follow. She led them out to the South Lawn, where the Sea King was waiting.

"Seeing you off in style," Quinn said, handing them both small blue tote bags with the White House logo on them. "A few things to remember us by. Be well."

Mike and Nicholas took the steps into the helicopter, settled into the seats. "Under two hours to home," the pilot said over their headsets. "Time to have a little snooze. Here we go."

Home.

Home to New York. Nicholas didn't think he'd ever heard anything better.

THE END GAME

New York

Nicholas slept twelve hours on Friday night, ate pizza Nigel made for him, and made his plans.

Mike slept longer, had a hankering for Thai food, and ate it three straight meals.

Saturday night, just before ten o'clock, Mike got out of the shower, pulled on a sleep shirt, and turned on the television to watch something mindless. Her parents' excitement had worn her out.

And she waited.

The doorbell rang.

Finally.

She padded barefoot to the door. "Who is it?"

"Delivery."

"What are you delivering?"

"A skinny baguette and Nigel's famous tuna salad."

She opened the door, pulled him inside, slammed the door, locked, chained, and dead-bolted it, took the baguette and carton of tuna salad from his hands, laid them carefully on the table, and turned.

"It's about time you showed up."

"That's what Nigel said. I like your T-shirt. *She Who Sleeps with Dogs*—does that include bad dogs?"

"Yeah, big lamebrain butt-biting, face-licking bad dogs." She leaned up and bit his ear.

"I, ah, I came to talk."

She backed up, folded her arms over her chest. "I've told you a dozen times, Drummond, there's nothing to talk about," and she gave him a manic grin and jumped him, her legs going around his waist, her arms around his neck, and he pulled her up hard against him, laughing, kissing all of her he could reach.

"Maybe you're right," he said into her mouth as he carried her down the short hallway to her bedroom, "maybe talk is overrated."

He pulled off her glasses and tossed them into the bathroom where they landed squarely on top of the laundry hamper.

She stopped kissing him, pulled back. "Nicholas? Do you know Handel's *Messiah*?"

"Yes, I suppose. Why?"

"I have this feeling that in a few minutes we're going to be singing the 'Hallelujah Chorus.'"

"Amen to that," he said. "Nice bedspread."

26 Federal Plaza
Monday morning

Mike hummed "Mamma Mia" as she stashed her newly replenished go-bag in her bottom desk drawer, and booted up her computer.

Nicholas had left her two hours before to go back to his house and change.

A red notice was flashing on her screen—a meeting had been scheduled with Milo Zachery. She and Nicholas had spoken to him a good half-dozen times over the weekend. Always, he had one more question. He'd never said a word when Nicholas had answered Mike's cell. Mike admired her boss for that. She supposed that since they hadn't heard from him in twelve hours, he'd made up a whole new list.

She grabbed a notepad and a pen, ran into Nicholas in the hall. She shoved up her glasses, gave him a silly grin, and patted the small butterfly bandage on his forehead, his only remaining injury from the mad time at Camp David. As for her face, her makeup was light since there was no more black eye, no more patches of green and yellow.

Nicholas got within six inches, but no closer. "Good to see you, Agent Caine. Been too long." He looked her up and down, from her shiny blond ponytail, vivid eyes gleaming from behind her glasses with pleasure at seeing him, and that made him feel very fine indeed. He'd swear she glowed from the inside out. He probably did, too, he'd have to ask Nigel.

She was wearing her signature biker chick black and

those butt-kicker boots. "I miss the little black dress, that was a visual treat, particularly with the boots." As if he couldn't help himself, he lightly touched his fingers to her cheek. "You'll get your Glock back today."

"I sure hope so. I mean, if we'd been attacked over the weekend, I'd have had to bruise my knuckles protecting you."

"Nah, you have your ankle piece, but if you'd like I could teach you to fight without using your fists."

She laughed, couldn't seem to keep it in. As for Mr. James Bond, he couldn't look more different from her this morning in a lovely gray pin-striped suit, white shirt, and Italian loafers shined to a high gloss. "I gotta say, you sure clean up well."

"Thank you, ma'am. Nigel wanted me to tell you he's practicing enchilada recipes, wants you to come over and be his taste tester."

That silly grin bloomed again, plastered itself all over her face. "I can't wait. Come on, we've got to go see Zachery."

They saw the updated threat matrix glowing on the wall of the conference room as they passed by. There was always something new, which meant, for them, that life was never boring.

They passed Ben Houston, who grinned and high-fived them. He stopped, cocked his head to the side, looked back and forth between them. Slowly, he nodded, smiled. "About time," he said, and gave them a little wave and headed to the conference room.

"About time for what?"

Nicholas laughed. "You, me, us."

She stopped cold. "But how could he tell? Am I wearing a red SS on my forehead?"

"SS?"

"Not telling. Work it out in that feeble brain of yours."

He was laughing when they walked into Zachery's office to see Savich sitting on the black leather couch, his leg swinging, fiddling with MAX.

He looked up when they came in. He rose, shook their hands. "Hi, Mike, Nicholas. Neither of you look worse for wear after the excitement at Camp David." He paused, then, "As for your weekend, I have to say it appears it was, ah, congenial. Sherlock sends her love and Sean is chomping at the bit for another video game knock-down, drag-out with you, Nicholas."

Congenial? Now, that was an understatement for the ages. Mike said, "It's great to see you, Dillon, but what are you doing at Federal Plaza? Are you here to take over the New York Office?"

Before he could answer, Zachery said, "No, he's not. Savich knows I'd fight him to the death, very likely mine. Come on in, you two, and shut the door."

Now, what was this all about? Nicholas closed the door, then sat next to Mike. He cocked an eyebrow at Savich. "What's happening?"

Mike said, "Please don't tell us Zahir Damari had a brother, a really nasty mean vengeful brother?"

Zachery said, "He does, actually, but thankfully,

they're not what you'd call a close family." He turned to Savich. "You tell them."

Savich set MAX aside, leaned forward. "Let me say that you two have proven yourselves to be an interesting problem for the FBI. You have a tendency to find cases that explode into something bigger. You're both excellent investigators, you're both out-of-the-box thinkers, actually, you're both unlike anything we've seen before. To be honest, too, you clearly don't care about flaunting the rules when you want to achieve a goal."

Zachery said, "Mike follows the rules, yes, but Nicholas, alas, would just as soon burn them."

Mike felt like screaming. *Who cared about rules? Where was this going? Were they going to be booted out?*

Zachery continued: "But the fact is, we are an organization of rules. Nicholas, it's obvious to all of us who work with you that you are inclined to feel occasionally hampered by our constraints and procedures."

Mike shot Nicholas a look. Another vast understatement.

Savich said, "I think we've come up with a way to make sure you two can follow your instincts, be wild-hairs when you feel it's necessary, and the U.S. government won't have to arrest you and throw out cases because you've overstepped legal bounds. We're creating a special unit, authorized by Vice President Sloane directly. We know the president will sign off, too, once he's better."

"A special unit?" Mike said, her heart beginning to pound.

Savich nodded. "You're going to be a small mobile unit, handling some of our more esoteric cases. Your scope is international, your budget is unlimited. Well, if you decide to buy a small country, I imagine there would be questions raised. You are a black ops line item, as of this moment."

Mike clamped her jaws to keep her mouth from dropping open. *Black ops line item?*

Nicholas raised an eyebrow. "We're still FBI, correct?"

"On the surface, yes, absolutely," Savich said. "But your unit will have exceptional powers. You will be able to move through all areas of the government as needed with no roadblocks. You will pick your team, though we have some suggestions. We think Gray Wharton, Ben Houston, Louisa Barry, and Lia Scott would be excellent teammates. You've proven your ability to work well with all of them in the past."

"Adam Pearce," Nicholas said. "I want Adam Pearce, too."

Savich nodded. "An excellent idea. Talk about keeping you humble."

Mike said, with a half-smile, "Who runs this unit?"

"You and Nicholas are joint chiefs," Savich said. "I trust you to keep each other in check. You'll report directly to Mr. Zachery and you'll continue to have your base of operation out of the New York Field Office. You will have your own section that, I understand, is being set up for you as we speak. After this meeting, you will meet with your team, get settled in.

"I might add that you will have your own transportation for any trips you need to take so we don't have to keep borrowing other people's planes."

Zachery said, "We vacated a space on the twenty-second floor for you. It will fit all of you nicely, plus there's a good-sized conference room. You can put it together however you'd like."

Savich said, "You will have access to everything the Hoover Building, the New York Field Office, and Quantico have to offer."

Savich glanced at Zachery. "We both feel this is the only way to keep you two out of jail. So, what do you think?"

Nicholas looked at Mike. Her eyes glittered, she looked ready to leap out of her chair and dance and hoot and holler, like she would burst with both astonishment and wild happiness. He felt his blood pumping fast and hot, and couldn't help it—he stood up, grabbed her, and whirled her around.

He set her down and both of them turned and said in unison, "Yes!"

Nicholas shook Savich's hand, then Zachery's. "Thank you both. We like the sound of this new unit. We would like to do this."

"Good," Savich said. "Now, let's go over how you're going to structure this. And we need a name for you. What do you think, we could call you the Double Os?"

Mike said, "It has a ring to it, but unfortunately there's quite a tradition of the Double Os getting killed in the line of duty."

"More like replaced, at least in the movies," Nicholas said. He looked thoughtful a moment, then a smile bloomed. "How about we call ourselves For Your Eyes Only."

Mike knew this was good, it was exactly right. She stood straight and tall and said formally, "As of this moment, we're your official covert eyes."

When they broke ten minutes later, Mike hooked her arm through Nicholas's and nearly danced him down the hall. "Let's get a cup of coffee and talk about this."

He stopped, an eyebrow raised. "What? You really want to talk? Well, it's about time. Let's go tell the lads and lasses first, though."

Mike said, "I can't wait to see who yells the loudest. Nicholas, can you imagine? We'll have power over our own cases, and as a black ops line item? Do you have any idea what this means?"

He did. Autonomy, being in charge, no limits, exactly what he liked. He gave her a manic grin.

"Of course you do. Now, we'll have to come up with a way to break ties, in case you and I disagree about how to go forward on an operation. I like rock, paper, scissors. Do you think that will cut it?"

He could imagine future arguments, knock-down, drag-out fights, but not which cases to take, but how they'd proceed, how close they could get to the edge without swan-diving over. The list would go on and on. He felt excited, content, and, he suspected, as happy as she was. He felt—*giddy*, Nigel's word. Yes, that was it.

"I can't wait for our first argument," he said.

"You'll lose," she said immediately, then, "We have so much to do—you know, so many procedures to establish and set into motion, so many rules to see everyone follows—"

He burst into laughter. "I can see our very first argument right over the horizon."

"That was a joke, lamebrain. Well, mostly."

Their announcement to Ben, Gray, Louisa, and Lia ended in a tie. Shouts all around, loud ones. While everyone was clapping one another on the shoulder, already arguing about who would have the better space, Nicholas called Adam, explained to him about the new unit, For Your Eyes Only, or Covert E for short.

Adam was silent for a long moment, then said, "Like if you tell me to hack into the CIA, it'll be okay? I won't go to jail again?"

"Not for even a minute."

Adam whooped. "Sign me up!"

"Get on a plane. We'll see you soon. I hope you won't mind having a cubicle?"

Adam groaned.

Ten minutes later, all of them were walking down the stairs to the twenty-second floor to scope out their new digs when Nicholas's mobile rang. He didn't recognize the number, hardly a surprise these days. "Excuse me a moment. Drummond here."

"Hello, Nicholas. I trust Michaela is nearby?"

"Yes," he said, his heart thudding. He signaled to Mike, and pressed the speaker button.

A familiar voice said, "This is Kitsune. I need your help."

AUTHOR'S NOTE

I failed to make the chess team because of my height.

—*Woody Allen*

Bobby Fischer and Donald Byrne evidently both met the height requirement. They played what has been dubbed *The Game of the Century* in 1956 in New York City. Bobby Fischer was thirteen years old and Donald Byrne was twenty-six, a leading American chess master. Midway through the game, Byrne saw that he would lose. Because Fischer was only thirteen, and because Byrne was a gentleman, he finished the game. It was exactly eighty-two moves.

So get out a chessboard and play the moves listed at the top of each chapter. (I've made them very clear so you should have no problems even if you're a beginner.) Enjoy this amazing game.

Why a chess game? This was J. T. Ellison's brilliant brainchild and played right into the title—*The End Game*. When she realized we had eighty-two chapters, the same number of moves that are in *The Game of the Century*, she knew it was meant to be. She could be heard singing the "Hallelujah Chorus" all over Nashville.

In a game of chess, toppling the King is the goal. In *The End Game*, the moves and countermoves made by the players of both sides lead to an actual end game where either side could win. Fortunately, for all of us, the right side won.

Rudolf Spielmann, 1883–1942, known as the Master of Attack, once said, *"In the opening a master should play like a book, in the mid-game he should play like a magician, in the ending he should play like a machine."*

—*Catherine Coulter*

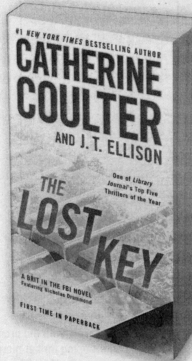